IGNITING THE SPARK

L. J. WEDE

CONTENT EXPECTATIONS

Certain scenes in this book may be upsetting for some readers. A non-exhaustive list of potentially upsetting content may be reviewed at https://ljwede.com/content-warnings/.

To my therapist, who made writing this a lot harder.

CONTENTS

Author's Note	i	Chapter 16	174
Chapter 1	1	Chapter 17	188
Chapter 2	8	Chapter 18	198
Chapter 3	17	Chapter 19	207
Chapter 4	27	Chapter 20	224
Chapter 5	37	Chapter 21	237
Chapter 6	44	Chapter 22	259
Chapter 7	49	Chapter 23	268
Chapter 8	62	Chapter 24	281
Chapter 9	72	Chapter 25	299
Chapter 10	87	Chapter 26	317
Chapter 11	101	Chapter 27	333
Chapter 12	114	Chapter 28	340
Chapter 13	132	Chapter 29	342
Chapter 14	142	Chapter 30	346
Chapter 15	158		

AUTHOR'S NOTE

I first thought of Sparks on a trip to visit my mother and sister in December of 2022 (sorry Astrid, you came a bit later). It was late, we had a long drive ahead of us, and I couldn't find a book to read. I could describe the book I wanted – a criminal protagonist skirting around a persistent vigilante, a love triangle that couldn't possibly work due to their complete philosophical differences... until it does... kinda.

I texted my then-fiancé to complain about how this book didn't seem to exist, at least not in the way I wanted it to. Boldly, I stated I was going to write it. Over that thirty-minute drive, we threw ideas back and forth until Sparks was born. The rest of the plot, well, that took a lot longer.

A year and a half later, the manuscript was finished. This novel took me through many phases of my life – leaving my job in marketing, getting married, and deciding to leave the corporate life behind to write full-time. Even now, I look back on my initial notes and storyboards and wonder how the hell I got here.

Sparks has been my reprieve and comfort, and I am so thankful to be able to tell her story. When anyone ever asks about this novel, I tell them that the book is fictional, but the emotions are real. I hope that this book can help others unpack their depression and anger, and work towards healing.

Special thanks to my husband, Alex, for putting up with my endless brainstorming, to my four-legged supervisor, Morticia, who provided special comfort during hard scenes and enforced my union-mandated hot chocolate breaks, and to my therapist (really enough said there).

Further thanks to all of you for taking a chance on this novel. I hope you grow to love Sparks and Astrid as much as I do.

-L. J. Wede

CHAPTER 1

Electricity. The driving force propelling life, a spontaneous eruption of energy. I've always felt a special bond with electricity, how it ebbs and flows as a current. I can understand its paths, anticipate where it wants to go, and send it on its journey.

The fuse box in front of me speaks a language I understand so easily, it should be considered my native tongue. The homeowner who called me clearly can't fathom the power of a surge, but after a few replaced fuses, I can feel the electricity restlessly humming. I run my fingers along the switches, gently releasing a flow of energy. I lightly probe, searching for weaknesses in this house's electrical wiring. The microwave is certainly pulling a fair percentage of the kitchen's circuit, but with the new fuses, the building should be safe from any more electrical problems in the near future. I withdraw my hand and close the door to the fuse box. After gathering my tools, I go to collect my pay and leave.

"Hey, everything looks good. Text me if you have any more issues and I can swing by."

"Oh, thank goodness," The young man exhales as he grabs his wallet. "You said cash only, correct? Fifty dollars?"

I nod from my spot, leaning against the wall. I was looking forward to going home to my apartment and having a drink. The homeowner interrupts my thoughts.

"That's a pretty necklace you have on. Where did you get it?" I stop fiddling with the chain and tuck the necklace back under my shirt.

"It's just something my mother made once. Don't worry about it," I snap. His posture stiffens from my terse response. I sigh and stuff the wad of bills into my pocket. "Thank you for giving me a call. I'm available if any more fuses pop. Just be careful of how many kitchen appliances you have running at a time."

With that, I start my walk home. In the brisk autumnal air, I pull my leather jacket tighter around my chest. My unruly curls are ruffled by the wind drifting down the alleyway. A spiced scent wafts by, giving me a feeling of warmth. Out of curiosity, I follow it to a coffee shop. The tables and booths are laden with pillows, bookshelves line the wall with their worn covers peeking out behind each other. College students are hunched over notebooks, while older patrons are engaging in pleasant conversation. All the while, a single employee is flitting amongst the tables, checking on coffee levels and removing empty mugs. Her blonde ponytail bounces as she laughs at a customer's quip.

A sudden gust of wind reawakens me from my trace. The fifty dollars in my pocket has to last the rest of the week, so a drink is probably not the best purchase. I continue to my studio apartment. As I fit my key into the door, a voice shouts from within, "Yo Sparks, where've you been?" My hopes of a relaxing evening are dashed as I open the door to Jack doing sit-ups in the entryway.

"Dude, please put a shirt on." I grab his abandoned tank from the knob and toss it to him, then go to set down my tools.

"Aw sweetie, don't like what you see?" He playfully gestures to his sweaty torso. Admittedly, it was not a bad view, but Jack never had problems losing his clothes.

"Jack, you know it's always a pleasure to see you, shirt notwithstanding." I grab an open bottle of whiskey and pour myself a healthy serving. "Do you want to tell me why you stopped by?"

Still sans shirt, Jack reaches into his bag and pulls out an opened package of black licorice. "Maybe your friend wanted to spend an evening with you." I reach over and grab a few sprigs of licorice. I take a bite and look at him expectantly. Nothing from Jack comes without a catch, and after being his friend and companion for eight years, nobody knew this better than me. "Okay fine, we can cut to the chase. I figured out how to find those behind Synergy Labs."

I forcefully set my glass down. "Don't mess with me, Jack. I'm not in the mood."

"Sparks, I know better than to joke about this. You know I lost someone too." He takes a step toward me. I clasp onto my necklace. My mother was recruited to develop a machine. That was, before the device killed her and Jack's brother. I don't fully know what it does, but I know it's dangerous.

I lock eyes with Jack. "I would do anything to destroy them, to watch those bastards go down in flames."

"Listen to me, I met someone who works for them now. He would be willing to give us an in... for a price. We need seven million dollars."

"Shit Jack, we don't have that kind of money. Why would you even bring this up?" I throw back the rest of my drink and grab the bottle, turning away to hide the tears in my eyes. If I had even a percentage of that amount, then I wouldn't stay in this shitty apartment for fuck's sake. But the landlord lets me pay in cash and doesn't ask questions. I take a big swig from the bottle, relishing the burn of the whiskey on the way down. Although the accident happened years ago, there is still a sharp pain from the memories.

Jack comes up from behind and wraps his arms around me. "Baby, shhh, it's okay, it's okay. I told you, I have a plan." He turns me around and tucks a curl behind my ear. "You and me, we're going to rob a bank."

I take another swig from the bottle, a dry laugh dying in my throat. "This isn't a game to me. If you're going to joke around, then just get the fuck out."

"This isn't a joke to me either!" Jack grabs the whiskey bottle and slams it on the counter. Liquid splashes onto the linoleum floors. "I might not have watched my mother die like you did, but that doesn't mean I don't care. My brother died in that accident."

"I didn't just watch my mother die," I snap. "I grabbed her necklace as the blast pushed her over the railing. I held on as I felt the electricity surge through my body, and when the chain snapped, I watched her lifeless body fall into a heap on the floor below. So when you share some ass-backward plan, I take it personally." The lights in the room flicker as my hands crackle with sparks, as I grip the necklace she used to wear, remembering that pain.

"I know..." Jack lifts my chin to meet his gaze and my sparks subside. "But that night is what gave you your powers." He gestures to my hands. "We can use your electricity to make this work! I don't call you Sparks for nothing."

"I don't think you fully understand my abilities. I can redirect electricity, not rob a bank! This is ridiculous."

Jack pinches the bridge of his nose. "You're not even considering this. If we hit a bank when they are getting a money delivery, we can be in and out with the cash in one go. We'll wear disguises so no one will recognize us. Plus, banks are insured anyway, it's a victimless crime. Please, just give this a chance..." Jack places a gentle kiss on my hand, then slowly leaves a trail of kisses up my arm to my neck. "... for me."

"I don't want to fight with you, Jack."

"You don't have to. All you have to do is let me be in control." He cups my head in his hand and deeply kisses me. I can't stop my back from arching at his touch beneath my shirt. He lowers his hands to my waist, my hips, my thighs, then he picks me up and places me on the counter.

"Jack..." He places a finger to my lips and shushes me. Slowly, he unbuttons my jeans and runs his hands along my hips. A soft moan escapes as I feel his hands drag along my sides and remove my shirt. The hair on my skin stands up in protest to the sudden exposure of air, but my attention shifts as Jack grips my shoulders and pushes me flat against the countertop. The coolness of the surface makes me gasp, and Jack chuckles as he holds me down.

The scent of his cheap cigarettes caresses me as he slowly bends over to whisper in my ear, "See, this is what happens when you do as I say." Jack tugs on my jeans and I arch my hips to help slide them off, leaving me almost bare to the cold. He grabs my discarded licorice from the countertop next to me and flips me onto my stomach. I can feel him drag the ropes up my back.

"Licorice is a very polarizing flavor," Jack taunts. "Some find it bitter-" I yelp as he abruptly slaps my ass. Jack leans in close to whisper, "and some find it sweet." He gently rubs the stinging area before taking a few steps back.

"Jack," I moan, pleading for more. "Stop fucking around."

"Then turn off the lights," he commands. I reach for the light switch, only to have Jack pin my arms down to the counter. "Turn. Off. The. Lights." The tone shift is subtle, but a hint of warning is in his voice. His grip on my arms tightens.

"Stop, you're hurting me," I object. I try to squirm out of his grasp, but Jack's hold does not waver. "We've talked about this, you know I don't like to use my powers."

"You don't want me to ask another time. Three."

"Jack, knock it off."

"Two."

"Don't patronize me!"

"One."

"Stop!" My anger flares through me, with sparks radiating off my skin. The lights in the apartment surge, before I sense the fuse blow and darkness encapsulates the room. Jack curses and nurses his wounds, his hands singed from my electric shock. "What the hell were you thinking, Jack? Why did you-"

Jack pulls me in for a deep kiss, his fingers getting tangled in my hair, which was now full of static. "See, I knew you could do it."

"But-" He silences me with another kiss, my annoyance at him piques, but fades fast. "Jack..." He picks me up and my legs wrap around his waist. Jack draws me into another embrace as he makes his way to my bed. He lays me down and crawls over me. "The fuse," I don't make it any further before I am silenced by a roaming hand glancing over my erect nipple. A moan slips from my lips, and I forget the rest of my sentence.

"You don't need to say anything," Jack murmurs. "Remember, I am in control, and this is the reward you get for obeying me." His other hand slides underneath my panties and glides over my clit. My body shakes from the tension, the emotional turbulence of highs and lows leaving me raw to him, desperate for his affection. He slips a finger in me and my legs buckle, any anger or resentment I had towards him vanishes. I can see him smile from the faint light of the streetlamps through the windows. Jack notices me staring.

In a low whisper I hear, "Close your eyes, or I'll make you turn those off too." As I shut my eyes, I can hear his belt buckle drop to the floor. He gently slides into my opening.

"Good girl."

CHAPTER 2

I wake to blankets strewn on the floor. Jack is gone. I reach for my lamp before remembering the incident the night before, recalling how my fuse needs to be replaced. I roll my eyes before fumbling to get dressed, tripping on my threadbare quilt. I'm going to need a new blanket before winter, especially since I can't afford the heating bill as it is. As I head toward the door, I catch a glimpse of my reflection in a mirror. Two angry, purple handprints encircle my biceps. I wince as I pull on my jacket, before grabbing my tools and heading to the complex's fuse box. Although I'm sure other angry residents have already bitched to the landlord about the power outage, I would rather fix it myself instead of waiting for a less experienced repairman to be called out. Besides, this is my building. The hum of the electricity is as much a part of my studio as the peeling paint.

I've just closed the fuse box door as my phone rings. The caller ID displays Jack's name on the screen. I begrudgingly accept the call.

"Good morning," I say sarcastically.

Sparks, I've picked a bank. Reschedule any freelance gigs you have today because I need you to case the joint and get some information.

"Whoa, whoa, whoa. Jack, we talked about this. No way."

You agreed to it last night. C'mon Sparks, don't chicken out now.

"I did not agree to this. There are so many reasons this is a bad idea."

The silence on the line is deafening. After the pause, Jack says two terse, clipped syllables. *You will.* I hear a click as the call ends.

I look down as my phone vibrates. A text. From Jack.

Golden Capital Bank on 54th Street. Stake it out, get every detail. Report back to me tonight. 6 p.m. Your apartment. -J

I groan with irritation. However, I didn't have any electrician gigs lined up, so I don't have a good excuse not to indulge him. But robbing a bank? Absolutely not. Right? No. I can't let Jack in my head like this.

Back in my apartment, I rinse yesterday off in the shower. The stench of whiskey fades down the drain and is replaced by the scent of my body wash. After toweling off, I pace around my studio. I know Jack. He isn't one to just drop an idea. He can be rash and impulsive, but he has always taken care of me. Ever since my mother died, Jack has been there to support me. Jack knows best, always.

Despite my apprehension, I decide to check out the bank. Perhaps with enough information, I could assuage his criminal notions. What does one bring to a stakeout? I have no fucking clue. I grab a backpack and stuff it with my laptop, snacks, some scrap pieces of paper, and pencil nubs. Feeling utterly unprepared, I wander toward Golden Capital Bank.

Standing in front of the grandiose columns, I am starkly reminded how bad of an idea this is. Guards with, I presume to be, fully loaded firearms make rounds outside of the building. Several security men are stationed inside surveilling the busy crowds of patrons. Cameras are installed periodically around the ceiling. I have no clue why Jack even began to think this would be possible. I cross the street to abandon this lost cause when I catch a familiar smell in the air. I stand on the sidewalk, confused, and search my surroundings to try and place the lost memory.

And there it is, the coffee shop from yesterday. A worn sign reads, "Brew for Two." I tentatively cross the street and retake my prior spot by the window. If anything, it is more welcoming and lively today, with the orange glow of the lights radiating from the ceiling. I can feel the buzz of electricity circulating within the shop like a comforting friend. And the girl, the same bubbly blonde girl, is bustling around the shop, her tray laden with fresh drinks and pastries. She looks up and we lock eyes, she gives me a soft smile. I impulsively enter the shop. Slowly, I wander toward the counter with a handwritten chalk menu.

"Good morning." The blonde sets down her now-empty tray and steps behind the counter. "Is this your first time here? My name is Astrid. I'd love to help you find something you enjoy." Her eyes twinkle as she wipes her hands on her apron.

"Um, I'm not really much of a coffee drinker, I'm not quite sure why I came in here actually."

"That's totally okay," Astrid reassures. "We have a large assortment of teas and hot chocolates. I'm sure if we work together, we can find something you like. And if we don't, you're always welcome to come in just to hang out, grab a book. So, what sounds good?" Positive energy radiates from her, and I just can't walk away.

"How about a challenge?" I banter. "I like strong spices, and my favorite candy is black licorice. Can't get enough of it."

"Do you want options," a gentle smirk spreads across her face, "or do you want a surprise?"

I place a ten-dollar bill on the counter with a wink. I'll be low on cash for the rest of the week, but for some reason, this just feels right. "I'll be over there when it's ready. Take your time."

I walk to a booth by the window, coincidentally, I'm sitting across from Golden Capital. Unintentionally, my sightline is perfect to try and discern a viable option to infiltrate the bank. I run my fingers through my hair, a futile effort to direct the strands away from my face. I grab my laptop and run my fingers across the keys. I open a document and recount my prior observations, hoping I'll discover a magical gap in their security. I'm lost in thought when Astrid brings over a steaming mug with a rich decadent smell.

"I strayed a bit from our standard menu and created something new." She sets down the cup in front of me, enclosed with a pile of whipped cream and chocolate star sprinkles. "This is a dark chocolate drink with anise, cardamom, brown sugar, and a few odds and ends. I hope I met your challenge." Astrid slides my ten-dollar bill across the table. "Just in case, this one's on me. I'll give you some space, but don't hesitate to flag me down if you need anything."

With that, Astrid is gone, back to flitting around the shop to care for other customers. I carefully grab the handle of the mug, testing the temperature of the beverage to avoid a burnt tongue. The whipped cream leaves a mustache on my lip as I take a sip.

It.

Is.

Heavenly.

The richness of the dark chocolate contrasts to the heavy seasoning, while the cream provides some levity. The drink is just hot enough to provide a comforting warmth without being scalding. I take another sip, trying desperately to not inhale the whole thing in one go. I cradle the mug in my hands, slowly enjoying the rest while gazing out the window toward the bank. Despite nursing the drink for what seemed like hours, it stayed the perfect temperature.

As expected, I finished my drink without discerning any bank robbing revelations. Who would have thought that banks, some of the most secure institutions in the country charged with storing and protecting valuables, aren't super easy to waltz into and clear out? Frustrated with my lack of solutions, I gather my things and bring my mug up to the front counter.

"So, what did you think?" Astrid pops out from behind the counter. "Did we find something to make the stop worth it?"

"Mmmm, I don't know," I reply with a sly smile. "I might have to get another for the road, you know, for further evaluation." She grins from ear to ear.

"I think we can make that happen. Give me one second." Astrid returns a short while later with a steaming to-go cup. "Any true scientist knows you have to run an experiment more than once to get an accurate result."

"Here's to good scientific integrity." I raise the cup and take a few steps toward the door before turning back. "Oh, and Astrid? Thank you." I gesture to the ten-dollar bill on the counter and walk out through the door, delightfully sipping on my beverage.

I begin the trudge back to my apartment while munching on a stick of licorice from my bag. The fallen leaves crunch under my feet, winter will be here before I know it. I pull my jacket tighter, wishing I had brought a beanie or a scarf. I take another sip of my drink, relishing the warmth in my chest as I swallow. However, it's not long before I am taken by the chill again, so I quicken my pace through the Boston alleyways.

Once safely inside my somewhat warm abode, I grab some veggies and a cutting board, then get to work prepping dinner. I place the chopped vegetables on a baking sheet and put them in the oven to roast just as my door slams open.

"Sparks, what's hanging?" Jack waltzes into my studio and tosses his jacket toward the counter. He misses, and it slides to the floor. "Do you mind grabbing that?"

"Jack, hi, thanks for almost breaking my door. I can't imagine how hard it is to knock." I crank the stove to high and set a pot of water on to boil. He digs through my bag and pulls out a twig of licorice.

"If I know anything, it's that you always have licorice on you." Ignoring the fact that he gave me the candy, he takes a bite and sprawls over my couch. "Now, let's talk shop. What'd you learn about the bank?" I groan and grab some ground beef from the fridge.

"Jack, this is nonsense. You need to put this idea to bed." I put the beef in a bowl, add some seasonings and a few odds and ends, then start forming small meatballs.

"Wait, did you even go to the bank today?" Jack sits up straight, frustration radiating from him. "Why couldn't you do just one thing for me?"

"Whoa, whoa, whoa." I turn away from the counter. "I didn't say that I didn't go to the bank. In fact, that's why I know that this is a bad idea. There is an insane amount of security, and guns. Guns, Jack! You and I have been through shit together, heck you've practically raised me after my mom died. But this, this is too much."

"Sparks, this is our one chance. This is everything we've worked for all these years. We can work around the guns and security if you can get a decent report back to me."

"Prison, Jack! Prison, or getting shot, are the only two outcomes. All of these years will mean nothing if I allow you to run headfirst into this. So no! The answer is no!" I turn back to the counter and continue making meatballs. "Jack, I can't lose you like that. I just... I can't."

Jack comes up behind me and wraps his arms around my waist. I can feel his breath on my ear. "Sparks..." he leaves a few gentle kisses on the nape of my neck. "Some sacrifices need to be made. We need money, and we need it now. Tell me what you saw, and I'll figure out a plan." He pulls me away from the counter and looks into my eyes. "Sparks, we can do this!"

"There were cameras, literally all over the place. Guards, inside and out, with guns - big guns." I set down my half-formed meatball, too flustered to make an adequate sphere. "I'm not risking my life over some half-assed, stupid idea."

In a moment, Jack's demeanor turns to rage. He flings my discarded cutting board off the counter toward my living room. Vegetable scraps go flying and the knife clatters to the floor, uncomfortably close to me. In a step, he is close enough to pull me against him, his grip on my hair forces me to look in his eyes. My breath catches in my chest, waiting for Jack to move or speak. My heartbeats fill my ear. *Tha-thump. Tha-thump. Tha-thump.*

Jack leans down to whisper in my ear. *Tha-thump.*

"I am not interested in your arguments today." *Tha-thump.* "I am not interested in listening to anything other than you screaming my name." *Tha-thump.* "As you are not in the mood to listen, I am not in the mood to fuck you."

Tha-thump.

"And seeing as I need you to go out tomorrow, I can't fuck up that pretty little face of yours. Bruises raise questions." His hand tightens on my scalp and forces my head back, looking toward the ceiling. His other hand trails down my body to the sliver of skin between my shirt and pants. Even his touch matches the ice in his voice. "Do better tomorrow."

Jack pulls away and I fall to the ground, no longer supported by his arm. I hear the door slam.

"Jack? Jack!" I run into the hallway. "Jack!"

He is already gone.

I stand there before I take a deep breath and go back to my studio.

Get ahold of yourself, this is embarrassing.

As soon as I open the door, I can tell that my dinner is ruined. I pull my burned veggies out of the oven and slam the pan on the counter. I stare at my charcoaled food and anger bubbles up inside me.

He's so selfish, and conceited, and impulsive, and just... just... arghh!

The charred vegetables fly across the room as I seethe through my teeth. Then I look around at the mess I've made, at the tray of meatballs that still need to be cooked, and the pasta still in the box.

Shit. You know what? No. I'm not doing this tonight.

I pick up my phone and order some pizza from a mom-and-pop down the street. I spend the next few minutes cleaning up, and then crash on the couch waiting for the delivery driver. My phone buzzes.

I don't care what you have planned tomorrow. You're going back to the bank and figuring out what you missed. Don't come back empty handed, or we will be having a different conversation than the one we had tonight. -J

I toss my phone onto a nearby blanket. I lay back and watch the slow-moving ceiling fan circle until I hear a knock from the door. Pizza in hand, I make my way back to the couch, grabbing a handle of whiskey as I go. I sit there for a while. Eating. Drinking. Ruminating. Much too drunk to worry about tomorrow, I allow myself to wallow in my thoughts and fears.

I stumble around the room and notice a vegetable scrap missed by my prior cleaning efforts, resting upon a dusty instrument case. I used to play my viola often, so often in fact that I wouldn't bother to fully zip the case. Just enough to protect it until the next day. I run my hands along the case, noting the partly closed zipper. You never know at the time that you won't be picking it up for a few months. You never know at the time that you'll walk away from it, leaving it to collect cobwebs in the corner. I wonder if Jack will ever do that to me. Slam the door on his way out and leave his favorite toy behind, waiting to be noticed again.

I shudder at the thought, and without doing so consciously, unzip the case. I use my cloth to wipe down the strings and fingerboard, before applying rosin to the bow and tuning my viola. For just a moment, I hold her in my hands, relishing her weight as a familiar comfort. I bring her up to my chin and pull a long silky note out of her, savoring the vibrations in my chest. I continue stumbling through a song I once knew, alcohol numbing the pain from my fingers as my callouses have dissipated. I don't remember falling asleep, but I wake cradling my viola in my arms, tears dried on my cheeks.

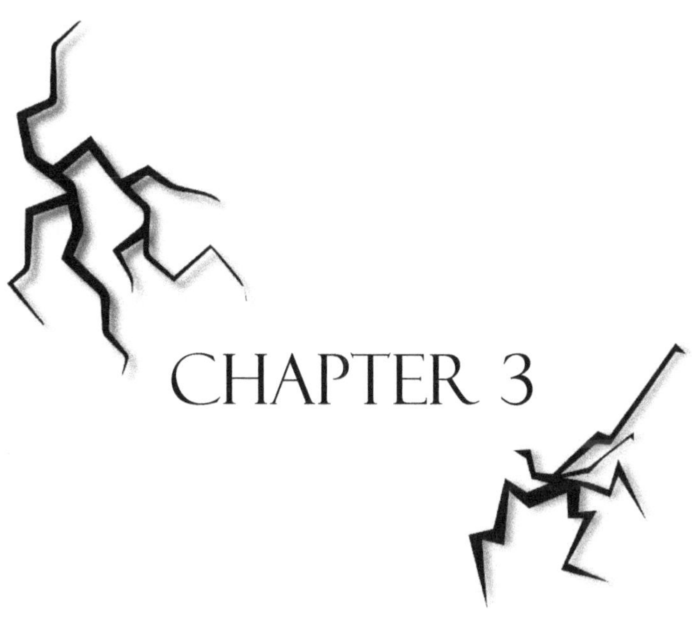

CHAPTER 3

I spend my morning at another electrician gig. Paid in cash. Of all the things to do hungover and cranky, electric work is my preference. It's quiet, and I enjoy working with my hands - although today my client has been hovering over my shoulder and my fingertips are sore from the sharp strings I played through the night. If only today's job was simple - troubleshooting a faulty electrical connection. In my haste to fix the issue, I am zapped quite a few times. Nothing dangerous, it hurts like a bitch though. Usually, I can use my powers to redirect the electricity before I get shocked, but I'm off my game today.

Finally, I finish up and grab my pay from the crotchety old man who pestered me all day. Then, I start walking toward Brew for Two. I figure if Jack is going to make me canvas the bank again, then I'm getting another hot chocolate.

I walk through the doors and the pleasant ambiance isn't enough to lighten my mood, even seeing Astrid laugh at a patron's joke leaves me twisted inside.

"Hi again!" Astrid greets me as she makes her way to the counter. "I'm so glad to see you back. How can I help you today?"

"Hey, um, can I get one of those anise hot chocolates from yesterday?" Her face falls.

"Oh shoot, we're out of anise flavoring. We don't get restocked until next week. Can I offer you allspice tea? Or we have a great fennel and clove-"

"It's fine," I cut her off. "I'll just have a regular hot chocolate then." Her cheery expression falters slightly at my terse interruption, but within a blink, she's back to her bubbly attitude.

"Alright then. I'll get that rung up for you." She starts punching it into the cash register before I grab her hand. We make eye contact, and she looks at me confused.

"I'm sorry," I say, and I mean it. "I've had an unbelievably rough day and I just really need... I don't know what I need. But I know that doesn't excuse me being cranky. So I want to try that again." I take a pause to compose myself, pushing my unruly hair back and putting a weak smile on my face. "Hi Astrid, can I please have a hot chocolate? I'll wait here so you don't have to make the trip over to my table." My feeble offer makes her chuckle. Her gaze softens and she nods.

"Absolutely. I'll get that right out for you." She pauses as if to say something else, but then turns away to steam the milk. When she returns, I see she added the same star sprinkles on top of the whipped cream.

"When I have a rough day," Astrid says, "sometimes all it takes is one thing to make the difference. One thing to turn the tides. If there's anything I can do to help you find that one thing, don't hesitate to ask."

She smiles as she slides the mug across the counter. I hold her gaze for an extra second, before thanking her and taking my drink to the booth I sat in yesterday. I get settled, pulling out my laptop as I hear the couple behind me discussing the newspaper in their hands.

"That's the second bust made in a week! The police say they don't know who did it, but the vigilante is coming hard for the Tributaries. Same story each time, the police got an anonymous tip that led them to an illegal gambling ring, but all of the men were tied up when they got there. Someone beat them to it. That guy must have a death wish to be messing with them."

I've heard about the Tributaries before, a gang that's been growing the past decade to the point where it's too big to take down. They specialize in offshore casinos. High stakes, and an even higher buy-in. Those who can't pay for their losses end up with fewer limbs and family members than before. Astrid walks up behind them.

"Now you both know that paper is just trying to rile you two up..." She lightly swats them with a towel. "Skip ahead to the comic section. Oh wait, can you actually check the local events for this weekend? I wonder if there's any good concerts going on."

They continue into a lively discussion on the latest in indie music and ticket prices, while I set my sights on Golden Capital Bank. I take a sip of my hot chocolate, it's good but... I don't know. Between my ebbing hangover and the stress of the past day, the drink isn't doing it for me. I slide it across the table and start taking notes of everything I see in the bank.

Three guards in front with guns.

Four guards on each side, same guns.

All guards wear body armor and helmets.

I continue in that manner for hours. Running my hand through my hair, I am so lost in thought that I don't notice the patrons leaving the coffee shop until I am alone in my booth. I look up at the empty tables with a startled jolt. Astrid wipes down the last table and grabs a binder, calculator, and some pencils.

"Oh shit, are you closed?" Flustered, I shut my laptop and tuck it in the crook of my arm. "I am so sorry, I'll let you finish up!" I hurriedly grab my bag and stumble to my feet.

"Sit back down," Astrid chides. "You are welcome to hang out here. That doesn't change just because the clock says so. Besides, I have some bookwork to do, and you seem like quiet company. Do you mind?" She gestures at the seat across the table.

"Well, I've got nowhere better to be." I give a half-smile and slide back into the booth. I reopen my laptop and she flips through pages of receipts and ledgers, making marks here and there. We sit for about half an hour before Astrid breaks the silence.

"Do you want something to drink while we're here? I can get you something-" Her eyes drift to my mug, still full. "Oh, you didn't finish your drink. Was there something wrong with it?" I shake my head.

"It was fine, I guess I just wasn't ready for my one thing yet," I sigh. "Anyway it's cold now." Astrid studies my face, seeing my exhaustion as I comb through my hair with my fingers. She gently grabs the mug and places it in front of me.

"Don't worry, it's still warm. You can still search for your one thing." I look at her and cock my head.

"Astrid, I ordered that hours ago. No way it's still..." My hand brushes the side of the mug, feeling heat from within. I stare at the drink, astounded. "... warm?" I raise it to my lips and take a drink. "What? How?" Astrid chuckles at my puzzled expression.

"I buy really nice mugs, that's how," she teases. "You think any of these college students remember to drink their coffee? I have a very distractible group of clientele. Speaking of, what's distracting you today?" She examines me intently. I shrug her off.

"It's nothing. Not worth bothering you over." With that, Astrid doubles down.

"Excuse me," she gasps in mock offense. "By visiting this cafe, you have become one of my patrons. That is a title I do not bestow gently. All of my patrons are my friends, so everything that troubles them is worth getting 'bothered' about. Now." She grabs my mug out of my hands and sets it on the table. "Spill."

Her command is firm, but kind. I hesitate. How do I describe to her that my friend is waiting for me to gather intel on the bank across the street?

"This is going to sound crazy, like such a strange problem to have," I start to ramble. Astrid puts her pencil in her binder and closes it, moving it to the end of the table. Her attention is solely on me, and whatever story I can come up with.

"I'm trying to figure out - hypothetically, of course - how one would rob a bank."

"Are you a writer?" Astrid furrows her eyebrows. Yes! A plausible excuse for researching a felony. I slump in my seat.

"You caught me," I lie. "I'm not a professional by any means, writing my first book. I was thinking that one of my characters would try to rob a bank, but I have absolutely no clue how that would even work." Astrid bursts out laughing.

"So you've been sitting here, checking out Golden Capital across the way?" She gestures toward the bank. "That's the funniest thing I've heard all day. Lucky for you, I live right upstairs so I tend to know a lot about Golden Capital." I breathe a sigh of relief.

"That is fantastic. Okay, hypothetically, how would you rob the bank?"

"Well, that depends." Astrid rubs her hands together. "Every Friday at 10 p.m., they have an armored truck move their excess to the Federal Reserve. I remember because they're loud and keep me awake. If you want the most bank for your buck - pun intended - you would want to intercept it then. That way, you don't have to open the safe yourself. However, that also means more guards. They like, I don't know, triple around then?" I type furiously trying to keep up with Astrid's rambling.

"I guess if you want the least amount of opposition, you would want to do it when there are the least number of men, so after business hours. They all go home around 5 since the bank doors are locked. So Friday afternoon is the most money, with the fewest guards. But then you have to open the safe yourself. Most banks have a timer on their vaults so they can't be opened outside of business hours, very high tech, wired right into the electrical grid of the building. Now the hardest part of either plan is the alarm. Your character really doesn't want that."

"Why?" I interject. "What happens then?" Astrid mulls it over.

"Well, for starters, the police would be there in a few minutes," Astrid explains. "That would put a damper on things. But some alarms have other countermeasures, like locking doors or whatnot. I don't know about Golden Capital specifically, but you can always just write what works best for your story."

"Would there be any booby traps?" This draws a chuckle from Astrid.

"Like what, spears falling from the ceiling?" Astrid jokes. "No, nothing like that. But yeah, that alarm is the crux of the plan. Unless you can figure out how to turn it off, I don't see a real way of getting in and out before the police show up."

"Thank you." I smile at her. "This has been super helpful for my book. It's a lot easier to draw hypothetical solutions from reality."

"Anytime!" She grins. "I always have time to chat. I look forward to helping with your next writing problem."

"I should probably go, let you get back to the rest of your day." As I gather my things, Astrid pops up from her seat and squeezes me in a hug.

"Hope to see you soon!" She grabs my now empty mug and flits to the back of the cafe.

I ride my warmth the rest of the way home, not even noticing the brisk breeze knotting my hair. I walk up the steps to my apartment. It is already unlocked. Jack is here. I open the door quietly and find him eating the rest of my pizza, which was meant to be my dinner. I set my bag down, trying to gauge his mood.

"Hi Jack, are you enjoying the pizza?" He swallows his bite and tosses a glance my way.

"I was looking forward to eating your meatballs," he mumbles accusingly. "But it seems you ordered in last night." I hurry toward the kitchen.

"Give me ten minutes." I start rustling pans together. "I have them ready to make, just give me ten minutes."

"Doesn't matter anyway." He throws the pizza back in the box. "I came here to talk, not eat." He grabs my arms and leads me to the couch. "Where have you been?"

"I was getting information on the bank. It's all on my laptop."

He rifles through my bag and starts reading through my notes, completely expressionless. Once finished, he sends it to himself in an email and puts my laptop aside.

"I don't have much time to stay today," Jack says. "But I have enough time to reward you for following directions." His eyes have a feral glint in them, but something about them is unsettling.

"Jack-" He shushes me before I can say anything further.

His hands grab me by the belt loops and pull me forward, before unbuttoning my pants. His hand traces the lace of my underwear, alerting my senses to his touch. He then pulls my shirt over my head, but leaves it around my arms, restraining my hands behind my head. Jack lowers me onto the floor and fondles my breasts. My nipples perk underneath my bra, displaying my arousal to Jack. He leans down to place kisses down my collarbone, while pulling my cups down to release my breasts.

"You speak anything, one word," Jack whispers, "and I leave."

Immediately his fingers pinch a nipple and twist, eliciting a gasp from my lips. His other hand grabs my chin, warning me of his threat. He continues to pinch and twist, harder and harder as my sensitivity grows.

Out of nowhere, Jack slaps me before aggressively planting a kiss over my mouth. His tongue explores my mouth possessively, and I begin to tremble with need. Jack smirks, pleased with my reaction to his touch. A finger drags down my torso to my panties, which he then slides down. The cold air sends a shiver down my body, as Jack leers at my display for him. Slowly, he reaches down and rubs my opening before slipping a finger in. I shudder as Jack continues his circular motions, occasionally pulling out to pay attention to my clit. It is becoming harder and harder to stay silent under his touch. Jack is aware of this and increases the intensity of his hand movements to taunt me.

Two more fingers enter, and I can no longer obey his command. I cry out as my back arches from the sensation. Immediately, Jack withdraws his hand, tsking me.

"Naughty girl," Jack says condescendingly. "Guess you didn't want to come today." I whimper from need, dissatisfaction on my face.

"No, Jack, please. Jack, don't go." I writhe on the ground. His response is a swift slap to my face. He grabs my chin and stares into my eyes.

"I warned you, and you understood the game. I can't help it if you break my rules." Jack pauses, mischief visibly crossing his mind. "I guess I will have to make sure you don't cheat and finish on your own."

"What?" I lean away from him, apprehensive of his next move. Jack sees my mistrust and narrows his eyes. He roughly grabs me and drags me to my bed. I try to regain my footing but end up stumbling to the floor. Jack ignores my fall and yanks me onto the mattress. He removes my shirt from my arms and instead grabs a scarf from the floor, using it to bind my hands to the bed frame. I struggle against my bonds and receive another slap.

"Behave, or your punishment will get worse. I will not warn you again." Thoroughly intimidated by his threat, I lie still, trying to stop my fearful shaking. Jack leans over to retrieve my discarded panties, then moves to face me. "Open your mouth." I comply and he gags me with the fabric.

"Here's what is going to happen next. For breaking my rules, I am going to bring you right to the edge of release. Right before you have the privilege of coming, I'm going to walk away. I'll be back sometime tomorrow to untie you if you've been a good girl. If I come back and you've been bad, we'll just have to do this again." He straddles me and grips my chin. "Do you understand?" I manage to nod through his grasp. "Good."

His hand returns to my entrance to rub my clit and insert his fingers into me. I grind against his hand until my breathing quickens. My toes curl into my sheets. I arch my back on the brink of release, but he pulls away. After placing a kiss on my forehead, he leaves my apartment, locking my door behind him. In his absence, I am left alone. Shivering from cold and displeasure, I fall into a restless sleep.

IGNITING THE SPARK

CHAPTER 4

The sun's blinding light glares into my eyes, and I am unable to shield myself from the rays. I know. I've tried. My wrists are raw from struggling against my constraints, and bruises from last night are splotched across my torso. My shoulders ache from the uncomfortable angle of my arms. A shiver causes me to tremble, my feeble attempts to cover myself with a blanket only led me to tousle my sheets.

Across the room, I squint to read the clock on the wall. Is the hour hand pointing at the 10? Or is that 11? My stomach growls in frustration. The pizza still sits on the counter, taunting me. I rest my head on my pillow and close my eyes. Astrid's silhouette appears, flitting between imaginary tables passing out drinks and bussing empty mugs. I can hear her laugh filling the room, accompanied by soft jazz from the radio. The spices of anise and cardamom tingle my nose, and there I am, joking about bank robberies and bookkeeping.

My daydreams are interrupted by the sound of a key in

my lock. Oh, thank god, Jack is back. He saunters over, eyefucking my naked body along the way. Jack sits along the edge of the bed and removes the gag from my mouth. He pets my hair, pushing it out of my face since he knows how much having hair in my face bothers me.

"Good morning," Jack smirks. "How'd you sleep?"

"Not well," I croak, my voice hoarse and dry. His eyes travel up my arms and he traces a finger along my raw wrists.

"Oh baby," he murmurs. "I thought I told you to be a good girl." I wince as he firmly rubs the wound. Defeated, I look up at him.

"Jack," I whisper. "Please." Something in his expression softens.

"Sparks, were you a good girl?"

"Yes."

A traitorous tear slips down my cheek. Jack raises a hand, and I brace for the impact before he gently wipes the tear away. His hands deftly unknot the scarf, freeing me from my headboard. I dart to the bathroom to relieve myself. After locking the door, I sit down and wrap my arms around my chest, sobs wracking my body. The door handle jiggles a moment, then a soft knock.

"Sparks? Sparks, baby, let me in," Jack calls tenderly.

I flush the toilet and wash my hands, splashing water on my face and roughly toweling off. I open the door to find Jack waiting with a robe. I am enveloped in Jack's arms, then he picks me up and carries me to the couch where a hot cup of tea and toast are waiting for me. I ignore both and hug a pillow to my chest. Jack responds by rubbing my back, humming soothing noises. This was our routine for years, when the night terrors of my mother's death would keep me awake, but today it just feels empty. Jack holds the plate in front of me, encouraging me to take a bite. It scratches my throat as I swallow. I shake my head as Jack gestures for a second bite, so he places the mug in my hands and lifts it to my mouth. The liquid scalds my tongue but I don't care. I drink until the mug is empty and Jack embraces me, caressing my arms.

Jack gets up and grabs a spray bottle and brush, before returning to soothe my unruly hair. *Spray, spray, brush. Spray, spray, brush.* Before long, my locks are detangled, so he begins to braid, taking care not to pull too hard. When finished, he reaches over to the lotion and applies it to my irritated wrists. The coolness is calming, and I can feel my senses reawaken. Jack notices this shift, a small smile coming to his face.

"There you are." He guides my forehead to his lips, placing a soft kiss at my hairline. His thumb rubs along my cheekbone, continuing to coax me back to him. I return his smile before pulling him into a hug. He nuzzles me, breathing my scent in deeply. "I'm glad to have you back." We linger in that position, content in each other's arms, until Jack has to leave. Once again, I am left alone in my apartment.

I wander around the room before stopping in front of my viola case. I find comfort in the tedious tuning process, listening closely for any dissonance. When I am satisfied, I begin bowing at the lower strings, pulling a sorrowful melody from within.

Violas serve a strange role in the string family. Everyone is familiar with the violin, the star of the show. Everybody's favorite string instrument. Parents always hope their child is the next violin prodigy. Cellos also have their fan club. Harmonizing to contrast the brightness of the violin, getting their own melodies here and there. Well respected, with a flair for the dramatic. Then there's the string bass. Beloved in jazz music, basses lay the foundation for the rest of the ensemble, stabilizing the piece with a firm hand. But then, you have the viola. Often forgot about, or ignored, or even replaced by a second violin player. Their task is to highlight everyone else, finding space between the violin and cello to add depth of sound - the ultimate support crew, with no one to support them. Like me, the viola is alone.

I first found my viola at a garage sale. Its previous owner was a kid who dropped out of orchestra to be an athlete. Missing a string with a broken bridge, it was hidden shamefully with the incomplete board games and scratched vinyls. Something about it called to me, maybe like attracts like. I took her home and learned step by step how to repair her. Over the years, I've learned to understand her. Warm, deep notes singing out, longing for the melody. Maybe that's why I've never played with anyone before, because I'm unwilling to force her back into her role of submission, supporting everyone else while falling apart.

I play until my fingers are numb, and then I play some more. When I can no longer press down on the fingerboard, I allow myself to return the viola back to the case, wiping her down thoroughly.

With nothing else to do in my apartment, I change into some warmer clothes and meander down the Boston city streets. I dwell in the sound of crunching leaves and honking traffic, while the bitter wind stings my cheeks. Winter will come any day now, but I will savor the last of the fall, the last of the birdsong, light jackets, and strong spiced drinks.

Wait, spiced drinks? I look up and I am back at Brew for Two. For some reason, this cafe has a magnetic pull on me. I decide not to resist the urge to go in. As I open the door, for a brief moment, all is right in the world.

"Hey!" Astrid beams at me from across the cafe. "I've got great news. We've got anise back in stock." She's grinning ear to ear, anticipating my surprise - which she receives.

"What?" I am pleasantly shocked. "I thought you said you weren't getting any in until next week?" She bashfully looks at her feet.

"Yeah, that's when my next shipment comes in." I wait for her to meet my gaze. In the silence, she continues. "I ran to the store after we closed yesterday. Got enough to hold the shop over for the rest of the week." I pull her in for a tight hug.

"Thank you," I mumble before letting her go. Astrid nearly glows with delight.

"Genuinely my pleasure." She hops behind the counter, returning to her professional demeanor. "Now, can I get something going for ya today?"

"I would love my usual to-go. I'm enjoying the city today, and I can't keep you past close every day." I rustle in my pockets for some cash, and I catch a glimpse of the pastries in the counter window. "Ooh, are your pastries any good?" A glimmer fills her eyes.

"I make them every morning, so I'd like to think so. Actually, hold on, I have some maple pinwheels in the back that I made for the first time today. Would you mind being a taste-tester and letting me know if they're any good? I'm always nervous to sell a new product, but since I try to rotate the stock, I need to keep coming up with new sweets."

"Grab me two." I wink at her. "The last time you picked my order went pretty well, so I'm willing to go out on a ledge twice."

"I'll go get those heated up for you, hang tight."

Then Astrid is off, flitting around the shop preparing my treats. While she's busy, I take a moment to reflect on the eclectic charm of the coffee shop. People from all walks of life feel welcome to stop in, from young students studying on the couches to older couples people-watching by the window. Bookshelves line the wall, full of well-worn tales and thriving green plants. The mismatched rugs and wall art add to the warm and cozy vibes. This place is special, and I can tell that the ambiance was delicately and intentionally crafted, purposefully serving as a haven from the outside world.

Astrid returns to the counter and sets down my cup and bag. "I won't make you try the pinwheels in front of me, but I expect a full report next time you come in." A playful glint crosses her eyes, and I chuckle at her jest.

"I'll write a whole essay," I tease. "Be prepared with your red pen."

"Then I'll just have to stay up all night to read it." Astrid smirks as she leans onto the counter, propping herself on her arms.

As I chuckle, I swipe a flyaway strand of hair out of my eyes. The motion causes the sleeve of my jacket to ride up slightly, exposing the raw irritated abrasion encircling my wrist. Astrid's hand darts across the bar to grab my wrist, examining the mark with concern etched on her face. Her other hand gently slides the fabric up to reveal further bruising along my forearm. She gasps as she scrutinizes my injuries. Embarrassed, I jerk my arm back and fix my sleeve.

"Thanks for the drink," I stammer, flustered as I grab my cup. But Astrid doesn't let the moment slide.

"Did someone do this to you?" She asks in a hushed voice, worry evident. I don't answer, instead I drop my change in the tip jar and leave.

"Wait," she calls after me. I turn back to face her, but I can't meet her eyes. She puts a piece of paper in my hand and wraps my fingers closed around it. "That's my phone number. If... if you ever need something, anything, I'm here for you. Even after close, I live right upstairs."

"I'm okay," is my only response. So quiet I'm not sure if she hears it. I don't wait to see if she believes me. I don't even know if I believe me.

Although I've lived in the same neighborhood for the past year, I've never taken the time to get to know it. Yet, this walk through the autumnal air is one of the best things I've done all week. Quaint galleries featuring local artists, food trucks with delectable steam, and hodgepodge thrift shops line the streets. The corner features a bar with live music and daily karaoke. Why haven't I explored these stores? I stumble onto a local park and breathe deeply, before finding a relaxing bench to claim.

Comfortably seated, I reach into my bag and pull out a maple pinwheel. It looks similar to a cinnamon roll with finely crushed nuts encased by the spiral. The flavors are rich and decadent, but still have a homemade rustic essence. I make a mental note about my comments for Astrid, but then I allow myself to enjoy the people watching.

My quiet evening is disrupted by the ringing of my cell phone. I check the caller ID - Jack. I mull over letting it go to voicemail, unsure if I want to talk to him, before my better judgment leads me to answer.

"Hey dude, 'sup?" I say.

Sparks, I need you. I can hear a layer of seriousness in his tone, and I sit up concerned.

"Jack, what's wrong?"

You need to get to Golden Capital right now. I gasp.

"No, Jack. What did you do?" I frantically gather my things, shoving my trash into a nearby bin. "Just stop a moment before you do something you can't take back."

This is happening Sparks, and if I have a chance in hell of getting my plan to work, I need you with me.

"Shit, shit, shit. Jack, listen to me. Just please." My

heart is racing, and no words come to my aid. "Jack, you're all I have."

If you truly care about me, come. If you truly mean all the things you say about your mom, be here. This is our only chance.

"Jack," I spin around to gauge my surroundings. "I'm about ten minutes away. Just stay put and I'll fix this. Don't do anything."

We're a few blocks away at 5th and Montgomery.

"We? Who's with you? Jack-" The line goes dead. "Fuck, goddamn it!"

I orient myself toward Golden Capital and start sprinting, pushing slow walkers out of my way. "Excuse me! I'm sorry! Move!" Grumbled protests follow, but I don't hear them. I reach the meeting spot, desperately searching the now desolate streets for him. Where is he? I panic when I can't find him and begin to hyperventilate.

Somebody grabs me from behind, a hand wrapping tightly around my mouth muffles my screams. I struggle against his grasp as I am pulled into an abandoned shop and flung to the ground. I look up, and in the dim light I can see Jack among three of the bulkiest men I've ever seen. They all wear black utilitarian clothing with the bottoms of their faces covered, gloved hands wrapped around their automatic firearms. My previous captor rubs his hands on his shirt as Jack kneels next to me.

"Hiya Sparks," he says with his trademark smirk. He passes a duffel bag to me. "Get changed."

"Don't do this. We can still walk away."

"No," Jack snarls at me. "We can't." He nods at the closest man and his pistol is aimed at my head. I hear a click as the safety is turned off.

"Jack," I breathe. "What have you gotten us into?"

He doesn't give me a response. I unzip the duffel and pull out combat boots, leggings, a black hoodie, gloves, and a lightweight tube of fabric.

"Will you at least turn around?" None of the men move, but they do avert their eyes while I change. When I am finished, Jack shows me how to drape the fabric tube around my neck and over the bottom half of my face. With my hood up, only my eyes are visible. He shoves a small key into my hands.

"Once we clear the vault, get to the motorcycle parked outside and drive to the studio," Jack commands with an air of authority. "Don't wait for me or get in our way. Let the men do their jobs."

"Why am I here?" I struggle to remain calm. "How do you know these guys?" He grabs my hand and gives it a soft squeeze.

"I need you to stop asking questions. If you just follow directions, you will be safe. Everyone ready?" He directs that last question to the group. I doubt my input would be invited. "Let's go."

The group moves as a horde. One of the men keeps a firm grip on my bicep to prevent me from leaving the merry band of criminals. Another man carries a duffel bag, full of additional bags. I see a motorcycle parked at the corner, surrounded by nondescript vehicles. We arrive at the back entrance to the bank in the early evening, the sun has begun its descent. Then I realize, it's Friday sometime between 5 and 10 p.m. This is my plan, Astrid's plan. I am shoved against the door and Jack moves to my side.

"Ready?" He asks, looking at me. I just return his stare, pleading with my eyes. "Reach out with your powers. Feel the electricity of the building?" I close my eyes and extend a tendril of power into the bank. My breathing settles as I relish in the hum coursing through the bank, and now, me.

"It's strong and steady," I report back.

"Cool," Jack scoffs. "Turn it off." My eyes widen. "Don't give me that bullshit. Next you'll say that you can't, but that's a lie. Just the other night you blew the power to an entire apartment complex. So I don't care how you do it, figure it out. The alarm is wired into the electrical grid. Shut down the power, and the alarm isn't in play."

There it is. That's why I am here. Not some personal connection or moral support. He needs my powers. A gun is raised to my temple again.

"Hold, hold on." I breathe in deeply, clearing my head. I feel the electrical grid again, poking around for a weakness. There. I found the central line from the power company. If I can create a surge, then maybe it would fry the connection. I start mentally collecting all of the flowing energy into one location. Sweat drips down my forehead from the exertion. Jack grabs my jaw.

"I am losing my patience, Sparks." I push him off me and the crew bristles.

"You're distracting me," I seethe. "Do you know how high the voltage is in this building? It's not like flipping a light switch. So, either go in on your own or back off!"

Jack blinks at my sudden display of resentment and takes a step back. He gives me a single nod and I close my eyes to continue my work. When all the energy is pent up and raucous, I force the ball into the connection with a strong mental thrust. A visible flash comes from within the bank as the power surges before dissipating. I stagger with the effort and Jack catches my fall. After a few shaky breaths, I check my work to find the bank is completely cut off from the main grid.

"Done." Jack victoriously pats me on the back before pulling me to a standing position.

"Alright then," he exults. "Let's go rob a bank."

CHAPTER 5

One of the goons kicks the door in. My babysitter grabs my arm again and brings me through the previously employee-only area. For some reason, he and Jack are the only two with pistols. The other two are armed to the teeth with assault rifles. In these close quarters, I am now able to differentiate between the three mystery men.

First is my babysitter. He has two holsters under his arms, one is empty as he is holding that pistol in his hand. While he is much more muscular than I am, we are the same height. However, he carries himself with such self-assurance that makes me think him being the shortest of the group isn't something he's worried about. He's wearing black cargo pants and a tight t-shirt. His left sleeve has ridden up, and I can see the very bottom of a tattoo. When he notices my gaze, he hastily pulls down the fabric.

"Shit," the second man groans. "This is a brand-new glove." He picks a razor blade off the floor and continues flipping it around in his fingers. I can see a thin slice through his glove where the blade nicked him as it fell to the floor. Despite breaking the silence, he speaks clearly without a hint of shame or awkwardness. I make a note that he must be comfortable hearing his own voice at inappropriate times. He's wearing a loose-fitting bomber jacket, and a belt of tools is clipped to his jeans.

The last man brings up the rear, towering over the other two with broad shoulders and a stoic presence. He is dressed the most utilitarian of the group - black canvas pants with a cargo vest. He hasn't said much, in fact, I don't think he's spoken this whole time. The only thing that sets him apart from any other gun-for-hire is a small keychain on his belt loop with a single penny. We briefly make eye contact before my babysitter shuffles me forward.

I've never seen this part of a bank before. In the lobby, the high vaulted ceilings are decorated with opulent displays of wealth. In the back, it is a maze of tight hallways. Our footsteps on the marble floor echo through the silent halls. Something isn't right. A tingling runs through the hair on my arms, a warning I don't understand.

"Jack," I call out. "Something's wrong." The group's attention snaps to me.

"What?" His eyes scan the area before landing back on me.

"I can't tell, but I know we missed something."

Jack scoffs before gesturing for the men to continue. The man holding my arm pulls me too roughly and I stumble behind him.

"Hey, babysitter. I'm not resisting, so if you could return my arm to me, that would be great." He rolls his eyes and loosens his grip on my bicep. I hear a snicker from behind.

"Yeah, Babysitter. Be gentle with your precious cargo," taunts the man with the razor blade. I'm not sure if he's trying to insult me or the man next to me. I turn to face him, irked.

"Be careful, or you're going to get singed, smartass." Babysitter pulls me further down the hallway, as another sarcastic comment is passed to me.

"Your nicknames are all spot on. Babysitter, Smartass, I bet he's beginning to feel left out." Smartass gestures to the solitary man behind him. Babysitter looks down at me.

"Ignore him," he says. "Or else he won't shut up."

I examine Babysitter's body language compared to the two trailing behind. They are both casually strolling through the bank with a relaxed hold on their rifles, while he has a firm grip on his pistol with his head on a swivel. As we walk, he's holding me back slightly, turning corners himself first to look down the passage.

We enter the lobby of the bank. Just as I remember, the ornate entrance looms over the squad. I am pulled behind the teller's counter, and the group crowds down to avoid being seen by those few passing by. Smartass puts his razor into his tool belt and reaches onto the counter. He closes his hand around a pen and jerks the chain free from its anchor. Pleased with himself, he starts playing with it, holding the chain in his hand and swinging the pen in a circle. I try to hide my quiet chuckle, and Babysitter rolls his eyes. As we leave the lobby for the relative safety of another hallway, I glance up at him.

"Are you a better shot at close range?" I inquire. He's taken aback by my question.

"What do you mean?"

"Everyone else has massive guns. You have two pistols. It seems like you're either underdressed or underprepared. I'm just curious why." He takes a second before answering.

"Pistols are better at close range, but they also allow me to keep a hand open."

"Why is that relevant?"

"Sparks," Jack cuts in sharply. "No more questions."

"You know what, I don't think you're a better shot close up," I theorize. "I think you have a different mission than the others." He raises an eyebrow.

"And what, pray tell, would that be?" Before I can wager a guess, Smartass interjects.

"Use your context clues! He's here to make sure you get out in one piece. We're all here to rob a bank, but he's running a damn daycare."

Jack whirls around.

"Shut it, all of you," he scolds. "We need to keep our focus on the mission."

The men sober up, refocused on being scary, hulking henchmen. I digest the new information. Despite being forced to come along, Jack ensured that I would have a bodyguard for our suicide mission. Our walk returns to its uncomfortably quiet state as we turn the final corner.

And there it is.

The vault.

The reason we're all here, sweaty and covered from head to toe in black. The reason why I am being held at gunpoint. The door is taller than I am, an ominous hulking wall of metal. The screws holding the hinges in place are bigger than my fist. Next to the locking mechanism is a two-foot-tall screen, intended to serve as the control panel, now useless without electricity. Again, I am forced to the front of the pack, face to face with the vault control panel.

"There are two types of locks on this safe," Jack explains. "One mechanical, which my... friend, can take care of." He loosely gestures toward Smartass. "The other is electric. Sparks, we need you to disengage it."

I look at him confused. "What do you mean?"

"Do your thing." He gestures at the mechanism vaguely. I look at him, exasperated.

"Let's make sure I'm understanding you correctly," I sigh and rub my eyebrows. "You need me to run a specific voltage of electricity through this circuit to trick it into unlocking..." I pause while glancing up for confirmation. After receiving it, I continue, "After I already cut power to the entire building."

"Well yeah," Jack shrugs. "Just make some electricity and shoot it."

"I can't just 'make' electricity." I elaborate. "I *redirect* it and take advantage of already in-place electrical systems."

"Why can't you make it?"

"Umm... the law of conservation of energy?" Seeing their blank stares, I clarify. "Ya know, 'energy can neither be created nor destroyed.' Electricity is just electrical energy."

"When did you learn this shit?" Jack grumbles. "You didn't even finish high school."

"Sure, but I've been through middle school." I gripe back. After my mom died, I went underground to hide from those responsible for her death. For all they know, I died. My lack of education has always been a sore spot for me.

"Okay, if you can only redirect electricity, then fucking do that." Jack is getting visibly frustrated from my physics lesson. I sigh again.

"Jack, redirect it from where?"

Realization dawns on him. There is no electricity here to redirect. I made sure of that when I exploded the electrical box earlier.

"Shit, um okay." He looks at Smartass. "Start doing your part of the lock. The rest of you, spread out. Find any batteries you can. Look for flashlights, laptops, everything."

I lean against the wall and slide to the floor. After my earlier stint, I am drained and need to rest. But the nagging feeling returns, a familiar memory pulling on my mind. What am I missing? I allow my mind to settle, examining the tug further. It's a very low voltage of electricity. The power is amplifying, exponentially gaining traction. The lights flicker on as the power grows. I jolt back to reality.

It's a back-up generator, and it's about to sound the alarm.

I jump up and use all of my strength to push the electricity back into the generator, crying out from the effort. The lights go back out and Jack whirls to face me, alarmed.

"What's wrong?" He tenses at my strain.

"Back-up generator." I grunt with the effort.

He swears and hollers at his group. "New target, mission critical! Find that generator and disable it!" He looks back at me. "Sparks, how long can you hold it?"

All I can do is shake my head. Any second it could be too much for me. The generator is gaining power and I am desperately clinging to any last bit of strength to keep it restrained.

"Boss," Smartass calls. "Could she use the generator to finish opening the safe? I'm on my last pin."

I whimper, tears in my eyes. It's too strong. If I let any of the power out, it'll slip from me entirely. Jack turns to look at me.

"Vault or the alarm." I hiss through gritted teeth. Jack nods, meeting my eyes. If he wants the vault open, I can't keep the alarm from triggering. Every moment is agony for me.

"Hold on. Sparks, please hold on." He turns back to the locksmith. "Hurry the fuck up! Team, form up! When that vault pops, we'll have minutes to grab and then retreat. Pass out the bags and stand at the ready." The men regroup into their rehearsed positions.

"Done!" The locksmith steps back, hands in the air.

All eyes turn to me. Jack gives me a single nod, and I fling the build-up of energy into the vault. A crackle of lightning flashes across the room, and static fills the air. Smoke wafts from the circuit and the door pops open. I collapse to the ground as the air is filled with a blaring siren. No one is there to catch me, preoccupied with stuffing bags full of money. The smoke plume grows steadily, and I realize there must be a fire from the surge. Water dribbles on my face as the building's sprinklers are engaged.

Someone grabs my arm and drags me toward the exit, I'm too exhausted to stand. His hand tightens and we stop moving. I roll my head up to find that our path is blocked. Babysitter clicks off his safety.

"You guys are in a hurry. Where's the fire?" chuckles the stranger.

A woman stands in our way, hands firmly on her hips. She is dressed in a skin-tight full body cobalt outfit, with a diaphanous gossamer fabric draped over her torso and arms, like a toga with sleeves. A mask covers her face, but she doesn't try to hide her blond ponytail.

It doesn't matter, I would recognize those eyes anywhere. Recognize that voice. That laugh.

Astrid.

CHAPTER 6

Bang! Bang! Babysitter fires twice at Astrid.

"No!" I cry out and pull at his arm, forcing his shots to go wide. I look towards Astrid and she is gone, a thick wall of ice stands where she stood.

"Get the fuck off me," Babysitter rips himself from my grip. "I'm trying to protect you, you brat."

He readies his second pistol, now dual wielding his weapons. He peaks around the wall, and motions for me to follow. Jack and Smartass run from the vault, duffels stuffed with cash. Fear flickers in their eyes at the ice wall, and the alarm continues to blare in the background. Jack spits out a slew of profanity.

"How the fuck did the Water Weaver find us?" He curses. "We don't have time for this. Plan B, let's move!"

The men spur into action. Smartass takes the lead, rifle at the ready. The stoic man hands his duffels to Jack, then takes his position at the rear. Jack scurries after Smartass with the money. Babysitter holsters one of his pistols and then slings me over his shoulders.

"Put me down," I plead weakly.

Despite my wishes, I know that I couldn't keep up with the group on my own. I used up most of my strength holding back the generator. Babysitter doesn't respond, just moves forward in formation. The ground is slick from the sprinklers, and my clothes cling to my body. We enter the lobby and the group closes rank, moving as a mass to protect each other's blind sides.

"I didn't know the Tributaries had female members." Astrid appears perched on the teller's counter. "Sweetie, you don't look so good. How ya doing?"

Her persona is cocky, but I can see the concern underneath. She sizes up the situation, trying to figure out where I fit in. Meanwhile, I'm terrified she's going to recognize me.

She ducks behind the counter as Smartass fires his machine gun in three round bursts. In the gap between shots, she pops up and slides down the counter. A tendril of water snakes up from the floor and flows into the weapon, before freezing and shattering the barrel. Smartass gapes at his hands, now without a working firearm. He recovers and pulls out a concealed knife, visibly on edge.

"I don't like being shot at," Astrid chides, back behind the counter. "But I'm feeling generous. Leave the money and the girl, and maybe I'll let you escape." Jack growls at her suggestion.

"She's stalling," Jack whispers to the group. "The Water Weaver knows the police are on their way. Normally, I'd love to kill her, but today we can't afford to get caught. If we find an escape route, we're going to take it."

He's met with a few grunts of confirmation, and the huddle moves toward our exit. Babysitter slides me off his shoulder onto the floor. He grabs my hand and wraps it around his belt before unholstering his other pistol.

"Keep a hand on me," he directs. "I need both hands right now, but I'll grab you if we need to run."

While we were planning, so was Astrid, or the Water Weaver as they're calling her. A line of water trickles across the room, flowing by my leg and curving in between me and Babysitter. Suddenly, it lunges toward the ceiling, the impact pushes me away before the wall freezes. The divide stretches from the teller counter to the opposite wall, effectively splitting our group in two. Jack, Smartass, and Babysitter are on the side toward the escape route, leaving me with the final member of our group.

"Sparks!" Jack thunders. I hear banging on the ice, but I know it won't break. Gunshots fire against the wall, but the bullets ricochet to the floor. "Get her out of there!" My compatriot circles an arm around my shoulders.

"Boss," he calls. "I've got her! We'll meet you at the rendezvous point."

I hear a clamor beyond the barrier, and then retreating footsteps. Smoke is billowing out of the hallway we came from. The fire apparently wasn't doused by the sprinklers and has begun to spread through the building. We are trapped between a wall of fire and ice.

"Release the girl." Astrid's voice calmly floats across the room. Tendrils of water rise from the floor wrapping around his legs. He attempts to shake them off, but new ones take their place.

"You want her, you witch?" He roars. I yelp as he grabs my scalp and holds his rifle to my head. "Get your magic off me or you'll be scraping her off the ground." The water sloshes to the floor, releasing her hold on him. Astrid stands atop the counter as a tidal wave surges behind her.

"Find somewhere else to point your weapon." A quiet rage lines her words.

I'm afraid. Not afraid for myself, but for her. I don't know who the Water Weaver is, but to me, my friendly neighborhood barista is staring down the barrel of a gun. My captor shifts his weight, and a soft jingle draws my attention.

His penny keychain.

I move purely on instinct, unsure if my scrap of a plan will work. I twist my body to grab his keychain. The chain breaks and I am rewarded with a single cent. I draw a small amount of charge into the coin, and with the last of my power, I fling it across the room at Astrid. Confusion crosses her face, and she reaches out to catch the penny. As soon as it makes contact with her hand, she convulses from the shock and falls behind the counter. The ice barrier splashes onto the floor.

My new bodyguard wastes no time grabbing me and hauling ass out of there. I stumble, trying to keep up, but am dragged most of the way. When we get outside, he breathes a sigh of relief but keeps up the pace. We arrive at the motorcycle left for me.

"Okay kid." He looks at me. "You still have the key right?" I nod, a mix of emotions in my head. "You're on your own now. Boss said you were to go to your apartment, alright? Get a move on before the police get here."

With that, he turns and runs toward where his getaway car was stashed. But I stand there, horrified about what I did to Astrid. Sure, I prevented her from getting shot, but she could be hurt. I turn toward the bank and see the tendril of smoke rising in the air. It's still on fire, and she's still inside. I take a breath, and against my better judgment, run back into the burning building.

I force the back door open and make my way back to the lobby. Smoke spirals up toward the ceiling, and I am thankful for the mask over my face. I crawl over the counter where I saw her fall and find her laying soaked in a puddle of water. In the distance, I can begin to hear the faint sounds of sirens. I shake her, hoping she wakes. When she doesn't, I panic and rip off my glove. I roll up her sleeve and to my relief, find a pulse. She's alive, just out cold.

Between the impending fire and first responders, I don't have the luxury of time to wait for her to revive. I lift her by her arms and start to drag her toward the exit. I make it to the end of the lobby, but there's still so far to the exit and I know that I'm not going to make it in time.

"Damn it." I crouch down over her, splashing her with the puddles on the ground. "Wake up! Please just wake up!" Desperate, I reach for her hand and firmly pinch the skin between her thumb and index finger. Her face contorts in discomfort. "Yes! Wake up!"

Slowly, her eyes flutter open. She is groggy and disoriented. I pull her to her feet, and she sways. I guide her arm over my shoulder. With most of her weight supported by me, we stagger out of the bank. I help her get a few blocks away, far enough from the police and the fire to be out of danger. I lower her to the ground and fall next to her, exhausted. I lean my head against the wall behind me and just try to breathe normally again.

"Are you okay?" She asks me faintly. I can tell that question took a lot of effort from her. I now start to realize the stupidity of my plan. This close to Astrid, I'm not sure my disguise is enough to keep her from recognizing me. I grunt and force myself to my feet. Leaning on the wall, I start to walk away.

"Wait!" She also tries to get to her feet, but falters. "Let me help you. I can get you out of the Tributaries." I pause.

"Can you get yourself home?" I ask, lowering my voice to try and sound different, still facing away from her.

"I'll be fine," she responds. "But what about you? Let me help you!"

My voice cracks and a tear slides down my cheek. "You can't."

CHAPTER 7

Wind rips into my face as I drive the motorcycle down the highway. I yank my hood off and slide down the scarf, suddenly struck with a sense of claustrophobia. A sob escapes from my chest. I think I might be crying. The cold droplets on my face could be rain, snatched by the wind before they can fall, disappearing into my hair and the road behind me. But I think I might be crying. I was told to go straight back to my apartment, but right now, anywhere else feels better than home. Anger, fear, and despair all swirl together into one singular sense of pain. I scream to the lonely night road, wishing to just drive forever, but I know that I have to go back. My hair is falling out of what's left of my braid, and I feel as disheveled as I look.

Eventually, I park next to my apartment. There's a glow behind the door, so I take a breath before opening the door to Jack. He's shirtless on the couch, talking on his phone. He quickly hangs up as I walk in.

"Goodness, Sparks. There you are!" He wraps me in a

hug. "I was worried about you." I wait for him to withdraw from the hug before I walk to the kitchen and splash some water on my face.

"I have all your stuff here." He pats the duffel bag with my clothes. "I couldn't call you because I had your phone. My colleague said you got to the bike safely... but you weren't here. What took you so long?"

"I needed to take the long way home."

I sit on the couch to take off my boots and unbraid my hair. Jack sits next to me and pulls me onto his lap, straddling him. He tangles his fingers in my hair and passionately kisses me. I gently pull away from him and move to my closet, stripping out of the wet clothes clinging to my body.

"Why are you acting like this?" Jack complains. "Tonight was a success! We should be celebrating." He runs his fingers down my bare back. Normally, that touch would drive me wild, but now it just feels sickening.

"Success?" I scoff. "Which part? Jack, what just happened?"

"What do you mean?" He asks incredulously. "We got in, got out, became richer. Even better, you were fucking awesome with your powers. Our colleague told me about your move with his lucky penny. You knocked that bitch out!" I shudder as the memories rack my mind.

"Did he tell you he threatened to shoot me?" I whispered, still processing the evening's events. I sit on the edge of my bed. "I had a gun to my head the entire time I was in the bank. Who were those people? Why do you know them?" Jack straddles me on the bed.

"Does it even matter?" He leaves a trail of kisses from my neck to my collarbone, his hands roam my body freely.

"I'm scared of you," I whisper softly.

His hands still on my body, Jack leans close to my ear and speaks so quietly I almost don't hear. "You should be."

He grips my shoulders and pushes me flat on the bed. He rips the cups of my bra down and aggressively fondles my chest.

"You should be grateful," he berates. "I'm doing all of this for you. For years, I've been taking care of you. All I ask is that I get a good fuck now and then." He yanks my hair and I tumble to the floor, crying out in pain. "You're going to show me how grateful you are."

Jack holds his dick in front of my mouth. I part my lips and let my tongue swirl reluctantly over the tip. He clutches the back of my head and forces the rest inside me. I gag on the length as saliva drips from my mouth. He moans, relishing the feeling, before thrusting vigorously and rapidly. My lungs scream for air as he rams into me again and again, each thrust driving deeper into my airway, stealing my breath with brutal force. Tears blur my vision, running down my face. They only seem to encourage him. His breathing quickens, movements becoming frantic, and with a final violent stroke, he hits the back of my throat and shudders. Hot liquid lines my throat as he finishes inside me.

"Swallow, whore," Jack commands as he pulls out. I obey him, but he isn't satisfied. "Show me." He grips my jaw as I open my mouth to let him see inside. "When did you become such a selfish slut?"

I close my eyes as I am knocked to the floor, covering my head as blows fall on my exposed abdomen. He lifts me up by my hair, drawing desperate cries as I try to assuage his wrath. His fist strikes me across the face, and I crumple into a ball. His footsteps echo as he walks to the bathroom, washing his hands in the sink. The slam of my front door rings out through the apartment after he leaves.

Abandoned on the floor, I allow myself to break down and sob. I gingerly wrap my arms around my stomach, all too aware of the ensuing bruises. I lean against the wall and stagger to the bathroom.

I don't recognize the person in front of me. My gray eyes are dull and a bruise is forming on my cheek. My long, red hair has lost its curls, and is now full of tangles and frizz. "Love" bites are sprinkled along my neck but whatever just happened to me wasn't love. I start to hyperventilate when I see the marks across my chest. More of my torso is coated in contusions than not, and breathing is painful. I can't stand looking at myself, weak and battered. A wave of emotions floods my mind and I lash out at the mirror. It shatters into shards of glass that cut my hands. I rip the rest of the mirror off the wall and force it into my trash can. I grab a broom and rid myself of the remnants of my fractured reflection.

I turn my shower as cold as it will go and walk into the piercing stream of water. I watch as the water is dyed red and bleeds into the drain. Astrid tried to stop this. She wanted to help. But I can't put her in danger by bringing her into this. I could never leave Jack, he's all I have. He took me in after my mom died. Taught me how to evade social workers when I dropped out of school, how to only pay in cash to prevent a paper trail, and how to never give my real name out to anyone. I died along with my mother. Sparks is all that is left.

My mother was recruited to create a weapon, leaving people exposed and vulnerable. It is my responsibility to undo her work. I got my powers from the accident that killed her, a constant reminder of my burden. Jack is the only one who knows my secret.

Although a part of me is begging to run, there's nowhere for me to go. I step out of the shower and towel off. I grab a compression bandage from the medicine cabinet and wrap my torso, hoping to prevent further swelling. I pull on some soft sweatpants and a flannel.

As I leave the bathroom, my eye catches on my duffel

from earlier today. For a second, I worry that Jack went through my things and found Astrid's number. I tear through my clothes and find the crumpled piece of paper right where I left it. Still in a panic, I decide I need to call her, to make sure she's okay. I pick up my cell, but then shakily drop it on the couch. Jack pays for my phone. How do I know he doesn't go through it? What if he figures out who the Water Weaver is? I grab some change and run outside to a nearby payphone, before dialing the number.

This is crazy. *Ring.* I shouldn't be calling her, it's the middle of the night. *Ring.* Or maybe it's morning. *Ring.* Why isn't she picking up? *Ring.* Oh god, what if she's dead. *Ring.* Or... sleeping. It's the middle of the night. I go to hang up the phone as she answers.

Hello? She sounds groggy, but otherwise fine. *Hello? Who is this?* I cover my mouth to prevent her from hearing my relieved sobs. *Hello?*

The line goes dead, and I hang up my handpiece. I return to my apartment and hide the slip of paper in my viola case. Jack doesn't even know I play. He also doesn't know that I have a friend.

⚡   ⚡   ⚡   ⚡

I spent the rest of the night and most of the next day in bed, only getting up for pain medicine, the canned soup from my cupboard, and the occasional glass or two of whiskey. Feeling the warmth in my cheeks, the throbbing pain turns into a dull ache. All day I was worried about Astrid. I shouldn't have left her alone in that alley when she could barely stand. Yeah, she made it home, but what if she's injured? What if Jack tracked her down after I called her yesterday? I don't have to go in, I can just walk by. Make sure she's okay.

I decide that the fresh air from a walk would be good for me. I replace the bandages on my stomach and put on a clean turtleneck and a pair of jeans. A slight bruise has formed on my cheek, so I apply some concealer and foundation to cover it. After checking to ensure that there were no visible injuries, I pull on a baseball cap and jacket before heading out the door.

I wander over to Golden Capital. Police tape covers the building. The fire must have spread after we left as the entire lobby area is covered in ash. My face pales at the memories, and I walk toward the corner of the street. I look across the street at Two for Brew, not brave enough to get any closer. Astrid is smiling and happy, waving goodbye to the last couple leaving the cafe. She pulls the door closed and fiddles with her keys. She looks up at me and our eyes meet. I freeze, worried she recognizes the scared stranger from the bank robbery, but instead she waves me over. I take a breath and jog across the street.

"Oh my goodness, hi!" Astrid beams. "Funny running into you here." I give her a light smile.

"Hi Astrid, sorry for coming by so late," I sweep my hair over my shoulder. "I heard about the fire at Golden Capital and I wanted to make sure you were okay. And well, here you are. Not on fire." Astrid holds out her hands.

"Nope, not on fire," she chuckles. "But honestly, I appreciate your concern. The fire was really tough for them to put out, but luckily, the firefighters didn't let it spread further."

"Do they know what happened?" I pry, searching her eyes for any sign she knows more than she lets on.

"Yeah, apparently there was a bad electrical fire," she says nonchalantly. "Crazy."

"Yeah, crazy." I rub my arms. "Well, I should let you get on with your day. I'm sure you have plenty to do."

"Actually, my schedule's all free if you want to hang out.

I'd be down to play board games at my place upstairs or check out some local shops," she offers genuinely. It's hard for me to say no.

"I should probably get home. I can't stay out too late."

"No worries." She smiles. "Let me know if you change your mind."

I take a step to walk past her, but a pebble slips from under my feet and I fall. Astrid jumps forward to catch me, but as her arms wrap around my torso, my bruises erupt in pain. I cry out in agony and twist my hands into Astrid's jacket.

"Oh my god, what hurts? What happened?" She lowers me to the ground, eyes frantically scanning for the source of my scream.

"I'm fine, I'm fine." My chest is heaving, but I force my breathing to normalize. Astrid notices the cuts crisscrossing my hands. She examines my face closer and brushes her thumb over my cheek. I flinch with the contact, and she looks at the smudge of makeup on her thumb. I can tell she smells the lingering whiskey on my breath.

"If I lift up your shirt, will I find more bruises?" Astrid gently asks. I just look at her, my deception lasted all of two minutes before she found out. "You don't have to tell me what happened or who did this to you, but can you come upstairs so I can treat your injuries? Please?"

"I trust you." She takes my hand in hers and squeezes. I move to stand, and she helps me up.

I let her lead me up the stairs to her apartment and unlock the door. Her apartment is gorgeous. Light wood floors, gauzy curtains, and cozy rugs fill the space. Knickknacks line the bookshelves and end tables, giving it an authentic lived-in feel. The decor is warm and homey, unlike my threadbare, linoleum abode. She leads me to a chair in the kitchen and helps me sit down. Astrid then pops over to the stove and puts a kettle on, before sitting across the table from me.

"So, you know my name is Astrid, but I don't know your name..." She's right. I don't give out my name. I'd always steer the conversation away from it. I haven't used my real name since my mom died.

"This was a mistake. I should just go." I turn to leave before Astrid backtracks.

"Hold on, wait a minute. No names, got it." She grabs my hand. "I just need something to call you besides, 'Hey you.' So is there like a nickname you're cool with?"

"I can't give you my name," I explain. "It's not safe for you to know. And the only person who uses my nickname is... him."

"Would you be okay if we came up with a new nickname?" She suggests. "We could make it something completely random, like um, oh, I got it! You like anise flavoring a lot, right? What about Anise?" I ponder it for a second before smiling.

"Anise. That's okay with me." A sigh of relief passes over Astrid's face.

"Dang, you really made me work for that one," she teases before taking a deep breath. "Can I ask you some less fun questions? You don't have to answer them." She pats my hand reassuringly.

"You can ask." I pull away a bit, already defensive. The kettle whistles to interrupt our conversation, and Astrid stands.

"You know what, let's start with a beverage first. Tea or chocolate?"

"Surprise me," I taunt. She rolls her eyes and pulls out some tea bags and spices. After meddling with the mugs, she slides one over to me.

"Give it a minute to steep before you start drinking. Oh, I also have some leftover pastries. Are you hungry?" I shake my head no, but she is already up getting a plate. "I'll grab some just in case."

At that moment, I realize Astrid is nervous, fretting about trying to make me comfortable. She sits back down with the pastries and fiddles with her hands.

"Astrid, why are you so nervous?" I ask. She seems shocked at my question.

"Oh, don't worry about me," she laughs it off. "I'm just trying to be a good host."

"Nope," I call out her lie. "That's not it." I pause for a moment. "You want to know more about me, right? Why should I answer your questions if you don't answer mine?" Astrid pinches the bridge of her nose and takes a deep breath.

"I guess that's fair. Yesterday evening, I met someone who was in trouble, like really bad trouble." Oh shit. She's talking about the bank robbery. "I tried to help her, but she wouldn't let me, and I honestly don't know if she's still alive. Even if she is, I don't know how long she'll be alive for. I genuinely see you as a friend, and I'm worried about what will happen when you go home tonight." Her honesty stunned me for a minute. I reach out and grab her hands.

"Astrid," I pause until she looks at me, tears pricking her eyes. "I promise, I will be okay." Her next question comes as a whisper.

"When did he hurt you?" She looks scared to hear the answer, both wanting to know and wanting to remain ignorant. She holds her breath as I respond.

"Late last night," I reply. "Really late last night."

"Oh god." Her face pales in realization. "Last night, someone called me. I think it was like 3 a.m. Was that you? Oh god, you needed help, and I didn't do anything." She buries her head in her hands.

"No, no, no!" I reassure her. "Or... actually yes, I did call but I didn't want anything. I just needed to hear your voice, remind me that there was something good in the world." Astrid takes a deep breath and shakes out her hands.

"Goodness gracious," she giggles, flustered. "I'm supposed to be taking care of you right now, but I'm the one getting emotional. I'll go back in my history and add your number, so I'll know when you call."

"Won't help. I called you from a payphone," I admit. "I didn't trust that he wouldn't find your number. He can't find out about you, full stop."

"So, I'm assuming you won't give me your cell phone number then? Or your address?"

"Off the table." I stress the importance of this. "Astrid, he would kill you. He can't know you exist, and he can't pop over for a visit and find you there."

"Your boyfriend doesn't live with you then?" Astrid clarifies.

"He's not my boyfriend," I explain. "Yeah, we have sex, but he's never claimed to be exclusive with me. He has a key to my place though, and he stops by pretty much whenever he wants sex or to... fight." We sit there silently drinking our tea and munching on the pastries. When we're done, Astrid puts the empty plates and mugs into the sink.

"I would like to make you a poultice to put on the bruises," Astrid states, watching my reaction. "It's not as good as pharmaceutical drugs, but it'll help. Would you be okay with that?" I nod and she continues, "I'll need an idea of how much to make. Would you be comfortable showing me? Or could you outline over your shirt where it hurts?" Astrid wrings her hands, obviously nervous about my reaction.

"Are you sure you want to see?" I ask, knowing how

emotional she was earlier. I run my hands through my hair. "It's not pretty."

"It's important to me that you are taken care of," Astrid reaffirms. "Of course, I don't enjoy seeing you hurt, you're my friend. But helping you heal is worth it. So if you'll have me, Dr. Astrid is at your service."

I stand and take off my jacket and ballcap. I cross my arms to take off my sweater and wince at my muscles flexing. Astrid places a hand on mine, a sincere look on her face.

"Can I help you?" I let go of the hem of my sweater and allow her to pull the fabric over my head. She quietly observes the hickeys across my chest before moving down to the bandages. "May I?" I give her permission to remove the bandages, she is horrified at what she sees.

"Anise, how are you walking? Sit down!" She ushers me back into my chair. She turns away from me and holds a hand on her head. She mutters to herself. "I respect your decisions. You know your situation better than I do. I respect your decisions..."

"Quite a mantra you have there," I tease her.

"You don't have to worry about him hurting me." All light has left Astrid's eyes, and a glimmer of the Water Weaver persona appears. "If he ever comes near me, I'll make sure he can never touch anyone again."

She recites her mantra a few more times, calming herself down. After a minute, her bubbliness reappears, and she starts grabbing items to make her poultice. She focuses intently on grinding the herbs and oils together. It's strange to see someone care about me so much. I don't really know what to do with that information. Astrid gets a clean cloth and wipes the table down and then grabs her poultice.

"You might be more comfortable laying down for this," Astrid suggests. She helps me get settled and washes her hands. I look up at the ceiling bracing for how much this is going to hurt. One of my hands grips the edge of the table, and I focus on my breathing. Without thinking, I reach out with my other and grab her left hand, finding support in a gentle squeeze from Astrid. She leaves one hand in mine and uses her other to spread the paste over my abdomen. I groan and grip the table until my knuckles turn white, while Astrid makes soothing noises.

"You're doing great. Just a few more minutes, hang in there. Almost, almost, and done!" My forehead glistens with sweat, and Astrid ties off the end of the bandage. I sit up and she helps me slide my turtleneck back on.

"What time is it?" I ask. "I should probably get home."

"I don't like not having a way to know if you're okay," Astrid fidgets with her hands again. "I'm scared that something could happen to you, and I wouldn't even know."

"The payphone isn't far from my apartment." I wrap Astrid in my arms. "I'll call you, I promise."

"Compromise with me," she begs. "Leave me your cell number and address in a sealed envelope. I promise I won't open it unless there's a true emergency, and you can come over anytime and check that I haven't opened it. I promise, I just need to know that you're okay." I take a step back and look into her eyes.

"If he ever even thinks you exist, he will kill you," I warn. I'm becoming friends not only with Astrid, but the Water Weaver. If Jack learns that I've been in her apartment, he'll probably kill me too. She's unfazed. I slump my shoulders. "Get me some paper."

Astrid scurries to grab a writing utensil and some stationery. The yellow paper has a polka dot border with a matching envelope. I cover my writing as I go, careful to ensure she can't see my information, before sealing it away.

Despite her eagerness, she waits patiently for me to extend the envelope to her. Her hand grazes mine, and sparks dart between our fingers. She pulls back in shock and we both blink, each wondering if what happened was real. After a moment, she pulls me into a hug and then walks me out, the only evidence of our encounter is a scorch mark on the corner of the envelope.

CHAPTER 8

In the next few weeks, life settled into a comfortable routine. Most days, I would stop by Brew for Two, sometimes for a few hours or others for a few minutes. Astrid learned about my freelancing and has since referred me to several of her clients. With my "new" motorcycle, I can travel further distances around Boston and take better jobs - still cash only. Currently, I am wiring an entire commercial build for what will end up being a boutique store. A lot of work for one person, but they pay well and I work quickly. A lot of the cafe regulars have become good acquaintances of mine, and we engage in idle chit chat. The coffee shop has become a second home. Sometimes I help Astrid bus tables, and other times I flip through the books on her shelves. I was never a strong reader, but I can trudge through the stories.

On days when I can't stop by the cafe, I make sure to give Astrid a quick call from the payphone, never from my cell. I occasionally go up to her apartment, and each time she shows me the intact seal on the envelope, hidden in the back of a drawer. Although my bruises have healed and no new ones have formed, she still worries about me.

Jack has deigned to return to the normal state of our relationship as fuck buddies. He never apologized for the bruises he left and comes over intermittently for rough sex. For him, it's as if that night never happened. For me, that's all I think about. I don't find pleasure in his touch. Where I used to feel ecstasy and euphoria, I am left with dread and contempt. I forcefully scrub myself down in the shower when he leaves, trying to purge myself of each fingerprint that lingers in my mind.

Those nights are the ones where I tear through the countryside on my motorcycle. The helmet Astrid begged me to buy is left on my end table. I crave the feeling of the wind battering my face and ripping through my hair. I drive until I'm free of the city limits and pull over to rage and cry out into the darkness. My powers are truly unleashed then. I reach for the power lines above and shoot sparks across the sky, painting the world with my fractured brokenness, a beautiful, haunting mosaic of crackling flashes. I don't know why I was so afraid of my powers. Using them makes me feel strong, untouchable. Maybe I don't need to be afraid anymore.

The sun glares through my window far too early. Last night was one of those nights, and my body groans from the memories of my episode. After far too little sleep, I walk into the cafe and strike up a conversation with a lovely group of elderly women, but Astrid can see right through my fake cheery disposition. Across the room, our eyes meet and for a second, my mask slips. In a blink, my internal torment is plastered over with a pageant smile. I force a laugh at the tales of grandsons' accomplishments before stepping away to the back of the house. I roll up my sleeves and scrub the dirty plates in the scalding water. Astrid slips into the room. I pass my finished dishes over to her and she loads them into the sanitizer. We work quietly. She offers her silent support as I channel my frustrations into dried chocolate patches. A bell rings as a new customer enters the cafe, and I wave her off. Hesitantly, she goes to assist them, and I finish cleaning.

The electricity of the coffee shop is a familiar hum in the back of my brain, like a pleasant earworm. I feel the shifts as Astrid powers up the coffee grinder or the espresso machine, a subtle comfort that almost allows me to sense where she is as she moves behind the counter.

I walk back to the front of the house, more relaxed now that I've shown those chocolate stains who's boss. Astrid is filling up a pitcher of water for some college students working on a group project. In the corner, a child and her father are stacking blocks. The kid giggles and Astrid smiles, a soft light glimmering in her eyes. I lean against the doorframe, contentedly watching her work. Her ponytail sways as she multitasks, wiping down the counter as she waits on the water. Astrid drapes her towel over her shoulder once the pitcher is full, grunting as she lifts the heavy container. She's got better things to do than deliver a pitcher, that's something I can do for her. I jog towards her, but before I can intercept the jug, the child cries out, her block tower toppling to the ground. The sudden noise startles Astrid. The pitcher slips from her hands as her head whips to the commotion, water splashing onto her apron and puddling on the counter, dripping onto the floor. I sense a change in the electrical current of the room and scrunch my eyebrows, trying to figure out the unusual shift.

"Shoot, how clumsy am I?" Astrid laughs it off, unbothered by her soaked apron. There's a new circuit near the counter, but what would cause that?

"Astrid, can you hold still for a moment?" The water. Something changed when she spilled the water, but what?

"I've got this, Anise." She grabs the towel from her shoulder. "Take a step back so you don't slip."

Astrid turns to the spill, and time slows. Her hand reaches down, ready to sop up the electrified water. I'm not thinking as I leap forward. She briefly makes contact with the water as I knock her over, but I reach out for the current, redirecting it to absorb the shock myself. My muscles seize as we fall to the floor, and my nerve endings cry out as the spasms ripple through my body.

After what feels like a never-ending eternity - which is really only one or two seconds - the last of the charge flows out of my limbs into the ground. I scrunch my eyes closed as I turn onto my hands and knees, disoriented and sore. Motherfucker, that hurt. Why did I do that? I know better. Idiot.

"Anise, are you okay?" Astrid kneels in front of me, unhurt. I cough and nod as she helps me to my feet.

"I'm fine." My voice comes in ragged pants as I brace myself on my knees. "Don't touch the water."

It wouldn't matter if she did. I've pushed the awry current back against the grid, but I don't want to take any chances.

"Are you sure you're okay?" Astrid frets over me, tucking my hair behind my ear to see me better. It's kind of cute how worried she is. I take a deep breath and roll my shoulders back, stretching my neck and loosening my tense muscles.

"I'm good," I confirm, shaking out my hands. "Happens more often than I'd like to admit at work. Now, just give me a second, I need to focus."

She stands back as I examine the counter, slowly releasing my hold on the current to follow it to the guilty culprit. There. A stripped wire tucked behind an appliance. Astrid passes me her towel and I wrap it around a pair of rubber tongs, unplugging the faulty cord. It's mostly posturing since I've pushed the current back to where it belongs, but with Astrid watching me so intently, the showmanship is necessary. My powers recede and everything goes back to the way it should be. I turn back to Astrid, a teasing smile on my face.

"Congratulations Astrid, you have won a complimentary electric audit from your favorite handywoman. As part of your winnings, I'm not leaving here until I know every inch of the cafe is safe." I am smothered by Astrid's hug.

"I'm glad you're okay," she whispers. I relax in her embrace, gently wrapping my arms around her waist. The faint smell of peaches and honey tickles my nose before she pulls away. "Thank you for saving me."

"It's nothing." I shrug. "You would have been fine either way. Just hurt like a bitch."

"Accept my gratitude," Astrid scolds, smacking me with the towel. She tries to come off playful, but there's a shadow of unease in her eyes.

Most of the cafe patrons are blissfully unaware of the minor emergency behind the counter. The few that do notice seem satisfied with the resolution, returning to their conversations. I luckily have my tools in the saddlebag of my bike, so I grab those and get to work, scrutinizing every piece of equipment at her barista station. A few cables get reinforced with tape, but the one cord was the only real concern. I replace the entire casing of the wire and wrap the whole length with tape for good measure. I plug it back in with a stern look, daring it to try me again. All of the outlets meet my standards, but I install redundant groundings and safety cut-offs where I can, then go outside to check the fuse box for good measure.

Satisfied with Astrid's future safety, I duck back into the warmth of the cafe, freezing from the incoming winter. She's slumped on one of her couches, all of her patrons long gone. Guilt and regret are written all over her face as she makes no effort to conceal her true emotions from me. I wriggle into the space next to her and pull her into my shoulder, mumbling soft reassurances as I stroke her arm.

"I don't understand what happened." Astrid's voice is faint, and I have to strain to listen. "It was just a spill, but then we were on the floor, and you were convulsing. I was fine and you... the pain in your eyes..."

"It won't happen again," I promise. "You're safe."

"How did you know?" She pulls away, looking into my eyes. "You tried to warn me. It should've been me, not you. How?"

"I must just be a better conductor than you," I tenderly tease. "But honestly, I'm just a really good electrician. The instinct comes with the job, shocks and all." She nods, accepting my half-truths though her lips stay set in a grim line.

After a while, Astrid pulls away and paces the room, biting her fingernails. She turns to me. "I could use a drink. You in?" She asks, wiggling her eyebrows at me. "I'm buying."

"I will never turn down free booze." I grab her hand and she pulls me up. "Bar or club? Looking cute or a mess?" She ponders this for a moment.

"Club, and we're going to look hot!" She cheers.

We make plans to meet at a local dance club, and I ride my bike home to get ready. I skim through the clothes in my closet and pull out a strappy mesh bodysuit. Strips of fabric selectively cover parts of my body, but the see-through material leaves plenty of midriff and cleavage on display. I select a tight, leather miniskirt and pair it with a scuffed pair of boots. Since my bathroom mirror lines my trash can in shattered fragments, I use my phone camera to apply a smokey eyeshadow and bright red lip, smudging my eyeliner until I am pleased with both eyes. My scarlet curls are falling down my back in nice enough ringlets, and I know better than to try to force my hair to do anything else. I set my phone on my counter and decide to leave it at home. Tonight is about cheering up Astrid, so I don't intend to need it.

I trudge through the snow, wishing I pregamed to have something warm in my veins. I arrive at the Tonic Room and pull my arms close to my chest, waiting for Astrid. I can feel the thump of the bass through the wall, and I know it's going to be loud once we're inside. It's been years since I've been to a club. Jack was so possessive, it was hard to enjoy myself. I shake him out of my head. Tonight will be fun.

Astrid waves to me as she crosses the street. She looks absolutely stunning in a shimmery gold dress that hugs her curves. Her legs are exposed due to her strappy heels, but the cold doesn't seem to bother her. She tightens her slicked back ponytail.

"I'm so excited," she says, pulling me toward the entrance. "Let's get some shots!"

We head to the bar, ordering two shots each. Whiskey for me, tequila for her. Her body glitter shines under the strobe lights. We down our liquor and then we are out on the dance floor, moving our bodies to the thumping speakers. A few guys cut in, attempting to dance with us. Astrid and I sway with them for a while but stay within arm's reach of each other. Despite the men jiving for our attention, we stay focused on each other and laugh at their brazenness. Needing more liquid poison, we saunter back to the bar and catch the attention of the bartender.

"Hello ladies," he says, giving us each a thorough examination. I am unimpressed but Astrid plays into his charms.

"Hi," Astrid bats her eyelashes. "My friend and I are not nearly drunk enough. Can you get us something to help with that?" She leans on the bar, giving the barkeep ample opportunity to glance at her cleavage.

"On the house." His eyes never make it to hers, and Astrid winks at me. Two cocktails are passed our direction and I take a sip.

"Damn." I grimace at the drink. "This is strong as shit."

"Good," she giggles. "It was free."

"I can't believe you're such a flirt." I tease her, batting my lashes. "Please, stare at my tits and get me inebriated. Maybe I'll give you a little kiss on the cheek." She punches my arm.

"I'll take your drink if you don't want it."

"I think I'll manage." I throw back the rest of my beverage. "Now c'mon, dance with me," I whine, pulling her back to the floor. She laughs and follows me toward the music. We return to the bar sporadically for more drinks, spilling more than we are able to get down, but most of the night is spent grinding on strangers and screaming along to the music.

Toward the end of the night, she pulls me close, and we dance on each other. Our bodies are in sync, and I can feel her breath on my neck. Her fingers tangle in my hair and my hands run down her sides. This has been the best night of my life, and looking into her eyes, I know she feels the same. I grab her hand and give her a little twirl, and she bursts out in laughter. As the overhead lights flicker on, we grab each other's hand and practically skip into the snow.

"I don't want the night to end yet," Astrid drunkenly giggles. "Walk home with me. I'll call you a cab from there." She runs ahead, pulling me along.

At one point in our journey, I slip on a patch of ice. Astrid laughs but extends a hand down to help me up. Feeling mischievous, I pull her down with me and we spend a few minutes in the snow, admiring the stars above. I don't get cold, and I suspect that Astrid has something to do with that. I turn toward her, staring at how the remnants of her body glitter are reflecting every bit of moonlight. She faces me and runs her fingertips along my cheek. My breath catches in my chest.

A squirrel runs near us, startling me, and I pull away. Astrid chuckles and stands, leaning down to help me. I brush the snow off her side, and we finish our walk to the coffee shop. Astrid waves down a cab and we hug before I get in. She passes a few bills to the cabbie.

"Make sure she gets home safe," Astrid says.

"I'll be fine," I slur back.

The taxi drives off and I tell him my address. I thank the driver when we arrive and stumble to my apartment, fumbling with my keys. The door is opened before I can get the key in the lock.

"Jackie, baby." I reach up to him and he picks me up. He sets me on the bed and steps back, analyzing my outfit.

"Where were you?" He probes. "You're drunk."

"Yeah, I had some shots." I struggle to untie my boots. I whine, "Can you help me?" He leans on the mattress, one hand on each side of me.

"Sparks, why were you out so late?" He refocuses me on his questions.

"I just went dancing. It's okay, I was good. No one even looked at me." Jack retreats.

"I highly doubt that," he grumbles, looking at my outfit. "Why didn't you bring your phone?"

"No pockets." I shrug. He looks me up and down one final time before accepting my story and untying my boots. My words slur together. "Thank you." I reposition myself to my knees and run my fingers through his hair. "Now I know why you're here."

Jack removes my hands, instead moving to take off my clothes. Naked, I widen my legs, determined to please him and avoid punishment. Instead, Jack takes off his shirt and helps me through the arm holes. He grabs a wet wipe from the bathroom and gently rubs away my makeup. I tilt my head at him, confused. Seeing my strange look, he tousles my hair and helps me under the covers. He curls up behind me and wraps an arm around my waist.

"Go to sleep, baby." He murmurs, and I drift away.

CHAPTER 9

I wake up nuzzled into Jack's chest with a massive hangover. I groan and shield the morning sun from my eyes. I have got to get some better curtains. I feel a lurch from my stomach and run to the bathroom. Jack holds my hair out of my face as I empty the contents of my stomach. When I'm finished, I close the lid and lay my head on the cool plastic of the toilet. Jack sits there rubbing my back.

"Good morning," he says softly. I groan, and he chuckles. "Sounds like you had a fun night."

"I'm never drinking again," I grumble. Jack grabs the ibuprofen from the cupboard and passes it to me. I swallow two and give him the bottle back.

"Come on, baby." He drags me to my feet and guides me to the kitchen. He starts to cook breakfast and I get out some clean plates. "So, what happened last night?"

"Um, not much," I answer. "I hadn't been dancing in years, so I just decided to go. Danced by myself until last call. When I left, I realized I was too drunk to walk home, so I took a cab."

"What club?" He probes further as he serves the eggs.

"Local one, the Tonic Room," I answer smoothly. "Super loud music, okay whiskey."

"Must be better than okay with how much you drank." He stabs a fork into his eggs.

"That's fair," I say. I gingerly take a bite of my eggs, aware of my uneasy stomach. "I'm sorry." He nods and runs his fingers through my hair.

"I'll always be here to take care of you." He pulls me in closer, cradling me in his arm. We finish our breakfast in silence. I take his empty plate and clean it in the sink when he reopens the conversation. "You know, if you want to go dancing, you could ask me to come."

"That would be nice." I smile at him. It would actually be very uncomfortable, but I'm not looking to start a fight right now. "Would you want to catch a movie after work tomorrow? You can pick the film, and I'll even buy us some popcorn."

"I'd like that," Jack smiles. "I'll pick you up from your job site. Text me the time and place tomorrow." With that, he kisses my forehead and leaves my apartment.

It's been a long time since Jack showed that he cared about me. When we were teens, we were inseparable. Every night, we'd spend time together going to concerts or staying in and watching sitcoms. As we got older, he grew colder and started to use me. The good moments faded away until one day we were here. I'd never asked for the reward and punishment system he set in place. This is not the Jack I fell in love with.

I've never taken the time to grieve all of the lives I lost. A happy family with a mom. Dating Jack properly, maybe even marrying him. Buying a house with a yard, instead of living paycheck to paycheck with a leaky ceiling. I cling to a pillow and allow myself to wish for a different life.

⚡ ⚡ ⚡ ⚡

The next day, I am at the worksite bright and early. Several contractors walk intently between the rooms, each with a job to do. I wipe my hands on my jeans before grabbing a spool of cable and lugging it to where I'm working. I'm dressed a little nicer than usual today since Jack is picking me up from here, with silver earrings and a bracelet. My curls are pulled back into a messy ponytail, but one spiral insists on staying free of the elastic.

Despite the harsh winter outside, I am sweating. My tool belt hangs low on my hips. I grab my wire stripper and clean the end of the wire. After threading the cable into the switch box, I roll the spool the length of the wall toward an unconnected outlet. I staple the cords up to keep them in place, and then cut the piece of wire from the main spool. I thread the last end into where the outlet will go once the drywall team is done. I repeat these steps a few times, making sure each wall outlet has a corresponding cable.

"Yo Anise, I got an electrical problem over here!" A framing guy calls out for me. I make my way over to his room. "We nicked a cable earlier and we need to know if it needs replaced before we put up the drywall. I've already sent my partner over to flip the fuse."

"What the hell?" I exclaim. "We have ungrounded wires all over the next room. All wires are live!" I warn the other contractors in the building and hear a chorus of responses.

"Wires are live!" "Heard." "Watch the wires!"

"Which wire did you nick?" I ask, and he gestures to a specific one on the wall. The wire in question has a thick gash in the casing. At the least, it will need some tape. More likely, it could need to be replaced. I take off my bracelet before slipping on two gloves. I feel the hum of the electricity running through the wires. Carefully, I hold the bracelet up to the gash and a few sparks fly through the air. Yeah, that casing is toast.

"Hey, electric girl?" A different contractor calls from another room. "I think we've got a problem over here." I turn to the first worker.

"Dude, can you get someone to turn off the fuse?" I sigh exasperated. I jog over to the next problem and see the service panel throwing sparks. Whoever worked on it last didn't finish insulating his wires.

"Hey guys, I've got this, but you need to clear the room just in case." The other contractors leave the room, and now I am free to use my powers to contain the issue.

I stick my gloves in my pocket and feel the dysfunctional circuit. The current circles around my bracelet, and I allow a low voltage to follow my nervous system and flow through me. Within a second, the current collides with my earrings, and I lose control, absorbing the shock. My legs give out and I land on the floor. Nothing is injured besides my bruised ego. I pull my gloves back on as the power is finally turned off. I remove the offending wires from the box and finish insulating them properly.

The rest of the workday passes by without any further incidents. Jack arrives to pick me up and I sling my toolbelt into his backseat before settling into the passenger side. Jack rests his hand on my thigh, and for a moment, I let myself relax at his touch.

"How was work, Sparks?" He asks nonchalantly.

"It was crazy," I rave. "There was this one guy who cut a wire and then started messing with the fuse box without asking. You think he would ask me, or any other electrician, before playing around but no. Could've been bad, but I'm too good at my job."

"Glad to know you spend every day showing off in front of idiotic men," Jack grumbles. "You know, you could be developing your powers instead of fawning like a schoolgirl." He aggressively pulls onto the highway, weaving between cars.

"Jack," I run my hand along his cheek. "There's nothing between me and any of those guys. I'm just one of the boys at work. And, I have been experimenting with my powers more. Just today I-"

"You use your powers at work!" Jack whips his head to me, enraged. "Are you trying to draw attention to yourself? The only reason I let you work is because I trust you to be discreet."

"I am. I only use them when I'm alone, and even then, barely." My heartbeat is thumping in my head. "If someone walked in, they wouldn't even be able to tell." Jack's hand strongly grips my leg, his nails biting my skin.

"So," he seethes. "What did you learn about your powers today?"

"I practiced running electricity through my bracelet." I explain passionately, despite Jack's anger. "It was actually really cool. The bracelet was charged, and probably would've shocked anyone who touched it, but it didn't shock me. My earrings, however, they knocked me on my ass. I can't explain it, but it's like it disrupted my internal circuits."

"Interesting." Jack looks straight ahead, expressionless. The rest of the ride passes in silence. We arrive at the theater, and as we walk in, Jack possessively wraps an arm around my waist.

"What movie sounds good to you?" I ask. Honestly, I hadn't kept up with the new releases, so I had no idea what was on. Jack is disinterested.

"You choose," he says with a flippant wave of his hand. I point at a colorful poster.

"That one looks fun?" I offer. He scoffs.

"I'm not seeing some girly chick-flick." He walks over to the ticket booth and selects two tickets for "The Crawling from Beyond."

"I can get it. My treat!" I move for my wallet, but his hand grabs my wrist in an icy vice.

"I can afford two tickets, Sparks." Jack is fuming. "What, now that you have your new fancy job, you think you're better than me?"

"Not at all." I lower my head in submission. "I was just trying to show you how much I appreciate you coming with me." He throws my hand down and pays for the tickets. He escorts me to our seats. We don't stop for popcorn.

We claim our seats in the back row of the mostly empty theater. As the lights dim, Jack pushes the armrest up and pulls me onto his lap. I can feel his breath on my neck as he leans in.

"You want to show me how much you appreciate my company?" Jack nips my ear and his hand slides underneath my shirt. My breath hitches and I squeeze my eyes shut. "Be my little whore. Let me use you like those horny construction men do."

His hands roam up to my breasts and erect nipples. He gives them a bitter twist, eliciting a powerless squeak from me. He condescendingly shushes me before continuing down my chest. He scrapes his nails down my stomach. I try to distract myself with the gore of the movie, but it only intensifies the adrenaline flowing through my body.

His fingers move down to my jeans, deftly releasing the button and inching down my zipper. I writhe in his lap and whimper a protest. Jack reasserts his control and tugs me further into his lap. One finger hooks around the string of my panties while the other hand envelops my throat. He applies a deliberate amount of pressure, restricting my airflow but not releasing me to unconsciousness, forcing me to endure his torment. He thrusts his fingers in between my legs, scraping my folds and plunging inside me. I want to cry out, beg him to stop, but I know it wouldn't help. He isn't gaining pleasure from his actions, only operating in a manner of jealous hatred.

The movie credits roll and Jack shoves me onto the floor. I pull my jacket around myself tightly, feeling vulnerable in his gaze. Impatient, Jack pulls me to my feet, and I stumble along after him. We weave through the bystanders in the lobby, some sparing worried glances my way as Jack's grip tightens on my arm. He rushes me back into the car and speeds off. I cling to my seatbelt as he recklessly snakes through traffic. I see our exit pass by, Jack makes no effort to slow down. We drive for another few minutes, ignoring exit after exit.

"Jack," I whisper. "I think we missed the exit."

"No, we didn't," is all I get in return.

"Where are we going?"

"Wherever I say."

$$\mathscr{N} \quad \mathscr{N} \quad \mathscr{N} \quad \mathscr{N}$$

It's dark when we pull up to a sketchy warehouse. Jack unlocks the door and gestures for me to go in. A table has several boxes laid across it, and a few trucks are lined up along the wall.

"I got you a job," Jack says smugly, crossing his arms over his chest.

"I have a job," I state, suspicious of his intentions. I blink and his hand is dug into my hair, yanking my neck back.

"I did this for you," Jack spits. "Be grateful." He lets go and I collapse to the ground. He walks over to the table, and I follow obediently. "You say you've been practicing your powers, huh? Prove it. These boxes are GPS trackers. Disable the first one, however you want."

"Does it have to work afterwards, or are you looking to destroy it?" I ask, running my hand over a box. They are about the size of a loaf of bread, with a thick black plastic casing.

"Dealer's choice, but just the first box," he clarifies.

I raise an eyebrow at him, surprised at how easy the task is. Without breaking eye contact, I feel for the lights overhead. I forget my earlier lessons from the construction site as the flow is disrupted by my earrings and my body spasms as I fall to the floor.

"Motherfucker!" My breath hitches in my chest as the last of the charge leaves my system. I mutter a few more profanities as I remove my jewelry and shove it in my pocket.

Try number two. The bulbs flicker momentarily as I throw a pulse down at the first box. The outside casing is melted, and the electrical components are fried. Jack is intrigued by the display, but content with the resulting dead GPS tracker.

"Earrings," he mulls. Jack confirms the box is defunct. "Good test. But the next one isn't that easy. For the second box, you need to disable it using only its internal power source."

There it is - the catch I was waiting for. I place my hands on the box, identifying the hum of the battery inside. I gently pull the current out of the box, allowing it to pass through me on the way to the ground. Jack taps on his phone.

"Interesting." He doesn't actually seem to care. "Anyways, I want you to do the same thing to the third box before it hits the floor."

"I'm sorry, what-"

As I ask my question, Jack picks up the box and chucks it across the building. I jump on the table and reach out for the box. It's moving too fast. I can't find a grip. There. A small ball of power. The box is falling, falling. I panic and rip the power core and sparks shower the room as the box plummets to the ground. I pant as the adrenaline leaves my body.

"Why are you on the table?" Jack asks disinterestedly.

"I don't know." I say, unsettled by how my body took over. "It just felt right."

"Moving on," Jack yanks me off the table and leads me toward the trucks lined near the back. "These are all-electric vehicles. This is different from the GPS transmitters. You cannot destroy the trucks. They must be able to function after your specific tasks. We are now looking to see how you are able to selectively affect these vehicles."

"Hold on, you're testing me?" Offended, I protest. "I thought you were testing the quality of the boxes. Why are you testing me? And who's we?"

"You will not ask questions." Jack shuts me down. "Or else we might have a problem." A chill runs down my spine, feeling more unsafe than I ever have with Jack.

He refocuses on the trucks and reads off his phone. "You will need to engage and disengage one of these systems on each vehicle. Remember, they must be usable when you are done. Here are the systems: locking mechanism, radio, engine. One the fourth vehicle, you need to do all three as fast as you can."

"That's not fair." I try to process all that he's asking. "I've never even tried anything like that."

"While I may have all night," Jack threatens, "don't keep me waiting."

I am shaking as I approach the first vehicle. The engineering is complex, and I struggle to identify the different connections. My head is spinning and nothing is making sense. Wires and cables and circuitry blend into an overwhelming conglomerate of electrons, swirling aimlessly. Wait, no. That's wrong. Electricity is controlled, consistent. It follows patterns and simple rules. I know this, I am this.

My body moves subconsciously, and I press my fingertips into the side of the door. My mind melds with the circuitry and I am flowing through the electrical paths. Air conditioning, windshield wipers, air pressure sensors, radio. Radio, radio, radio! I reel back as heavy metal blasts through the car, breaking me from my stupor. I look at my hands and touch my face, checking that I'm back in my own body.

"What the fuck was that?" Jack stares at me in awe. "Your eyes, they were... glowing."

I don't answer. Instead, I take a devoted step back toward the vehicle, allowing my consciousness to be sucked back in. I retrace my tracks back to the radio to switch it off. Fueled by hubris at my newfound ability, I continue on, triggering the locking mechanisms, the engine, the headlights.

"Sparks, step away from the car," Jack orders. He shifts apprehensively. "I mean it."

The car is my playground, and I am sick from the invigorating high. My hair is fiercely yanked backward, and I am ripped from the truck, collapsing to the ground. Jack kneels beside me, and for a moment, what could be fear flashes across his eyes before being concealed.

"Do you feel it?" I mumble, entranced. I don't listen for his answer, drawn back to the truck's power. It's intoxicating and I find myself reaching back toward the door. "I can almost hear it calling me..."

"Sparks!" Jack slaps me across the face and I jerk to meet his gaze. Realization dawns on me as I gasp and scoot away from the vehicle. For the first time in my life, I was strong, powerful, in control. But Jack's always watching. Can he see how at home I was in the untold pit of energy? How in an instant, I was stronger than he will ever be? Stronger... but still so weak.

'I... I need to go home." I whisper, now afraid of Jack's scrutiny. If he knew... My mind flashes back to his aggression and rage. His possessiveness at the theater. His violence after I confronted him. He could never know. Jack examines me, dissecting my reaction. After a beat, he nods and takes me back to my apartment.

⚡ ⚡ ⚡ ⚡

I lock the door behind me and lean against it. After taking a shaky breath, I move to my kitchen and down the rest of my whiskey. The empty bottle stares back at me. It needs to be restocked sooner rather than later. I throw the bottle into the trash, the glass shattering in a satisfying manner.

The local liquor store is only a block away. After buying whatever whiskey was cheapest, I take my pillage to my couch and unscrew the top. I take a long draught from the bottle, and then another. My throat burns as it goes down, and I savor the pain, focusing on that feeling over the ones sprinting through my mind. The effects of the liquor start to creep in, numbing my brain.

I walk over to my viola case and fumble with the zipper. Although I am quickly losing finger dexterity, I pull my viola to my chin, not even bothering to tune. An aggressive, albeit slobby, tune comes out and I exhale, allowing my mind to clear.

Except that doesn't happen this time. Instead, my rage is amplified. My bitterness from Jack's indifference, my resentment from his abuses, my indignation at his controlling nature.

I remember a time when we were better. Licorice and popcorn for dinner, sharing a bottle of whiskey playing strip poker, whispering sweet nothings in my ear as we made love, not fucked. Back when his touch was invigorating, giving me life. Before I knew I was a bird in a silver cage, a prize to be kept hidden. He's never asked to be my boyfriend, and now I don't know if that is due to his sheer arrogance that I had no other prospects, or if he never actually loved me. But I loved him. Deeply, and with everything I had. And for years, he has been everything I had. Ever since my mother.

My viola screeches as the thought of my mother disgraces my mind. My mother. What an appalling thought. After all this time, her betrayal still cuts me deep to my core. I had a happy enough childhood. My father out of the picture, my mother and I were a good team. I got good grades, she tried to sprinkle smiles and laughs into my day. Fresh baked goodies, bandages with a kiss, reading spooky stories to me in candlelight. I had always thought my mother was the loveliest mother one could have, before she started working for Synergy Labs. Her workdays became longer, and she didn't notice when my grades slipped. Dinner came from a microwave, scrapes went unkissed, and I did my homework alone. I would already be in bed before she came home, a quick peck on my forehead was our only daily interaction.

But that wasn't why I hated her. Her abandonment I could excuse. No, I hated her for Synergy Labs. For betraying the image of the person I once knew. I could never forgive her for her part in the project.

The machine was almost operational when she died. I went to work with her that day. The nightmares keep the memory as clear as the day I lived it. The flash that cut through the facility. The blast of air as if a bomb went off. My mother was thrown over the railing, dead instantly. I desperately clung to the necklace around her neck, hoping, praying she was still alive, though I knew she wasn't. The chain snapped from her weight.

The same necklace hangs around my neck as a constant reminder of my duty. It is the reason I stay with Jack. The reason I can't allow myself to get distracted by anyone else. My happiness is irrelevant so long as those responsible for Synergy Labs are alive, devising plans to build weapons of mass destruction. My mother contributed to this establishment, and I must atone for her crimes.

My fingers flit faster and faster on the stringboard, matching my spiraling thoughts. It's not fair. It's not fair! A child responsible for her mother's actions. A mother who died before she could face the accusations I thrust upon her. My teenage years were thrown away, orphaned and relying on the generosity of another grieving stranger. I met Jack because of her, stumbled into this relationship because of her, and now I am doomed to be beaten and raped because of her, unable to leave.

A part of me dreams of leaving this cage and flying away. I first think that I'd have nowhere to go, but a part of me knows that's not true. There's one place I'd be safe. *No.* A place full of warmth and light. *No.* Where the aroma of coffee roams the air, and laughter flits through the room. *No!* Where blue eyes and tender hands wait for me. *No!* Inside a small cafe, a pair of arms wait to caress me, to shield me from harm and show me love. *No!* Inside a small cafe, Astrid waits for me.

"No!" I cry out. A viola string snaps and whips my cheek, drawing me out of my mental spiral. Thoughts like that aren't helpful, aren't productive. My personal happiness is irrelevant. My duty comes first. Everything is a means to an end. I take another drag of whiskey, desperately trying to drown out my thoughts of impossible realities. Desire is cruel. Desire hurts more than any bruises Jack could paint on my flesh. It's better to stamp the callous embers, before a spark could ignite a flame that burns from the inside out.

But Astrid refuses to be stamped out of my brain. She's there, all day, every day. Smiling, laughing, adding sprinkles on my hot chocolate, singing in the club, lying in the snow...

"No, no, no!" I sob delirious. I fall to my knees, pulling my hair. It's of no use. She's entrenched in my life, and there's no amount of whiskey that can drown her out. I am overtaken by the need to hear her voice and I stumble to the payphone. Dropping quarters on the ground, I fumble to dial her number. I don't need the little slip of paper anymore, all of her is ingrained in me.

Hello? Anise? She picks up after just a few rings. I slur out a greeting, unsure of the words coming out of my mouth.

Are you drunk? The familiar sound of her concern comes through the phone. I can almost picture her expression, clinging to my low words through the phone.

"I had to hear your voice."

Are you hurt? I can pick you up.

"It doesn't matter, nothing matters."

Anise, what's wrong?

"I can't leave him." I bang my fist on the plastic wall. "I'll never be able to leave him."

Let me come get you! I'll help you pack, you can stay with me.

"No! You don't understand." The cold air bites my cheeks where tears leave wet trails. God, I should've put on some warmer clothes before coming outside. "I don't stay with Jack because I'm afraid of him or I love him, although I used to love him. He's my only way of taking down the monsters hiding behind Synergy Labs."

Synergy Labs? What's going on?

"My mother did this to me. How could she do this to me? I hate her so much, Astrid."

Anise, you're scaring me. Come to the cafe, we can talk this out.

"Mothers are supposed to protect you." I talk over her, drunkenly rambling about my burdens. "All I want to do is be with you. In a heartbeat, I would run away. Find a place where no one can hurt us, where I could keep us safe."

I could protect you, Anise. Please, believe me.

"You can't. I know you think you can, but this is big. Big enough that I can't allow myself to be happy." I barely whisper out the last sentence, but Astrid picks it up.

What would make you happy?

"To be with you. To spend the rest of my life with you. To hold you in my embrace and feel your heartbeat in my chest, listening to your pulse as you fall asleep..." I pause, hearing how ridiculous I sound. "I'm sorry, I'm drunk and don't know what I'm saying."

Drunk words are sober thoughts.

"Goodnight Astrid."

I hang up the phone and shuffle back to my apartment, passing out as soon as my head hits the pillow.

CHAPTER 10

I wake in a heap of blankets on the bed, squinting at the bright light coming through my window. Goddamn sun. I really need to get curtains. A bottle of whiskey hangs from my fingers, or what's left of it. Less than a quarter of the bottle still has amber liquid swirling around. I groan and scurry to the bathroom, retching into the toilet. Fuck, I hate drinking. No, I love drinking. I hate the day after. I start the shower and stand under the icy downfall, cursing the morning but waking promptly.

Somewhat refreshed, I towel off and walk into my living room. Quarters are haphazardly strewn across the room. I must have called Astrid last night. I pause to think. I remember walking in the door after Jack's weird tests, but nothing else. My viola is resting on my couch. Aw shucks, a string snapped. I carefully place it back into its case, making a note to buy new strings. I'll probably do that when I get curtains. I gather my discarded quarters and head out to my trusty payphone, dialing Astrid's number.

Good morning, sunshine. I can hear her smirk. *How'd you sleep?*

"Ugh, I called you last night, didn't I? I can't remember a thing. Did I say anything embarrassing?"

Nah, you were just drunk.

"What did I say?" She hesitates before she answers.

Nothing abnormal. Just some ramblings. I could tell you were upset, but you were slurring too much for me to make it out. For some reason, I feel as though she's leaving something out, but I choose to take her at her word.

"That's good. Sorry I bothered you last night."

Anytime! I love drunk Anise.

"I should let you get back to your day."

Wait, um, actually... I was about to make some lunch and I have enough to feed an army. Would you be interested in coming over for lunch... and, um, hanging out?

"I'd love that." I smile a genuine smile. "Be over in like forty-five minutes?"

Sounds like a date. Plan! Sounds like a plan!

We hang up and I head back to my apartment. I'm giddy as I open my closet. I feel like putting effort into my appearance today, looking cute. I pull a maroon turtleneck over my head to hide the bruises on my neck, then pair it with black jeans and a flannel. I apply some mascara and deep red lipstick. Since I'm riding my bike over, I don't bother doing my hair. I grab my leather jacket, mittens, and helmet, before heading out the door.

⚡   ⚡   ⚡   ⚡

I park my bike outside of the cafe and remove my helmet, fluffing my curls. I see a light on through Astrid's apartment window, and smile as a mischievous thought crosses my mind. I lean to the ground and carve out a snowball. *Pmph.* I pause before rolling a second and tossing that at her window too. *Pmph.* Another pause. *Pmph.* The window opens and Astrid pokes her head out.

"Did you just-" She is cut off as a snowball bursts in her face. She cackles. "Oh, it's on!"

I take cover behind a dumpster and start mass producing my snowballs. I hear the door open and lob a few projectiles at her direction. Astrid squeals as my aim is true. She ducks behind a car and begins her own stockpile. Snow is flung in all directions and our laughs fill the air. My breath fogs in front of me and I start to shiver. I decide to approach my end game, so I can get into the warmth of her apartment. I form a massive snowball and army crawl through the snow away from my impromptu fortress. I sneak sufficiently close enough to her and then stand, heaving my monster ball in her direction. It was much heavier than I imagined, so it shattered a foot away from me. Astrid whips toward me, the element of surprise lost.

"Oh, you little twirp!" She chucks a few snowballs toward me, but I tackle her into the nearby snowbank. She throws her head back laughing as I lay on top of her, her body heat radiating through her clothes. I lean in closer, feeling the warmth of her breath on my face. She stops laughing, an earnest look in her eyes. Astrid reaches up to tuck a dangling strand of hair behind my ear, and her hand settles on the back of my head.

I close my eyes and delicately close the distance between our lips, a soft graze before I withdraw. Swiftly, Astrid wraps her hands in my curls and lures me back in. She passionately kisses me, and I return the fervor, hands gripping her jacket, pulling her against me. A kitchen timer signals in the distance, and we separate. I pause, taking in the sight below me. Blonde hair spread across the snow, cheeks rosy from the cold. I'll remember this for the rest of my life.

"I think that's the pork," she whispers, and I stand, helping her to her feet. There's a moment of silence, before I run my fingers through my hair and follow her inside. After hanging up my coat, I stick my hands into my pockets, awkwardly floating around the kitchen.

Astrid glances up at me smiling, taking me in. After a moment, she cocks her head, confusion in her eyes.

"You don't like turtlenecks," She states plainly.

"What do you mean? I like turtlenecks," I tease.

"No, you don't. You think they're itchy and scratchy, they give you claustrophobia. You only wear them when..." Realization crosses her features, and she trails off mid-sentence.

"When what?" I snap, defensive.

"How bad did he hurt you this time?"

"Not that bad," I say indignantly, but she's not convinced. I sigh and lower my guard. "Astrid, it's not bad. It's just colorful and looks worse than it is. I'm just... just a little embarrassed, I guess."

She grabs some plates and starts serving, mulling over what I said.

"Anything I can do to help?" I ask, running my hand through my hair, already nervous from the terrible start to our meal.

"Sure," she smiles, dispelling the tension. "Can you grab the water pitcher from the fridge? I'll meet you at the table."

I open the fridge and snag the pitcher, then fill both glasses at the table. Astrid pulled out all the stops for this meal - tablecloth, nice plates, table already set. And as always, she looks gorgeous. Her hair is normally in a high ponytail, but today it falls past her shoulders. Her white, lacy top flows past her wrists, in stark contrast to her light-wash jeans lining her legs.

"So, today we have a spiced pork loin with succotash," Astrid passes me a plate. "Plenty more if you're still hungry."

"Thank you for cooking!" I gaze at the plate, which smells fantastic. "I've never had succotash before. I'm looking forward to trying it." She picks up her fork and scoops some up.

"I grew up in a pretty rural town," she reminisces. "There were a lot of farmers, and we ate a lot of vegetables. Really living off the land type of people. Succotash reminds me of home. What about you?"

"My friend and I move every few years, always somewhere urban." I state plainly, matter-of-fact. "Easier to blend in, but that also makes it hard to put down roots. Heck, I've only been here about a year. I don't remember much about where I grew up."

"Wow," Astrid looks at me with pity. "That sounds awful."

"I guess I hadn't really thought about it." And that's true. It's just how it was. Jack said it was safer to keep moving. Blend in, hide your identity. Moving so often has some downsides, it's easier to avoid making friends when you know you'll just be leaving.

"Sounded like you had a lot of fun last night," Astrid teases. "What all did you do?"

"I can't remember a thing!" I laugh at her jest. "I woke up in a pile of quarters, so that's why I know I called you."

"Your fingertips look pretty raw," she notices. "What caused that?"

"Oh!" I exclaim. "That one I do know. I played my viola last night, apparently a little too long." I glance down at my hands and see the irritated fingertips, a sure sign that I got sliced by the wires. "I was pretty bummed this morning when I found out I broke my G string." Astrid chokes on her food out of shock.

"Excuse me?" She's a little startled.

"Oh my goodness." I am mortified. "I did not break my underwear. One of the strings on the viola is tuned to the note G, making it the 'G string.' I found it snapped this morning, so I need to go buy more strings."

"That is the funniest thing I've heard all day." Astrid blushes behind her hand, trying to maintain some decorum after our underwear discussion. "I didn't know you played."

"Eh," I shrug. "I just kind of play what the instrument tells me to. Somehow, it always knows how to say what's inside my mind. I'm not good with words, but I'm good with music."

"I'd love to hear you play," Astrid suggests genuinely. "Maybe you could play in the cafe sometime, if you want an audience."

"Maybe." I give a slight smile. I don't think I'll take her up on either offer, but I appreciate her interest regardless. "What's the story with the coffee shop anyway?"

"What kind of story are you expecting?" Astrid shrugs. "It's a rather simple one."

"Really?" I probe, unconvinced. "A young twenty-something moves from the middle of nowhere to the big city, somehow wrangling enough entrepreneurial spirit and cash to own their own cafe."

"I lease," Astrid rolls her eyes at my assumption. "I just make it work, ya know?"

"But why?" I waggle a piece of squash at her. "Why do

you do this?"

"It's silly," she downplays. I sit and wait expectantly before Astrid gives in, playing with her cuticles. "I think that water has a... spirituality, it's healing and powerful. I don't know how to explain it, but it feels like there's something more there. When I make someone a coffee, or a hot chocolate," she glances at me here, "it feels like I'm contributing to something more. That an act as simple as giving someone a warm drink can somehow make their day better. I became a barista to help people, to make a difference in my community."

"I think that's wonderful." And I mean it. But something about this doesn't feel completely resolved. Water has a spirituality? Is she referring to her powers? "I'm really glad I stumbled into your shop that day."

"Would you consider staying here? For more than a year or two?" She looks at me hesitantly.

"I think I would like that very much." And I would. Although I don't know how much choice I would get in the matter. Jack decides when and where we move. Astrid grabs my hand from across the table, pulling me from my train of thought.

"You can set down roots here," she suggests. "The patrons at the cafe love you, and we can keep finding you electrician gigs. And... I'm here."

Our eyes meet. The lust in the air is palpable. Her eyes fixate on mine, and I can tell she feels it too. I push my nearly empty plate to the side and climb onto the table, crawling to her. She joins me and our bodies are taut against each other. We kiss, my fingers wrapped in her hair, her hands exploring between my turtleneck and flannel. Astrid's nails drag along my back and I softly moan into her mouth. I gently tug her hair to the side, exposing her neck. I plant soft kisses from her jawline to collar bone, leaving smudges of lipstick in my wake. She shudders, before gripping my jaw and guiding my lips back to hers. I gasp for air then return to taste my drug of choice, high from the thrill. I sit back on my knees and pull her onto my lap, caressing her ass through her oh-so-tight jeans.

Her hands tug at my flannel, pulling it off my shoulders. The fabric pins my arms behind my back, but I am unbothered, moving to massage her thighs. Her tongue runs against my lips, which I part for her. She slides against my teeth and I nudge into her. Chest heaving, she pants for air. I take the opportunity to take her bottom lip between my teeth and tenderly bite. Astrid moans and seductively whips her hair out of her face.

"How do you do this to me?" I groan, digging my nails into the denim of her jeans.

"I've been waiting to touch you for weeks," she murmurs. "To feel your body against mine, run my fingers through your hair, learn how you taste. I am reveling in every fucking moment."

"How do I taste?" I taunt.

"Ambrosial, like an exquisite blend of spices." Then, she's done talking as she reconnects with my lips, moaning again. Her hands move to my breasts, outlining the edge of my bra and squeezing. I shake my flannel the rest of the way off to free my arms. Then, I guide Astrid flat to the table and straddle her. My hands roam her entire body, her hair, her breasts, her stomach, her hips. Astrid intertwines her fingers into my hair and yanks me down to her, tongues mingling through open lips. I grind my hips into hers, and she arches her back.

She sneaks a finger under the hem of my shirt, running along the waistband of my jeans. I reach down to remove the obstacle when my phone rings. I roll my eyes and slide off the table.

"Ignore it," Astrid pouts. "Come back to me."

"I'm sorry," I run my hands through my hair, frustrated at the interruption. "I have to take this."

Only one person has this phone number, and he doesn't like to be ignored. Jack's voice sears through the phone.

Where are you!

"I went out for lunch," I defend myself. "We don't have plans so I didn't think it would matter."

Well, we have plans now. How soon can you get back?

"I need fifteen minutes." I rub my brow, kicking myself for answering.

This is important.

"I will get there as soon as I can, okay? See you soon."

I hang up and glance at Astrid. Although dejected, she's hiding her disappointment. I run my thumb along her cheek and place one last kiss on her lips.

"Next time, I'm leaving my phone at home," I promise.

"Tomorrow," she grasps my hand in hers, pleading with me. "Go ice skating with me. Just us."

"Wouldn't miss it for the world." I pull her into a tight embrace.

And with that, I leave her apartment and speed on my bike. A gloomy, dark cloud sets over me. The cold air pierces through my clothes, but I don't even feel it. I feel nothing as I am dragged away from her, my one good thing.

⚡ ⚡ ⚡ ⚡

"Thanks for joining me," Jack mutters sarcastically as I enter my apartment. I fling my jacket onto my coat hook and walk over to him. He stands, looking me over. "You look nice today."

"Thanks," I mumble. He grips my chin, pulling me to my

tip toes. He leans down and examines me closely.

"Your lipstick is smudged," he accuses, rage in his eyes.

"I just ate." A plausible reason.

"You must think I'm clueless," he sneers. He slaps me and I fall to the floor from the impact. My cheek stings as I avert my gaze. He crouches down to my level. "We don't have time to punish you now, but believe me, I won't forget this." My face pales at his words, terrified of his implication.

"Jack, please, listen to me-"

"Shut up, whore. I told you, we'll deal with your shallow excuses later." Hate drips from his words. "I need you to put this on." He tosses me a black object. I start to move toward the bathroom, but he stops me with a wave of his hand. "I think I'll watch."

I nod and remove the fabric currently covering my figure. His leering eyes trailing every curve, every contour. Mostly naked, I unfurl the clothing provided. It's a black bodysuit, with silver threads woven into the fabric. The material is thick and sturdy, constructed almost industrially. I pull it on and then zip it up to my chin. A hood hangs loosely from my neck.

"Braid your hair," Jack instructs. "Then I'll show you how to pin the hood on."

"What am I wearing, Jack?" I probe.

"A disguise. For our next heist." He states simply, daring me to challenge him.

"No," I shake my head, knowing it's the wrong thing to say. "I'm not doing that again. We barely made it out last time."

"Yeah, due to your shitty recon."

"My shitty recon?" I can't believe him. "Or the fact that

it was a fucking bank that was literally designed to not be broken into. Or that some crazy person broke into the bank to stop us from robbing it." He grips my neck, cutting off my airway.

"Maybe that's why we're changing plans," he says condescendingly. "We're stealing the money once it leaves the bank..." Images flash across my mind, the tests. "... in all-electric armored trucks."

No, not again. He tricked me into proving that I could do it, that I could take control of the trucks through their circuitry. I mean nothing to him anymore. No longer a friend or companion, just a tool. A possession.

As if to contradict my thoughts, Jack gives me a deep, passionate kiss. The edges of my vision start to fade when he drops me to the floor. I gasp for air and cough, shifting to my hands and knees. Jack kneels to the floor and places a hand on my back.

"Remember that the next time you look for a fuck somewhere else," he spits in my face. "Now, go braid your hair and get that shit off your lips."

A few minutes later, the hood hangs just above my eyes, with a front panel covering the lower half of my face. Jack shows me how to smudge charcoal around my eyes to disguise my face in the shadows.

"You see these silver-colored fibers?" Jack gestures at my sleeves and I nod, unwilling to speak to him. "This is actually aluminum filament. After last time, I wanted to give you a way to protect yourself, and after you told me about your bracelet story, I came up with this. Ideally, you can electrify your suit so no one can touch you but me." A gloved hand runs down my bicep, sinisterly indicating his dominance. "Let's go."

Jack leads me to a new motorcycle and settles me on the seat behind him, forcing me to wrap my arms around his chest. Snow falls from the sky in frantic flakes, and a brisk wind is creating drifts on the road. Not great weather for a bike ride. He starts the ignition, and we are off toward trouble.

⚡ ⚡ ⚡ ⚡

We arrive at an ominous house in a rough neighborhood. Jack escorts me down to the basement before handcuffing me to a pipe lining the back wall. He pulls a folding chair over to me and I slump into it, trying to appear uninterested by peeling at the chipping paint on the wall. He shakes his head and then pulls a whiteboard out of a closet, complete with markers and magnets. Jack then heads upstairs, out of sight.

A few muscular men trickle into the room, each taking a folding chair and getting comfortable. One of them comes over and crouches in front of me, a haughty sneer on his face. His facial hair is patchy, sticking out in places and razor burnt in others.

"My, my, my," he jeers. "What's a pretty little thing like you doing here?" I roll my eyes and turn away from the vulgar man. His eyes are drawn to my jingling handcuff.

"Oh, is the little girlie afraid?" He asks in mock concern, raising his hands to his cheeks. "Handcuffed in a room with big, scary men?"

"Let me be clear." I sit up in my chair and plant my feet firmly into the bedraggled carpet. I don't recognize my voice, icy and authoritative. The lies flow effortlessly. "These handcuffs are not to stop me from running. Oh no, they are to keep me restrained. Even so, they would not stop me from very easily taking the life of every one of you in this room. I would suggest you return to your seat before I am tempted."

"Your little costume doesn't scare me, sweetheart," he

taunts. "We all know you're just the boss's whore."

"Go. Away." My anger seeps out of me and the lights begin to flicker. I can feel a slight glow radiate from my eyes. The creep is oblivious, too busy staring at my breasts to see what every other man in the room was quietly backing away from. He licks his lips, disgustingly ogling his way down, and reaches for my thigh.

"Ahhh!" He cradles his hand, in searing pain from my electrified suit. "You bitch!"

Bang! A bullet flies into the wall near us, and Jack stands menacingly halfway down the staircase. He glares into my eyes.

"Sparks, stand down." A simple command. I recede into myself, content to withdraw from the flickering lights.

"The suit works," I casually inform Jack. He reholsters his pistol and nods, understanding my conveyed meaning.

"Excellent. Next time he touches you, kill him."

The creep scampers away to his seat, while the crew from the first heist follow Jack the rest of the way down the stairs. Smartass gives me a friendly smile before grabbing a chair and sitting near me. The stoic man finds his way to a dark corner, while Babysitter takes his usual place right next to me.

I make myself as comfortable as I can in my metal chair as Jack stands by the whiteboard going over an elaborate plan. Fancy magnets weaving between other magnets, markers drawing lines like a football playbook. Despite the intricate maneuvers he was drawing, my role was simple. I spend the rest of the time analyzing the men in the room.

Smartass is playing with his razor blade. I notice a few nicks in his gloves, and I imagine his fingers are laced with scars. Babysitter is watching Jack intently, moving his eyebrows extensively. Like seriously, the guy is an open book from just his eyebrows. Confusion, concern, understanding, excitement. I tap my fingers on my leg before passing my gaze over to the stoic man in the corner who tried to protect me at the last heist. He is unmoving, unreadable, until... there! As soon as Jack finishes his explanation, the stoic man mumbles a quick prayer. He catches my eye afterwards, noticing I witnessed his little secret. I make a quick note of his new nickname - the Reverent. The four other men filter out of the room, all pulling on identical gloves.

Jack heads over to me and unlocks the handcuff. I flex my wrist and stretch the aching muscles. Babysitter grabs my bicep and I groan.

"Please gentlemen." I wrestle my arm back. "I'm cooperating. Keep your guns and hands to yourself."

Before they can argue, I lead the way to our awaiting transportation. Four teams of motorcycles and sidecars line the road, and Jack mounts the only single bike. Smartass, Reverent, and the Creep strap into a sidecar. I take my seat in the last sidecar, and Babysitter straddles the bike. Three other men I don't know hop onto the rest of the cycles. Everyone except me dons a helmet. I guess Jack was more concerned with my fancy hood than my safety. Babysitter starts the ignition and follows the caravan toward the interstate.

CHAPTER 11

The earlier snowfall has escalated to a blizzard. The wind pierces my bodysuit and I shiver. I'm on edge. The power lines are a bit off the interstate, not a reliable source of electricity. Of course, there's always the other cars on the road, but those are infrequent. I start slowly siphoning a bit here and there from the passing vans and pickups, stockpiling the reaped energy in my suit. Babysitter is wearing gloves so there's little chance of accidentally shocking him. Still, I pull my arms close, nervous for him. I guess I'm also nervous for myself, speeding down an interstate toward no good.

Babysitter's body language stiffens. The three armored trucks come into view. My breath catches in my throat, and the intensity of what we plan to do finally sinks in. The three motorcycle duos ahead of us pull out their rifles and speed ahead. They weave through traffic and each other, like hockey players skating on ice. One of the pairs cuts off the last truck, while the other two flank their respective sides. Shots are fired and all hell breaks loose. The truck veers, looking for an escape route.

Babysitter pulls up close to the truck and I reach out with my powers. GPS tracker located, I effortlessly fry the hardware. The truck is another story, it's too complicated from a distance. I need to feel it, to let myself merge with the circuitry. I shiver, not from the cold, but from memories of the other day.

"Get closer," I call over the wind. Babysitter adjusts his position to better see the edge of the sidecar, and gently drifts toward the truck. With a deep breath, I make contact with the truck and allow my mind to lapse.

I exhale as I am surrounded with energy, lavishing in the warmth. I find myself traveling down the pathways of the wires, exploring the crevices. Voices call out to me, but I ignore them. Finally, I cross the conduit toward the locking mechanisms. Oops, looks like the doors are unlocked now.

The truck lurches, and I am ripped away as Babysitter swerves to avoid crashing, spewing profanities. I pant, slightly disoriented as I catch up on what I missed.

"Unlocked!" I yell to the nearest cycle pair.

Smartass nods and yanks open the driver's door. He grabs the driver by the collar and tosses him onto the road, before getting in himself. I scream as the man hits the road hard. The other passenger is shoved out the other side of the truck before Smartass turns on the hazard lights, signaling that he is in control of the truck. He slows and turns off at the next exit, and the caravan approaches the next truck.

The team resets but I am hyperventilating. My actions led to the death of two men. I didn't know, didn't realize what would happen to the guards. A bitter taste fills my mouth as we approach the next truck, knowing my tally is going to rise before the day is over. I harden my nerves.

After seeing the fate of the first vehicle, the second truck is not going easy. Swerving across several lanes, speeding up, slowing down. I struggle more to track down the GPS device, as this truck is an entirely different make and model than the previous. I dispatch the tracker simply enough, gesturing for Babysitter to bring us in.

"I can't get closer," he roars. "We'll crash before you can do your thing." My mind races, trying to feel for anything valuable from this distance, my efforts are unsuccessful.

I move to crouch on my seat. Every bump of the road shakes the sidecar, and I struggle to maintain my footing. "What the fuck are you doing? Sit the fuck down!"

"I can reach further this way," I counter and stretch toward the vehicle, almost, almost, allmoooost. The truck lurches to the side and I falter. Babysitter yanks me back before I fall to the pavement below. Jack's bike pulls up beside Babysitter.

"Is she trying to get herself killed?" Jack yells incredulously.

"Wait, Jack, stay there!" I call and slip behind Babysitter.

With one hand wrapped around Babysitter's chest holster, I rifle through Jack's saddlebag. I shift around looking for a rope of some kind. The closest thing I can find is a short pair of jumper cables. This will have to do.

I scooch back to my sidecar. I take one end of the jumper cables and tie them to a handle. The other end I wrap around my wrist a few times. Giving it a few hard tugs, I am satisfied enough with the strength of my tether. I crouch on top of my seat and gradually rise to a squatting position, one foot on the edge of the sidecar.

"Sparks, sit your ass back down!" Jack bellows. "Sparks! Do you hear me?"

I give the tether one last tug before I lean over the road,

trusting my entire body weight to the half-ass rigged cord. I curse under my breath, straining for the truck. Babysitter delicately veers right, and my hand lies flat on the side of the target. Quickly, I launch my mind into the fray, rushing to find my marks.

The entire truck is wired differently than the one prior. I am completely turned around, all of my limited experience is useless. The motorcycle dips in a pothole and I grip the jumper cable with both hands until we stabilize.

"Sparks," Jack screams. "Any time now!"

"You're welcome to give it a try," I holler snarkily. "You know, since this is so fucking easy."

I readjust my footing and give the tether several good tugs. After taking a few deep breaths, I turn back to the truck and reengage. I slip back into the electrical pathways, poking and prodding. After a few wrong turns, I am able to unlock the doors. On my way out, I stumble upon the engine block and turn off the power. I snap back to the real world as the truck slows abruptly.

I move back to a seated position, clenching my tether in my fist. Jack directs Reverent's bike pairing to apprehend that vehicle as we move forward to the final truck. We are left with one complete pair, a lone rider - Jack, and my pod. Gunshots ring out behind us, and I flinch, knowing what they imply.

We approach the last vehicle, the other motorcyclists already weaving around it. In an act of desperation, it suddenly veers off an exit and into the city. Luckily for us, the roads are devoid of other traffic, preventing interference or casualties. This truck is different still from the previous two, longer with a ladder scaling the back corner. I return to my crouched position, legs aching from the exertion. I put my foot on the ledge and begin to shift my weight forward.

I glance up as we drive over a patch of ice, losing

traction. I scream as I lose my balance. Babysitter flings his arm toward me, but I am out of reach. In a split second, I make the decision to jump off the motorcycle instead of allowing myself to fall.

My hands find purchase as I dangle from the truck's ladder. Babysitter spins out, and the bike crashes into a pole. I lose sight as the truck rounds a corner, and the remaining caravan follows.

I pull myself up and find my footing, clinging to the ladder desperately as the driver tries to shake the pursuing motorcyclists. My hood ripples in the wind and I'm too terrified to even think about dismantling the GPS tracker.

Ice covers the road ahead and the truck fishtails down the road. The motorcycles struggle to follow, the ice diminishing their driving abilities as well. The driver loses all control of the truck and ramps the curb, flipping the vehicle. I am flung from the ladder. Flying through the air, I brace for the impact.

Instead, I watch as the falling snow melts before my eyes, forming a wave that catches me and gently lowers me to the ground. One moment, I am sopping wet, water dripping from my body. The next, I am somehow bone dry and the snow resumes falling. I sit there for several minutes, staring at my hands, my arms, checking for injuries that aren't there, unable to comprehend what just happened.

The snowstorm increases ferocity until it is an all-out blizzard. I stand, but visibility is so low, that I am moving blindly. I hear Jack cursing, and I run toward the sound of his voice.

"I'm okay!" I call out. "Guys, I'm okay!"

I trip over something - more like someone. I look down and one of Jack's goons is lying on the ground, unconscious and hogtied with a thin band of ice. It is then I realize what is happening. The Water Weaver is here. Astrid is here.

⚡   ⚡   ⚡   ⚡

Sirens ring through the storm, and I hear Jack call out from behind me. The snow is disorienting, I can't tell which way I came from or where I should be going. I try to make my way toward Jack, and I start to make out some of his words.

"Let's get this truck unlocked!" He commands. "Take as much cash as you can hold and get back to base. Let's move!"

"We have to go!" I shout through the wind. A scream cuts out, Jack ambushed by the Water Weaver. I panic, frantically trying to find Jack and get to safety.

Swiftly, the snow clears and I am standing in the eye of the storm. I dust myself off and look down the street as the Water Weaver steps into the clearing, her untamed hair swirling with power. The fabric of her suit ripples with the force gusting from her. She moves with fluidity, strong in her motions but graceful and elegant.

"You're the girl from the bank," the Water Weaver realizes. "You're alive? I thought you were dead! Why are you here? What are you wearing?"

"Oh you know, I just thought it was good weather for a swim." I alter my voice, trying to speak in a lower register. Normally, I'd love to be alone with Astrid, but I really don't want to be alone with the Water Weaver. "Thanks for catching me earlier, assuming that you're the only one here capable of... whatever it is you do."

"You're welcome." The Water Weaver arches an eyebrow at me. "You need to leave, now."

"Already tired of my company?" I feign offense but use it as an excuse to take a few steps back. "Alright, I can take a hint. Let me go grab my idiot and we'll head out."

"They're not leaving unless they are in police custody." The Water Weaver slinks toward me, closing the distance between us by half. "I'm operating under the assumption that you're here under duress, otherwise, you'd be with them." A tinge of warning is in her voice, a thinly veiled threat.

"Don't for a second think that anything I did today was up to me." My offended reaction is real this time. I step towards her sharply. "Six innocent men died and that is something that I'll have to live with for the rest of my life. But this was a choice that was made for me, and I resent that."

"You always have a choice," she criticizes, inching toward me. "You never have to pull the trigger."

"I'm glad your world allows you to be so ethically black and white." I shake my head caustically, turning away and moving toward the end of the clearing. "You don't know me, don't try to impose your moral compass over my life."

"Okay, let's play this game." The Water Weaver quips, not letting me walk away from our fight. "You said six men died. Why? What are the lives of six men worth to you?"

"I'm not playing," I scoff.

"No." The Water Weaver comes up to me. "Help me understand. Six men are dead and you won't walk away. Six men who won't go home to their families. Tell me what is so important that their lives are worth sacrificing, and maybe I can help."

"Whelp, this has been fun," I chuckle, avoiding her question. "But it's far past my bedtime and I need to grab my jackass and get going. Can you cancel the whole storm thing you're doing?"

"Is that bothering you? I guess I can do something about that, but before you go, I want to say that I'm sorry." Her defenses are back up, but I can tell there is sincerity underneath her armored exterior. "I'm sorry that you feel trapped, I'm sorry that you've had to make some tough choices, and even though I really do care, I'm sorry that I've been stalling you."

"Shit," I suddenly realize how close the sirens are, how they must be here already. "Drop the blizzard and get out of my way."

I jog a few steps to pass her but slip on a patch of ice. I give the Water Weaver an evil eye and she shrugs sheepishly.

"I told you, the only way they are leaving is in police custody," she states calmly. "That does include your jackass." I rise to my feet.

"I don't want to hurt you," I warn. "But I need him."

"I don't want to hurt you either."

The Water Weaver stands in a ready position, pulling snow into liquid spheres in her hands. I reach out to the streetlights surrounding us, electricity crackling in my fingers. We lock eyes, each waiting to make the first move. Nervous, I lob a bolt above her head. The Water Weaver takes advantage of my hesitation, sliding down a path of ice and lashing out with a rope of water. I stumble back, wet, but uninjured. However, in the current weather, the water saps any remaining heat from my body. Now in close quarters, the Water Weaver pops up and jabs at my abdomen. As soon as her hand makes contact with the aluminum in my suit, she recoils from the shock.

"Fucking hell," she curses, shaking her hand.

I take a chance and sprint toward the edge of the storm, but slip from a snare around my ankle. I push a current down the line and the Water Weaver cries out. An ice wall is raised in front of me and I slam into it. I whirl around angrily.

"For fuck's sake!" I seethe. "I am genuinely trying so hard not to kill you right now, but you're making it so goddamn difficult. Don't you know water is a conductive material?"

"Give it your best shot," she taunts, but her heart isn't in it. My face softens.

"Please," I beg. "Don't make me fight you."

The Water Weaver expands her ice wall, fully encircling us in a hodgepodge arena. The sides are slick and unclimbable. I receive her message - I'm not leaving until she says I can. I nod, eyes tearing up. She raises her hands, beckoning for me to strike first. I oblige by sending a few quick bursts her way. Only one strikes home, but she falters in her step. She quickly recovers and lunges toward me, pelting me with water. I lasso her with an electric whip, and her muscles spasm from the charge. Her face contorts with pain, and she whimpers softly. I hear the sirens begin to fade in the distance. I drop the charge.

"No, no, no!" I slam my fist into the wall, praying for it to shatter or react at all, but it is immovable. I walk up to the Water Weaver, my whole body glowing and shooting sparks. "Let. Me. Out! They're getting away."

She shakes her head, and I see fear in her eyes. She's scared of me. That knowledge hurts worse than the guilt of the deaths on my chest. I kneel in front of her and bow my head, withdrawing all of my powers. Emotions overwhelm me, frustration, guilt, powerlessness.

After a few minutes of silence, I feel myself dry. I look up and she is gone. The ice wall has disappeared and the snowstorm is back to its normal level of intensity. I waste no time looking for the Water Weaver, instead hopping on Jack's abandoned motorcycle and racing toward the last remaining siren calls.

I am going ungodly fast on this bike, especially considering the weather. My connection to Astrid is compromising my duty. I need to refocus. This is my burden, my mess to fix. I can't let myself get distracted.

Despite everything I tell myself, deep down, I know I can't hurt her. For the first time, I consider her questions. Six men have died so far, and although I didn't pull the trigger, I am responsible. How many more deaths are worth stopping those who killed my mother? How many before I am no better than they are? I know it's worth giving up my own life, but is it worth Astrid's?

No, absolutely not. Astrid will not be another tally, another person murdered to fulfill my vendetta. I don't have an answer for the other questions, but I have drawn a line in the sand. A new question pops into my mind. Would I give it up for Astrid? Would I turn my back and walk away? For the first time, I hesitate. Could I live with myself if I do?

I don't have time to continue contemplating as the police cars come into view. There's two of them, driving one after the other. I carefully pull beside the one furthest back. Checking in the rear windows, I breathe a sigh of relief when I see Jack stewing.

I've found Jack, but I don't know what to do from here. It's too dangerous to try and fuck with specific components of the car while I'm driving. There's no way I could stay in control of my motorcycle. I'm going to have to be a little more brazen than I would prefer.

I sap into some of the car's power and start collecting it in one spot. In one motion, I force it all to the engine block, overloading the circuitry. The car falters, and then the engine lurches, unable to find a consistent rhythm. I slow down and follow the car as it pulls over, staying just far back enough to hide in the flurry of snow. The officer exits the vehicle and pops the hood. I have just enough power reserved to send to him, knocking him unconscious. I grab his keys and unlock Jack's door.

"Took you long enough," he grumbles.

"Excuse me," I retort dryly, shocked by his flippancy. I unlock his handcuffs. "I was a little busy."

He pushes me out of the way to straddle the bike. Irritated, I settle behind him, and we ride in silence the whole way home.

⚡ ⚡ ⚡ ⚡

I walk straight to the bathroom when I get home, eager to take off what's left of my eye makeup, although because of my frequent interactions with Astrid's water powers, most of it is long gone. I pull off my hood and let my hair down. For a brief moment, I break. The stress of the evening has been too much, and I need a reprieve. I hear Jack stomping around in the living room and force the pieces of myself back together. The night isn't over yet.

"Does it make you happy to see me fail?" Jack accuses.

"Where is this coming from?" I throw my hands in the air. "I worked my ass off out there. I almost died like three times."

"You always seem to get separated from the group," Jack sneers. "Why is that?"

"You know exactly how that happened. The motorcycle crashed, I fell out." I shift my focus to his behavior. "You didn't even come looking for me! You were too busy leeching every single cent you could."

"Yeah? And where were you?" He probes. "Didn't see you get caught."

"The Water Weaver cornered me." I bristle at his accusations. "We danced around for a bit, but I got away. The first thing I did was come for *you.*" I poke his chest, furious that my loyalty is under fire. He grabs my hand, crushing it in his grasp.

"What was it you said?" His words are full of venom. "I think it was that you resent me? That was it, right? I couldn't make out all of your conversation, but your distaste for me was clear." I pale when he misquotes what I said to the Water Weaver.

"That wasn't what I said." I stammer out, but Jack chuckles.

"No." He looks deep into my eyes. "You're lying. I would like to think I can tell the difference after eight years."

"It doesn't matter," I plead with him. "I am loyal to you. I came back for you."

"Are you?" He challenges. "Both missions I've taken you on have failed. Today, you came home with smeared lipstick like some common whore. I'm starting to think that you're in desperate need of a few reminders."

He steps toward me, and I stumble back, fall onto the couch, and frantically scoot away from him. He strides to the sofa and grabs my ankles, pulling me toward him. I panic, and a potent charge courses through my clothes. Jack curses as the shock reaches his palms. He pulls out a pair of gloves from his back pocket and slides them on, fire in his eyes.

"You're going to regret that," he whispers. I scramble away from him, but he lunges forward to grab my hair.

"No, no, no!" I scream as he pulls me to the bed. I struggle against Jack as he tries to undress me. Fed up with my disobedience, he throws me into the wall. The world goes black as I fall to the floor.

When I regain consciousness, I can tell I am bound to my bed, blindfolded. I am fully naked, exposed and vulnerable. I shiver, the cold air feeling like pin pricks in my skin. A gloved hand clutches my throat, and I gasp for air but find none.

"I could kill you right now," Jack whispers. "Maybe I

should."

His grip tightens, and my heart thumps in my chest. This is it. He's really going to kill me this time. The world slows and I go limp. Jack removes his hand and slaps me across the face, keeping me from slipping off the edge. My chest heaves, taking in the much-needed oxygen. I hear Jack rustling around before he sits on the edge of the mattress. His weight causes the mattress to slope, and I slide toward him.

"You're so beautiful like this," Jack murmurs, caressing my face. His hand pulls on my ear, and I struggle as he slips an earring in on each side. The backs are secured too tightly, pinching my lobe. "Now, you might feel a slight amount of discomfort."

I hear a slight crackle and then pressure in my ribs. Then I feel everything everywhere, all at once. Pain shoots through every nerve ending, my muscles spasming as an intruding electrical force overwhelms my nervous system. I've never been on this side of the current, always the one in control, never the incapacitated. I want to scream, I want to cry out, but I can't move, can't breathe, can't think about anything through the burning sensation.

It's over as quickly as it starts. I pant as adrenaline runs through my veins, twitching as the rest of the current leaves me. I hear the crackle once more, and brace for the searing pain that engulfs me entirely. I try to redirect the flux, some of it, any of it, but I realize that he crippled me by inserting my earrings. He planned this, thought this through. His betrayal stings, but as I seize from his torture, my mind is riveted on the agonizing stimulations.

"You deserve every second of this," Jack spits, and pulls away his device. I lose any ounce of composure I had left, screaming curses and soaking my blindfold with tears. I pull against my restraints and blood dribbles down my forearms. Jack unbuckles his belt and groans. "Something about seeing you bleed makes me so hard."

"No," I sob as he wipes his hand down my arm, then uses my blood to stamp his handprint on my thigh.

Jack then jabs me with the device in a rapid series of assaults, thigh, shin, torso, breast, collarbone, hip. Each lasting no longer than a second but feeling like an eternity. The last blow is held to my neck, a long, drawn-out blast full of scorn. With my eyes blindfolded, every sense is exacerbated. He pulls away, and I am left feeling hollow.

My legs are forced open, and Jack fiercely thrusts inside me. He moves vigorously, ramming against my walls with a callous ferocity. My body goes slack with no fight left. His nails dig into my flesh, scouting for handholds as his movements quicken. He stills, and I shudder at the thought of him coming inside me. He pulls out and struts around the room, reflecting on his recent pleasure.

"You're a monster," I whisper.

"So I am," Jack taunts. "But what does that make you?"

CHAPTER 12

Jack is gone. He's left but I don't feel safe. I feel vulnerable in the apartment he found for me, with locks he has keys to.

He almost killed me today.

I never thought he would ever go that far, but I guess he did. My fingers fumble as I remove my earrings, breathing a sigh of relief once they are discarded. My mind flashes back to his hands - squeezing, probing, dominating. I won't be treated like that again. Never again. I scurry around my apartment in a frenzy, collecting every single piece of jewelry I own and flushing it all down the toilet. I stand, watching the rippling water as the cheap metal is carried away.

I leave the bathroom and throw on a dirty shirt and a ripped pair of jeans. I grab an old duffle bag, put my Sparks costume in the bottom, and then start stuffing random clothes on top. I don't even know what I'm grabbing, just whatever is close. I run through my apartment to grab my stockpile of cash.

My mind is racing. What am I forgetting? What else do I need? I glance at my phone on the counter, no, the phone that Jack bought for me. I step backward, scared of it. Does he use it to spy on me? I suddenly feel sick. My hand goes to my stomach and my skin pales. I grab my helmet and duffle bag, then slide open the window to the emergency exit.

I nearly trip as I take the steps down, two to three at a time. I slide the strap of my duffel over my shoulders. Straddling my bike, I hear the roar of the motor revving. I sneak one last glance toward my apartment building, knowing that once I leave, I can't take it back. A single tear slides down my cheek as I drive away into the dark night.

There are fifteen steps to Astrid's landing. I counted all of them, doubting a step of my life with each one. But now I'm here in her doorway, all of my possessions in a single bag. I raise my hand to knock but hesitate. Jack likely doesn't know I'm gone. I could slip back to my apartment, and he would never know. Flashes of tonight flit through my mind, and my hand knocks on its own. I hear movement inside, and fear overtakes my body. I back toward the stairs, but the door opens before I can turn. A groggy Astrid walks out and blinks, adjusting to the darkness outside.

"Anise, is that you?" She asks, slightly dazed. She stretches as she yawns.

"I-I..." I stammer, not knowing what to say. "I can come back in the morning." What a stupid thing to say.

"Anise." Suddenly awake, she takes me in. Disheveled, covered in burns, huddling my duffel to my chest. I obviously didn't come for a normal chat. "What's wrong?"

"I..." A lump is lodged in my throat, making it hard to speak. My words come out as an embarrassing, vulnerable squeak. "I need a place to stay tonight. My apartment..." I shake my head, staring at my feet. "Can I crash on your couch? Just for tonight?"

"Of course." Astrid's arms gently encircle me, her hug transitions into a guiding arm leading me into the warmth of her apartment. "Do you want something warm to drink? I can put some water on the stove."

I am numb. I left Jack. No, no, no. I can go back. I can leave now, and everything will be okay. He won't hurt me again. I'll behave and maybe he will love me again. I can't leave him. I can't leave him. I have to go back.

Astrid's eyes meet mine, and I realize I spoke my thoughts out loud.

"Please stay," Astrid pleads, just above a whisper. "I won't force you to do anything, but please, don't go back to him."

"I still feel his hands on me," my voice cracks. "I feel dirty, used. I need to get him off of me." My heart starts to race, and I whip my jacket to the floor. I stare at my arms, reliving every caress and blow.

"Would a shower help?" Astrid keeps her distance, but I can see how much she wants to embrace me, replacing every negative touch with her own.

I nod, but I don't know if it's possible to wipe him clean. She escorts me to the bathroom and turns on the shower, before giving me space. I undress to my underwear. I catch a glimpse of myself in her mirror. I haven't looked at my reflection in months, and all at once, I am reminded why. Faded bruises cover my body, complete with brand-new electrical burns scattered across my skin. I don't like who I've become.

Something in me snaps and I fall to the tile floor. Clutching my chest, I cry out. My face is dry, out of tears to shed. I allow myself to mourn, to grieve for what I lost tonight. A friend, a companion. Jack and I never dated, but there was always a part of me hoping we could grow old together, white picket fence and all. But that was never going to happen, and I am left alone.

A quiet knock raps at the door.

"Anise, are you okay? Can I come in?" With no answer, she waits a moment before entering.

She kneels beside me, rubbing my back and humming soothing noises. I reach for the sink, and Astrid takes my elbow, guiding me to a standing position. She opens the shower door to test the water temp, and finding it satisfactory, steers me in even though I'm still wearing my bra and panties. I expect her to leave, but she walks in, sweatpants and all. The water soaks us both, my hair dripping and her clothes clinging to her frame. She reaches for the shampoo and lathers my curls.

"Your shirt is wet," I state.

"It'll dry," Astrid replies unconcerned. I catch her gaze on my neck, no doubt looking at the angry wound on my neck. She notices my stare and refocuses on my hair. "It looks like you were burned by a vampire," she comments uneasily.

"I think it was a stun gun," I whisper.

I flinch recalling the overwhelming pain and rub my hand over a burn on my stomach. Astrid washes the soap out of my hair, careful to avoid my eyes. She then passes me the bottle of body wash and a loofah, allowing me to take control. I take the loofah and start to scrub my arm vigorously. I dissociate, thinking only of getting the feeling of him off my body.

"Anise," Astrid interjects. "Anise!"

She grabs my hands, stopping my assault. The skin on my arm is raw and irritated. I blink, unaware of how violently I was scrubbing.

"Can I?" She requests.

I pass the loofah over to Astrid, and then guide her hand to my body, giving her permission to step in. She firmly yet carefully runs the loofah over my skin, and I allow Jack's touch to run off with the soapy water.

Astrid turns off the shower and passes me a fluffy towel. She ducks out of the room before returning with a t-shirt and shorts. She leaves again and I wrap myself in the towel before changing into dry clothes. I shuffle from the bathroom and find Astrid in her bedroom across the hall. She waves me in with a smile, and I realize that I've never been in her bedroom before. It's spacious and cozy, with rugs layered over plush carpet. A bed is against the far wall, with a bookshelf and comfy chair by the windows and a cluttered desk by the door.

Astrid has also changed into dry clothes and is finishing putting clean sheets on. A pile of fuzzy blankets is stacked by the foot of the bed. I grab the top one, a pale yellow cotton throw.

"Thank you for letting me stay tonight, Astrid," I say shakily. "I'll go crash on the couch, and I'll be on my way in the morning."

"Nonsense," she fusses. "You're a guest who is in desperate need of a bed. You can sleep in here tonight, and then we'll figure out the rest tomorrow."

"I'm not kicking you out of your own bed," I protest. But Astrid simply shushes me and ushers me into the sheets. They're soft. And warm. I feel her hands tucking me in as I fall asleep.

⚡ ⚡ ⚡ ⚡

I start to wake, nuzzled in soft sheets. Wait, I don't have a fleece blanket, just my patchwork quilt. I throw the blanket off me and sit up with a start, unsure of where I am. I don't recognize my surroundings, the blankets, the desk, the bookshelves. My eyes scan the room and land on a blonde curled up in a chair, Astrid. Last night hits me all at once and I struggle to breathe as all the air leaves my body. I scoot back until I am pressed against the headboard. I pull my knees to my chest and bury my head in my arms.

Astrid shifts, and I tiptoe out of the room trying not to disturb her. I grab my duffel and slink into the bathroom to get dressed. I didn't pack many great clothing options, so I settle on jeans and an old sweater. I'll have to get my clothes from my apartment soon. I walk out of the bathroom and carefully shut the door. I turn to leave but find Astrid bustling around the kitchen, filling mugs with cocoa powder and steamed milk. Despite my best intentions, I must have woken her.

"Good morning," Astrid greets me cheerily, setting the mugs at the table. "I made some cocoa, your favorite."

"You know my kryptonite." I set my duffel by the door and take a seat at the table, cradling the mug Astrid passes over. "Thanks for the drink. I'll be out of your hair in a bit."

"You don't have to leave," Astrid offers. "I don't mind having a roommate. We'll have to reorganize a bit, but we'll make it work."

"Nah, I've got some things to do." That's a lie. I have nowhere to go, but I don't want to be a burden. If I leave, I'll be homeless in the middle of winter.

"Where are you going?" Astrid probes, calling my bluff. She raises an eyebrow when I have no answer for her before sighing. "Anise, you're my best friend. Let me be yours."

I don't respond, instead I stare into my drink and take small sips. The conversation dies down as we sip our beverages. I lose myself in thought, ruminating over recent events.

"Do you want to talk about it?" Astrid suggests, noticing my distraction.

"It'll just upset you." I shake my head.

"Then I'll make more cocoa." Astrid deflects, creating space for me to share.

"He almost killed me last night," I confess. "Either way, it didn't really matter to him. I know that if there was a next time, he would choose differently. He would choose to kill me."

"We're going to need some more hot chocolate." Astrid puts the kettle back on the stove, visibly frazzled.

"I couldn't fight back." I pull my knees to my chest. "He blindfolded me so I couldn't see, I couldn't tell what he was going to do next."

Astrid slides another mug across the table, letting me monologue and process my experience out loud.

"I tried to fight back, but I was powerless." I'm embarrassed at my own worthlessness. "I... I gave up. He could have killed me, and I would have let him."

"Look at me." Astrid forces me out of my self-loathing. "You don't let him do that to you again. He doesn't get to ruin you, he doesn't get to have that power over you."

"He's a monster." I slump in my seat. "And that makes me his little whore."

"Look at me!" Astrid slams a hand down on the table, not angry but assertive. "You are not 'his little whore.' You are the woman who makes small talk to lonely old ladies, you are the friend who combed my entire shop for unsafe cords. You are so much more than him, and he doesn't deserve the privilege to even be in the same room as you. If he ever lays a finger on you again, you are going to fight like hell. You are going to do whatever it takes to get away and come home to me. He doesn't get to win this."

A small crack shows in her demeanor, and I am overtaken with emotion. I run around the table into her arms, and together we slide to the floor. We sat there in silence, Astrid petting my hair and my face buried in the crook of her neck seeking comfort. I pull myself together and shake out my arms. She's right. He doesn't get to win this.

"Astrid?" I twirl my hair nervously. "Do you think we can still go on our date? I was looking forward to it."

"Let's make a whole day of it." Her face lights up. "We could both use some fun."

"Do you have a leather jacket?" I ask.

"Um, I don't think so. Why?" She replies. I pull mine out of my duffel and pass it to her.

"I'm driving." I give her a wink. "And leather is safer to wear on a bike."

She smiles and disappears into her room. I just finish drying the dishes when she returns wearing jeans, a lacy shirt, and my jacket. Her long hair is swept over her shoulder, and I can't help but stare at how much better the jacket looks on her. She grabs a purse and I put on a denim jacket before escorting her outside. I offer my helmet to her and straddle my bike. She stands there hesitantly, helmet in her hands.

"There's only one helmet," she states.

"Yep." I get off the bike and gently slide the helmet over her head, buckling the strap underneath her chin.

"You're not wearing leather," she states again.

"But you are." I lean against the bike. "Trust me, I will drive extra carefully knowing I have precious cargo with me."

"This isn't safe," Astrid protests weakly, moving to the bike. I help her on and position her arms around my waist.

"Just keep your arms around me and everything will be

fine."

I rev the engine and then slowly drive off. Her arms tighten, but I am focused on driving. I might be reckless with my own life, but with Astrid behind me, I am definitely taking everything a bit more seriously. We turn onto the highway, and I feel a gasp behind me as we accelerate. I'm glad I braided my hair before we left, otherwise, I'm sure she wouldn't be able to see around me. A few pieces came out from the twists and currently fly around my face, and I relish the feeling of the wind's cold bite. Slowly, Astrid's grip relaxes, and I can feel her looking around.

I chose my route intentionally, aiming to drive down the most scenic route in the city. It's not rural by any means, but the road is bookended by trees forming a tunnel. I imagine the road would be breathtaking in the summer, with birds and squirrels scurrying through the treetops, but it is still stunning in winter where the branches intertwine with the sunlight.

At the end of my route, I pull over in front of a quaint little workshop. I get up first and then help Astrid who's a little wobbly from her first motorcycle trek. She unclips the helmet and shakes out her hair.

"Where are we?" She asks.

"We're at a paint-your-own-pottery place," I gush in excitement. "The owner needed some electrical work done a while ago, and it seemed like something you would be interested in."

"Well then," Astrid holds out her hand, which I quickly grab. "Let's go check it out."

We enter the workshop. Despite the paint-stained concrete floors, it ends up being toasty and warm inside. Shelves line the white walls, filled with a variety of knick-knacks, while tables are slumped around the middle of the studio. There's an orderly chaos about the place, complete with strewn paintbrushes and splattered paint. A decent amount of folks linger around, and an older plump woman wearing a smock waves as I enter.

"Well, how do you do?" She calls. Her work clothes are colorful but well-worn, and her gray hair is pinned up with the end of a paint brush. "I'm so glad to see you back, sweetie. Are you and your friend interested in painting today?"

"Hi Meredith," I chuckle at her warm welcome and pull out some cash. "I think some painting would be lovely. Got any open space today?"

"Absolutely! We're running a two-for-one special today." She beams. "I have way too many mug blanks and need to clear some inventory."

"I think mugs would be fitting," Astrid jokes. "I actually own a coffee shop downtown."

"Oh, no kidding!" The old woman is very interested in this new information. "Do you ever sell local artist work in your shop? I've been looking for places to sell my pieces, and I would give you a hefty commission."

"You know, I don't currently," Astrid mulls it over. "But that's a great idea. We have a ton of shelf space, and then patrons can have their drinks served in their new mugs."

"Oh, excuse my manners," Meredith chides herself. "You two are here for pleasure and I'm dragging business into it. How about when you are finished, you leave your address with me? After I've fired your mugs in the kiln, I'll deliver them to your cafe, and we can chat then."

"Looking forward to it." Astrid shakes her hand and I finish the rest of our transaction before we head to the wall of mugs.

There is a wide array of shapes and sizes. Some have thin, delicate handles, while others are more industrial. A few have etched patterns and carvings, but most of them are bare allowing the painter to fully flesh out their design.

I watch as Astrid mulls over a few, gently running her fingers over the clay. She lifted one, testing the weight before placing it back on the shelf. Two more fail her tests until she finds one that passes inspection. I love to see her in her element, deep into the physical qualities of the mugs that hold the beverages so near and dear to her heart. Her mug has soft, rounded edges that fit her hands as she cradles the body. I pick one that's hexagonal, intrigued by the unique shape. I sneak up behind Astrid and grab her mug from her hands and replace it with mine.

"Hey!" She protests. "That one is mine."

"I know," I grin, revealing my idea. "I'm going to paint it for you." She runs a finger along the edge of mine, raising an eyebrow.

"Hmmm," she ponders, a mischievous glint in her eye. "I suppose that's agreeable. Though I'll have you know, I'm very picky about my drinkware."

"I think I'm up to the challenge," I banter.

We claim a table by setting our mugs down, and then head over to grab our brushes. At least a hundred bottles of glaze are set out on the shelving. We each grab a clean palette and start squeezing colors onto it. I stick with a variety of blues. At a glance, it seems Astrid is focusing on deep reds and striking grays. She jokingly covers her palette.

"No peeking," she teases. "My idea is too cool to share."

"I don't need to copy you to create an ultra-cool mug," I playfully gloat, pushing out my chest and sticking up my chin. "I have a natural artistic talent."

Astrid sticks her tongue out at me as we head back to our table. Very quickly, I notice the difference in our techniques. Astrid moves methodically, using her brush in a precise manner and keeping her station clean. On the other hand, my quip about "natural artistic talent" was a bold-faced lie. I get paint on my face before my brush even makes contact with the mug. I roll up my sleeves. In no time, colorful blue splotches dot my arms. I definitely go more abstract, with no hope of trying to create an actual design.

I stick my tongue out slightly trying to focus and catch Astrid staring at me. She looks at my colorful mess, her eyes glinting with playfulness. She leans over with her paintbrush and dabs a red blotch on my cheek before returning to her mug. After her affectionate swipe, I feel a surprising warmth in my chest. We continue in a pleasant silence until we are both finished with our "masterpieces."

I grin like a child when I show off my mug with an enthusiastic flourish. The mug is covered with mottled swirls of blues and greens, and flecks of white reflections. Astrid leans over and smiles as she takes in the cerulean and teal splotches.

"This is gorgeous," she says.

"Thanks." I accept her compliment. "It's supposed to look kind of like water. I was thinking about our chat the other day about spirituality, and it just struck me."

"Wow." Her eyes mist up with the added backstory behind the mug. "You have no idea how much this means to me."

"I'm glad you like it." I blush at her affection, then change the topic. "What'd you paint?"

I glance at her mug and take in the curving stands of red weaving through each other. Strings of maroon, burgundy, and scarlet are layered with an impossible depth. Looking closer, occasional glints of silver peek out behind the crimson lines.

"I took inspiration from a few places." Astrid traces some of the strokes as she explains. "I tried to replicate the color and texture of your hair, but then I felt that it needed something else. Then I looked up and saw your eyes and got lost in them. I knew the mug needed some silver accents."

"I think you were right." I lean down to admire the mug. "The silver is stunning."

"Yeah, stunning..." Astrid whispers softly, but she's not looking at the mug.

My breath hitches in my chest as we lock eyes, neither one of us willing to sever the connection. I feel heat gather between my legs as Astrid licks her glossy lips. I am jostled from my trance as Meredith abruptly interjects.

"Hiya ladies!" She exclaims. "Are you two done? Don't worry about cleaning up, I've got you two covered. Oh, and Astrid sweetie, I'll be in touch. Have a great rest of your day!"

Meredith starts gathering up our materials after putting our mugs on a shelf to get fired. Astrid lets out a breath she was holding and extends a hand to me. We interlock fingers as we step onto the snowy sidewalk, but that's not enough for me. I whip around, pinning Astrid against the edge of the building. Her lips find mine before I can even blink. I weave my fingers through her hair as her hands pull me closer toward her. Her tongue flicks against my teeth as my hand explores under her jacket. She pulls away from me as a car drives into the lot. I smirk, unembarrassed by my display of affection. I run my thumb along her jaw before walking back to my bike.

I help Astrid with her helmet, covering her flushed cheeks. I wonder if they are pink from the cold... or from me. She straddles the bike behind me and for a moment I lean into her, relishing in the feeling of her warm body. Her finger wipes a spare strand of hair out of my face, and a moan escapes my lips. I start the engine and force my thoughts to clear, knowing we wouldn't make it very far if my mind is in the gutter. This proves to be more difficult than I anticipated as I feel her chest press into my back.

I pull over when my racing thoughts make it impossible for me to focus on the road. I dismount the bike and shake out my arms. Astrid is blissfully unaware of the effect she has on me, instead heading toward the restaurant I coincidentally parked in front of. She doesn't realize how the tight denim of her jeans cradles her ass, how badly I want to touch the exposed sliver of her hips when the lace of her shirt rides up. Seeing her in my leather jacket, the fluttering in my stomach sinks lower into a pulsing warmth. I run my tongue over my bottom lip before following her into the eatery.

"I didn't realize how starved I was." Astrid takes in the fragranced air as she plops into a booth.

I slide across from her and take a gander at the menu. It looks like we have stumbled into a French bistro, because I can't read a single thing on the menu. Luckily, there's a few pictures, so I know some of my options. A courteous waitress glides over the worn tile floor to us, pulling a notepad out of her apron pocket.

"Bonjour, puis-je prendre votre commande?" She greets. Well shit. I don't speak French. I sigh and prepare for a difficult and embarrassing social interaction when Astrid pipes up.

"Bonjour, puis-je avoir la soupe à l'oignon s'il vous plaît? Merci." She speaks in a rapid cadence with the confidence of a fluent speaker. I am stunned, sitting there gawking while not understanding a single thing going on. A few questions and answers are passed back and forth before the waitress turns to me.

"Umm, hi." I push my hair out of my face, feeling flustered. "Can I have the grilled cheese and tomato soup please?" I point to the picture on the menu.

"Crème de tomates et un sandwich au fromage grillé," The waitress translates to herself as she jots down my request. She politely nods at me before addressing Astrid and leaving. Astrid chuckles as I bury my face in my hands, mortified.

"You don't speak French?" She teases.

"My Spanish is better, and it's still abysmal," I groan. I feel her fingers rub my hair, before moving under my chin and guiding me to meet her playful gaze.

"Why did you bring us to a French bistro if you don't speak French?" She banters.

"Obviously, I thought they would still speak English." I stick my tongue out at her. "And I didn't pick this place on purpose, just kind of pulled up here."

"Really?" Her face lights up. "It's amazing. I come here about once a month, and their food is stunning, especially their soups."

"Good thing I got soup then." I wink at her. "So, how do you know French?"

"That was my foreign language class in high school," she says nonchalantly. "My teacher was amazing, so I really dove into it. My junior and senior year we could only speak French, which makes you pick it up really quickly. When I graduated, a bunch of my classmates and I backpacked around France for a while. I learned a lot about coffee there actually," Astrid chuckles, reminiscing about her high school adventures. "Did your school require foreign language classes too?"

"I don't know," I murmur quietly. I pull my leg under me and run my fingers through my hair. I feel small, insignificant from the ramifications of my life decisions.

"I didn't quite catch that." Astrid digs through her purse for something, unaware of my embarrassment. "What'd you say?"

"I didn't go to high school," I disclose. I make my statement as factually as possible, hoping she doesn't hear the shame in my voice, hoping I look unaffected by my confession.

"Huh." Astrid studies my body language, sensing she's on uncertain ground and unsure of her next move. "So how did you learn your trade?"

"I guess you could say it came... naturally to me. Or after you get shocked five times, you learn to not touch live wires." I laugh at my joke, but Astrid doesn't. She's still searching my face for clues. Desperately wanting to dig deeper, but tactful enough to respect my privacy. Luckily, the waitress returns with our food before Astrid can continue to pry.

"Bon appétit," the waitress wishes, and then returns to her work. I use the food's arrival to change the topic of discussion.

"What did you order?" I ask Astrid, looking at the cheesy bowl in front of her.

"French onion soup," she replies, cutting into the brown broth. "I adore it."

"Oh no, you're a brothy soup person." I fake shock and cover my mouth with my hand. "I don't think we can be friends." I dip my sandwich into my soup.

"What?" Astrid looks at me quizzically. "You don't like broth?"

"Cream-based or nothing," I retort. "If I ever get chicken noodle soup, I just eat it with a fork. Creamy soups though, orgasmic." I emphasize my statement with a spoon of my tomato soup.

"Oh c'mon," she pushes back. "Broths are great. They're warm, nutritious, and they make you feel better when you're sick. Didn't your mother ever make you soup when you didn't feel good?"

"Nope, she always made rice." I feel a glimmer in my eye remembering my mom. "In the mornings, she would throw in banana or apple slices. When I would feel a little better, she would sprinkle in a bit of ground beef to try and get me some protein. She tried so hard to be a good mom."

"She sounds wonderful." Astrid smiles and rubs her thumb over my hand, but I pull away.

"She wasn't," I gripe bitterly. "She put me in a series of impossible situations, and I'm left cleaning up her mess."

"Do you want to rant? I'm a good listener." Astrid looked at me without judgment, but I couldn't dump my family shit on her. That's what my viola was for. God, I miss my viola. I reached my hand back out to her as a peace offering.

"Don't worry about it. Let's just enjoy the rest of the day." Astrid smiles, and I know she has an idea for the next stop on our date.

CHAPTER 13

"Bend your knees," Astrid coaches. "Lean forward. Don't-" I trip over my skates and slam to the ice. "Don't go on your tiptoes."

I groan as I rise to my hands and knees. Astrid apparently loves ice skating, so after we finished lunch, she begged me to come. It's a beautiful outdoor rink, lined with snowy trees and packed with other families and couples. There's a range of skill levels represented, from damn near professionals like Astrid, to first-timers like me. I like to think I'm somewhat coordinated, but with the amount of time I've spent lying on the ice, I begin to severely doubt I have that quality. Snow flutters from the sky, getting caught in my eyelashes. I can see my breath fogging the air as Astrid bends down to help me back up. I scramble on the ice trying to find the slightest bit of traction.

"Whose bright idea was it to attach blades to a shoe and to twirl around on ice?" I joke, enjoying myself despite my lack of talent.

"You call this twirling? Anise, I hate to break it to you, but you're barely standing." I stick my tongue out at her and try to skate again. Astrid snaps back into cheerleader mode, "You've got this! Give me a step!"

I fumble out a few successful steps, starting an unremarkable glide. I reach out my mittens and Astrid grabs my hands, steading me. She positions herself in front of me, skating backward while dragging me along. Together, we gain speed and stability. A laugh escapes my lips and I throw my head back in exhilaration. Euphoria overtakes the both of us and I grow more confident on my feet. Too confident, as my blade catches on a ridge in the ice, and I stumble. Astrid braces herself and absorbs my weight until I can compose myself once again.

I blow at a stray tuft of hair in my face, determined to figure this whole ice skating nonsense out. I glance up to Astrid and see a slight look of concentration that wasn't there before. I return my focus to my skates and see that the ice is completely smooth. No more cracks, ridges, or tracks from other skaters. I flick my eyes back up to hers, which is back to her normal enthusiastic expression. Sometimes I forget that Astrid isn't just the owner of my favorite coffee shop, but also doubles as the Water Weaver.

It's a strange twist of fate that I stumbled upon Brew for Two so long ago. I'm fairly certain that Astrid doesn't know who I really am, but that makes everything so messy. Two people with secret abilities, both identities intertwined. The Water Weaver concerned with the safety of Sparks, unaware that Anise calls her almost daily. Sparks and the Water Weaver are pulling their punches every time they collide, aware of some connection between the two of them and unwilling to hurt the other. Astrid and Anise dance around specific details of their respective pasts, unable to reveal their alter egos. Little does Astrid know that my suit is in her apartment, hastily thrown into my duffel. If she ever finds it, our little game would erupt. The Water Weaver would discover what I've been hiding, upending the relationship we've built over the past several months.

There's so much I don't know about Astrid. What are her actual powers? Is she actually smoothing out the ice in front of my skates? Where did she even get her powers? And why is she so obsessed with Jack and the Tributaries? The longer I speculate, the more questions I have. How did she know about the bank robbery? The armored truck heist? Why did she let me go? What would she do if she found out my secret?

"Anise?" I snap back to the present moment to Astrid nudging my arm. "You still with me?"

"You bet," I rub my mittens together, chilled from the cold. "I've got a few more laps in my tank."

"Well, c'mon then." She tugs me forward, resuming her backward skating.

We skate faster and faster, laughter filling the air. Snowflakes are sprinkled in her hair and her blue eyes sparkle with bliss. I realize, for the first time in so long, I am happy. No ifs, ands, or buts. No looking over my shoulder or waiting for the other shoe to drop. Just happy. I take in the moment. The thrill of skating, the wind ruffling my hair, Astrid's eyes on mine feeling the same thing.

Another skater bumps into my shoulder, knocking me off my feet. Astrid drops to her knees to catch me before I can faceplant on the hard surface of the ice. I am unfazed, caught in my childlike glee giggling in her arms.

"It seems like you're always falling into my arms," Astrid pretends to chide me.

I barely register what she says, too enveloped in euphoria. In that moment, I don't think. I just grab her by the nape of her neck and pull her lips to mine. I feel her stiffen before relaxing into my embrace, her arms wrapped around my sides.

"I'll always be here to catch you," she whispers.

I gaze into her eyes and feel our energy shift. Happiness fades as a new stronger emotion takes its place. Despite the freezing temperature, a heat builds in the pit of my stomach. Astrid looks at me with an intense fire, full of passion and need. My heart races as lust overcomes my every thought.

"I think the rink is getting way too busy," I lie, desperate for any excuse to leave. "Maybe we should think about where we are going next..."

Before I can finish my sentence, Astrid is already dragging me off the ice, not allowing my clumsy skating to slow us down.

In a flash, we are sitting on my bike with Astrid straddling my lap, facing me. Her fingers are woven into my braid as her lips embrace mine. My hands roam her body. While I would love to make out with her on my bike for the rest of the night, I want more. I want to learn every inch of her body. I want to know what she tastes like. I want all of her. I break our kiss and wrap my arm around her torso, sliding her behind me. I hear her whine in protest, so I pass back her helmet and rev the engine. I feel her arms wrap around my torso, and when she's ready, I tear onto the street.

The Astrid who was hesitant to ride a motorcycle is gone, replaced by one much more brazen. I feel her hands exploring my body while I drive. Her hands graze my sides and my stomach, before being so bold as to slide under my shirt. The hem of my top rides up and I can feel the wind bite into my abs, but I am much too aroused to care. Astrid reaches up to my breasts, massaging and squeezing through my bra. A growl escapes me, and I accelerate faster, needing to get back to the apartment as soon as possible.

Astrid then drifts south, her nails scratching the denim covering my legs. She rubs the fabric over my inner thighs, driving me wild. I wonder if she can feel the heat radiating from where my legs meet? Almost as if an answer to my question, Astrid's fingers crawl toward there. My breath hitches and one of my hands leaves the handlebars to clutch hers. There's no way I can drive straight if she touches me there, no matter how bad I crave her fingertips. I place her hands back onto my torso, and she keeps herself busy the rest of the short drive playing with the hem of my sweater.

We're already a flurry of limbs when we burst through the door to her apartment. I toss my keys onto the entryway table, not caring when I hear them clink on the floor, obsessed with the soft lips pressed to mine. I hear a soft thud as Astrid drops her purse. Fabric flies as coats, hats, and gloves are discarded. None of it matters as fingernails trace my hips and my breath hitches at her simple touch.

Astrid struggles to take off her boots, so I walk with her until the back of her legs hit the couch, forcing her to sit. I drop to my knees and cradle a foot in my lap. I stare into her eyes as my fingers dance along her leg before unzipping her boot. I slide it off and leave a painstakingly slow trail of kisses from her ankle to her upper thigh, before giving the same treatment to her other leg. She starts to tremble, need taking over her body. She throws my jacket aside and draws her shirt over her head, sitting in her jeans and a nude bralette.

"Wow." Still on my knees, I stare up at her gorgeous figure above me, content to kneel in reverence for the rest of my life. Astrid is in more of a hurry, guiding me to my feet and dragging me into the bedroom. Her hands slide under my sweater and discard the fabric. She takes several steps back and I see the heat fade from her eyes, replaced with distress and anguish.

"Astrid, what's wrong?" I ask concerned. She's seen me shirtless before, surely she hasn't changed her mind? Surely my body is still good enough for her? I stand exposed and vulnerable in my push-up bra, dejected.

"I can't do this," she murmurs. "Not when I see his marks all over your body."

I look down and see the burns and bruises covering my arms and torso. I know there are plenty more underneath my jeans, as well. I could see how disturbing they would be to her. Damn it, Jack was not going to take this from me. I was going to fuck her tonight.

"Lucky for you," I speak in a low voice. "I don't need to see to pleasure you."

I retreat to the wall and flick off the light switch. It's dark outside, but the streetlights provide just enough light to see her silhouette. I saunter over and run my thumb along her cheek. She shivers with anticipation at my touch. I lean in close and whisper in her ear.

"Do I have your permission to fuck you?"

"Please," she begs, and I hold her body against mine and tilt her head to the side. I run my tongue against her exposed neck and nibble her earlobe. Astrid gasps and arches her back.

"Anise, I need you to touch me," she pleads, quivering where she stands.

I chuckle and drag my fingers from her shoulders to her waistline, where I unbutton her jeans and lead her to the edge of the bed. I quickly slide off my own pants and kneel in front of her wearing only a bra and a thong. Although every bit of me is aching to be touched, my pleasure doesn't matter right now. I have a duty to the goddess before me. I bite the edge of her underwear between my teeth and slowly slide it down her legs before she steps out of them. I blow a cool stream of air toward her sensitive folds and am rewarded when Astrid spews a profane word.

I unclasp her bra, leaving her fully naked before me. She lays down on the bed, allowing me to straddle her. I lean down and take one of her breasts in my hands. Her nipples are already hard when I run a finger over the tip. I can hear her breathing accelerate and I get wet from the sound. I roll her nipple between my fingers and pinch the peak. I continue that action as I bend over and flick her other nipple with my tongue. She whimpers as I take the tip in my teeth and swirl my tongue around. I continue to torment her as she writhes beneath me, flustered by my touch.

"Oh fuck, fuck, please Anise," Astrid sobs beneath me. "I can't take it anymore! I need, I need-"

I don't let her finish before I thrust a finger into her, and she screams in pleasure. I readjust to sit between her legs and place a kiss on her pelvis. Astrid wraps her legs around my head, desperate to keep me close to her. I oblige, flattening my tongue and sliding it along her opening to her clit. She is so wet, and her salty taste is heaven to my tastebuds. I continue to thrust my finger inside her walls and use my mouth to suck, nibble, and lick to my heart's content.

"Anise, I'm so close," she bawls. I feel her body tense around my fingers. "I'm going to come. Fuck, Anise!"

She orgasms with a feral recoil. I sustain my movements until I feel her come down from her high, then run my tongue over her folds to lick up every last bit of her. I suck her wetness off my fingers before I lie on the bed next to her trembling form, draping my arm over her chest. I trace the line of her collarbone, satisfied by her reaction.

Astrid stares at me with a fire in her gaze. She flips to straddle me and interlocks her fingers with mine, effectively pinning my hands by my head. But I'm not scared of her, of this intimacy. Instead, I feel safe and desired. Astrid mistakes my accelerating breaths for fear rather than my deepened arousal.

"Do you want this?" She checks tenderly. I crane my neck, reaching for her lips with mine, but she leans back firmly. "Use your words."

"Yes," I affirm breathlessly. "I want every part of you."

A growl rumbles from the back of her throat. She moves slowly, deliberately to my neck. Her warm breath caresses my sensitive nerves, and my cheeks flush. Her tongue glides along my vein, and I wonder if she can feel my racing pulse. A gasp escapes as she gently bites down where my neck meets my shoulder. My eyes roll to the back of my head as I feel her hand explore between my legs. I shift to open wider, allowing her full access to wherever she felt to venture. I moan from the little circles rubbed near my opening. I squirm, already overwhelmed by the sensation. Astrid tsks at my movement.

"Now we can't have that, can we?" She repositions herself to be kneeling between my legs, holding them still and easily accessible for her. "Close your eyes. I want you to feel every touch, every graze, every sensation. Close your eyes and just *feel.*"

I oblige, allowing my eyelids to close. I focus on the soft cotton sheets between my knuckles, the caress of her hair as the ends tickle my thighs. Her thumb steadily rolls around my clit, applying an unyielding amount of pressure on the nerve. Her tongue snakes in an indiscernible pattern - looping around my opening while flicking inside, figure-eights and spirals. The motions send me into a frenzy, biting on my bottom lip to restrain my moans. A firm pinch on my clit draws a desperate cry from my throat as I experience the intersection of pleasure and pain.

"I earn every sound that crosses those lips," Astrid reprimands from between my legs. "Don't keep my prizes from me."

A sharp bite in the same place draws a second cry. I fall apart in her hands, screams of ecstasy leave me as she returns to her work with a reinvigorated fervor. Every sensation draws me further and further down before I shatter with an ear-splitting shriek.

My orgasm is unlike any that I've had previously. Every nerve is hypersensitive, and the release is exhilarating. I throw my head back and lose control. The streetlights outsight surge as sparks shoot from their bulbs. I feel the electricity run through my fingers to the rest of the apartment. It is no doubt a spectacular display, but fortunately, I am able to contain my outburst to the outside of the dark bedroom.

The mattress shifts as Astrid crawls to lay next to me. She gently sweeps a stray hair off my face, unbothered by the sheen of sweat on my forehead. My eyes flutter open and the shape of her face is looking at mine in the dark.

"Are you okay?" She asks, caressing my cheek.

"Yeah," I respond, my throat hoarse and scratchy. "That was intense."

"Did I take it too far? Shit." She shakes her head. "Let me go get you some water." Astrid moves away but I grab her arm.

"No, it was perfect." I pull her into my embrace, and she snuggles into my chest. "It was perfect."

"Move in with me," she whispers, her eyelids growing heavier with each blink.

"Okay, so long as we can do that again." All thoughts of resistance melt away as I lay in this afterglow with her.

She nuzzles closer and drifts asleep with a content smile on her face. I pull the blankets over our intertwined bodies and pet her hair. I lay my head against a pillow and pull her tighter into my arms. Her warm breath caresses my chest. Hesitantly, I lean closer and lightly kiss her forehead.

So this was it. I chose happiness over duty. There will always be a part of me looking to exact my vengeance against those behind Synergy Labs, but not at all costs. I won't let my family curse ruin this. A warm bed with a girl who cares about me, the flutter in my chest when she laughs. Instead of seeking to destroy, I now have an obligation to protect this one bit of good in the world. My duty is now to her.

CHAPTER 14

Sunlight shines through the shimmering curtains covering the window. The fabric diffuses the light, allowing it to softly brighten the room. For once, I am able to wake up without being blinded by the sun's rays. Astrid shifts in my arms and stretches through her toes, the last traces of sleep fade from her eyes as she looks up at me.

"Good morning," I murmur towards her, loosening my hold so she can sit up.

"Morning," she chirps. "How'd you sleep?"

How did I sleep? I never sleep well. Normally my dreams are filled with visions of Jack, rapidly fluctuating between the good and bad days. Last night featured a different kind of terror. Instead of Jack screaming at me, he was screaming at her. His hands gripped her arms, pulled her hair. I forced myself awake in the early morning, and have kept watch since, checking often to make sure she was sleeping peacefully in my protective embrace.

"I slept well," I lie smoothly. "I dreamt of the cutest kitten."

"Awww," Astrid's nose crinkles. "I love cats. Maybe we should get one!"

"Maybe we should live together for more than a few hours before we adopt a living creature," I tease and roll out of the bed.

I take in the sight of the apartment after last night. A path of clothes leads back to the door. The contents of Astrid's purse have tumbled onto the floor. My keys fell off the entryway table, and I know they probably slid somewhere that will be annoying to find later.

I start to gather my discarded articles and make my way to my single duffel bag of clothes. I dig through it and find the only pair of clean underwear, leggings, and a ripped t-shirt. I really packed like shit before I left. Either I need to go shopping with what little cash I have on hand, or I need to go back to my apartment. A shudder flashes through my body, but I throw the clothes on and repack my duffel with my laundry.

A nagging feeling returns to my mind. Ever since I left Jack, I've had the feeling that something isn't right - be it paranoia or budding insanity. My fingers flicker to the familiar space around my neck where they can find comfort by fiddling with my mother's necklace. Yet this time, I only find a ghost of a memory. My eyebrows scrunch together as I pull the collar of my t-shirt away from my chest and feel for the chain, tracing the ridge of my collarbone.

How did I not notice sooner? My mother's necklace is gone. I never take it off, never. My mind clambers through the events of the past few days. When was the last time I had it? I think back to ice skating, the pottery studio. I don't remember having it. Was I wearing it when Jack...? My breath hitches as I force myself to think back, retracing the path of the electricity in my mind. From my leg, up my chest, to the metal earrings. Did the current travel to my necklace? No, I would've felt it. I stare at myself in a mirror and know my reflection and I have come to the same conclusion. We lost the necklace.

The disapproving glare cuts to my core.

It's been one day, my counterpart berates. *One day without the constant reminder of your family's misdeeds and you've already forsaken your duty. How pitiful. Is a pair of soft arms to hold you at night enough to make you forget the sins of your mother?*

I shake the voice out of my head. My necklace must be in my apartment. I'll just have to go get it.

Astrid is already flitting around the kitchen when I leave the room. She's wearing a sweater and baggy overalls, her tousled hair in a slouchy ponytail. She slides a teacup onto the table and gestures for me to drink it.

"You spoil me." I thank her for the drink and take a sip of the tea laden with honey. It soothes my sore throat and I gratefully finish the glass.

"It's the least I could do after last night." A mischievous glint dances around her eyes.

"Funny." I play along. "I seem to recall that last night was quite magnificent. There's nothing to make up for."

"I'll believe you when you lose the rasp in your voice." A speck of guilt creeps from behind her mask.

Before I realize it, I am striding toward Astrid. My hands grip her shoulders and pin her against a wall. My mouth finds hers, passionate and determined to overwrite her regret. She tugs on my shirt, bringing us closer until our torsos are touching. I pull away, and her lips cling to mine until the last second.

"I would lose my voice completely to have just one kiss with you," I speak lowly. Her eyes scan mine, seeing only lust inside with absolutely no remorse. "Believe me." She nods and I back away, moving to wash my dishes in the sink.

"Hey, I forgot to show you yesterday." Astrid fiddles through a drawer to pull out a yellow envelope - my envelope. She hands it out to me. "You can check the seal, still intact."

"Break it," I shrug, drying my cup with a rag.

"What?" Astrid stands with the envelope still outstretched, shock written plainly across her face.

"Break the seal," I say casually. "Open the envelope, go ahead and read it."

"I don't understand." She holds the envelope like a fragile eggshell, afraid to damage it. She runs her fingers along the edge, settling on the scorch mark in the corner. I place a hand on Astrid's elbow and guide her to sit on the couch.

"Open the envelope, Astrid."

She looks at me once more before sliding her finger under the flap and ripping the paper, officially breaking the seal. Her hand shakes as she pulls out the note inside, seeing I did in fact write down my contact information.

555-9375.

818 Park Street, Apartment B.

While I'm trying to be nonchalant, the hair on the back of my neck raises. I'm trusting her, I remind myself. Besides, I'm moving in with her, so it doesn't matter. It does though. My privacy is my most important possession. Jack has always taught me to hide my identity above all else. Even as I'm leaving him, I can't shake his voice inside my head. *Never let them know who you are, Sparks. You're only safe when you're a secret. You think the government will leave you alone if they find out about your powers?*

While I'm not about to give her my real name, I'm proud of myself for letting her this far in.

"I need to go back to my apartment," I murmur as I rake my fingers through my hair. My palms are sweaty, and I'm sure that I couldn't stand still if I tried. "I left a bunch of things there, like my viola. Plus, I only brought like one pair of underwear. I'll be heading back there today."

"I'll drive," Astrid states, her tone hard and matter-of-fact.

"I can't ask you to do that," I feebly protest, although I could bring back more things in her car than on my bike. The thought of being alone in the studio makes my stomach clench and my head dizzy.

"You didn't ask," she responds and walks over to a closet. She rummages around for a second before slinging a baseball bat over her shoulder. "Besides, I have the address now. Let's go."

"I don't think that's necessary." I follow her out the door, obliged yet exacerbated. Her only reaction as she walks down the stairs is to swing the bat in her hands, demonstrating her familiarity with the weapon.

♪　　♪　　♪　　♪

It's not long before her hatchback pulls up at my apartment. I force her to park near the fire escape, trepidation filling my mind. My leg is restless, and I've played with my hair enough to cause my scalp to be sore. Astrid opens her door and I scramble out of the vehicle.

"Hey, we need to set expectations." I grab her wrist before she can cross the street. "You can't go in, but you can wait in the hall."

"Just let me help you pack, Anise." She rolls her eyes. "If he's there, I'll beat his ass. If he's not, then there's nothing to worry about."

"This is still my apartment. Coming in is a privilege, not a right," I bristle at her arrogance, before taking a breath to calm down. Astrid shifts her weight from foot to foot and bites at her cuticles.

"I'm sorry, I'm just worried about you."

"And I'm terrified for you," I admit. "I'll compromise, you wait in the hall until I know for certain he's not there."

"I'm not promising I won't come in bat-a-blazing if he is." Her face hardens into a cold line.

"I'm going to pretend I didn't hear that."

We cross the road and walk to the front door of my apartment complex. It doesn't feel the same as we step into the lobby. The tile floor is still cracked, missing several squares. The paint is chipped and flaking off. The rundown dilapidation hits too close to home, too stark a reminder of my own treatment. I find my door and stand before it, my hand frozen on the knob. Astrid places a hand on my shoulder, allowing me to take my time, yet reminding me that she - and her baseball bat - is there. I turn the knob and open the door just wide enough to slip in, closing it behind me.

I'm horrified at what I see. Slashes run up and down my sofa, stuffing flung onto the floor. Shattered glass covers the floor by my empty kitchen cabinets, the doors hanging from bent hinges. My clothes are tossed from my closet, draped from my upended mattress and cracked bed frame. I take a second step into the room as my heart breaks. Not from my trashed apartment. I couldn't care less about the holes in the drywall. No, what kills me is placed in the middle of the floor, encircled by the destruction, as if a spotlight shines on it. The damage is caused intentionally, done to send a message, to wound. The fretboard is snapped in a clean line, dangling by the three remaining strings.

My viola.

I hear a desolate wail as I fall to my knees, hands clenched to my chest. I don't recognize the scream as my own. The door bursts open behind me, but I don't acknowledge the presence standing to my right, baseball bat at the ready. Consumed with my wretched sobs, I gently lift my viola to my lap, burying my head in grief as I mourn the absolute fracturing of my being. I am pulled into Astrid's embrace, her hands soothing and rubbing my back. My chest heaves as my fingers run over the splintered edge. I wince as the wood slits the pad of my finger, and a small drop of blood paints the dark wood. A twisted grin warps my face.

"Look, I've put my blood and tears into this viola," I cackle as hysteria latches onto me. "He broke it. It's broken. I'm broken. The whole world is broken. Everything is broken."

"Broken things can be repaired," Astrid consoles, slowly taking the viola from my hands and setting it in the case.

I watch the blood drip from my finger, forming into a small pool on the linoleum floors. Astrid finds a rag in the kitchen and holds it against my cut. Silent tears stream down my cheeks as she helps me stand. She ushers me to the bedroom, and we start to go through my clothes, stuffing the salvageable pieces into whatever we can find.

After we fill a few bags, Astrid takes a load to the car, leaving me to continue packing. I've always hated being alone in this apartment, and that feeling is exacerbated while standing in the midst of destruction.

A ringing cuts through the silence. Once more. It's my phone. I left it here when I ran away. I follow the ringing to the kitchen where it's charging in an outlet. Jack's face lights up the screen before I shakily accept the call.

"Jack," I whisper. I hate that he affects me this much. He hasn't said a word, but I'm quaking on the other end of the line.

Hello Sparks. I can feel his smirk through the phone. *Did you like my decorations?*

"What do you want?" I spit out the question, forcing myself to fake an air of confidence despite his taunt.

Well, isn't it obvious? I want you by my side, where you belong.

"You don't get to hurt me anymore. I left." I try to convince myself of this as I say it, but I don't feel safe at all.

Ah, but you loved it, didn't you? You'll come crawling back to me soon enough. I stiffen at his words, the taste of fear violates my senses.

"You're wrong." I shake my head. "I-I'm moving on, I'm making a new life without you."

I'm sure whatever dick you fell onto isn't keeping you satisfied like mine would. What pretty little lies did he tell to lure you away from me?

"There's not another guy, Jack. I'm leaving *you*." I flinch as a growl rumbles through the phone.

You'll come crawling back to me, the sniveling mess you always are. Just you wait.

"I don't need you anymore, Jack. You might have broken me for a while, but I'm stronger now. Maybe I should thank you for that, but you don't deserve the wasted air."

If that's how you really feel, then perhaps I should be leaving. Perhaps I'll say hello to the pretty blonde before I go. She looks like she'd be down for some... fun.

"No..."

I feel the breath leave my lungs. Questions I didn't think to ask race through my head, most prominently - how did he know I was at my apartment? He knew I would be here to answer his call. Even more alarming, he knew I brought Astrid. My head jerks up. Astrid. She's outside. I run to the fire escape and lean over the barrier. She's not there. I sprint across my apartment to a window facing the front entrance, stumbling over the remnants of my furniture. Across the street, Jack leans against a motorcycle. Our eyes lock and he gives me a little wave. The sunlight glints off a small piece of metal in his hand - my mother's necklace.

Goodbye Sparks.

He winks before pocketing his phone and driving off. I can't breathe. Astrid. Where is she? I hear the door open behind me.

"How we doing? I was thinking that-" Her voice cuts out as I hold her tightly in my arms. "Are you okay?

"Am *I* okay? Are *you* okay?" I fuss over her, examining her for possible injuries. She swats my hands away.

"What is going on?" She demands. "You're acting weird. Well, weirder than normal."

"He was here."

"Yeah, I know. He tore up your couch." She smooths out her overalls.

"No, he was here thirty seconds ago." Her hands stall on the denim fabric. I brief her on the phone call she missed. "He said he was going to hurt you, and then I couldn't find you... I thought I was too late." I pull her into another hug. "I would've done anything to save you, and I will never forgive myself if you ever get hurt."

"I can take care of myself." She rubs my back. "Don't worry about me."

There's a part of me that knows she's probably right, I've seen what the Water Weaver can do. But I don't want her to be in that position, and I know Jack wouldn't hesitate to kill her, even before he knows her secret. No, that can't happen. I have to be more careful.

Ding!

The phone chimes from the floor, a text pops up on the screen.

I look forward to meeting your friend. -J

A picture appears a moment later. Handcuffs lying near a stun gun. The image of a tortured Astrid crosses my mind, her screams echo in my ears. I feel the blood rush to my head as the phone falls from my hand. My legs move on their own until I am kneeling in my bathroom, emptying my stomach into the toilet. Astrid grabs a stray hair tie and manipulates my hair into a messy updo.

"He's just trying to get to you," she murmurs. "We're going to be okay. Let's just grab the last few bags and get out of here."

I lean against the cool porcelain of my shower, giving her a feeble nod. She passes me a cold washcloth and I clean myself off. Astrid looks at the wall above my sink.

"Huh, there's no mirror," she comments absentmindedly. "You can see a faint outline of where the paint is sun-bleached, but no mirror. If he broke it, there should be shattered glass all over the sink and floor. But it feels strange to think he would just... take it."

"He didn't touch it," I say offhandedly. "That mirror and I had a disagreement a few weeks ago. I won."

I force myself to shove everything down and lean into the all-familiar cold, standoffish side of my personality. I see the blurry outline of my silhouette in the shower tile reflection. Her shoulders square as she stands above her trauma, leaving the traces of her vulnerability on the floor. I grab the last few boxes and Astrid holds the door as we leave the apartment complex. I don't bother to lock up.

The drive home is quiet, Astrid is cautiously waiting for a safe moment to break the silence, but there doesn't seem to be one.

Astrid parks by the cafe and twists her keys from the ignition. She doesn't unlock the doors, so I sit in the passenger seat as the cabin lights dim. Seconds pass, then a minute, then two.

"I'm going to start taking some bags in." Astrid says. I blink free from my trance and move to open my door, but she puts a hand on my shoulder. "You can sit here a bit longer if you need to."

"Nope, sorry, I'm good." I am. I have to be.

We're able to grab everything in one trip and we stack the bags in her room by the closet. Everything I own, all in just a few duffels. Astrid is also staring at the bags, I imagine she's having similar thoughts to mine. She moves the few steps to sit on the edge of the bed, her gaze dropped to her lap.

"I didn't realize how bad your life was." The words leave her mouth softly yet sting fiercely on my skin. I bristle at her commiseration.

"I don't want your pity," I bite. "And I don't need your charity. That was my life, and while it might not have been an idyllic fantasy, it was mine."

"Anise, the bloodstains." She looks up at me, her fingers fidgeting. "There was so much blood. Your bedsheets..." She shivers at the memory.

I kneel by the first duffel and pull the zipper open. One rumpled shirt, a loose sock, some shorts it's too cold to wear. I start sorting my clothes into piles on the floor.

"I just don't understand," Astrid continues. "You seem so self-assured and confident. Why did you let him hurt you?"

"It's not as simple as that." I find the missing sock and complete the pair. I feel tears prick the corners of my eyes, so I distract myself by folding a turtleneck.

"You know what," Astrid turns to me, frustration evident by her clenched fists. "It actually is that simple. Dating you is a privilege that he did not deserve. You should have left him months ago."

"I made the best decisions that I could." My vision blurs as I struggle with the misshapen fabric. "You can't just insert yourself into a narrative you created. You have no idea what actually happened."

"Then tell me!" The bed squeaks as she stands. She throws her arms out. "Tell me because I don't understand how you stay with someone who doesn't care about you."

"He loved me!" I clutch the sweater to my chest as the first tear falls. Wet paths streak my face as others follow. "Maybe not at the end but he loved me for years. And I loved him. That means something. He took me in when we had both just lost everything. We didn't have anything but each other, us versus the world."

"H-h-he," I stammer through my tears as an arm glides over my shoulders. "He loved me, Astrid. He loved me."

"Tell me a story," she whispers as she strokes my hair. "Something happy and sweet."

"We bought two train tickets to anywhere," I sniffle as I drag my sleeve over my cheeks, drying my skin. "That was normally how we picked where we were moving next. Cheap, quick, easy to travel anonymously - everything we needed. We only had two bags each. I'm pretty sure he just packed clothes, but one of my bags was my viola. I wouldn't leave it behind."

"We were about twenty miles from our destination when the train broke down. He instantly got all paranoid, worried that they found us. Was he right? I don't know. Regardless, we grabbed our bags and broke a window to climb through. We walked and walked until it started to get dark. By pure luck, we found a farm with a giant flock of chickens. We reasoned the farmer wouldn't miss one or two birds, so we stole our dinner."

"We set up camp near the edge of a forest. With the abundant wood source, it wasn't too hard to start a fire to cook our chicken. We didn't have any blankets or tents, so we used our clothes as makeshift pillows. That night, we ate like medieval kings under the starlight."

"Wow," Astrid soothes. "That sounds nice."

"It was."

"Who were you running from?"

"What?" I pull away as the memory crumbles from my mind.

"You said he was scared of someone on the train," Astrid nudges. "Who?"

"Oh," My mind goes blank as I try to think of a lie to cover up how close I've gotten to the truth. Synergy Labs, the government, whatever mess Jack had drug us into. "Don't worry about it. I don't think they know where I am."

"Are you going to have to move again?" Her voice is barely a whisper.

"Not if I'm careful." I reassure her, although I'm not sure if I'm being honest.

"This is why you don't give out your name." Astrid pieces together and I nod. "Will you tell me what it was?"

"I haven't used that name in eight years," I shake my head with a chuckle. "Anise feels more like my name at this point, and I quite like it."

I guide her lips to mine, hoping the affection satisfies her need for personal details. She hesitates, aware of my blatant use of distraction, but pulls me in regardless. We curl into each other's embrace, lying on strewn piles of clothes. As we drift asleep, I know a new happy memory is forming.

※　　※　　※　　※

A sweaty sheen covers my skin when I jerk awake. My eyes dart around the room searching for the monster from my nightmares as I sit in the dark and unfamiliar setting. As my breathing slows, I settle on the sight of Astrid gently snoring on the floor next to me. I quietly untangle myself from her limbs. I run my hand through my hair as I pace the length of the room, still on edge.

Astrid shifts in her sleep and I freeze in place, hoping I didn't wake her. A breath. A heartbeat. Another. Fuck. She moves again. Wait - she shivered. I allow myself to relax as I pull the quilt off the bed and carefully drape it over her sleeping form. A small smile graces her lips and a part of me breaks. She's so perfect, and I'm so broken.

I fumble for my keys and sneak out of the apartment before the first tear can fall. I rev my bike before peeling onto the street. My hair whips around my face as the wind pierces my skin. I yearn for the pins and needles from the blistering cold. Faster. Faster. Faster!

The streetlights blur in my periphery and disgruntled drivers honk as I bob and weave through the Boston traffic. I don't hear their curses of profanity. I wouldn't give a shit if I did. The light turns red, and I swerve through the oncoming traffic, skidding around the corner as I intermix with traffic.

I throw my head back as I laugh maniacally, relishing the rush of adrenaline. So many thoughts are competing in my mind - the guilt of leaving Jack, the fear of Astrid's safety, the shame of losing my mother's necklace, and the guilt of her involvement with Synergy Labs. I am drunk on the danger that my motorcycle provides, high off of recklessness. The thrill of nearly dying has my heart beating in my ears, drowning out every voice in my head.

I don't know how much time passes before I finally pull over, still relishing my hysteria. My old apartment looms above me, ominous and foreboding. I search the ground before finding a rock that fits comfortably in my hand. The jagged edge slices my palm as it hurls through a window. Glass shards twinkle in the moonlight as they cascade to the ground. Another stone follows the first, drawing forth another display of brilliance.

I clamber up the fire escape and through one of the broken windows which slash my arms and legs. Once in my apartment, I'm unsure of what to do next. Whatever part of my subconscious drew me here isn't providing further instructions. Blood drips onto the linoleum floor, a fresh puddle forms beside the dried stains. I chuckle as a macabre ink blot takes shape. What does it show? A pretty butterfly? No. I see a flame with the splatter forming embers floating away from the destruction.

All at once, I feel something feral rise within me. Too long I've been a doormat for Jack's cruelty. Too long I've taken the backseat in tracking down those behind Synergy Labs and extracting my revenge. There's power in my veins, and it's about time I use it, even if it means burying the humanity inside of me.

I look back down at the growing puddle at my feet. Yes, I think I understand. I reach out to the electrical current running through the apartment. I smirk as I feel the charge tingle around my fingers, eager to run free. Who would I be if I didn't oblige their wishes? I brandish my hands as sparks rain from the ceiling. The flares touch my skin, but do not burn. Instead, they greet me as a beloved old friend.

"Ready to have some fun?" The energy surges in response. The lights flicker and the smell of smoke taints the air. I pull deeper, amassing more and more power. "Let's play."

As the words leave my mouth, a blinding flash bursts from every light in the building as the circuitry is overloaded. My callous rage is unleashed, and the furniture turns into tinder as a blaze erupts. The gust from the broken window ruffles my hair as the flames are fanned higher, licking the wall and ceiling. The air blackens as smoke swells throughout the room. I stride toward the window. The cold pierces my face as the blistering heat singes my back. I make my way down the emergency exit and straddle my bike across the street. Sirens sound in the distance as I watch the fire cleanse and destroy.

"Goodbye."

CHAPTER 15

The past few days since the fire have been pretty calm. Astrid either hadn't noticed or hadn't commented on the lacerations on my arms. The fire marshal declared the incident at the apartment complex a freak accident, but I've kept a low profile just in case.

The smell of smoke keeps me awake. What did I do? Since when do I let myself lose control? But I couldn't stop myself, couldn't push down the power and the anger bubbling inside me. I need to be stronger.

My internal admonitions are shoved aside as I enter the job site. I had missed working, so I wasn't too upset this morning when I had to wake before the sun and strap on my tools. This will probably be the last day I work on this commercial build before returning to gig work or looking for another long-term job, but I'm proud of how much I've been able to accomplish on my own.

Regardless, all I'm concerned about is finishing up the wiring so I can turn in my timecard and receive the last of my pay. I fiddle with a stubborn wire as a colleague walks up behind me.

"Hey Anise, how's it going?" He asks casually.

"Eh, you know, something's always gotta be a bitch to configure or else my job would be too easy." I smile as the laborer chuckles at my joke. "How can I help you?"

"Hopefully nothing too big, there's some guy here asking to see you. At least, I think he means you. 'Looking for a redhead called Sparks' is all he would say to me." My hands slip at the sound of the name and for a second, I forget to breathe. He notices my reaction and tenses as well. "If this guy is trouble, we can get rid of him for ya."

"No, no, no." I fake a calm demeanor and wipe my hands on my jeans. "I'll take care of it. Thanks for letting me know he's here."

"Sure," he says, unconvinced. "Shout out if you change your mind."

He wanders over to a group of other laborers and gestures toward me, no doubt telling them all to keep an eye open. I tighten my ponytail as I head toward the entrance of the construction site, subtly taking stock of power sources within range.

I shove my hands into my pockets as I step out of the framed building into the harsh winter gale. A smarter person would have grabbed a jacket before leaving the relative warmth, but I was focused on my visitor. He had his back to me, leaning against a lamppost smoking a cigarette. He turns when he hears my footsteps crunch the snow on the sidewalk.

"Hey, it's Sparkie!" Smartass, the brazen gun-for-hire, smirks. "What is it they're calling you now? Janice?"

"Sure," I say gruffly, intentionally not correcting him. "You're not welcome here. Leave."

"That's no way to greet a friend." He wags his cigarette at me. "Especially not when I've come to offer you a job. No thievery this time, just mechanical work."

"Thanks," I flash a fake smile. "Not interested."

"Look." Smartass deflates as he drops his cheeky demeanor. "I don't know what trouble you've gotten yourself into, but the boss isn't going to take no for an answer. I really think you should reconsider."

"I'm not in anymore." I cross my arms over my chest, partially for warmth. "I left him."

"He told me to mention a necklace he found at your apartment." Smartass pauses before continuing, as if he was enjoying this about as much as I was. "We have a machine that can help with some 'Synergy Labs' problem, but it's broken and I'm no mechanic. If you help fix the machine, you can have the necklace back."

I take a step forward as the lamppost flickers. Another step and Smartass flinches from the burst of sparks. I grip his lapel and yank him closer.

"What do you know about Synergy Labs?" I hiss.

"I don't know anything," he replies cautiously. "It's all above my paygrade. The boss told me to drop the name if you wouldn't take the job. But I've seen the machine. It's real and very broken. All you have to do is fix it and you get your necklace back." I drop his jacket and release the lamppost from my mental hold.

"If this machine is so important, why didn't Jack come himself?" I accuse.

"Would you have listened?" He chuckles. "Besides, I'm a fairly nice guy once you get to know me. I guess the boss figured I could be your friend."

"I don't need your pity, Smartass."

"Derek."

"What?"

"My name. It's Derek. And it's not pity, it's kindness. Like yeah, I kill people for a living, but I'm not a bad guy."

"Fine, then prove it by answering me honestly. Does Jack know where I live?"

"I don't think so." Derek's face looks sincere. "I mean, I would rather have this chat over a nice dinner at your place and not with those angry looking men over there. But again, I'm lower on the totem pole so I might be wrong."

"I need a minute to think about it." I run my hand through my hair as thoughts race through my head.

"Dude, it's freezing out here," Derek grumbles.

I scowl at him while I trudge over to a nearby bench. Am I crazy for not tossing Derek on his ass? Actually, scratch that. I'm past crazy. I shouldn't even be considering this. Honestly, I'm not sure I can even be in the same room as Jack without killing him - with good reason. Even if I excuse his transgressions against me, he's manipulated me into murdering people. Innocent people who had loved ones and family. I can't ignore the fact that this is probably another scheme of his.

But what if it's not? What if there's even an ounce of truth to Derek's story and this has something to do with

Synergy Labs? I can't just walk away, even if it means trouble for me. And my mother's necklace. I need it. The weight of the pendant around my neck grounds me, keeps me focused on what's important.

And what's the worst that can happen? A simple machine repair - that's not even illegal. Sure, I'm not a mechanic, but it can't be that hard right? In and out in one day. I can do that. Yeah, I can do that. I take a deep breath and steel my resolve before giving Derek a slight nod. He grins and sits down on the bench next to me.

"Here's how this is going to work." He fishes around in his pocket and pulls out a small rectangular device. "This is called a pager. Super old tech that isn't used much anymore, but it gets the job done."

"I'm not stupid. I know what a pager is."

"Well I didn't, so thanks for the compliment. Skipping to the end, blah blah. When we're ready for you, we'll send you GPS coordinates via the pager. Show up with your tools and whatever. Sound good?"

"Just one thing." I grab the pager and clip it to my toolbelt. "You're going to be my coordinator from here on out. Tell Jack that if I see him, at the rendezvous point or in public, I'll kill him."

Derek chuckles at first, then shifts nervously when he sees the resentment behind my glare. He nods before sauntering away, and I stand in the icy gale, too stubborn to even shiver. Satisfied with his departure, I release the breath from my lungs and shove my hands into my pockets.

I made quick work of the rest of the wiring, resolved to finish all of my remaining work today. I forgot that Jack knew I was working on this project, and if he's willing to send goons my way, I don't want to be here when the next one shows up.

When I pull up at the cafe, I see Meredith, the pottery shop owner, unloading crates of ceramic goods from a truck. Astrid is struggling with a box, so I jog the few steps to hold open the door.

"You're back early," she says. "Can you spare a set of hands for a few minutes? There's a ton of boxes, I have customers, dishes are piling up, and-" The phone ringing interrupts her compiling list and her usual happy demeanor cracks as she glares at the offending phone.

"I'll grab the phone then jump in where I'm needed," I assure her.

"No, I'll answer it in just a second. I just need to set this down." She shuffles inside.

"It's all good. I've got it." I grab the phone from the receiver. "Brew for Two. This is Anise speaking. How can I help you?"

"I need the owner." A gruff voice clips.

"She's a bit preoccupied at the moment. Maybe I can answer your question?"

"I'll wait."

"Okay... I'll let her know."

I set the phone on the counter and walk over to Astrid, who's furiously running around trying to find more room for boxes. I take the crate from her hands and set it on a nearby chair and pull her in for a hug.

"Take a breath baby," I whisper. "Everyone can wait an extra thirty seconds for whatever they need."

"There's just so much to do. Maybe I shouldn't have agreed to help with Meredith's local artist project."

"Shhh," I stroke her hair. "The project will be great. Selling handmade ceramic mugs is such a smart idea. I know you've put a ton of work into the logistics, and it will work so smoothly once we figure out all the kinks. Don't give up on it yet."

"Okay," Astrid takes a deep breath, and her usual smile returns to her face. "I'm going to start setting these up. Can you bus the tables and help Meredith carry in the last few boxes?"

"Consider it done. Also, there's some guy on the phone. He said he would rather wait for you than talk to me." A hardness flashes over her eyes so quickly, I wonder if I possibly imagined the reaction.

"Interesting," she tilts her head, with a grin. "I wonder what he wants."

I watch her walk away and answer the phone with a smile plastered on her face. She takes the call in the backroom, and I can't help but feel something is not right. I grab a tub and start gathering used mugs and plates and quietly tiptoe into the back. As I walk through the swinging doors, Astrid hangs up and slides the phone into her back pocket.

"You can just leave those on the counter. I can run them through the dishwasher in a bit."

"Sounds good." I place the bin near the sink. "What did the guy want?"

"What?" She turns her head to me as we walk back into the main room.

"The guy? On the phone?"

"Oh," she giggles. "That was just my supplier. Wanted to confirm our shipment for tomorrow."

"Oh, glad everything is okay." I shake my head as thoughts run through my mind.

What's gotten into me? One weird phone call is enough to rattle my trust in Astrid? I need to be better. I can't let my past relationship with Jack ruin what I have in front of me.

I force myself to focus on my next task and grab the last box from Meredith. She waves as she drives away, and I carefully balance the box on my knee to open the door. In the short time I was outside, Astrid has already unpacked most of the crates. New paintings and photos are stacked and ready to be hung, small price tags hanging off the corners. Mugs and teacups with matching saucers line the shelf closest to the cash register, carefully placed around small ceramic figurines available for sale. The two mugs we painted are set aside, waiting to be brought to our apartment upstairs.

"This already looks great, Astrid!" I set my box onto a nearby table.

"I feel a lot better now that I can see everything laid out." Her genuine smile is back, admiring the new decor in the shop. "I could use a few more shelves, but it works well for now."

I grab a few photos from the pile and start sliding their frames onto nails in the wall. Most are cityscapes capturing the shift from autumn to winter, but there are a few portraits of pets and scenes with cozy imagery. Astrid returns to her usual flitting around as I finish setting up the display, then walk to the back to start on the pile of dishes. I feel content as I sort out the various shapes, trying to fit as many cups inside as I can. A bell rings as the door opens to new customers, and I can hear Astrid's voice as she greets them. Pleasant chatter floats through the air as patrons play board games and gossip.

Memories of my first visit to Brew for Two drift through my mind. In just a few months, so much has changed. Yet, Brew for Two stays the same. I lean against the wall and slide to the floor, peacefully lost in the ambient noises that soothe and comfort. There's a place for everyone here, even me. The coolness of the tile seeps through my jeans and tingles my thighs. I rest my head against the wall, and a wave of serenity settles my busy mind. All of the thoughts of the day dampen, my eyelids grow heavy, and I peacefully drift asleep.

⚡ ⚡ ⚡ ⚡

Later that day, Astrid laughs as she wipes the whipped cream off her nose. We're sitting on the couch after finishing the brownies we salvaged from the cafe.

"Be careful with that, you're making a mess!" She reaches for the aerosol can, but I hold it out of her reach.

"Is that such a bad thing?" I straddle her lap and squirt a dollop on her cheek. Before she can rub it off, I lean down and lick the cream from the side of her face. Astrid takes advantage of my distraction and snatches the can from me. "Hey!"

"I want dessert too," she hums as she sprays a line along my exposed collarbone. She delicately sweeps her tongue along the trail until she meets the neckline of my shirt. Her eyes widen with pretend concern, "I think I missed a spot. We'll need to remove your shirt for closer inspection."

Her fingers curl around the hem of my tee as she raises the fabric over my head. As soon as I'm clear, another blob of whipped cream appears on my chest. She leans in and follows the curve of my breast while goosebumps form along her path. Her thumb passes over my bra and circles my nipple. I pull her in for a passionate kiss, digging my hands into her hair. The can of whipped cream falls to the floor, forgotten within seconds. Astrid shifts and pushes me flat against the couch, hands roaming my body. She tugs the cups of my bra down, displaying my erect nipples.

"How are you so fucking hot covered in whipped cream?" She growls.

"I'm just curious if I taste as good as I look," I tease.

"Somehow, even better."

She swirls my nipple between her lips before nipping at the bud with her teeth. I squirm beneath her, every touch setting my nerves on fire. Her fingers travel down my stomach before landing on my jeans. She pops the button free and moves toward the zipper, until- *Beep, Beep, Beep.*

"Crap, is it eight already?" Astrid fumbles off the couch to turn off her phone alarm. I sit up, flustered and unsatisfied.

"What's up?" I ask.

"I have to meet with my supplier now." She frantically grabs a bag and her coat. "I'll be back in an hour or two."

"I thought you said your supplier was coming tomorrow?" I walk towards her and button my pants, abandoning hope of getting laid.

"Did I? Oh, the shipment is coming tomorrow, but I have to meet with him today to confirm the order." She doesn't look at me as she flounders for words.

"Where are you going?"

"I'm sorry Anise, I have to go." And with that, she abruptly closes the door behind her, leaving me standing in my bra covered in whipped cream.

I grab a paper towel to clean off my chest. After a few minutes, I hear the squeak of a window frame. Intrigued, I meander over to the window to look outside. Down below, Astrid crawls out the back window of the cafe. What concerns me, however, is that she's not wearing what she was before she left the apartment. No, she is dressed as the Water Weaver.

"No, no, no," I whisper. "What are you up to?"

I run to the bedroom and grab a black sweatshirt. Ideally, I would have loved to change into my bodysuit, but I didn't want to risk losing Astrid's trail. I race downstairs and into the alley and I see the swish of her skirt as she turns the corner. I nearly trip on the rough cobblestones in my desperation to catch up to her, to protect her. She thinks she knows what she's doing, messing with the Tributaries, but I fear the day she slips up. Do the Tributaries take prisoners? Would it be more merciful if they didn't? I don't want to find out.

I follow the Water Weaver through dimly lit backroads, gradually growing closer but far enough away to be hidden in shadow. Her skirts swish with her steps, graceful and reminiscent of flowing streams. She embraces the movement of water, winding around corners with ease. Finally, she slips out of the alley and onto the road before entering a building.

I read the sign on the door, "The Jordan River Sanctuary." Huh? A church? I take a step back to look at the structure. The steeple stretches upwards in an impressive feat of architecture. Meanwhile the front door is flanked by glistening stained glass, depicting some kind of river scene. I'm not religious enough to understand what's going on. I pull open the massive doors and creep inside. A preacher stands in front of a large array of pews. A modest number of patrons sit, listening to his sermon. After a quick glance, I don't see the tell-tale ponytail of the Water Weaver.

I notice a small staircase to my right, and slowly tiptoe up the steps hoping for a better view. I freeze in my tracks about halfway up the staircase when I hear two familiar voices.

"What do you have to report?" The Water Weaver.

"You're late." A gruff voice, the one from the phone. It sounds familiar, but I can't place it yet. "When I agreed to work with you, I expected more professionalism."

"You didn't give me much notice." She responds unshaken. "I had to rearrange other commitments. However, you will note that I did make it happen, five minutes late or not."

The man grumbles a bit. I take this opportunity to climb a few more stairs, praying they don't squeak. The staircase opens to a dimly-lit balcony. A few parishioners sit toward the front, but the Water Weaver and her mystery friend sit in the very back. I see his face and immediately duck back into the stairwell, sitting on the second step. It's one of Jack's goons - the Reverent.

My mind immediately fills with questions. How do they know each other? Didn't they try to kill each other in the bank? What the hell is happening?

"There's been another theft, but this one is... odd," Reverent says.

"How so?" The Water Weaver inquires.

"Firstly, it was kept very quiet. Beyond need to know. I just found out when I called you, and apparently, we've had it for a few days."

"It? They didn't steal money again?"

"No, it's some kind of machine."

"Huh, what does it do?"

"That's the weird thing, it's a hair away from being rubble itself. The Boss has had several people try to fix it, but they haven't had a clue. But it's important to him that it gets repaired, and quietly. He's killed the people that've failed."

My breath catches in my throat as I ingest this information. I'm willing to bet that this is the machine I've been hired to fix. Now I know, failure would mean my death - not that it would take much for Jack to decide to kill me regardless.

"Do I need to intervene?"

"Not yet." He sounds less sure. "At least, I don't think you can as of now. The Boss is keeping it in a very secure location. I'll keep a tab on it, see if anyone gets close to repairing it. I don't know what its intended purpose is, but I have a feeling we don't want it functioning."

"Anything else I need to know?"

"That's all I have."

I scamper down the stairs before I hear the Water Weaver's voice once again.

"And the girl? Any news?"

I freeze as her strong demeanor cracks, her voice hopeful yet forlorn.

"Nothing since the failed heist about a week ago. I know the Boss came into work the next day with bruised knuckles... and burns on his hands."

I don't stick around to hear the rest of the conversation. Instead I hurry out of the church toward the cafe, needing to make it home before Astrid knows I followed her.

I start walking in the direction of the cafe, overwhelmed with all that I'm trying to mull over. I am still reeling when I walk into the liquor store on impulse. I don't remember buying that cheap bottle of whiskey. I also don't remember drinking enough to send me over the edge of tipsy, but alas, I am stumbling over cobblestones in the alley. But as the edges of my vision blur, the thoughts in my head become clearer.

I know I should be worried about Jack and the new information I learned about the mysterious machine. I know I should be finding ways to hide or run, instead of facing what will surely end in my death. But I couldn't be less concerned with my own safety at the moment.

I don't understand. The Water Weaver was all but mourning me - er, Sparks. She doesn't realize that she's the one who saved me. I've spent years running and hiding and just trying to survive, whereas with her... it's different. I have the opportunity to put down roots. To meet people, make friends, thrive. Maybe even, be something more than roommates. She thinks I'm dead when I've never been more alive.

Which is also kind of sad, ya know, because Jack will likely kill me the next time he sees me. Bummer.

But hey, maybe I'll kill him instead. Yeah. That would be nice.

I fumble up the steps into our apartment and slump onto the couch. Minutes later, Astrid walks in with red-rimmed eyes. We lock eyes and say nothing. Instead, I tilt the bottle toward her, an offering. A night together of silent companionship and liquor. No painful questions or futile efforts to fix the problems of the other.

Astrid gratefully sits beside me and takes the bottle. Her face scrunches as the whiskey burns her throat. She takes a few large gulps from the glass before she passes it back.

"Suppose I better catch up," she jokes, leaning her elbows on her knees. "Seems like you've made it a decent way through that bottle."

"Maybe so." I hold the bottle up to the light to see how much liquid is left. "But the thoughts are quieter. What more could I ask for?"

"Cheers to that." A sip for her. A sip for me. Another for her. A long pull for her. She pulls her knees to her chest, nestling the bottle in a sad embrace. "Hypothetically... how do I help someone who doesn't want to be saved?"

"What a depressing quandary." I lean back against the couch. "I think it depends on the why. Is it that they don't want to be saved or can't be saved?"

"I can't tell." She picks at a hangnail. "She's strong enough to walk away, and no one could touch her. Yet she stays in a situation that causes her and others to suffer. I can see the pain in her eyes. I never know if I'll see her again when she leaves."

"You have to let her make her own choices." In my boozy haze, I'm starting to think Astrid might be talking about me, but the fog encompassing my mind is diluting my thoughts. "People have been making her choices for her, and she'll resent being forced to leave as much as she resents those controlling her now. The best thing you can do is keep holding a door open until she's ready to run."

"I just hope she runs before they kill her, if they haven't already. Hypothetically, of course."

"Of course... hypothetically." I nod and place a hand on her knee. "Either way, it worked for me."

"Yeah, it did." A tear slides down her cheek as she forces a somber smile. "I'm glad."

CHAPTER 16

I am greeted with the smell of cinnamon when I open my eyes. That, and probably the worst hangover of my life. I groggily sit up, squinting at the soft light filling the room. Ugh. I throw back the covers and proceed to fall out of the bed. The carpet softens my landing, but it still hurts. I groan out a few curses before I follow the smell into the kitchen to find a similarly bedraggled Astrid standing over the stove.

"Good morning," she says quite unconvincingly. I nod and lay my head onto the cool counter. "How are you feeling?"

"Eggghhhh."

"I'm not surprised," she chuckles. "You got a head start on me and I still couldn't keep up with you."

"Mph."

She slides a mug across the counter to me. I lift my head and pull it closer, taking in the mug's design. Crimson stripes interwoven with scarlet and flashes of silver. The mug she painted for me. I trace the lines with my finger, in awe of how the colors ebb and flow. It was beautiful in the shop, but now once the glaze has been fired and sealed, the colors are vibrant and fiery.

"This is gorgeous," I whisper.

"Thank you." She reaches over and tousles my hair. "Now drink up. This is a hangover remedy passed down by my great-great-grandma. If it doesn't help you, nothing will."

Astrid sits on the counter, her feet dangling in the air. She has a drink of her own, held by the cool blues of the mug I painted for her.

"Will you tell me about your family?" I ask. A soft warmth glimmers on her face.

"Oh, there's so much I could say." She sips her drink and kicks her feet idly. "My father is the most kind-hearted person you would ever meet. He and my younger brother, Liam, would shovel snow for all of our elderly neighbors after a snowstorm. It would take the whole day to clear all the sidewalks and driveways. One year, the street pitched in and bought him a really nice snowblower as a thank you. The idea was that they would be finished faster and could go back inside, but my dad just started doing the next block over too. Liam would also make a quick buck by walking their dogs. He started with one or two, by the time he graduated he was walking a whole herd of them!"

"I would pay money to see that," I chuckle at the thought.

"Hold on, let me grab my scrapbook." Astrid jumps off the counter and makes her way to an end table in the corner to retrieve a binder adorned with colorful stickers from a drawer within. She flips through the pages as she walks back. "Here it is."

She passes the book back to me, and sure enough, there was a photo of a teenager being pulled by German shepherds, golden retrievers, and a dalmatian. His smile peeks out from behind his mop of blond hair. Even though his mittens are ratty and worn, he's giving the camera a thumbs up.

On the next page is a gray-haired older woman stirring a pot while a child clings to her leg. A middle-aged woman stands next to them slicing oranges, a laugh frozen in her eyes.

"That's my mother and my grandma, Mimi, and of course there's little me at the bottom." She points at each figure as she introduces them. "We were putting together a simmer pot. Mimi insisted on doing one at least once a month, if not once a week. They bring positive energy and auras into the home, and they smell amazing. It sounds silly but..."

"Water has a spirituality," I say, remembering her earlier phrase.

"Exactly." Astrid's eyes twinkle. "Water has a spirituality."

I flip through a few more pages as Astrid explains the memories behind the photographs. Astrid and her brother competing on the swim team, the family grilling burgers at the lake, her mother painting watercolor landscapes in the backyard.

"You look so... happy. All of you do," I utter. She snaps the book closed and turns to me.

"Tell me about your family, before you ran away with your friend." She looks at me eagerly, but I don't have any pictures to pull out and present.

"I didn't run away." I twist a stray strand of hair around a finger, avoiding her eyes.

"Then where's your family?" She's confused now.

"I don't know anything about my father," I try to be frank, matter-of-fact. Pretending like this is no big deal. "My mother never talked about him and I wasn't old enough to wonder why. She died eight years ago in a workplace accident. I was only fifteen."

"Who took care of you after?"

"I met someone at the memorial service. His brother also died in the accident. He took me in, and the rest is history."

"Your ex?"

"I guess that term works," I chuckle, "though he always avoided any labels."

"I can't even imagine what that would be like." She rubs her hand over the scrapbook cover. "My family is everything to me."

"Shit happens." I shrug. "I learned everything you need to know - cooking, driving, tax evasion."

"You don't pay taxes?" Astrid asks incredulously.

"What are you, the government?"

"I have so many questions..." She glances at the clock on the wall. "Shoot, I have to get downstairs to the cafe. I'll see you afterwards, okay?"

"You bet." I lean over and kiss her on the cheek. "Make lots of good coffee." She waves as she walks out the door. I take our mugs over to the sink and quickly rinse them out.

I lean onto the counter and take a breath. After the past few crazy days I've had, it's nice to have a slow, calm day. I turn and look across the apartment until my eyes catch on the scrapbook, still sitting on the counter. Astrid would probably appreciate it if I put it away for her. Scooping it up in my arms, I head over to the small end table in the corner.

I don't know how I hadn't noticed this table before. Lots of trinkets are scattered over a gossamer tablecloth, similar to the material that flows off of her costume. I lift the edge of the fabric to open the thin drawer underneath and place the scrapbook inside. A small worn stool sits underneath the table. That catches my attention. Why would she sit by this end table?

I take a closer look at the display and realize the trinkets are placed intentionally as a makeshift altar. A copper bowl inlaid with aquamarine crystals sits along the far edge of the table, filled halfway with water. It is flanked by two light blue candles, wax beading down the side as the wick's length is dwindling. A small burlap pouch holds a few sprigs of herbs and dried fruit rinds, next to that, a decorative box contains a few tan seashells.

Placed in the center of the deck is a white tarot deck with copper foiling detailing the phases of the moon. Some of the edges are slightly warped, showing its use. I run my finger along the design, picturing Astrid shuffling these cards.

"I didn't know she was into tarot." I mull over the artifacts on the altar. I've never been one for superstition or destiny, but just this once, it might be fun to pretend.

"Alright then, what is my future?" I chuckle as I shuffle the cards. I place the deck back onto the table and reveal the top card. I gasp as I see a man suspended upside-down by his ankle. The card reads, "The Hanged Man." I quickly place the deck where I found it and back away from the table. As I calm down, I laugh at how spooked I got over nothing.

"Well... that didn't look like a good card. It's just a fun little game though, it doesn't mean anything."

Beep-beep. Beep-beep. The pager from Derek chirps from my bag. So much for my slow, calm day.

✣   ✣   ✣   ✣

The gray waters of the Boston Harbor lap against the docks as I approach the *Flash Flood*. I tried not to think about bad omens as the ship rocks in the waves.

The message on the pager was just a series of numbers, which after a quick Google search, proved to be latitude and longitude coordinates leading me here. I feel out of place in my bodysuit, complete with the hood, scarf, smokey eye makeup, and my electrician belt slung over my shoulder, but I'm not taking any chances with any of these goons. I need to be prepared for anything, and my anonymity might be helpful later.

The irony isn't lost on me. The Hanged Man? As I'm walking to certain death? I don't have to know the deeper meaning to see the humor of the card I drew.

The armed guards out front intimidate me, but I try to stand composed. They search me for weapons before declaring that I wasn't a threat. I smirk at their ignorance, as electricity tingles my fingers. I'm tense and alert, feeling defensive and I haven't even boarded the boat yet. The guards speak into their earpieces and Derek pops onto the top deck, waving me on. The men step aside, and I apprehensively make my way toward the boat.

The dock sways underneath my feet and my stomach drops. Though I have a tough exterior, I'm scared shitless.

Yes, the guns and big men aren't reassuring, but that's not what is making me queasy. With every step, I am further and further from land, suspended over the sea by rotting planks that could snap with a misplaced step. Or once I'm on the boat, a whole mess of problems could arise that end with me in the water. The churning, swirling, murky water. The kind that swallows a person in seconds.

I can't swim. I never learned how to swim, and everything is insistent on rubbing it in my face. Birds swoop and dive, cackling through the air. The waves are crashing and pulling, eager to knock me off-balance. The dock creaks and rocks, pleading to be put out of its misery. I can feel the color drain from my face as I reach the gangway where Derek is waiting.

"You'll get your sea legs in a minute," he jests. I'm not too sure. "We've got a room set up for you below deck. I'll walk you down."

Derek places a hand on my back and gently steers me toward the staircase. To the rest of the deck crew, I look like a prisoner being escorted to the dungeon, and it occurs to me that perhaps I am. However, Derek's touch doesn't seem to be imposing or restrictive, and he uses a slight pressure to direct me to turn when needed. It feels respectful, as it allows me to move at a comfortable pace yet feel assured in my movements. We traverse through a few narrow hallways lined with closed doors until Derek motions at me to stop. He punches a code into a keypad, and we enter.

It's clear that this room was retrofitted to be a workstation, as a tarp covers the beige-covered carpet. There's a small porthole along the wall letting natural light filter in. In the center of the room, something is covered by a sheet. I pull it off to reveal the machine everyone's been up in arms about, and to be fair, it looks important... but also broken beyond repair. It's taller than I am and several feet wide. The casing is cracked, showing peeks of frayed wired and chipped circuit boards. A motor is situated on the side, rusty and dented. I scan over the whole contraption, tallying every defect in my mind.

"You have got to be kidding me." I say after a moment. Derek leans against a wall and chuckles.

"How long will it take to fix it?" He smirks at me.

"I'll need a bit to do some math, but it'll definitely need parts I don't have."

"Make me a list."

"I don't know what to do with this. I'm an electrician, not a mechanic. You haven't even told me what it's supposed to do."

"I've been told it's a generator." How reassuring.

"Then buy a new one."

"Not an option. This was too much work to swipe." I can't imagine how many guys it took to lift this. I scan it again. Many. It took many guys to lift this.

"Totally legal enterprise you got here."

"I just promised you wouldn't do anything illegal, not that we didn't." He meanders to a chair in the corner and plops down. "Now make me a list of what you need."

I huff and turn to the contraption. My hair falls into my eyes as I thoroughly examine every inch of the casings, wires, and circuitry. It's impossible to test what does and doesn't work with any real accuracy, as the machine won't even start. To begin, I start disassembling it piece by piece. I figure that if I can figure out which pieces do work, I can start to repair and replace what doesn't.

After an hour, I am surrounded by trails of cords and loose screws, yet it seems as though I haven't even made a dent of progress. Grease is smeared across my face, my hood and scarf long discarded. Derek is still slouched in the corner, fiddling with his phone. The room is silent, except for the sounds of my tinkering. This is taking for-fucking-ever. There has to be a better way.

"This would be so much faster if this would start," I grumble.

"Have you tried turning it off and on again?" Derek suggests flippantly. "Or maybe a hard reboot."

"Wow, your mind is extraordinary," I say dryly.

I sit for a second and consider his words. I don't think he meant to, but he didn't make a bad point. If I can force it to turn on, I could better tell which parts aren't working. And I might be just the person to animate the dead. I quickly reassemble the pieces I removed before standing and taking a step back. Derek looks up from his phone, glances at me, then smartly scoots his chair back.

The electricity from the boat nearly jumps into my hands, eager to move, to flow. I chuckle at the familiar enthusiasm before gently redirecting the current into the machine. My eyebrows scrunch at the cold, distant tingling as the device greedily absorbs the energy. It feels... off. The lights flicker as the machine sucks more and more electricity in an insatiable suction. I focus on my diagnostics knowing the sooner I make note of the failures, the sooner I can get the fuck off of this boat.

When I'm satisfied with my examination, I withdraw my powers. My shoulders sag, and I slump into a nearby chair, sweat glistening on my brow. I feel drained of vivacity in my core. My eyelids flutter and my breath comes in shaky gasps.

"Are you okay?" Derek cautiously stands and steps toward me. "Do you need anything?"

"I'm fine," I grunt, struggling to sit up. I shouldn't be this tired. What is going on? "I need paper to make a list before I forget everything." Derek disregards my statement and dials a number.

"Oliver, we need two coffees downstairs." He pauses as he listens to the voice on the line and turns to me. "How do you like your coffee?"

"I'm fine," I insist, although my hands are shaky as I scribble the materials I need in illegible handwriting. Derek returns to his phone call.

"Just bring some cream and sugar on the side. Thanks man."

"I'm okay, Derek. I'm just tired."

"Then coffee should help." He straddles a chair and looks over my shoulder. "Jeez, your handwriting is worse than mine."

"Get over it," I retort.

"I'm the one who has to place the order."

A few minutes pass before the door opens and I am accosted by the bitter smell of coffee. My nose scrunches, but I keep working on my list, which takes up most of the page by now.

"Derek, I've got your drinks here."

"Thanks, Oliver." A cup is placed next to me, along with sugar packets and creamers. "Drink."

"I'm working."

"Consider this your union-mandated break." Derek plucks the pen out of my hand and slides the paper to the other side of the desk.

"Didn't know criminals could unionize." I begrudgingly take the cup and dump all of the sugar and creamer in, hoping to disguise the astringent taste. As I take a sip, I am disappointed to find that it did not work. I grimace as the liquid assaults my tongue.

I look up at the two men sipping their coffees. I'm surprised when I recognize Oliver as Babysitter. It seems he was promoted from childcare to being the gang's barista. Good for him.

"I wish we could unionize, maybe then we could get dental." Derek shakes his head. "The water filters on this boat aren't that good. We have to boil the water, hence, we drink a lot of shitty coffee."

"You would think that illegal work would pay better," Oliver says. "We risk our lives for that asshole."

"Careful, that's the boss's girl," Derek scolds, his voice hushed.

"Not anymore," I grumble.

I want to shout. I want to scream across the city. I'm not his! I left him! I ran away and he can't hurt me anymore! But all I can manage is two words, just above a whisper.

Yet, I'm not sure if I'm telling the truth. Sure, I moved out, but here I am on some random boat just because he requested my presence. He didn't even have to ask me in person. God, I must look so pathetic. Their conversation continues in the background.

"How am I supposed to know who the boss is dating? I don't-"

"I'm told you I'm not-" I cut myself off before my temper can escalate and take a breath. "I'm not the boss's girl. I left him." Derek looks me up and down, assessing my body language.

"Good for you." He looks over at Oliver, who nods, and then pivots the conversation. "What shit does the boss have you working on, Oliver?"

"Ugh," Oliver groans. "I'm tallying up accounts that are past due to pass to the shake-up team. I miss shake-up duty. No two schmucks are the same."

"Accounting duty?" Derek clutches his stomach as he laughs. "Who'd you piss off to get assigned there?"

"Very funny," Oliver narrows his eyes. "I better get back to it before I get posted outside. It's too cold for sentry duty."

Derek chucks his empty cup at Oliver as he leaves, playful banter concluded. He fishes through his pocket and retrieves my stolen pen.

"My lady." He extends the pen with a flourish and a deep bow.

"Thank you, sire. How honorable of you." I accept the pen as he winks and plops back into his chair.

"So, how much longer until we wrap up for the day? You already have quite the shopping list."

"Well, there's a bit of a problem." I walk over to the machine and point. "Have you seen the markings on the fuel tank?"

"No, that's your job." He rolls his eyes.

"One I am so eternally grateful to have," I retort. "Either way, it says CH_3NO_2. That's the chemical formula for nitromethane. Judging by the size of the tank and the amount of energy this machine requires, we're going to need a lot of it."

"Add it to the list."

"It's really expensive," I caution. "Especially in the quantities we'll need."

"That's my job to figure out. Yours is to add it to the list."

"Fine." I shrug my shoulders and sprawl out my best guess for the necessary quantities of the product. "That should do it."

"Cool." He folds up my paper and shoves it into the pocket of his jeans. "Let me call an escort for you. I'll page you again when I have the supplies."

Derek dials a number on his phone as I hurriedly replace my hood and scarf over my face. A burly man walks through the door and grabs me by the arm. I quickly snag my toolbelt as he yanks me into the hallway.

"Ow! I'm not resisting." He pays me no mind as we climb the stairs onto the main deck. "Lighten up, would ya?"

"I can escort her from here." A gruff voice comes from the side. My captor sneers and pushes me into him before heading back below deck. I look up and see Reverent helping me regain my balance. "Where are you heading?"

"Off this ship," I clip back and briskly stride toward the dock.

"Haven't seen you around in a while." He chooses his words slowly and carefully, like a fucking politician. "I don't think we were properly introduced earlier. My name is Jeremiah."

"I didn't know you were this observant." I intentionally disregard his introduction. We tread down the gangway onto the dock where I expect him to turn around, but he instead follows me ashore past the last of the sentries.

"Fun project you're working on?"

"Unfortunately, no." We move from the sand into the parking lot. He's not getting the hint. I don't trust him and have no interest in being friends.

"What is your role in the group?" He's talking around what he really wants to ask, and it's grinding on my nerves.

"I don't have to prove myself to you."

"No, no. Of course not." Jeremiah shuffles behind me as we approach my bike. "You staying around after your project's done?"

"Not if I can help it." I stow my tools in the saddlebags. Damn, this guy is persistent.

"Strange that the boss is so secretive about his girl."

"I'm going to let you off with a warning because I have better things to do than kick your ass right now." My voice is crisp and cold. Jeremiah shrinks from my gaze. "I am not 'the boss's girl.' In fact, I have every intention of killing that asshole the next time I see him. Relay the message to all of your dim-witted friends because I will not be so forgiving if I must explain it again. I am only here because I have to be, and as soon as that changes, I am gone. Now, back away from my bike or I will run you over."

He stumbles back, and I rev my engine before peeling away. As the port recedes in the background, I finally exhale and drop my shoulders. I hate boats.

CHAPTER 17

As soon as I step into the apartment, I am engulfed in a tangle of limbs and kisses.

"I've missed you sooo much!" Astrid smothers me with affection, and I am glad I had the forethought to change out of my bodysuit before coming upstairs.

"I missed you too, babe." She rubs her thumb along my eyebrow, and I remember the sweat, soot, and grease splattered on every visible section of skin. "Get off me, I stink and need a shower."

"I don't care." She nuzzles my neck.

"Astrid, I will be the most thorough and doting lover in ten minutes when I don't stain our sheets. Ten minutes to wash away the day."

"Okay..." She mopes over to the couch and dramatically drapes herself over the cushions.

"Oh my goodness." I roll my eyes playfully. "You are so dramatic."

With my up-and-coming actress waiting, I hustle into the shower. The grime flows down the drain as the hot water soothes my aching muscles. Today was awful, but it doesn't matter. I'm home, and the most beautiful woman in the world is waiting for me. I can't help but smile as I duck underneath the stream. Just a few minutes in, I hear the bathroom door open. Clothes fall to the floor in soft thuds and affectionate hands roam the skin of my back.

"Ten minutes is twenty too long," a sultry voice whispers in my ear.

"Hmmm, I'm not sure what I could possibly do to appease you."

"I think there's only one thing you can do... pass the soap." I oblige, passing the bottle to Astrid. "What is this?"

"What do you mean? It's my soap." I turn to face her. Horror is etched on her face. She's examining the bottle intently.

"This says 'five-in-one shampoo, conditioner, body wash, shaving cream, and hand soap." She perks an eyebrow. "You use this?"

"It smells nice," I defend. "And it's efficient."

"After this, we're going shopping," she protests incredulously.

"If you can walk after this, I didn't do my job." I reach for her.

"Nuh-uh, both hands on the wall of the shower." Astrid steps back, holding the soap hostage. "You wanted to be clean, remember? We need to do this right."

I chuckle and face the wall as she squirts some of my soap out of the bottle. The smell of sandalwood and bergamot fills the air. Her fingers rub the suds in my hair, massaging my scalp. My eyes flutter at the magic feeling. She gently nudges me under the shower stream and tilts my chin up. The shampoo glides down my neck into the hollow of my back. She runs her fingers through the strands of my hair, detangling with careful precision.

When Astrid deems me shampoo-free, she tilts the shower stream toward the wall and lathers her hands with the soap once more. Residual water drips down the curve of my waist and hips. Soft kisses trail down my side all the way down to my ankle, where Astrid truly begins her work. She kneads the foam into my sore muscles. I moan and allow my stiff body to droop, exhaling the tension I've held all day.

"There you go," Astrid coos. "I've got you."

"That feels so damn good," I sigh. "Thank you."

"Oh, sweetie," she chuckles. "I'm not nearly finished with you yet."

She makes her way up from my calves to my thighs and lower back. My eyes roll into my head when she smooths the knots out of my shoulders. Astrid's hands then roam to my front, fingers barely grazing my stomach.

"How was your day?" She nibbles on my ear, and I struggle to find the breath to answer.

"Fine," I gasp. I don't care about my day. I just want her.

"That's not a real answer," she scolds. Her nails scratch my ribcage, and my heart skips a beat.

"Stressful, my client has a generator that's totaled." Her hands find my breasts and I can't think straight. "They insist on fixing it, and uh... it's a big project."

"Sounds important." Her breath is warm on my neck. "What's wrong with it?"

"Everything." Astrid takes a nipple between her fingers and a strained groan escapes my throat. "I'm not sure a single piece of it works."

"What a shame," she teases, rolling the nub between her fingers. "Is the client at least nice?"

"I don't want to talk about anybody else while you're toying with me," I mumble. As a response, she tsks and tweaks my nipple harshly. "Ahh, um, the client is a... a group of guys." Shit, I can't even remember with her hands on me. "One is a real piece of work, but I think the rest are trying."

"Is that why I smell coffee on your breath?" One of her hands stays on my breast, while the other trails to my inner thigh. "If I remember right, you don't even like coffee. Is there another barista who you've been sleeping with?"

"I was trying to be nice," I moan. "I took a few sips of some shitty coffee. Nothing more."

"Mmmm, no barista then? No pretty girl who whispers sweet nothings while fingering your clit?" She teases me, deliberating running the pads of her fingers over my inner thigh higher and higher, stopping right before she gets to where I want her the most.

"There's no one else, Astrid. You're all I want." I can't take it. I reach for her hand, but she takes a step back.

"Hands on the wall, baby. I haven't said you're clean yet. In fact, I think you're about to get a little dirtier." Her eyes gleam with mischief, and I force myself to turn back to the wall. "Good girl."

I gasp as her fingers slip between my legs, finding my throbbing clit. Astrid rubs small circles as she nips at my ear. I lose myself in the feeling of her. My breath comes in shallow pants, and I can't stop the strained moans that leave my throat. She runs her fingers along the rim of my opening before thrusting inside. I yelp at the sudden entrance before grinding against her hand. I let loose a string of profanities as I get closer and closer.

Suddenly, Astrid grabs my waist and spins me, pushing me against the wall of the shower. She clutches my face in her hands, her lips passionately meeting mine. I feel her body pressed against me, her soft chest, her legs. The stream from the showerhead cascades over the two of us. The rest of the world fades to just the two of us, together under the outpouring of water. One of her hands is tangled in my hair, keeping my lips locked on hers. The other slowly slinks down, finishing its earlier work. I come undone almost instantly, screaming as the ecstasy of the moment fills my mind.

"There's no one else, Astrid." I lean against her chest. "It's only you, always you."

N   N   N   N

My target is in my sights. Their back is to me, trusting and unaware. They will receive no mercy from my assault. Three... two... one... *Pmph.* Bullseye.

Astrid whips around to face me, a mischievous gleam in her eyes. She drops the rope of the sled and plants her hands on her hips.

"Anise, did you just throw a snowball at me?" How accusatory. I should be offended, except...

"Of course not," I lie, my hands behind my back.

"Mmhmm." Damn, she's not falling for it. I now have two options: abort or stick to my guns. Good thing I made two.

Pmph.

"You did not!" Astrid shrieks as she drops to the ground, forming snowballs at an impossible rate. Perhaps picking a fight with the Water Weaver wasn't the smartest idea. I duck behind a tree and assemble my own ammo. Snow flies through the air, bursting upon contact. Flakes freckle my hair and eyelashes.

I dive for cover behind a different tree, peeking around the trunk to catch sight of my rival. Scanning the horizon, I see no sight of her. I turn around to lock eyes with a massive ball of snow, cocked and ready for launch.

"Surrender," Astrid commands. I kneel before her.

"I will not yield," I say with dramatic stoicism. "If I shall perish, then so be it."

With a solemn nod, Astrid slings her sphere at me. Direct hit to my chest. Hand clutching at my "injury," I slump to the ground. I exhale and close my eyes. As a finishing touch, I stick out my tongue.

"Get up you drama queen," Astrid teases. "Loser has to pull the sled."

I groan through my smile and trudge up the rest of the hill, sled in tow. When we reach the summit, we see families sliding down the slope in all sorts of makeshift toboggans, from garbage can lids to yoga mats and tarps. While I'm glad we were able to find the sled at a nearby rental stand, it does look like fun to scrounge for a substitute. We patiently wait in the short line until it is our turn. At Astrid's insistence, I sit in the front of the toboggan. She wraps her arms around me, and I clutch the reins.

"Are you nervous?" She asks, seeing my grip.

"I've never done this before," I whisper giddily. My pulse is racing, and I can feel the flush of my cheeks. "I'm so excited I can barely sit still."

"Well, make sure to keep your arms and legs inside the vehicle at all times." I can feel her warm breath on my ear, and my heart starts racing for a different reason. "Let's go!"

Astrid pushes off and we quickly gain speed on the well-worn tracks. The wind bites at my cheeks, but I don't spare the cold a second thought. I squeal as my periphery blurs, eyes darting wildly at the sensations.

"Want to go faster?" Astrid prompts. I nod, and Astrid removes one of her hands from my stomach.

She subtly touches the ground, and almost imperceptibly, the texture of the snow changes and glistens in the sun. A slight rainbow shimmers over the drifts. Immediately, the sled surges faster. We careen around trees and bushes, and I can't stop the roaring laughter the wind rips from my lips. We go over an elevated patch of snow, and I swear the sled leaves the ground for a split second. Out of nowhere, a snowman appears in front of our sled.

"Look out!" I point at the sudden obstacle.

"Bail!" Astrid shouts.

Before I can react, she grabs the side of the sled and jerks to the side. The toboggan capsizes and I am thrown through the air. I hit the ground hard, rolling with my momentum for a few feet. The impact makes me gasp for a deep breath of air. In a blink, Astrid is crouched next to me, her eyes darting over my body.

"Are you okay?" Her voice is shaky as she panics. "I'm so sorry. I made us go too fast. I should have been more careful. I am so, so sorry."

I try to stifle a giggle. Instead, I end up holding my stomach as I laugh, tears steaming gleefully down my cheeks.

"That was so much fun!" I wheeze. "Can we go again?"

Astrid rolls her eyes, sitting back on her heels. We end up going down the hill again and again, although I don't see the glistening snow again and Astrid keeps her arms wrapped tightly around me. Even at the slightly slower speed, I am lost in the thrill. The gusting air invigorates me, and I feel euphoric, intoxicated by the high of the adrenaline and endorphins.

When the sun brushes the horizon, Astrid pulls me away from the sledding lanes. We return the sled to the rental stand and make our way to the parking lot. Her cheeks are rosy, flushed from the chill. Her eyes glisten and reflect the nearby streetlamps. She's never looked more beautiful. I grab her hand and give her a little spin as we walk toward my bike.

Wait, what was that? I glance past Astrid to the barely illuminated figure in the distance. He's leaning against a lamppost, lit cigarette dangling between his fingers. It falls to the ground, and he doesn't even bother to snuff it out.

"He's here."

I can't find any air in my lungs to say anything else. I drop Astrid's hand, struck by a torrent of emotion. He's here. He's here. Is he alone? Did he bring any goons? He takes a step toward me, and I instinctually take a step back. The shadow of a smirk crosses his face. Jack.

"What was that?" Astrid looks up at me, a soft smile on her face. My mind goes completely clear except for one thought. I need to get her out of here. Her smile wavers at my expression. "Anise?"

"Get to the bike. Now."

"What's wrong?" Her smile is completely gone now.

I don't answer, instead I grip her arm and take off into the parking lot. She stumbles a step before overtaking me, towing me at her faster speed. With her guiding pull, I risk a look over my shoulder and see him walking toward us, lackadaisically.

He's planned this. We're playing into his hand. We need to flip the script. I scramble for a plan before reaching out with my powers. I don't feel much, we are in a public park for fuck's sake, but I do feel something. Streetlights. Impulsively, I force the power lines to surge. Astrid screams as the lights go dark and glass shards cascade down to the pavement.

I straddle the motorcycle and rev the engine. Astrid fumbles with her helmet strap as I yank her onto the seat behind me. I don't bother putting mine on as I peel out of the lot. I erratically weave through traffic as I make a series of random turns. Left. Right. Left. Left. Right. Astrid tightly wraps her arms around me, clinging to me in distress as the bike careens through the streets. I scan the nearby cars, hoping that none of them are following us. None of them look familiar, but I don't trust going back to the cafe quite yet.

Out of the corner of my eye, I see a group of motorcycles pull into a diner parking lot. I cut across several lanes to whip into the lot and park among the other bikes, feeling safer as part of the herd. I usher Astrid to a booth in the back where I can plainly see the parking lot and door. I slide her a menu and look over the contents, trying to calm down.

"What do you want?" I ask casually.

"Excuse me?" She grabs the menu out of my hands. "We're not going to talk about how you almost killed us with your reckless driving after freaking out at the park? What the fuck is going on?" Her gaze is agitated and direct.

"I saw my ex." I run my hands through my hair. "I had to get you out of there."

"You don't think that was a bit of an overreaction? Did he threaten you or something?"

"No, but he walked toward us." I get flustered trying to explain. "He was standing in the shadows smoking a cigarette. I thought-"

"Hold on, you saw a guy across the parking lot and just assumed it was your ex?" She shakes her head, her posture softening. "It would've been too dark to be able to tell who he was."

"No... No, I saw him." I protest, but my mind betrays my confidence. Did I really see Jack? Or did I just panic at the sight of a random smoker? I know Jack. Surely, I can recognize him after eight years... right? Right?

"Anise, it's okay." She puts a hand over mine, soft and reassuring. "You're okay. He can't hurt you anymore."

As we sat in the diner, I desperately wished that was true.

CHAPTER 18

That moment invaded my dreams. The lit cigarette. The tilt of his head. The arrogant swagger. It must have been him. It had to have been him. I saw him. I swear I did. Didn't I see his piercing eyes? Didn't I see him pull a knife and plunge it into my-

I jolt awake, pulse throbbing in my ears. I'm home. Astrid is curled in my arms. My breathing slows as I tug the blanket up to cover her shoulders. She's safe, so everything is okay. I can't let her down again. I need to get better, faster, stronger so I can protect her.

Astrid shifts in her sleep, burrowing closer to me. Ever so softly, I brush my fingers over her hair. A small smile creeps onto her face. I have to keep her safe. I stay awake for the next few hours, content with holding her until she wakes. Content with acting as her sentry as she sleeps.

The next day passes quietly enough. I help out in the cafe. The local pottery collaboration has been very popular, so Meredith brings several batches of mugs and teacups to restock the shelves. Astrid clears off more shelf space to open the opportunity to other goods. Now there's an array of jewelry, paintings, and trinkets for patrons to peruse while they wait for their drinks.

I spend most of the day bussing dishes. Astrid is a natural at striking up light-hearted conversations with all the patrons, but I prefer to stick to polite smiles as I take their empty mugs. Every once in a while, I would get called over to referee a board game dispute or assist with today's crossword (four down was "spool"). Everything was calm. I didn't realize how much I craved something stable and orderly.

As the last patrons leave, I am rinsing the final dishes and placing them in the sanitizer. A pair of arms wrap themselves around my torso, and a soft kiss is placed on my neck.

"The customers love you," Astrid whispers.

"Nah, they love you," I chuckle. "I'm content to just be liked-ish."

"You should give yourself more credit. Dolores never lets me help with her crossword."

"I'm not sure if she'll let me help again after I misspelled 'calendar.' I had to scribble it out in pen."

"Oh..." Astrid grimaces. "She might just kill you for that one."

Together, we walk up to the apartment. Astrid instantly cocoons herself in a blanket on the couch. I pick up the latest book I've been working on and sit in the lounge chair.

I figured it was finally time to start picking up what I missed in high school, so Astrid borrowed a few books for me from the library. This one was about the Italian Renaissance and the Enlightenment. I have no idea what's going on, but the pictures are neat.

"Do you have any opinions on the ideas of Machiavelli, yet?" Astrid quips from her nest.

"He, um... makes good pasta?" I answer.

"Machiavelli is a political philosopher, not a chef," Astrid teases. "Let me know when you get there, and we can chat about his debates."

"Maybe we should have pasta for dinner tonight?" Suddenly, I am in no mood to read about stuffy, old men. "We can look up a recipe and get flour all over the kitchen."

"Ugh, that sounds so good," Astrid groans. "But I've got to run some errands for the cafe tonight."

"Maybe tomorrow then." I purse my lips. "What kind of errands do you have?"

"I-I have a delivery order," she stammers. "It's not something I normally do, but they are paying extra."

"That's great! Is it far?"

"A bit, it's the Jordan River Sanctuary."

"Interesting." I try to hide my facial expression as I set my book down. Isn't Jordan River the name of the church she met Jeremiah at? Astrid really is terrible at cover stories. "I was thinking about going for a drive tonight, so I might not be here when you get back."

"Make sure to wear your helmet."

"Of course, of course." Probably not.

We continue reading for about an hour until Astrid gets up to leave. She kisses my cheek and waves goodbye. As soon as the door latches, I run to my room and dig out my bodysuit. Right on schedule, I see the Water Weaver duck out of the back of the coffee shop. I take the fire escape down, following a few blocks behind until we arrive at the Jordan River Sanctuary.

Once again, mass is being held at the front of the church. A small choir sings a hymn about loving thy neighbor as I sneak to the balcony staircase. A few steps from the top, I can hear familiar voices.

"Thanks for being on time."

"I was five minutes late one time," the Water Weaver groans.

"Relax, I was trying to lighten the mood," Jeremiah chuckles lightly, before speaking again in a grim voice. "I don't have good news. Our mutual friend is back."

"Are you sure?" I can barely hear her voice waver.

"Unfortunately so. I talked to her myself." Jeremiah sounds no happier than her. "Left me with more questions than answers."

"What did you find out?" Astrid presses.

"She has some amount of autonomy, as she was allowed to leave the compound, but at the same time, I don't think she was there willingly." No shit. Fuck that boat. Jeremiah continues, "She was escorted on and off the ship. I think she's being coerced somehow to fix the machine."

"The one they're killing to fix?"

"The same one."

"I don't like this." I can hear footsteps. I think she's pacing. "We need to get her out."

"She made it clear she doesn't trust me, but I'll try to reach out to her again. Weaver, I'm doing all I can to keep an eye on her. It's hard to do without raising eyebrows."

"I know. You're risking a lot to help me."

"I didn't sign up for this shit. Murder wasn't in my job description." A tinge of anger colors his voice. "The way the organization is heading, trouble is coming. The boss isn't treating the contractors right. Pay is late, and often short. He's pushing boundaries, and it won't be long until he's pushed back. Who knows what the fuck will happen then."

"The last thing we want is a power vacuum in the biggest gang in Boston." Astrid groans at the thought.

"Honestly, I think the girl will be the crux of it all. She's already causing waves."

"How so?" The Water Weaver asks.

"Firstly, she's outwardly hostile toward the boss, undermining his authority. I mean, the only girl in the group being the boss's ex? Not a good look."

"Wait, they dated?"

"Maybe, hard to say. Either way, despite the boss trying to keep it quiet, rumors have been spiraling out of control. Combine that with the fact that half the gang knows about her... abilities, it changes the power dynamic."

"If she's there when everything collapses, she might be used as a pawn," the Water Weaver hypothesizes.

"As if she isn't already," Jeremiah scoffs.

"Can you try to figure out what leverage the boss has over her? Maybe if we can neutralize the control over her, she'd be willing to run."

"I'll see what I can do."

"Let me know when you find something out."

"Wait, there's more!" Jeremiah interjects. "What do you know about nitromethane?"

"Science isn't my strongest subject. Ask me about the various monarchies in Europe, however, and I would be more useful."

"I've heard through the grapevine that the gang's put in a big order for it. It's like gas, but more intense."

"Are they building bombs?"

"We can only pray they aren't. Anyway, that's all I have. I'll call you when it's time to meet again."

The concluding pleasantries continue, but I take my leave. I mull over their conversation as I walk home. The nitromethane is for me, so I feel reasonably confident that bombings are off the table. The rest of the talking points are not as easy to dismiss. I heard Derek and Oliver griping about their working conditions, but I had no idea things were this strained. What would happen if the gang fractured? What would that mean for me? I shiver as grisly thoughts cross my mind.

I turn the corner that leads to the cafe, but instead of climbing the stairs, I hop on my bike. I'm going for a drive. As I dart through traffic, I settle on three facts.

One, I am a valuable asset to many groups of people. Jack did one thing right raising me after my mom died. Keeping my powers secret prevented the wrong people from learning about me. My anonymity afforded me a certain level of protection from being extorted and manipulated. However, he brought me into the spotlight after his two failed heists, so I need to watch my back... no one else will.

Second, I am vastly underprepared. While I've had my powers for eight years, it wasn't until a few months ago that I started to explore them and get a feel for my limits. I have virtually no experience using my powers to protect and defend, leaving me and the one I care about vulnerable to other people.

Third, there is no escaping the Boston underworld. Too many people know of me. The only path out would be to up and run, and I refuse to leave Astrid. Something is brewing that threatens the current standings. I have to get stronger.

Out of the city, I find an isolated field beneath a junction of power lines. Perfect. I dismount the bike and stretch. Let's fucking do this.

I start by slowly pushing and pulling the current of electricity, moving larger and larger amounts. Feeling thoroughly warmed up, I direct it in a circle above myself. A faint silver line appears in its path, growing thicker as I feed more energy into the loop. Before long, I have a substantial hula hoop hovering in the air, sparks crackling in the dark. I feel the pulse, wanting to run, discontent being static. I appease its appetite, spinning the wheel. *I have to get stronger.*

A drop of rain falls onto my cheek, then my hand. I can hear the trees rustling their leaves in the wind as water drips from down above. Rumbles of thunder roll from nearby hills. I cackle as I revel in the energy. I allow some of the electrons to flow through me, drunk from the rush, from the thrill. How much energy am I commanding? I feel powerful, lit up from the glow. The light twirls through my hands, looping around my arms. As more electricity is fed into my ring, it speeds faster. The draft from the current has my hair whipping around my face. *I have to get stronger.*

I split the hoop into strips. The light radiates intensely, taunting me with its power. I start throwing the bolts around, weaving and crisscrossing through the sky. The lattice stretches overhead, vibrant against the inky darkness. Deep purple clouds cover the moon and stars, leaving only nothingness above. Static makes the ends of my hair reach toward the sky. Fat raindrops fall quickly, dampening my clothes and turning the field to mud. A shiver ran down my spine, not because of the chill of the water dripping from my fingers, but in awe of the flares above. *I have to get stronger.*

I extend my hands up and push the pulses higher and higher into the sky. Bits of light splinter off of the branches, crackling into a silver spiderweb. *I have to get stronger.*

Push. Harder. Higher.

I have to get stronger.

It's not enough.

I have to get stronger.

I'm not enough.

I have to get stronger. I have to get stronger. I have to get stronger.

A bright light flashes in the sky above.

I have to — CRACK!

I don't know how long passed before I opened my eyes again. A faint ringing echoes in the distance. Wait, no. That's not right. My ears are ringing. The smell of acrid smoke assaults my nose. As rain pelts my body, I realize that my clothes are absolutely soaked. Has it been raining that long?

Mud coats strands of my hair as I move to sit up. I prop myself on my left arm and immediately fall back to the ground, pain shooting through my hand. I carefully lift my hand as my nerves scream in agony. An angry red burn starts in my palm stretching down my forearm, small offshoots branch from the main vein ending in sprawling feathers.

What happened? I don't understand, I don't know, I don't... A flash of light. The crack of thunder. Fragments start to piece themselves together. Pushing the strand of electricity higher and higher, reaching toward the sky. The flash. The fear. Pushing the light down, out, anywhere. The feeling of a million stabbing needles. Being thrown to the ground as the air surged past me.

I stand up, cradling my left arm to my chest. The burn stings with every raindrop plopping onto the raw skin. The ground in front of me is scorched with the same sprawling pattern as my hand. Ash slowly turns to mud as the frigid air pierces through my clothes. I flex my fingers, wincing through the pain. A crack of lightning strikes in the distance and thunder rumbles through the hills.

"Fuck. You." I mutter through clenched teeth. "Fuck you. Fuck you. Fuckyoufuckyoufuckyou. Fuck you!" I am screaming now, shaking from rage or the cold I don't know.

"Is this some kind of sick joke?" I stare at the sky, spinning, trying to find something, anything to direct my anger towards. "Is the universe playing some twisted game? You've taken everything from me! My mom! My childhood!" I stomp in a puddle, indifferent to the splash on my already drenched clothing.

"Well, you can have my life! Go on, take it! It hasn't been mine in years." Another lightning strike flashes. "You can have whatever you want, but you can't have her!"

I fall to my knees as thunder grumbles. Tears well in my eyes, but I don't let them fall. Only a whimper escapes, "You can't have her."

I have to get stronger.

CHAPTER 19

Days pass. My rage doesn't. The pain in my arm slowly fades. The scar doesn't. I keep practicing, finding ways to push myself, become stronger, test the limits of my abilities. I go out every night, driving my motorcycle with reckless abandon, coming home after she's fast asleep and staying awake until the sun rises. I see the unease in her eyes, her worried, anxious glances as she bandages my hand. I wait for her to yell, to scream that she hates me and claim I'm distrustful and ruinous. Say something I truly deserve. But she doesn't.

Instead, she gently rubs salve into my burned skin, places my helmet next to my keys, leaves a pastry on the counter when she goes to work. I don't understand.

I wake in the middle of the day under a soft blanket, a bookmark placed in my textbook. I've nearly finished the text on the Renaissance, and she quizzes me while I scrub caramel off of plates.

"The Peace of Lodi was signed, and war ceased between which city states?" Astrid wipes down a mug.

"Milan and Venice," I answer. That was like the first chapter of my textbook. "The cost savings from not having to pay for armies led to an influx of spending on cultural products, like art. Ask me something harder."

"I'm getting there." She smirks as she dries her hands on a towel. "All this new art, how was it different from previous art?"

"It celebrated the human form," I recite.

"Use your own words." Astrid nudges me with her elbow. "If I wanted a dry recounting, I would've read the book myself."

"In essence, they painted and sculpted hot people. You would have been a model in like a thousand paintings if you were alive then." Astrid smirks as I continue. "Lots of art prior focused on the story of the scene, but those Italians, man, they just liked to look at naked people."

"That's one way of looking at it."

"That's the best way of looking at it!" I splash some water in her direction. "Michelangelo literally painted naked people all over the Sistine Chapel. Have you seen the Creation of Man? You can't tell me he wasn't horny as fuck that day."

"I wouldn't blame him if he was." She stands behind me with an arm wrapped around my waist. Her other hand dollops a daub of soap suds onto my nose. I turn to face her and run my fingers through her hair. I pull her in for a kiss, gentle and deep.

"Maybe tonight, we could gather some inspiration," I whisper in her ear as her hands explore beneath the hem of my shirt. "Venus is quite the muse."

"Or we could have some fun now…" Her hands find their way to my chest and caress my breasts. Her fingertips trace the lacy edge of my bra as she nibbles on my ear. I close my eyes and savor the warmth of her breath dusting my neck. I grab the strings of her apron and pull her body against mine.

The bell on the front counter dings, pulling Astrid's attention away.

"The worst timing," she moans, fixing her apron strings.

"Tonight baby." I smooth her hair down. "Just a few hours."

She gives a quick peck on my cheek before walking into the front room, a friendly smile on her face.

As if to pile onto the bitter sting of my fading arousal, I hear the obnoxious beeping of my pager. I groan as I watch the series of numbers scrawled across the screen. It's GPS coordinates again, but different from the last. Fucking of course it is. Upstairs, I change into my bodysuit and an overcoat. Quickly, I scribble a note for Astrid.

Emergency call from a client. I'll be back soon.

-Your Michelangelo

With that, I sneak out the fire escape and drive the irritating thirty minutes to a new pier. A brisk walk later, I find the same boat as my last excursion. I try to hide my scowl as I step onto the dock. Despite its haggard appearance, it seems to be much sturdier than the previous port's. Even so, fuck boats. A new hunk of muscle is waiting for me as I approach the gangway.

"Name?" He side eyes me gruffly. His hair is cropped close to his head, revealing the tattoo of a skeleton on his neck. I don't respond. Instead, I hold his gaze and cross my arms. He puffs up his chest and glares down at me. "Give me your name or get off this dock."

"Step aside." I speak with a clear tone, unimpressed with his intimidation efforts.

"You little bitch," he growls and takes a step forward. "I'm not messing around."

"Wait, hold on!" A voice calls out from the top deck. Jeremiah jogs down the gangway, waving at the piece of meat blocking my path. "She's cleared to board."

"She hasn't provided identification."

"This comes from the Boss himself." Jeremiah grabs my hand and tugs me past the guard. "Thank you." I roll my eyes as Jeremiah pulls me up the ramp like an overeager summer camp counselor.

"A word of advice," he's speaking to me now. "Things tend to go smoother if you don't pick fights with every person on the ship."

"Noted," I scoff.

"I'm serious." We go below deck into an isolated hallway. "It's not you versus the world. There are some people here who are looking out for you."

"Maybe I don't need saving." I jerk my arm back and lift my chin indignantly. "I can take care of myself."

"But you don't have to." Jeremiah stops next to a door and gives it a few raps. "Derek, we're here."

"Janice!" I hear Derek fiddling with the lock on the other side of the door. Does he really think my name is Janice?

Well, not my real name. My fake name. My... nickname? Doesn't matter, either way. Janice? Nuh-uh. The door flings open, and Derek pulls me into a one-armed hug, much to my chagrin.

"Sparks. You call me Sparks or you'll be calling me from your grave."

"Oh Sparkie, glad to see you are still as bubbly and delightful as ever." He gives a nod to Jeremiah. "Will you be back to escort her out?"

"Just call me over the walkie when she's done," Jeremiah confirms before turning to me. "See you soon, kid."

"I'm fully an adult, you know," I call after him. "I don't care if you're two feet taller than me!"

Derek chuckled as he ushered me into the workroom. The immense machine loomed over me, casting a deep shadow over the sprawled tarps. After a quick scan, I can tell that everything is more or less how I left it.

"We haven't secured the metro-, uh netro, the..." Derek stumbles over the word as he fishes out the list I made him the last time I was on this godforsaken boat.

"The nitromethane?" I offer.

"Yeah, that. It's going to be a bit longer for that." He plops down in his swivel chair. "I was able to get the rest of the supplies though. Just do as much as you can without it."

With that, Derek pulls out a razor blade and starts flipping it between his fingers. It moves with a practiced agility, however, the scars on his knuckles show proof of clumsier times. He notices me watching and does a special trick - flicking it up, catching it flat on the back of his hand, tossing it back up, and then grabbing it midair. With that, he gave a mock bow and then gestured to the machine for me to start my work. What a pompous dick.

I start to dig through the boxes laid next to the wall. Screws, wire casings, adapters, a new alternator, standard stuff. I get to work tuning the exhaust system and replacing the rusting metal.

My mind wanders as I work. As usual, all thoughts lead to Astrid. This wire casing has a unique blue color. I bet Astrid would think it was pretty. I open a new box of screws. Hehe. Screw. Gradually, my thoughts veer towards more serious topics, namely the Water Weaver.

I still don't understand how she got mixed in with all of this. With Jeremiah. With the Tributaries. With Jack. She's practically enemy number one for a crime syndicate.

But Jeremiah is the sore spot. Is he her source? Or is he planning on betraying her? I have to test him somehow, but how? He can't know that I know he's been speaking with the Water Weaver, and he *definitely* can't know that I know her. That doesn't leave many options.

Three knocks shake me out of my head as Derek gets up to open the door.

"Oliver, my man!" The two men fist bump as Oliver enters with a tray of coffees. "Sparkie, union-mandated coffee break."

"I don't know why you care so much," I grumble as I dust myself off and walk toward the small collection of office chairs. "One would think I should spend my time working so we don't have to be here longer than we need to."

"Too much work leads to burnout," Oliver teases. "Consider us your HR reps. Now drink." He dumps milk and sugar into a coffee before handing it to me. Apparently, he noted my preferences last time. I take a polite sip and try to steel my face against the bitter attack on my senses. The two men across from me chuckle, so I can only assume it doesn't work.

"Thank you for the beverage, Oliver," I say. I do appreciate the thought, although… coffee? Ick.

"You're welcome," he grins and gives Derek a light punch on the shoulder. "It sure beats twiddling my thumbs like an asshole. Would much rather hang out with you two."

"What do you do here anyway?" I ask. "I doubt you're a professional barista-for-hire."

"Ugh, nothing right now," Oliver groans. "I've been on call for weeks now. Normally, I'm a bouncer for the casino boats, sometimes I work overtime in accounting. I'm good with numbers and don't mind the extra pay. However, Boss has everything locked down right now, so I just clock in and fuck off."

"Hear, hear!" Derek raises his cup. "The most action I've gotten in forever is just watching you with your wrench. I enjoy your company, sure, but it's not the same as tracking down defaulters. Much slower pace."

"Do you normally like your jobs?" I press. "Being gunmen and fists?"

A moment passes. Then two. Oliver swirls the brown liquid in his cup. Derek is the first to respond.

"Nobody dreams of being a murderer when they grow up, and I haven't met anyone who wasn't desperate when they were recruited." His voice isn't angry or forlorn but is instead very candid. "They join up because they have to and stay because it's what they know."

"Plus, the pay normally ain't too bad," Oliver adds. "You learn to live with it, compartmentalize."

"I told you earlier," Derek continues. "I'm not a bad guy. Oliver here has a family, wife and kids. Jeremiah, the guy who just escorted you now, actually went to seminary. He won't say what happened, but it must have been pretty bad for him to end up on this side of the aisle. Either way, he joined before the Boss escalated the contract work to murder, used to just be breaking kneecaps and sending threats."

"Now, don't be spreading this around," Oliver leans in and lowers his voice. "But the well is running dry. Apparently, he commissioned those bank robberies to fill his coffers and didn't get as big of a haul as he needed. Paychecks might start bouncing."

"Oh shit," I say. "Correct me if I'm wrong, but I don't think it's a good idea to not pay freelance murderers." This gets a chuckle out of the group. Oliver leans back into the worn chair, content with the buzz from spreading juicy gossip. "Why did you two join the Tributaries?"

"For me it was real simple," Oliver starts. "I dropped out of high school so I have no career prospects in this shitty economy. The wife got let go when her company went bankrupt, and I refuse to let my kids make the same mistakes I did. I took this job so they could stay in school and go to college without worrying about us."

"I'm what you would consider a legacy," Derek chimes in. "My family's been in the gang world since they immigrated to America many, many generations ago. This is all I've ever known. My dad and my brother were both shot when our organization collapsed a decade ago, but the Tributaries took me in. Without them, I probably would also be dead."

"Damn, that's pretty grim." I recline back in my chair and take another sip of my coffee. Still gross.

"Well, it is nice keeping personal and business separate, not that I have too much of a personal life," Derek chuckles at a memory. "Growing up, family dinners were always business meetings. 'What numbers did we pull this week?' 'Pass the salt.' 'We need to retaliate after the murder of our cousin.' I'm glad that now I can go to my room and relax in silence after a hard day's work."

"So, Sparks," Oliver says. "What's your story?"

My eyes meet his and the lights in the room flicker once. I keep myself composed despite the painful memories and very slowly set my cup down on the table. Derek sits up, no longer feeling comfortable with the conversation.

"It's okay," Derek speaks calmly. "You don't have to share."

"No, it's alright." I take a controlled breath and then continue. "My mother died in an explosion. Jack helped me get off the streets. We have since fallen out and are no longer on speaking terms. Once I finish this mission, we are parting ways." The tension in the air lifts once the guys know I'm not about to go apeshit on them. They both lean back in their chairs, sipping at the last dregs of their drinks.

"I've never heard of anyone leaving," Oliver muses. "Have you Derek?"

"Nah." He shakes his head. "Just those who find early retirement at the end of the barrel."

"Well," Oliver gives me a sincere look. "I wish you the best when you tender your resignation. I think I speak for us both when I say that we're rooting for you."

A small grin slips from my mask. I decide to let it stay. Maybe it wouldn't hurt to have some... I dunno... friendly acquaintances? Hell, I suppose I could learn to like coffee. I take another sip. Yuck! No on that second count.

"I'll make sure to throw a party!" Derek teases. "We can get streamers, balloons, oooh, a cake!"

"Yeah, yeah, yeah." I roll my eyes as I stand up. "There will be no retirement if I don't fix this piece of shit, so I better get back to it."

After a round of fist bumps, Oliver departs with the empty coffee cups and Derek resumes playing with his razor. I go back to my mind-numbing project. At least I can use this time to think.

I don't like the meet ups between Jeremiah and Astrid. Why does she trust him? More importantly, should she? I need to test his loyalty to find out whether it's to Jack or her. But how?

Jeremiah doesn't know that I'm onto him, but based on my eavesdropping, it seems he's feeding information to the Water Weaver. I need to know if what he's telling her is accurate, or if artistic liberties have been taken. I can't tell if his reports have been accurate so far, I can barely tell what's real myself. The only way to verify his story is if I control the narrative. So... I need to feed Jeremiah a message compelling enough to spread to Astrid, but without being obvious. Easier said than done.

Subtle breadcrumbs. What's juicy enough that he would have to tell the Water Weaver? Me! Astrid has been torn into knots about the "mysterious girl." If I can trick Jeremiah into getting intel on me and he is truly loyal to Astrid, he would run to her immediately.

I'm obviously not going to reveal my identity. If Jeremiah takes this intel to Jack, then I'm screwed. No, it needs to be something else. A cry for help? No, that could get messy if Jack is involved. Plus, I want Astrid to be as far away from this floating hellhole as possible. What about a calendar event? A time and place.

Pros: It's vague enough to arouse curiosity and interest. Furthermore, I can control the environment. If Jeremiah is planning on ambushing the Water Weaver, I can get there early to disrupt their plans. Otherwise, I can lurk in the darkness to see if Astrid shows up, then leave.

Cons: Where? When? Also, how do I get the info to Jeremiah?

From the corner of my eye, I see the notepad and pencil on the table. A note! I believe Jeremiah is going to escort me off this boat, so I could get a note to him then. I slink over and grab the materials for my plan.

Okay... where should this rendezvous be? Not somewhere too busy, we want seclusion. I think through the city of Boston for places I'm familiar with. The only place that comes to mind is a small park. I remember sitting in the park eating a pastry when I got the phone call from Jack - the one begging me to come to the bank. Damn, I wish I sent that call to voicemail.

I scratch the name of the park on the bottom of the page. Cool, got a place. Now what time? Sunset is early afternoon in December, so really anytime in the evening should be dark enough to provide me with enough cover to hide. 8? 9? 9:30? Snap judgment - 9:30. That way I can go to bed early. Stupid reason, but it works. What day is it? Shoot, I can't remember the date. Umm... it's a Wednesday today at least. I scribble "Thursday, 9:30 p.m." down next to the park name. Good enough.

I rip the bottom of the page off and stuff it into my pocket. I write some random gibberish down on the rest of the page. Alternators, electrical flow, this and that. If

Derek asks, I was writing down machine things. Not like he would understand it was nonsense anyway.

"I think that's good enough for today." Derek yawns as he stretches his arms above his head. "Do you think you could finish the rest when we get the nitromethane?"

"Probably," I shrug. "It doesn't come with a manual."

"Fair enough." He sends a text on his phone before standing. "I know the Boss is getting antsy for this. Either way, Jeremiah is outside to escort you off the boat."

"Thanks Derek." I give him a light punch on the shoulder. "I suppose you aren't half bad to hang around."

"Whoa, was that a compliment?" He teases, a laugh sparkles in his eyes.

"I mean, the coffee is shit, so that's making you look great in comparison."

That earns me a chuckle as he opens the door. I wave back to him as I step into the hallway. Jeremiah gives me a polite nod as we meander toward the top deck. He lets me walk on my own this time, instead of guiding me by my arm or my back. I guess he trusts that I'm not going to go crazy and try to blow up the ship. Although that option gets more appealing the longer I'm here.

"How's it going?" Jeremiah starts the conversation with a smile. I try to avoid narrowing my eyes. He has to earn my trust, but that doesn't mean I have to be a complete dick. Who knows, he might be useful.

"If I look at any more wires today, I'll go cross eyed." I force a small smile, but I'm not sure it reaches my eyes.

"Hopefully you can find something relaxing to do tonight," he offers.

"I am going to get laid," I state bluntly.

"That works." Jeremiah stifles a laugh. "What a lucky guy."

"Girl." I correct without thinking. Shit. Should I have said that?

"Apologies." Jeremiah seems unbothered. "What a lucky girl." We walk in silence for a few steps, both of us unsure of where the conversation should go next.

"What about you?" I reopen the topic. "Any relaxing to do later?" He seems surprised I asked. To be fair, I am too.

"I'll be attending mass later tonight," he answers. "I try to go twice a week, if not more frequently."

"Interesting," I muse. "Does your priest know about your day job?"

"To some extent," Jeremiah sighs. "He and I spend a lot of time in confession."

"Isn't it a bit odd?" I look up at him. "Doesn't this line of work directly conflict with religion?" I expect anger, or at least annoyance. I'm surprised to see sorrow.

"It's my burden to bear." His shoulders sag. "My whole life, I've been an honest person. My mama would take me to church, and we would analyze the sermons at a coffee shop afterward. It was my favorite part of the week. Just the two of us."

"That sounds nice." We've made our way off the deck and onto the shore.

"It was." He smiles sadly. "Until it wasn't. My ma got sick. My professors told me to pray, that God works in mysterious ways. But I know God. I've spoken with Him every day for as long as I can remember. I heard Him speak to me, and he led me here, to the Tributaries. My salary is paying for my mother's treatments. My soul is damned, and I accept that. But this is His will."

"How is your mom?" By this point, we have made it to my bike, so I lean against the seat.

"She's doing well." The ghost of a smile appears on his face. "She's still sick, but she's hanging in there. Thanks for asking."

"Anytime."

I fish in my pocket for my keys and feel the slip of paper. Shit, I almost forgot. I pull out my keys and "accidentally" my note falls to the ground. I'm already driving away before Jeremiah can reach down to grab it. In my rearview mirror, I watch as he uncrumples the scrap and reads the note. The drop has been made. Now we wait.

⚡   ⚡   ⚡   ⚡

"Astrid, I'm home!" I plop my keys down on the entryway table and tousle the wind out of my hair. I changed out of my bodysuit before I got home, so I'm in my regular jeans, t-shirt, and leather jacket. "Where are you?"

"In the bedroom," she calls in a sing-song voice.

"What's got you in such a good mood?" The hardwood is cool against my bare feet as I saunter toward the bedroom and open the door.

"You," she whispers.

My mouth falls open in shock as I take in the sight before me. Astrid is draped in a white bedsheet, her skin bare except for the fabric dangling over her shoulder and around her waist. Her blonde hair cascades down her back in gentle waves. She stands poised in front of the bed, reminiscent of Botticelli's *Birth of Venus.*

"Wow." The breath leaves my lungs as my eyes take in every inch of her body. "You look... wow."

"Are you going to stand there all day or are you going to worship me like the goddess I am?" She cocks her hip dramatically, though her eyes are sparkling with mischief.

"Fuck yes." In one motion, I shrug my jacket to the floor and cup her face in my hands, pulling her in for a deep kiss. My hand goes to the fabric over her shoulder before I am swatted away.

"Tsk tsk," Astrid chides. She places a hand on my shoulder and guides me down to my knees. "I said worship."

Happy to oblige, I lower my head to the floor to kiss her feet. I slowly and methodically make my way from her toes to her ankles, to her shins. Gently, I lift her leg and drape it over my shoulder, leaving tiny kisses from her knee to her inner thigh.

"Would you allow me to bring bliss to your divine self?" I tilt my head back to meet her gaze, inches away from her center. She runs her fingers through my hair.

"You may."

I proceed tantalizingly slow, first only allowing my breath to reach her. I feel her thigh muscles clench from the anticipation. I brush a kiss against her clit, almost imperceptibly soft. But she feels it. Her head rolls back, and a slight moan leaves her lips, almost imperceptibly quiet. But I hear it.

My tongue lightly traces the outline of her lips, already wet. She squirms from my shoulder, but I hold her tight against me, a hand on her lower back and thigh.

"You're not going anywhere," I whisper, sending another gust of air toward her exposed nerves.

Her hands grip my hair as I resume my tracing in deeper, faster circles. Closer to the clit, then further out. Two fast, one tortuously slow stopping just shy of the bud. Then I flatten my tongue and lick her entire opening, flicking my tongue at the end. Astrid is nearly hyperventilating, leg quivering around my neck pulling me closer. Time to go in for the kill.

I focus on the clit, flicking my tongue on the clit over and over. I listen to Astrid's voice repeating my name, "Anise! God yes, Anise!" Her moans drive me to go even faster, even harder. Her thighs clench around me and I can't breathe, but I fucking love it. At last, I lightly nip directly on her clit, and she screams as she finds her release, the most perfect sound I've ever heard.

"Was my worship satisfactory?" I tease.

"Fuck off." Astrid grasps my shirt and pulls me into a deep kiss. "Take off your shirt."

"As you wish, my lady." I toss my shirt to the floor and shimmy out of my jeans before she leads me to the bed. I just now notice it's covered with a plastic tarp. Seems I was a little distracted earlier. Astrid guides me to sit on the bed. She picks up a palette from the nightstand and straddles my lap, her toga draped over my leg.

"I thought now would be a good time to show me what you learned from your book." Astrid dips her thumb into a pastel blue paint and caresses my cheek, leaving behind a smear of color. She leans in close and whispers. "Paint me, my Michelangelo."

I dip my index into a soft pink and draw swirls across her temple. The fabric slips off her shoulder and I take the opportunity to leave a handprint on her collarbone. As the clothes shed, more pigment is used. I outline hearts on her abdomen, she traces my scars, I write "mine" on her upper thigh.

The rest of the night passes in a vibrant blur. Our bodies are both covered in blue and pink. The colors blend into a creamy lavender as our limbs intertwine. There's blue in her hair, pink on my lower back, purple on both of our chests. Together, we become an intimate display of ombres and gradients, slowly becoming more and more lavender as we touch, rub, and kiss. After a long night, the paint dries, and we make our way to the shower. As the lilac paint washes down the drain, we hold each other close, not ready to let go. We fall asleep intertwined, out of breath and energy, but still desperate for the other's touch.

CHAPTER 20

The morning sun is diluted by the gauzy curtain, but Astrid's blonde hair shimmers in the light. I could watch her sleep all day, clinging to my side underneath the warm comforter. I've never seen someone sleep as calmly or as peacefully as her. I am happy to act as her sentry, ensuring her sleep remains undisturbed.

She shifts and nestles deeper, using my shoulder as a pillow. I slowly reach up and softly stroke her hair. Her eyes flutter open and meet mine.

"Good mornin'," she says groggily.

"Good morning, beautiful." I sweep her hair out of her eyes. "I love waking up next to you."

"Well, I plan on waking up next to you for the rest of my life." Astrid leans in and I pull her in for a deep kiss.

"Sounds perfect to me."

She rolls out of bed wearing my t-shirt from the day before. I follow her into the kitchen and pull out the two mugs we painted. Astrid patters around the kitchen, pulling out powders, creamers, and other flavorings. She makes cocoa most mornings, mixing together something that is always delicious. Today it seems we are going with the standard spiced anise chocolate, my favorite.

Astrid passes the warm mug to me, perfect temperature to drink. I don't know how she does that. Her phone vibrates across the room, and I grab it for her.

"Jesus, you've got like twenty-seven missed calls from a random number." I furrow my brow and pass the phone to her. The caller isn't saved to her contacts. "Who would call that many times and not leave a voicemail?"

"Oh, that's Je-." She freezes as she glances at the screen. "Jerry. That's Jerry. I need to call him back." I swear, this girl cannot lie worth a damn. She steps out onto the fire escape, phone already up to her ear.

I quickly tiptoe to the living room and slide open a window close enough to overhear her conversation, but not close enough for her to notice.

"-know, I know... I was busy! Jeremiah, not everything is... wait, what? Slow down, I can't understand you."

She paces back and forth on the landing, confusion etched on her face.

"You're blowing up my phone because she littered? Jeremiah, be for real... That's all it said? A time and place? That could be anything. A family picnic, a doctor's appointment, a-... Okay, probably not a doctor's appointment."

She's getting frustrated. I can't quite make out the voice on the phone, but I can hear him rambling on and on.

"I don't know what I'm walking into here." Astrid gestures wildly with her hands. "For all we know, this could be a trap for me. You said you haven't heard any chatter for tonight? This could be unrelated to the Tributaries entirely."

She pauses her pacing and sits on the top step, head in her hands.

"I know it's her. You said it fell out of her pocket? Did she see it fall?... If she's there, I have to be there too. She needs help, I can feel it. Ugh, this is a bad idea. Can you text me the time and place? Thanks... I'll check in with you tomorrow. Thanks, Jeremiah."

I shut the window and stand in front of a bookcase as Astrid reenters the apartment. I turn over my shoulder.

"All good?" I ask, pretending to step away from looking for a book.

"Oh yeah, he was just worried... about a cat." She wrings her hands and stares at the floor.

"How's the cat?" I take a sip of my drink and stare at her innocently.

"The cat?" A glimmer of confusion crosses her face before she stumbles back into her lie. "Oh yeah, he's fine now."

"Glad to hear it."

We lounge on the couch together and finish our drinks in comfortable silence. Astrid leans her head on my shoulder while my thumb traces circles on her arm. Just the two of us. If only we could stay like this forever.

However, it eventually becomes time to open the cafe downstairs. Astrid rises from the couch and stretches her arms above her head.

"Am I going to have my favorite busgirl today or am I working a solo shift?" She teases.

"Put me to work, baby." I give a little shimmy as I move toward the closet. I pull out a clean shirt and jeans and toss Astrid her favorite sweater. She excitedly pulls it over her head and hugs her arms to her chest, relishing the soft fabric.

Once ready for the day ahead, we hold hands as we head to the store. We tie our matching aprons around our backs. I unlock the front door and already, a few regulars start to flow in. Luckily, Astrid is already behind the counter filling mugs with steaming liquid. I take over the cash register with quiet pleasantries and a friendly smile.

Within minutes, the familiar murmur of conversation fills the room. Dolores calls me over to help her with the crossword (three across is Guatemala) as some college students pull out a board game. Life is good.

Eventually, mugs become empty and plates are left with only crumbs, so I gather dishes to wash in the back. Before long, I am elbow-deep in warm suds mindlessly scrubbing and rinsing.

I have a bit of a problem. Jeremiah actually called Astrid. I really didn't think he would. I can't nail him down. Is he trustworthy? Playing both sides? I'm starting to think he's someone who could be an ally. But his good nature created a bit of a pickle where Astrid now expects something to happen this evening at a park down the road. Unfortunately, I don't have anything planned...

Damn it.

This could be a great opportunity for Sparks to pass a message to Water Weaver directly. But what? And how?

Astrid doesn't know about my double life. Do I want her to know? No, that's stupid. I don't want her involved with that shitty aspect of my life, and that would only draw her in deeper. But what would I even want to tell her?

Astrid gives me a quick peck on the cheek as she grabs some extra clean mugs. Suddenly, the life I could have is all I can picture. Waking up on lazy Sunday mornings, drinking hot cocoa in bed, living with our limbs intertwined. I could stay here in Boston and not look over my shoulder. I could be happy.

Stop. Stop torturing yourself. I splash the water in frustration. It doesn't matter what I want, it never has. My burden must come first. I can't walk away from who I am, who I need to be. But Astrid has to be protected. I can stay with Astrid, only as long as I can keep her safe. But if my life ever puts hers in danger, I have to walk away. Even if she begs me to stay. Even if every fiber of my being screams in agony. Even if it kills me.

Back to the problem at hand. Take all of my wants and lock them behind a wall. What does Sparks need to tell the Water Weaver, and how do I pass along the message?

The Water Weaver has seen Sparks a few times, but never up close and always with my face obscured. I tempt fate every time we come in contact and risk her realizing my identity. Perhaps I could leave a message of sorts for her to find. A pang of guilt hits my stomach for so brazenly deceiving Astrid, but it has to happen. A message. Maybe I could write a note, just like before. Good enough for me. I can leave it somewhere she'll find it.

The rest of the day passes in a blur - coffee, board games, dishes, friendly conversations. The number of customers dwindles until just a few are left. I untie my apron and hang it behind the counter.

"Hey Astrid," I get her attention. "I got a text from a client. They're having issues with their fuse box. Are you okay holding down the fort if I go and see what's up?"

"I think I can manage." Astrid teases and her nose crinkles in the cutest way. "I have a bit of experience taking care of these crazy folks."

"See you tonight then." I kiss her cheek and head upstairs. I quickly change into my bodysuit and then throw some clothes over it. I also shove a pen and paper into my toolkit. My bike revs as I pull onto the road, the brisk winter air stinging my face. It doesn't take long to arrive at the park, but I drive a few blocks past and park my bike behind a dumpster in some random alley.

Hours pass with me sitting on a park bench staring at a blank page. All of the words I want to say speed through my head, but I can't pick out the perfect ones. Though as the sun trickles down in the sky, I know I don't have more time to mull it over.

Dear Water Weaver,

Glad you got my message. Sorry it came in such an unorthodox way, I didn't know who I could trust.

There's a lot I could say, but it all comes down to one point. You need to back off. The Tributaries aren't safe, and I can't protect you from them. I imagine you probably have your reasons for intervening, but you need to cut your losses and save yourself.

Hypocritical, I know, but I'm almost out myself. One more job and I'm free, but I can't leave if I know you're still in. So, we must go together.

Please.

-Sparks

I grab a staple gun from my kit and stick the note to a tree. There. After stowing the staple gun, I stand near my bike. I should ride off now, leave the note and trust she'll find it. But... there are a lot of trees in the park. Despite my best intentions, I find myself walking back to the park. I find a tree within eyesight of the note.

"It can't be *that* hard to climb a tree, right?"

Wrong. It is in fact hard to climb a tree. However, I figure it out without too much damage to my pride. Once safely in the branches, the view is actually quite nice. Streetlights cut through the darkness, creating a forest of shadows and icicles. I lean against the trunk and watch my breath fog.

After a while, I hear a soft crunch of snow. In the distance, I see an ethereal figure in blue slowly snaking through the park. Her golden ponytail sways as she steps from shadow to shadow, searching for something or someone.

I sit there in the tree for a few minutes, observing her movements, guarding against any double-crossing from Jeremiah. Only the Water Weaver shows. I take a breath and make a rash decision.

I reach out for the electricity running through the nearest streetlight. I borrow some of the current and the light dims slightly. Instead of flinging the energy as I normally do, I try to manifest a small burst of sparks close to her. The Water Weaver jumps back in surprise as the light spooks her, but carefully leans over to examine the fading glint. Another burst shines further from her in the direction of my note. Like a trail of breadcrumbs, she follows one after the other directly to the tree. I cling to the shadows of my trunk, blending in amongst the darkness.

The Water Weaver plucks the note from the tree, disappointed I left it behind and didn't meet her in person. She reads it quickly, folds it, and tucks it in her shirt.

"You could just talk to me." Her sudden statement startles me, and she hears the branches creak. She turns over her shoulder, scanning for the noise. "I know you're here, you know I know you're here. I mean, you led me here, so you must be close. Why won't you just show yourself?"

She starts walking toward the grove of trees I'm in and I panic. She can't find me, I can't be here. I reach out for the streetlights and all at once, turn them off. She yelps in surprise at the abrupt darkness, but I'm already moving. Unfortunately, I also can't see. I only make it halfway down the tree before I slip and fall. I grunt as I land on my shoulder. It's going to have a nasty bruise, but the rest of me is fine.

"Don't do this," the Water Weaver pleads. "Turn the lights back on. We can talk this out. I know there's a way we can help each other."

I don't say anything. I only run, stumbling over tree roots, dodging low-hanging branches. As I leave, I allow the streetlights to flicker back on one at a time. In the end, the Water Weaver is left calling out to an empty park.

⚡ ⚡ ⚡ ⚡

When Astrid gets home, I am lying on the sofa icing my shoulder. The purple hues have already spread to my shoulder blade.

"Good evening, babe!" I greet cheerily. "Did you have a fun outing?"

"Looks like I had more fun than you." She sits next to me and examines my shoulder, her gentle probes causing me to wince and grit my teeth. "How come you are always injured?"

"Well, it turns out the problem wasn't with the fuse box, it was with the transformer outside." The lies flow smoothly, and I hate myself for it. "You know it takes ages for the power company to get around to fixing anything, so I thought I'd just do it myself. I was climbing down the pole, and I missed a rung."

"You need to be more careful," she chides. Astrid goes to the bathroom and returns with a poultice she rubs on my bruise.

"I don't know," I tease. "I kind of like the attention I get from my lovely nurse."

"There are other ways to get my attention instead of throwing yourself off a ladder." She brushes her hand down my cheek. "For one, seeing you on the couch in just a sports bra is quite captivating."

I imitate a raunchy trumpet showtune while fiddling with my bra strap, and Astrid chuckles.

"Nuh-uh." She slaps my hand away. "No sexy time while you are too injured to move your arm."

"I can move my arm!" I attempt to lift my shoulder to prove it but can't make it above my head without pain shooting through my side. "Ow, ow, ow! Okay, well, I don't need both hands to be a sexy-time team player."

Astrid grabs a blanket from a basket and drapes it over me, tucking me in. She caresses my forehead tenderly.

"Later, I promise. In the meantime, have you had dinner?" She opens the fridge and pulls out cheese and crackers. "We can snack on the rest of these."

"Say less." I sit up and reach for a cracker to assemble my sandwich. Astrid places a pillow on the floor and plops down next to me. "I can scoot over. You don't need to sit on the floor."

"I'm good down here." She pats her pillow. "I think everyone needs some floor time now and then."

"If you believe so strongly in it," I toss a pillow down, "then I'll join you."

"I feel like we're having a slumber party," Astrid laughs. "Like we should be playing Twenty Questions or Never Have I Ever."

"Let's do it then." I suggest.

"What?"

"I'm calling your bluff. Three fingers up." I nudge her with my elbow as I hold up my three fingers. She rolls her eyes but obliges.

"Okay, but you go first."

"Fine," I say. "Never have I ever learned to swim." Astrid lowers a finger.

"Never?" She asks. "Man, I love to swim! My ma used to call me her little fish."

"That is adorable." I grin, picturing a baby Astrid splashing in a pool wearing arm floaties.

"We should add swimming to our list of summer date ideas," she suggests. "There is an adorable pond near where I grew up that would be great to learn in."

"Let's not get ahead of ourselves," I tease. "Your turn next."

Astrid looks up at the ceiling as she thinks. "Never have I ever... been to a baseball game."

"You live in Boston," I say incredulously as I put a finger down. "It's like a law that you have to go."

"I haven't always lived in Boston, you know," she explains. "I was a small-town girl first. Lived in a town with under a thousand residents."

"Either way, this summer, we're going to Fenway Park."

"Only if we can get some peanuts and Cracker Jacks." Her eyes light up. "I want the full experience."

"Throw in some hotdogs and you're on." I wink at her. "My turn. Never have I ever flown on a plane." Her finger drops.

"It's not that exciting, but it gets you places quickly." She shrugs. "Why haven't you flown before?"

"Need a government ID." I take another bite of cheese. "Don't have one."

"You've never explained to me why you're underground." Astrid offers me a cracker. "What's that story?"

"Not one worth telling." I change the subject. "Your turn."

"Hold on," she interjects. "You have to give me something. What's your name?"

"Anise."

"No, it's not." Astrid moves the cheese plate out of my reach. "What is your name?"

"Anise suits me just fine," I retort. "Plus, you're the one who gave it to me."

"Because what else am I supposed to call you!" She throws her hands in the air. "You're so secretive, and for what? We live together, we've fucked, and I don't even know your name! I don't really know anything about you. Most people don't hide from the government unless they're murderers or something. I don't need to know everything, but you need to give me something. Please."

"Every other name I've had was given to me by someone who betrayed me," I quietly confide. "So if it's alright with you, I'd like to stick with the one given to me by someone who cares about me."

"Why are you hiding?" Astrid asks softly, placing a tender hand on my thigh.

"It's a long story." I pull my knees to my chest. "My mom was involved in some pretty bad shit. There are a lot of people who are interested in her work - the government and some... unsavory people. It would be best if neither found me."

"But your mom's dead, isn't she?" Astrid leans in. "What do they want from you?" I flinch as images of my mom's death flash across my eyes.

"Her work ended up... affecting me." I glance at the lightning scar covering my palm. "I don't know exactly what she did, but I know more than I wish I did. That's enough for them. As far as being a murderer, some people have died but I wasn't the one pulling the trigger."

"Would they kill you if they found you?" She spoke so faintly I could barely hear.

"No." I shake my head. "They'd do much worse." I shiver as I picture myself as some lab rat, poked and prodded to find the cause of my powers, or worse, tortured into being a weapon to kill tens, hundreds, thousands of people. "I haven't spoken my 'real' name in eight years, and I never will again."

The room is silent. I feel the tears prick behind my eyes, but I lock up the reopened memories and push all of the sadness away. I don't have the luxury of being vulnerable. I straighten my spine and toss my hair over my shoulder.

"Next question." I state as I reach for another slice of cheese.

CHAPTER 21

The next few days pass uneventfully. I know Astrid went down to the church a few times to strategize with Jeremiah, but I can't find the motivation to follow. Instead, I stay in the apartment, hiding in the dark beneath the covers. I can't sleep. My ghosts haunt my dreams. Visions of snapping locket chains, vibrant pulses of electricity, my mother laying on the ground like a discarded porcelain doll in a pool of crimson. Every time I close my eyes, I see her limp frame dangling from the railing. I hear her final scream in the silence of my solitude.

I drag myself to the kitchen, scavenging until a bottle of nearly empty whiskey calls to me. I oblige, bringing the glass to my lips. The amber liquid burns as it spills down my throat. Hopefully it will cauterize the wound of my recurring memories. But after way too few sips, the bottle is empty.

Disgruntled, I discard the useless container on the counter. This won't do. I trudge to my closet and pull on the closest t-shirt and jeans. The shirt is cropped with well-worn rips in the material, but my jacket will protect my midriff from the brutal winter chill. With that, I duck into the wind and embark on my search for emotional pain relief.

Somewhere between a few blocks to a few miles, I step into some grungy dive bar. I really wasn't paying attention. I ignore the hoots from belligerent patrons as I sling my jacket over a bar stool and flag down the bartender.

"Whiskey. Double. On the rocks... Leave the bottle."

I slide a wad of cash onto the counter which compels the barkeep to move quickly. I throw the first glass back as soon as he sets it down, and he is gracious enough to top it off before moving onto other customers.

The sticky floorboards creak as a patron strolls to a worn-down jukebox. The lights flicker with the strain as a bass-heavy punk song spurts through the staticky speakers. Dusty taxidermy deer hang from the ceiling next to creased black and white photographs of things I couldn't be bothered to care about. Several glasses of self-deprecation later, I feel a hand trail across my back as a man straddles the barstool next to me.

"Evening foxy." The tobacco on his breath is assaultive. I force the liquid in my mouth down, trying not to gag. "Have I seen you around before?"

"I'm not interested in company." I set my glass down and reach for the bottle. The man snatches it from my grasp and sets it back down.

"C'mon sweetheart," he purrs. "I can be a lot of fun."

I turn and very slowly look him up and down. The middle-aged man is puffing his chest, showing off his stained shirt with text faded beyond the hope of legibility. A flame tattoo snakes up his arm with patchy ink. His hair is greasy and combed into a tight rattail. His expression sours when he notes my unimpressed examination.

"I stand by my original statement." I refill my glass and place the bottle away from him. Asshole.

"That's not very polite, kitten." His wrinkled eyes make their way down to my chest where they appear to get stuck.

"Get lost." I polish off my glass and smack my lips. Whiskey hurts so good. How much have I had to drink?

"I think I'll stay right here and enjoy the view." The creep leans against the bar, ogling my exposed midriff.

"Fucking hell," I curse and slide to the next stool down. If he's going to eyefuck me, I at least don't want to smell him. Mud splatters onto my jeans as he clomps his feet onto the stool next to me. "Seriously? You massive prick. Barkeep, can I settle my tab?"

I can drink at home. I'm not putting up with this shit. The bartender brings my bill and looks at the amount of whiskey left in the bottle.

"I can't send you home alone after drinking that much." He shrugs, indifferent to my groan of frustration. "Do you want me to call a cab or a friend?"

"This must be the worst fucking bar in all of Boston."

I scribble Astrid's number on a cocktail napkin and pass it back. The creep skulks off, resigned to the fact that he was not getting laid by me. I lay my head on my arms and give in to the swirling thoughts inside my mind. Although heavily diluted by alcohol, fragments draw my attention.

Astrid's naked body. Robbing Golden Capital Bank. Sledding for the first time. Fighting the Water Weaver in the blizzard. Astrid's naked body again. Baking cookies with my mother. Playing the viola in my apartment. Astrid's naked-

A rusted bell clanks instead of rings as the bar's door opens. Light footsteps as someone approaches the bar and strokes my hair. Astrid.

"How much did she have to drink?" She asks the bartender.

"Enough." Not true.

"Aw sweetie," she murmurs. "Let's get you home."

She guides my arms into my jacket and zips me in. I stand and the room sways as the alcohol hits my bloodstream. The bartender might be better at his job than I gave him credit for.

"Evening foxy." A familiar voice purrs at Astrid.

"Excuse me." Polite yet firm, such an Astrid response.

Mine is a little different. With his attention solely on Astrid, I land a square blow on his cheek. As the creep falls onto the guy standing behind him, Astrid grabs my shoulders and pulls me stumbling to the door. Chaos erupts behind us as fists fly in the bar fight I accidentally started. Whoops.

The winter air pierces through my jacket as we step outside. As the horizon starts to buckle and bend, I lean onto Astrid. Her hair smells of peaches and honey. It's slowly becoming my favorite scent.

"You should keep this shampoo," I giggle as I murmur into her neck. Astrid fumbles with her car keys as we near the passenger seat of her car.

"I wasn't planning on getting rid of it, silly," she teases me as she pulls open the car door. I fumble with the seat belt until she takes it from me and clips it herself.

"It smells like good smells. Good smells." I give my hair a sniff. "Ew, I smell like the tobacco guy. Fuck him."

"We can get you showered in the morning." Astrid shifts into drive and we pull onto the road. Her right hand is resting on my thigh drawing little circles.

"I don't want to smell like him," I drunkenly pout. I grapple with my zipper until I can wiggle out of my jacket. Next, I clumsily yank my shirt over my head.

"What are you doing?" Astrid tries to pull my tee back down, but it's too late. I fling it in the backseat.

"It smells. I don't want to smell." Next, I attempt to unbutton my jeans, but I don't have the dexterity to maneuver the fabric.

"Anise, you can shower when we get home. You need to keep your clothes on." She grabs one of my hands and clamps it to her leg.

I slowly gaze over her body. Oh-so-tight leggings leading up to a puffy coat and soft blue earmuffs. Strands of wavy hair fall out of her messy ponytail. God, I want to fuck her. I take my free hand and curl strands of her hair around my finger.

"Man, you had a lot to drink, didn't you?" She speaks absentmindedly as she puts the car in park. "Let's get you inside."

Astrid tucks my discarded clothing under her arm and helps me out of the car. As the snow crunches under our shoes, I'm transfixed by the soft pillowy snow drifts lining the alley. In a moment of impulse, I run up to a drift and fall backwards into the fresh powder. The freezing snow chills my bare skin, but I giggle like a child as I lie enveloped by the walls of snow.

"Anise, what are you doing?" Astrid chides. "You're not even wearing a shirt!"

She reaches her hand down to help me up, but I pull her down on top of me. Her cheeks flush as she notices my erect nipples, visible through the black lace of my bra.

"You're cold, we need to get you inside." But she remains straddling my hips.

"Is that so?"

I grab a small clump of snow and drag it down my neck, to the ridge of my collarbone, and along the curve of my breast. I moan as I caress my nipple with the snow, my body heat sending melted droplets down my side. I continue rubbing small circles until the clump disappears and my bra is soaked. More snow. Repeat on the other side. My clit is throbbing with need.

Astrid eyes me hungrily, her pupils slightly dilated. She holds my gaze as my hands reach back up to my bra. I fold the fabric of the cups down and my tits bounce free. My hands are ice-cold from the snow. I arch my back as I pinch my nipples, softly yet firmly massaging them amidst the freezing sensation. Yet, Astrid keeps her hands on her thighs, digging her nails into her leggings in restraint.

"Touch me, Astrid." I whisper seductively under my breath. She closes her eyes and clenches her fists. When she opens her eyes, the passion is undeniable.

"Fuck it." She curses and suddenly plunges into a deep kiss, fingers interwoven in my hair, craving a closer and closer connection. Simultaneously, heat radiates from the snow below, soothing my shivering body. She grinds against me as her hands explore my body. Hair. Shoulders. Stomach. Breast. Nipples. I arch my back as she fixates on my nipples. Rubbing, Pinching. Twisting.

"God, yes!" I cry out.

My screams encourage the frenzy that is Astrid. She deftly unbuttons my jeans, pulling them down over my hips. She doesn't bother removing my panties. Instead, she just slides the fabric over, exposing my lips to the frigid air. A shiver runs up my core, and I could swear another pulse of warmth rises from the snow below.

Astrid lowers herself just below my thighs and glances up at me. Her playful eyes taunting me. I am at this point a complete mess, squirming and gasping for air. Astrid soaks in my desperation before pinning down my legs, presenting my entire body to her. I shift underneath her weight, anticipation driving me insane.

Ever so slowly, Astrid leans down and exhales a long breath of warm air directly on my clit. My eyes roll to the back of my head. I scrape my nails up my torso and massage my breasts, relishing in the feeling. I continue to fondle myself as Astrid dives in, drawing circles around my clit with her tongue. Slower. Faster. Wider. Deeper. I feel my core tighten as I near climax. Astrid senses the shift. She replaces her tongue with her fingers, replicating the same speed and pressure making my toes curl.

"Tell me you'll stay with me," Astrid whispers in my ear.

"What?" I can't think straight. I'm so close. I'm so close.

"Tell me you'll stay with me," she orders, her voice sultry yet demanding. "Tell me that you want to be with me. Tell me that through thick and thin, I'll wake up next to you every morning, no matter how bad life gets. Tell me that this means as much to you as it does to me. Tell me that I'm yours."

"I'll stay." I cup her face in my hands. "No matter what, Astrid. Always."

And as I cry out her name for the final time, she passionately bites the side of my neck.

⚡　　⚡　　⚡　　⚡

The purple bruise is still visible on my neck after a few days. It probably doesn't help that Astrid keeps touching it up, but I'm not complaining. The sight of the mark turns her on, makes her lust insatiable. Again, not complaining.

Unfortunately, we couldn't stay in our love nest forever and the real world was calling. Or paging. Derek has the nerve to page me early in the morning this time before the sun even rose. I barely resist the urge to throw my pager across the room, and instead try to drag myself from the warm cocoon of blankets.

Astrid is already downstairs by the time I manage to put myself together. I groggily sit on the counter while she takes croissants out of the oven.

"Aw shucks, looks like my favorite dishwasher is busy today," she teases me. "Otherwise, I have no idea why you're out of bed so early."

"Duty calls, I suppose." My feet swing in the air. "Honest question, do you mind if I use the coffee maker?"

"You don't like coffee." Astrid raises an eyebrow as she moves the bread onto a rack to cool. "Why would you want to use the coffee maker? Second question, do you even know how to use it?"

"I'm sure it's just a button or something." I slide off the counter and follow her. "There are some guys at work that I hang out with on break, and they always complain about how bad the coffee is. I thought I would bring them some of the good stuff."

"Are you making friends? Tell me everything!" I don't know how this woman is so enthusiastic before eight in the morning.

"I don't know if we're 'friends' but they always make sure I take my breaks, real company culture advocates." I lean against a different counter recalling our coffee chats. "Then we tell stories, make fun of one another... Holy shit, they're my friends, aren't they?"

"That's amazing!" She claps giddily. "How many coffees do you need? Do they take cream or sugar?"

"Umm..." I stare blankly. "There's three of us. They always make their own coffee."

"I'll make four, just in case you make another friend." Astrid takes off to the front of the house to start the coffee. "Grab a to-go box and load up some of those croissants!"

"Astrid, we don't need food, and I can make the drinks myself!" I protest. "I'm not trying to make more work for you."

"I won't take no for an answer, even if it means I have to come in and cater your break." I hear the machines gurgling. "You'll repay me by setting up my Christmas decorations when you get home. Trust me, I'm getting the better end of the deal."

Oh boy. Sensing I was not going to win this battle, I resign and box up a few of the fresh croissants. Before long, I am out the door with my toolbelt thrown over my shoulder and a bag of goodies.

I drive down to the address that was sent to me. It's the busiest port we've met at so far, meaning there are two boats docked instead of one. The other is much larger, but I pay it no mind. I stuff my jacket in the saddlebags and pull the hood of my bodysuit up. While Derek and Oliver have seen my face, I don't trust pretty much anyone else on this boat. As I finish wrapping my scarf around my face, a car pulls up a few spaces down from me. Jeremiah gives a friendly wave from the driver's seat. He's driving a sedan, old but well-maintained, with a small cross dangling from the rearview mirror.

"Good morning, Sparks," he says cheerily as he closes the car door. Ugh, a morning person. "Sorry to see that you got the early wake-up call."

"If you find the person who set the schedule today, tell them to fuck off for me." Jeremiah chuckles as we walk toward the pier. "By the way, I brought some coffee for Derek and Oliver. You're welcome to a cup."

"I would really enjoy that." Jeremiah smiles and pulls out his phone. "Let me text Oliver so he can meet us downstairs."

"You have his number?"

"Why wouldn't I?" After pressing a few keys, he slides the phone back into his pocket. "He's my coworker."

"I assumed secrecy would be a big thing for you guys." I gesture at him. "Committing crimes and such."

"Eh," he shrugs. "We work close enough that you tend to let things slip. First you mention your family. Then the job you had last summer. Before long, you just know everything about each other. It also is just easier to be able to contact each other, in case you want to grab drinks or you know, meet for coffee."

"Touché."

We continue our walk to the boat. Fortunately, walking in with Jeremiah made going through security much easier. It's nice not having someone manhandle you onto the boat. Instead, I just trailed behind him as he exchanged light pleasantries with the guys we passed. I stayed quiet, lurking in his shadow. A few men give me a polite wave, which I acknowledge with a quick nod. Finally, Jeremiah knocked on the door and Derek opened it wide.

"Sparkie!" He grabbed me in a tight bear hug. "It's been too long."

"You'll crush the croissants if you don't let me go." I say, though I'm muffled from his squeeze.

"Croissants?" I hear Oliver perk up in the back. "Derek, put her down or I'll knock you down."

I'm released from Derek's hold, and I offer the bag to the hungry scavengers. To-go cups are picked out of the tray and sugar packets are passed around. Oliver takes a large bite of the bread, ripping the flaky layers. His eyes roll back into his head savoring the still warm pastry.

"Jesus, Sparks," he moans orgasmically. "I think you're my favorite person."

"Hey! I didn't realize I was so easily replaceable." Derek punches his shoulder. He takes a sip of his coffee, looks down, and then looks at me. "Actually, no. He's right, this is amazing."

"Oh, Brew for Two." Jeremiah reads off the label. "My mom and I used to go there every Sunday. They give a discount on every second drink purchased, which made it easier for us to afford. Good to know the cafe is still doing well."

"I just drove by on my way here," I lie, trying to look nonchalant. Shit. Maybe this wasn't a good idea. "First time going."

"I should stop by sometime and say hello to Astrid," Jeremiah mulls. "She was so supportive when my mom got sick." Wait, he knows Astrid? Like actually knows her?

"Who's Astrid?" Oliver asks.

"The owner. Real sweet girl, unmatched barista," Jeremiah elaborates. "Haven't spoken to her in what feels like forever."

Now, I'm confused. Does he know she's the Water Weaver? I remove my hood and grab a croissant, tearing off a small tuft. Damn, these are good. This must be why Astrid trusts him, she knows him! My thoughts are spinning faster than I can keep up with them.

"The scones there were delicious - lemon blueberry," Jeremiah continues. "Chef's kiss. Mwah."

"Scones?" I say. "That's your go-to? Seriously?"

"What?" Jeremiah says. "Scones are great."

"No way," Derek scoffs. "Everyone knows the proper breakfast treat is a muffin, especially ones with a crumble topping."

"Man, I love scones." Jeremiah takes a sip of his coffee. "They're so light and flakey. Muffins are too heavy."

"Nooo," Derek corrects. "They soak up the coffee. It's perfect."

"You both can't be this passionate about breakfast pastries," I say in disbelief.

"All I know is I only eat scones when I drink tea." Derek reclines in his chair.

"Really?" Jeremiah leans forward. "When do you ever drink tea?"

"When do you ever see me eating scones?" Derek points at Jeremiah. "Got you!"

"Actually, you're both wrong," Oliver interjects. "You see, bagels are-"

"Get out of here," Jeremiah cuts him off.

"What are you? A New Yorker?" Derek teases.

"Oh, come on guys," Oliver says.

"No."

"Invalid."

"I'm outta here." Oliver grabs the last croissant and heads toward the door. "See you losers later."

"Bye." I give him a wave as he ducks out.

Jeremiah and Derek continue debating the benefits of muffins and scones while I grab my toolkit. The heater must be running overtime because the room is uncomfortably warm. Fortunately, I chose to wear a sports bra today, so I unzip my bodysuit and tie the sleeves around my waist. I see the last of the needed parts in a tub, so I get to work reassembling the engine. Eventually, Jeremiah leaves and Derek plays with his razor as usual.

"Sparks, once you're done with whatever you're doing, we've got the nitromethane," Derek says casually. "We'd like to do a test run today if possible."

"Gotcha." I wipe the sweat from my brow. "Give me ten minutes, maybe fifteen."

"I'll have it brought down."

Derek sends a text on his phone and then resumes killing time in his corner. Slowly, the box of parts dwindles until it's empty. A knock on the door and Derek receives a gas canister from an unknown man. I continue fiddling with a few wires, checking connections to ensure everything is in its place. Although, who could say for sure. I motion for Derek to pour the fuel into the tank.

After he steps away, I light the ignition. Gears turn and I can feel the current come alive. It twists and turns through the wiring, and then- Wait. It's going there? No, that's not right. I cock my head and crouch down, analyzing the movement of the engine compared with the flow of the electricity. The current is growing, almost pulsing. *Thump. Thump. Thu-thump. Thu-thump.*

"Something's not right," I warn Derek.

"The fuck you want me to do?" His eyes go wide as he gestures at the machine whirring in the center of the room. "Fix it!"

I disengage the ignition, but the machine keeps vibrating. I see sparks fly in the corner as the resistor cracks. The lights in the room flicker as the battery becomes overloaded with more power than it can sustain. Yet, the engine keeps chugging, burning more and more fuel. Then, everything freezes, and I can feel the energy compacting, compressing itself into a smaller and smaller package. Uh-oh.

"Derek, get down!" I fall to the ground as Derek leaps behind an upset table.

An explosion rocks the boat. Visible streams of electricity streak from the machine. I desperately throw out my arms, pushing the flares up and away from Derek. The energy is parasitic, leaching strength from my limbs and breath from my lungs. Spots flash before my eyes and I let go, hoping my redirection was enough to protect him.

The dust settles. Derek runs over and kneels next to me. My eyelids flutter as I try to lock in on his face.

"Sparks, are you okay?" He scans my body, searching for injuries. "Oh god, oh god."

"Did you get hit?" My voice is strained and raspy. "I tried to... I... I tried."

"I'm fine, don't worry about me." He helps me sit up and I lean against him. He's so warm. Or am I cold? "The light, it bent away from me. I don't know how. Was that... you?"

"I wasn't sure if I was fast enough." I slowly stand up, though Derek sits me back down.

"Your first reflex wasn't to save yourself," he says. "It was to save me. Why?"

"You're my friend, dumbass." My strength is gradually returning to me, although my head is throbbing and I feel like shit. My body feels foreign, like something is missing. I can't place the sensation. "Now, what the fuck just happened?"

Derek has no answer. I take a breath, tighten the sleeves around my waist, and carefully approach the machine. I examine the wiring and mechanics from top to bottom with no clear answer.

"It appears the resistor couldn't withstand the electrical charge, but that doesn't make sense," I muse. "Even with a broken resistor, the reaction doesn't fit. I've never seen or heard of this type of electrical explosion."

"So how do we fix it?" Derek asks.

"Fuck if I know." I brush my hair out of my face. "I'm guessing maybe a better resistor."

"But you just said that the resistor wasn't the problem," Derek counters.

"Derek, answer me honestly." I turn and face him. "What is this? What is it supposed to do? This is not a generator."

"I don't know." He shrugs.

"Derek, we both could've died right now. Do not fuck with me."

"I don't know!" Derek throws his hands up. "Honest."

I stare at him, examining his facial expression and body language.

"If I find out you're lying," I threaten. "I will personally kick your ass."

I turn back to the machine and pull my hair into a messy ponytail. There's got to be an answer here somewhere. That electric pulse was like nothing I've ever felt before, and I've been struck by lightning. Something about this machine feels malicious. I reach out and to feel the machine and... nothing. I can't sense the electricity. I stumble back in shock.

No, no, no. No. No! My head is running a million miles an hour. I reach out everywhere, nothing. Is there even electricity in the room? Of course there is. The light right above me is on. I reach for the light specifically, still nothing. The strange feeling. It wasn't something new, it was the lack of something. My power's gone. My breathing quickens, and it's not long until I'm on the verge of hyperventilating.

"Sparkie, what's wrong?" Derek walks back to me, concerned with my behavior.

"I... I..." I take a breath and put on a calm exterior, though my interior is hysterical. "Nothing. Everything's fine. Do you have a piece of paper I can use to write down a shopping list?"

"I don't believe you," Derek examines me skeptically, "but I'm going to give you the benefit of the doubt. Here's a pen."

My shaking hands refuse to steady as I take the writing utensil from him. The list is short, and more of a guess than a known guarantee, but I can't focus enough to search for any more conclusions. I'm more concerned with why the powers I've had for eight years have decided to hide.

As I continue writing, I feel deep within myself. There. I find the familiar knot of energy within myself. Weak. Feeble. But there. Gingerly, I reach out again. It feels like crawling through layers of foam, but I can touch the current. Hesitantly, I try to redirect the flow, but my connection snaps. My powers are still there, just weakened. Don't love that, and it certainly raises many, many more questions.

"Hello baby." A hand grips my throat and jerks me back, while another encircles my torso.

"Sir-" Derek starts to object but is shushed.

"Go stand outside," Jack orders. Derek hesitates. "Go. Outside. Now."

"Yes, sir." Derek leaves and closes the door, and I am left alone with Jack.

"It's been some time," He purrs in my ear. His hand rubs my exposed stomach. "You look good, feel good."

"Take your hands off of me," I order, hoping I sound more confident than I felt without my powers.

"You shouldn't be in a sports bra around my men, some of them are less behaved than others." His voice is smooth and velvety. Once it would have sent shivers down my spine, now it makes me want to hurl.

"Fortunately, Derek is a gentleman. The same can't be said for you," I snap. I try to writhe out of his arms, but Jack only tightens his hold.

"Have you made progress on the generator?" He questions as a hand slips beneath the opening of my bodysuit.

"I know it's not a generator." My hands grasp at the one around my throat, but his hold is unshakable. "Jack, stop."

"Answer my question." A finger traces the outline of my panties.

"I need another day." My mind is racing. How am I here again? I left and it means nothing. Every road leads back to Jack's arms. "I would be faster if I knew what it was I was actually fixing."

"I expected more from you." His breath tickles my neck, and my body clenches in repulsion. "I thought for sure my Sparks would have this done by now. Perhaps you need some motivation?" His hand inches lower.

"Don't touch me!" I struggle and he tightens his grasp on my neck. His other hand inches lower still. I won't let this happen. I stomp on his foot. Hard.

"Fucking hell, you bitch!"

I fall to the ground, gasping for air. I scoot away from him, but my back runs into the machine. I turn and crawl away as his foot connects with my stomach. Ignore the pain. Get away. Get away. Get away! I yelp as he yanks my ponytail, stopping my escape.

As Jack forces himself on top of me, I see his face for the first time in weeks. He looks the same, but older, more tired. His nostrils flare with anger at my resistance. Then his eyes change from impatience to fury. I know what he sees. The fresh hickey on my neck.

"Are you serious?" Jack drops the facade of sensuality, leaving only sour resentment and flat rage. "Are you that much of a whore? Are you already letting some drifter mark you? How much do you charge for a mediocre ride?"

"No, Jack, it's not like that!" I plead, but my words aren't heard. A sharp slap stings the side of my face. A sob escapes and I abandon my strong exterior. "Help! Derek, help!"

"How dare you!" Jack screams, spittle flying. He punches down and I try to block the blows with my forearms. "I own you!"

Suddenly, the smoke alarms ring out. Derek charges in.

"Boss," Derek shouts. "Fire in the laundry! They need you!"

Jack's mania is broken. He runs out of the room in an instant, discarding me behind him. I break down sobbing in a pile on the floor, scared and in pain. Derek kneels beside me, flustered.

"You've got to go," he rambles. "I've only bought a few minutes. Can you walk?"

I lay there stunned, confused by the shift in events. Derek doesn't wait for a response and pulls me to my feet. I hiss as he grips my arms, likely bruised. He hustles me to the door and points down the hallway.

"Jeremiah is waiting around the corner." Derek gives me a starting push. "Hurry!"

"Thank you." I glance up at him before sprinting down the hall.

True to Derek's word, Jeremiah was right around the corner. Together, we race off the boat. We don't stop running until we're in the parking lot, crouched behind a retaining wall. In that relative safety, I sit and bawl, not caring a bit that I am a sniveling mess in front of Jeremiah. He just sits there holding me and petting my hair. Slowly, my sobs lessen, and I start to pull myself together. Jeremiah silently offers me a tissue, which I accept.

"Thank you." I can't speak above a whisper, my voice raspy from screaming. "I hope you and Derek won't get in trouble."

"Nah." Jeremiah waves a hand. "Oliver actually lit a fire, so it was a real-ish emergency."

"Why did Oliver light a fire?"

"Derek texted as soon as Jack arrived," he explains. "We can't directly oppose him since he is our boss, but we did what we could. Sorry it took so long."

I look Jeremiah in the eyes. I see sincere pain and concern. I pull him in for a hug and nestle my head on his shoulder. Maybe I do have friends.

"Will you tell them I'm okay?" I ask.

"They know. It takes a lot more to take down our Sparkie." Jeremiah softly smiles. I chuckle and punch him on the shoulder. His face grows more serious. "Do you trust me?"

"I think you've earned it," I answer bluntly.

"The Water Weaver would like to meet - in person this time." I startle slightly at the abrupt shift in conversation.

"What? No." I shake my head vigorously.

"Why?" Jeremiah presses. "She's trying to take down the Tributaries. We're all working toward the same goal."

"Because..." I don't have a good answer.

"Please." He takes my hand in his. "As a personal favor. Hear her out."

"Okay." Wait, no. Shit.

"Okay? Great!" Jeremiah does a celebratory fist pump. "When are you available?"

"Same time and place. Today." At least then it's a place I know. And it will be dark.

"Same what?" Jeremiah feigns confusion.

"Don't start." I roll my eyes. "I know you got my note."

"I knew that was on purpose!" He seems vindicated. I now wonder what his conversation with the Water Weaver was like. "I'll set it up. Keep this between us, Derek and Oliver aren't involved."

I give a succinct nod. He pulls me in another hug, this one tighter than the one before. We stay there for a few minutes, comforting each other. Eventually, he lets go.

"Oh, I almost forgot." Jeremiah fishes for something in his pocket. "I got this for you. I know it's a bit early, but Merry Christmas."

He passes me a small white box. A green bow is taped to the top of the lid. I gently open the box and pull out a silver keyring with two charms - one is a lightning bolt, the other a solid circle. Since my powers have slowly started to regain their strength, I can easily tell the round object is a battery.

"It's so you always have a bit of electricity on you," Jeremiah explains. "So you can protect yourself in an emergency."

"Wow." I examine the charms further. They are both simple, but elegant. "I didn't know we were doing gifts. I don't have anything for you."

"Don't worry about it." Jeremiah dismisses with a wave. "Just take care of yourself. That's all I want in return."

We sit there for another moment as I rub my thumb over the ridge of the lightning bolt. I feel tears prick the corner of my eye. I haven't received a Christmas gift in... eight years. Jack ignored the holiday every year, and I stopped trying after a few disappointments. Maybe this year, I'd celebrate.

"One last thing before I go," Jeremiah says. "I wasn't lying earlier when I said I used to go to Brew for Two often. The barista there, Astrid, she is a good person. If you ever need anything, I mean it - anything, go there. She will help you."

Jeremiah leans over and clips the keyring to the zipper of my bodysuit. The silver lightning bolt shines in the sun. He hands me my helmet and I slide it on, mounting my bike. With one last appreciative nod, I peel off toward the main road.

CHAPTER 22

I spend a few hours lollygagging around town, passing time until sunset. I could go home, but I don't feel like telling more lies to Astrid. "Where were you today?" "Why are your arms bruised?" "Why can't you tell me the goddamn truth for once?" I can't lie to her right now. I can't, so I don't.

However, hiding from the truth doesn't make you exempt from facing the consequences of your own actions, and soon it is time for me to meet with the problem I created.

I lock the door of the public bathroom and allow myself to grimace at the grime coating the walls. It's hard to apply face paint in the flickering light, but I need to pull out all the stops so Astrid doesn't recognize me. Unfortunately, that includes painting this mask on my face and hiding behind my scarf and hood. After ensuring all of my fly aways are pinned securely down, I shake out my arms.

Am I really doing this? I leave the bathroom and start my three-block trek to the park. What would I do if Astrid recognized me? Worse, what would she do? Fuck, we live together. Face paint won't stop her from recognizing me, no matter how dark it is. This is reckless and stupid. And yet, I step over the threshold into the park.

I'm a bit early, nerves always make me punctual. I assume the Water Weaver will meet me near where I left the note the first time, so I reluctantly step over tree roots toward the back of the park. The shadows from trees seem to reach out and grab at me, pulling me deeper into my anxiety.

This is a bad idea. I shouldn't be here. What am I doing? I can feel my heart pounding in my chest. Each beat is hammering a spike of doubt in my psyche. *Tha-thump.* Don't do this. *Tha-thump.* You have nothing to gain. *Tha-thump.* Just go home.

I sigh, watching the cloud of frozen air leave my lips. Maybe I'm right. My remaining confidence dwindles, and I re-make up my mind. Fuck it, I'm leaving. I turn to walk away and come face-to-face with the Water Weaver.

"Didn't think you would make it." She crosses her arms as she leans against a tree nonchalantly. "Though I guess you weren't planning on staying."

I take a step backwards but say nothing. She scans me quickly, and I pray the shadows are deep enough to provide a semblance of cover.

"Let's keep the lights on this time, m'kay?" She says bluntly. The blue tones of her outfit shimmer in the faint glow. "Do you want to start by telling me your name?"

"Tell me yours first." I bluff while trying to deepen the pitch of my voice. She smirks.

"Fine." The Water Weaver steps out from her tree, and I take another stride back. "We can keep this professional."

"Works for me." I breathe an internal sigh of relief, glad that she isn't going to push for personal information.

"I need to know what you're doing with the Tributaries." She studies her nails, trying to appear disinterested. "Why are you sticking around?"

"Do you want the short answer or an essay?" I shoot back.

"I'm not in a hurry." She cocks an eyebrow. "Are you?"

"Short answer, I'm on my last job now, then I'm free." I release a deep breath and sit down, leaning my back against a trunk. I grab a dead twig from the ground and twiddle it in my hands. "So I'm not really 'sticking around' as you say. The essay version is a long story."

"I'm listening." The Water Weaver sits on the ground attentively, legs crossed. The wind blows gently, fanning out the gossamer fabric behind her. I bet the fabric shimmers beautifully in the sunlight, much like the blonde highlights in her hair.

"You're really going to make me monologue?" The Water Weaver's expression doesn't change. "If only you were braiding my hair, this would be quite the slumber party."

The Water Weaver blinks, still waiting.

"Goddamn," I curse under my breath. "Fine. Monologue it is. The story starts nearly ten years ago. There was this research company that was developing a dangerous technology, one that ended up killing people. Someone close to me died, and I decided to do something about it."

"What's the name of this company?" It's clear she's trying to appear nonchalant despite her obvious probe. I pause, unsure how much detail I want to give.

"Synergy Labs," I say after a moment. A flicker of recognition flashes across her face before she wipes it off.

Shit, have I mentioned them before? Worse, does she know about them?

"I made it my goal to take down those responsible, but after eight years of work, I have nothing to show for it." The stick in my hand takes the brunt of my frustration, snapping in half. "I had an agreement with a member of the Tributaries to work together, but it seems I've just been wasting my time."

"How is robbing banks supposed to help you with your vendetta?" The Water Weaver questions. No venom behind her words, only a search for clarity.

"Apparently my contact knows someone who was willing to give us an in… for a few million dollars," I chuckle bitterly. "I'm not even sure if that was true anymore. But in my defense, I was against that plan. I didn't know we were going to rob a bank until I was shoved through the doors."

"Then you were in too deep?" She concludes.

"Something like that." I draw squiggly lines in the snow with my twig remnant. "After the armored car fiasco, I walked away. Told him to fuck off. But then he promised this last gig was it. This was real. Something tangible."

"What are you working on?" The Water Weaver asks, the act of disinterest long gone.

"You don't have to pretend you don't know." I glance up from my stick drawings. "I know you've been talking to Jeremiah."

"I wish he knew more," she admits. "He mentioned a device, possibly a bomb, using some special gas."

"Oh, the nitromethane?" I smile. "It's not a bomb, you can relax."

"Then what is it?" Her hands are clasped tightly together. She's probably trying not to bite her cuticles. Cute.

"It's a little fuzzy." My shoulders slouch as I confess my uncertainty. "Everyone I've spoken to insists it's a generator. Now, I'm not an expert mechanic by any means, but I know electricity." I summon a few sparks betwixt my fingers to prove my point. "This is not a generator. I don't know what it is, and I have a weird feeling in the pit of my stomach about it."

"What makes you say that?" She's leaning in, hanging onto every word. I'm surprised she's not taking notes, but I can tell she's committing this conversation to memory. "Stop being so vague."

I set my stick to the side and think about being on the boat. My stomach clenches as I recall the energy that lashed out from the machine, temporarily losing my powers, Jack trying to touch me, what almost happened. No. Don't go there. Not here, not now. Later.

I breathe out a shaky breath and raise my eyes to hers. For the first time in this park, I don't see the Water Weaver. Instead, I see Astrid behind that mask. Her blue eyes shine through and meet mine. I just want to reach out and grab her hand, bury myself in her arms and lay there until the cold takes me away. Or maybe she'll do that thing where she warms the snow, and it'll feel like the softest embrace.

"I've decided, I'm going to trust you," I say softly, "though this might be the stupidest thing I've done all day, and today has not gone great for me. My powers are connected to Synergy Labs. Don't ask me any questions, I won't answer them. Hell, I'm not sure if I would even know the answers myself..."

"Regardless, we turned on the machine today," I continue. "For a moment, everything was fine, it was producing electricity similar to a generator. But then, it went wrong so quickly. All of the power it was holding lashed out. I redirected it before anyone could get hurt, but one of the bolts hit me."

"I..." My eyes shift to the distance, staring blankly at the horizon. "I lost my powers. I couldn't redirect a charge, couldn't create sparks, couldn't even feel it." My arm subconsciously wraps around my torso, feeling exposed and craving some form of security. "It was like I was naked."

"That sounds awful." Astrid, not the Water Weaver, speaks to me. "I couldn't even imagine how scared I would be."

I don't respond. A single tear slips from my eye. I stand up and face the tree, running my gloved fingers over the bark.

"Do you need anything?" She slowly stands, keeping her distance. "A hug or something?"

"No, I'm fine." I pull myself together, internally placing brick after brick back into my wall. "It doesn't matter anyway, my powers are back now. Full strength. Bursting with lightning."

"It's okay to be vulnerable," she says. "I can help you."

"I'm not weak!" The streetlights flicker from my outburst. I turn to face her again. "I'm fine. I don't need your pity, just thought you should know to give it a wide berth, in case your powers are like mine or whatever."

"Noted." The Water Weaver mask clicks back into place. Which is fine. I don't care. "So this machine, we don't know what it does, but it shoots out electricity?"

"I guess that kind of sums it up." I shrug. "It needs to be repaired anyway. The parts weren't able to keep up with the amperage, so they burnt out."

"Interesting," the Water Weaver muses. "It sounds like it was only meant to do one charge."

"Well, it will be able to do several ideally once I'm done with it," I boast. "But then I'm wiping my hands of the whole thing. Synergy Labs or not, I'm not working with the Tributaries anymore."

"Then what will you do?" She asks. "Planning on sticking around Boston or heading out?"

"None of your business," I defend. "What's it to you anyway? Why are you even bothering with the Tributaries?"

"I take care of my neighborhood." She picks an imaginary piece of lint off her sleeve. "They need to be turned in to the authorities, and I had some extra time on my hands."

"Is this just a game to you?" I accuse, raising my voice slightly. "You know they won't pull their punches, right?"

"I can take care of myself," the Water Weaver bristles. "I'll have you know that my actions have led to several arrests already, without any casualties or major injury."

"Yeah, yeah," I scoff. "That all sounds fine and dandy until a pistol is leveled at your head and it's kill or be killed."

"That would be murder." She raises her chin indignantly. "And I won't stoop to their level."

"You say that now." Scorn drips from my words.

"I'm serious," she protests, stomping her foot.

"Look, I'm glad you're an optimist." I look her in the eyes, speaking slowly and concisely. "But if you are ever alone in a room with them, kill as many as you can."

"No-"

"Yes. Kill. Them." I stalk toward her. "Or else you will find that they can do things to you that will make you cry out for your death. Trust me, I know. If the options are a stain on your moral transcript or your blood staining the floor as they torture you, kill them. If you absolutely can't do that, then kill yourself."

"You don't mean that." The Water Weaver is standing with her arms crossed, trying to look tough. But I can see the doubt in her eyes, her confidence shaken.

"I'd want you to kill me." I'm only a few feet from her now. Close enough that she can see the sincerity in my eyes. "The second I'm no longer useful to them, I'd want you to kill me. Better you than them."

This time, she's the one to turn away. She leans against a tree, resting her head on her arms. This isn't a game, this is serious. I didn't mean to upset her, I just... I can't stand the thought of Jack's hands on her - caressing her body, cutting her skin, drawing screams from her lips. I walk back to my tree and curl up at the base, pulling my knees to my chest. For a few moments, we both exist in silence. Neither willing to break the tension that has settled in the air. Seconds pass, then minutes. I watch my breath fog in the frigid air. Eventually, I get sore from sitting on my tree root and stand, dusting the snow off my legs.

"Whelp, this was fun," I say somberly. "Anything else you wanted to ask before I bounce?"

"One more question." She turns slowly to look at me, eyes grim behind her mask. "Do you think you're a good person?"

"What?" I ask, taken aback.

She repeats the question. No explanation, no elaboration. Just, "Do you think you're a good person?"

The question was heavy, akin to a child desperate to believe in Santa Claus or a sinner searching for religion. Those seven words bring forth so many memories. A few are good - helping Dolores with the crossword, labeling fuses for an elderly client - but those are nothing compared to all of the good Astrid has done. There are also so many memories that are bad - robbing banks, stealing food and whiskey when my funds were low, starting fights in shitty bars, lying to Astrid for months. I don't believe in heaven and hell, but I don't want to consider what my outcome would be if I were wrong.

"Do you think you're a good person?" She asks.

"Probably not," I answer, then walk away into the dark night.

CHAPTER 23

If that question wasn't enough to start an existential crisis, the Santa iconography might have been sufficient. The next day, Astrid threw her whole self into decorating for Christmas. Garland, string lights, window decals, even holiday-themed to-go cups. A small chalkboard lists a few winter flavorings Brew for Two is promoting: peppermint, gingerbread, white chocolate cranberry, and a few others.

Astrid puts me to work hanging paper snowflakes from the ceiling until I run out of string. She nearly sends me to the store for more, until she realizes that we haven't begun to decorate the apartment upstairs. That problem takes up the rest of my afternoon. Then Astrid has the great idea to make a popcorn garland as we watch Hallmark movies, so I end up trudging through the snow to the store to buy string anyway.

It's worth it, though, to see her smile as she throws popcorn at the TV when the big city lawyer threatens to close the town Christmas tree farm (right before the big hot chocolate festival, gasp!). It's worth it to see her yell at the TV when the plucky journalist runs back to New York since she's so afraid of commitment. It's worth it to see her cry as the journalist brings a sprig of mistletoe to the hot chocolate festival and holds it above the tree farmer. It's worth it.

Astrid gets inspired from the movie and drags me out to a live tree farm so we can pick the freshest, greenest, smelliest tree in the lot. Never mind that neither of us own a pickup. However, the salesman helps us strap it to the top of her hatchback and the tree doesn't lose too many needles as we maneuver it up a flight of stairs into the apartment. I vacuum the floor as she untangles the lights. Once adorned with lights, popcorn, tinsel, and ornaments, the tree looks like Christmas threw up on it, but Astrid is beaming with happiness. And it's worth it.

"I wish you could come home with me for Christmas." Astrid laments as she pulls the cutout cookies from the oven. Golden trees and snowmen line the tray, and she moves them onto a rack to cool. "My Mimi's cranberry sauce is legendary. She won't give out the recipe no matter how much we beg. She just smiles and says that she left her cookbook to Ma in her will."

"That's kind of morbid, isn't it?" I let a few drops of food coloring fall into a bowl of icing and get to work mixing the color in. Soon, a yellow batch will be ready to join the waiting red and green.

"That's just Mimi," Astrid chuckles. "And my dad makes the best roast duck in the state. You would just love it."

"I'm sure it's great." I smile at her. "But Christmas and I have an understanding. Every year, I get my own version of milk and cookies and that's how I celebrate."

"Oh yeah?" She puts the next batch of cookies into the oven. "What makes your milk and cookies so special?"

"It's pretty great." I give a little shimmy as I scoot onto the counter. "I go to the dollar store and buy a pack of gingerbread cookies, whatever is cheapest. Then I hop over to a liquor store and buy a fifth of whiskey."

"Don't tell me you dunk the cookies in the whiskey," Astrid says, disappointed in my lack of jolliness.

"Yup!" I lean back against the cabinets. "I finish the cookies, drink my bottle, and call it a night. Been doing that for the past five or so years. My ex never wanted to celebrate, and we didn't do anything Christmas-y in my childhood, so I'm content with my whiskey and my gingerbread."

"Really?" She looks heartbroken, a hand on her chest and her head tilted to the side. "No caroling, no gifts, no driving around looking at Christmas lights, nothing?"

"Nah." I shake my head. "At least, I don't remember doing it if we did. But it's okay. I don't really get it anyways."

"It's not okay." Astrid grabs some butter knives and places one in each frosting bowl. "Next year, I'm doing it all with you, even if I have to drag you kicking and screaming. If I wasn't going home tomorrow, I would try to fit it all in now. Dang it, what time is it?" She turns to look at the oven clock. "We might be able to still catch some lights tonight after we finish the cookies."

"Let's just frost these cookies," I say, and I pull her into my arms. "Tonight, I want to stay in and hold you until the sun comes up."

"I'm going to miss you," she whispers into my shirt. "I wish you were coming with me."

"I'll miss you too." I squeeze her tightly. "I'll miss you so much. Call me every day, okay?"

"Okay." She takes a step away and rolls her shoulders back. "Now, an essential part of celebrating Christmas is decorating a buttload of cookies. If we don't start now, we won't finish. Plus, I don't have any counter space for the cookies in the oven." She's right. Every space is filled with a star, snowflake, tree, snowman, or some other shapes I can't even discern.

"Looks like we have... three minutes on the oven timer, so we need to get frosting," I say.

The next few hours are filled with laughter, messy cookies, and overflowing tupperwares. We make cookies for the neighbors, for me to deliver to some of the cafe regulars, and for her to take home - and presumably some for those neighbors as well. The two of us snack on some of the broken snowflakes that didn't survive coming off the pan with the leftover frosting remnants, like Christmas chips and dip. Their flavor is simple, nothing fancy, but they make you tingle inside with warmth and love.

"So I know you don't celebrate Christmas," Astrid says, fidgeting with her fingers. "But I got you a gift anyway. I'm not expecting anything in return, but I was wondering if you wanted your gift tonight or when I get back."

"I got you a gift," I say casually. "I was just waiting on you."

"What do you mean you got me a gift?" She stands surprised. "But... you don't celebrate?"

"You do. It's not that hard of a logical leap that you like giving gifts." I finish my cookie and wipe my hands on my pants before gesturing at the piles of presents underneath the tree. "Plus, I like you and I wanted to give you something."

"I don't know what to say." Astrid looks at me. I can't read her expression right now. Her head tilted ever so slightly, her lips barely parted, thoughts moving rapidly behind her eyes.

"Of course you don't," I tease. "You haven't opened it yet. I'll go grab it."

I walked into the bedroom and pulled the box out from under the bed. The wrapping isn't as clean or crisp as all of the presents Astrid wrapped - my corners are bent, there's a bubble of air on one side, and the cardboard is exposed on the other, but I did stick a bow on top, so... perfect. Or at least, good enough. I meet Astrid back in the living room and we both sit on the plush rug. Now, she has a box from underneath the tree at her side. I slide my gift to her and patiently place my hands in my lap.

"Open mine first," I say, suddenly nervous. I tried hard to think of a good present, but I don't have much practice in the area. "I hope you like it."

Astrid carefully peels back the wrapping paper and removes the lid. She gently pulls back the tissue paper inside and holds up one of the new ice skates. The clean white leather stands out in contrast to the soft blue laces I picked out.

"These are beautiful." She runs her finger along the stitching of the sole. "They're perfect."

"The salesman said they take time to break in," I say. "He recommends thick socks the first few times you wear them."

"Does this mean you're willing to go skating with me again?" Her eyes light up. "The rink will be open until at least February, maybe March if the weather holds out."

"If you're willing to hold my hand, I'm willing to bruise my ass falling as long as you like," I tease. "We can go when you get back."

"I can't wait!" Astrid giddily puts the skates back in the box. "I might even come back a few hours earlier so we can make it to the rink that day."

"Okay ice princess." I roll my eyes playfully. "The ice will be here when you get back."

"Your turn!" Astrid hands her box to me, barely able to stay seated. "Open it, open it, open it!"

The box is an odd shape, almost like a pear with a wide bottom and narrower top. It's not very heavy, but it's large. Despite the weird angles and curves, the red wrapping paper is pleated neatly around the edges. I slide my nail under a piece of tape, trying to slice it as cleanly as Astrid did, but end up ripping the paper instead. My unwrapping skills could use some work. I attempt to remove the rest of the paper delicately. A heavy black canvas shape emerges from beneath the paper, and I freeze.

Is this? No. Yes? Wait, yes? I glance up at Astrid and she gives an excited nod. Holy shit. I rip the rest of the paper off, no longer concerned with decorum. I feel the tough and sturdy fabric beneath my fingertips and slowly make my way toward the zipper.

"Before you get too excited, it's not new," Astrid rambles. "But the woman at the store assured me it was in excellent condition with high quality wood. She also put new strings on it and some other things. I didn't really understand much past that point, but she seemed really knowledgeable and..."

The zipper glides effortlessly along the curves of the case, exposing the deep cherry wood of the base. The fretboard glistens in the light, obviously freshly cleaned. I press my fingers onto the strings and savor the sting of the wire. A viola.

"I don't..." I stammer. "This is too much. I... I don't know what to say."

"Don't say anything." Astrid smiles. "Just play me something."

"I've never played for anyone before." I pick up the viola and pluck the strings, adjusting the tuning pegs until I'm satisfied. I apply some rosin to the bow and then bring the viola to my shoulder. "Um, what do you like to listen to?"

"Are you seriously taking requests?" Astrid asks incredulously. "Are you that good?"

"Meh, I can figure it out." I close my eyes and try to remember the song from the movie we watched the other day. The bow glides against the strings. I play a few quick notes to sketch the melody in my mind. After a few seconds, I feel ready and begin the song.

"Oh, it's 'Silent Night,'" Astrid sighs. "I love this song. It's so beautiful."

"You know the name of the song?" I raise my eyebrow. "I thought the movie just made it up."

"You're kidding." Astrid shakes her head. "No, this is an actual Christmas carol. You're really playing this after hearing it once from a movie?"

"Relax, it's not a hard melody." I shrug dismissively as I continue playing. "After learning some Telemann, this is nothing."

"Who?"

"Georg Phillip Telemann," I explain. "You don't know him? His concerto took me forever to memorize."

I switch out of "Silent Night" into Telemann's "Concerto in G Major." It's not a perfect rendition as I'm quite rusty, but I find myself smiling, happiest I've been in a while. My fingers dance along the fretboard as Astrid stares entranced. After a few minutes, I transition to some traditional fiddle music and Astrid claps along to the music before getting up to dance. She pulls me up and together, we spin in circles as the viola fills the apartment. Admittedly, my playing gets worse the more I move, but Astrid doesn't seem to mind, or even notice. I play through all of the folk songs I have memorized, then start making them up. We dance until I can't feel the tips of my fingers and Astrid collapses on the couch laughing.

"That was so much fun!" Astrid claps. "I had no idea you were an expert."

"Whoa, let's not get carried away." I blush and wave off her compliments. "I just taught myself in my room. Besides, I think that's the first time in over a year I've played the viola sober."

"That sounds like a party," she teases. "Either way, you should try out for an orchestra or something. You're really good!"

"I'm content with my audience of one." I wink at her as I place the viola back in its case, carefully securing all of the pieces. "Thank you for the present. I can't even begin to thank you enough."

"My pleasure." She smiles and gives me a hug. "If you play like that often, I think I'll get plenty of benefit as well."

"I can arrange for that to happen." I grab her hand and lead her to the bedroom. "Unfortunately, you have a long drive tomorrow. You need to get to sleep."

"Why does my family live so far away?" Astrid groans and flops onto the bed. "Everyone should just move to Boston."

"You're the one who moved, babe," I remind her. "Where did you grow up again?"

"West Haven, middle of nowhere northern Pennsylvania." West Haven? That sounds familiar. I shake the feeling away as her muffled voice continues through the pillow. "A town with a few thousand people and absolutely nothing to do except swim. Then again, it's winter, so we are back to nothing."

"I'm sure you can find something entertaining." I pull back the covers and lay next to her.

"Pray for me." She rolls over and finds her way into my arms.

"I'd rather just hold you," I whisper.

Astrid mumbles something, nearly asleep already. I hum the song from earlier, "Silent Night" I believe it was called. As her breathing deepens, I stroke her hair. The moonlight just barely filters through her gauzy curtains, casting a soft glow around her face. She's perfect. I let myself dream of future Christmases, full of lights and songs, running through hot chocolate festivals with a sprig of mistletoe. I think about all of the work we put in the past few days to enjoy this time, all the decorations, the mountain of cookies. As I drift into a festive dream, one thought remains. It's worth it.

*   *   *   *

Astrid leaves early the next morning. I helped her load all of the presents into the trunk of her car and fill the passenger footwell with cookies. She stood with her suitcase in her hands, stalling, but I took it from her and placed it in the backseat. With a hug and a kiss, she was on the road. I waved from the street corner until she was far gone, and immediately regretted my decision not to accompany her.

But meeting the parents? Celebrating a holiday that I knew nothing about? Strolling down a memory lane full of childhood memories? It just wasn't a good idea. Besides, I did have my milk and cookies tradition to keep.

I curl up on the couch and finish reading my book on the Renaissance. By the time I flip over the last page, it is solidly midday, which I figure is late enough to deliver cookies. I pack them up and then get on my bike. Astrid left a list of her regulars and their addresses. I drop off all of my packages with a smile. Many of the patrons invite me inside, and while I appreciate the offers, I decline, blaming the mountain of cookies I have left to deliver. Although, I did stay to help Dolores with her crossword (seventeen across was candy cane).

By the time I get back to the apartment, I'm not sure of what to do. I finished my book, and I'm not really in the mood to start a new one. I could drill my viola scales, but my fingers are still sore from yesterday. My callouses have gone soft. It seems I'm at an impasse.

My final decision was to deep clean the apartment, hoping to surprise Astrid. I turn the music up loud and start scrubbing. I nearly miss the ringing of the phone, but I answer before the call goes to voicemail.

"Hey Astrid," My face lights up as I read the caller ID. "How was the drive? Did you make it okay? How's your family?"

One at a time, baby. Astrid hiccups through the line, her words slurring. *I made it to West Haven, and I found something to do. Ma made eggnog and Christmas music is on the speakers. We're having fun!*

"I've never had eggnog. Is it good?" I tease, knowing what the answer is.

Very good. Good very. Much good. Goodness gracious, she is drunk. This is amazing.

"How's your family?" I ask.

They are all doing well. Liam is doing well at university, honor roll student. He's still annoying though. Hey! Liam, stop! I can hear a male voice in the background. *He's throwing pillows at me, proving my earlier point. Wait, Liam. Wait-*

Hello? The male voice, I assume Liam, comes through panting. *Is this Astrid's girlfriend?*

Liam! The phone line is disconnected before I can react to Liam's question. Girlfriend? I... I guess I am her girlfriend. Huh. The phone rings again and I answer.

Anise? Astrid is on the line now.

"Hi baby," I respond.

Sorry about that. Liam took off with my phone, but I'm safely locked in my room now. Did he say anything embarrassing?

"Nah, just typical brother stuff." I brush off the earlier query from Liam. I can dissect that later.

I'm sure you're lying to protect my honor, but I thank you nonetheless. Anyway, how was your day?

"Nothing too interesting." I lie in bed and prop myself on a pillow. My feet kick in the air as I get comfortable. "I delivered all of the cookies, helped Dolores on the crossword, standard stuff."

You are a lifesaver. Thanks for doing that.

"It's no biggie."

It's a biggie, at least a medium-ie. But the regulars all love you, and Dolores barely even likes me.

"Well, I was happy to do it. Saved me from boredom all day."

Hear, hear.

The line is quiet for a few moments. We're both comfortably sitting in each other's company, despite being hundreds of miles apart.

Drive down tomorrow. Astrid says quietly.

"Huh?" I sit up, unsure if I heard her correctly.

Please, tomorrow is Christmas Eve. All I can think about is you and how Christmas is supposed to be spent with your loved ones. It doesn't feel right to celebrate without you.

"Are you sure?" I ask. "I don't want to intrude on your family's celebrations."

Please. She begs. *Drive down tomorrow.*

"Okay," I relent. "I'll leave first thing in the morning."

Really? Thank you! Grab a pencil to write down our address. If you get lost, just ask for directions to the Larson's house. Everyone at West Haven knows where everyone else lives, so you'll get pointed in the right direction.

"Astrid Larson. I like it." I chuckle as her drunken rambling continues. Eventually, she says goodbye and rejoins her family.

Wanting to leave early, I grab a duffle bag and shove some clothes inside. What do you wear to meet your maybe-girlfriend's parents? I figure sweaters and jeans are never wrong. Do I bring makeup? Probably. Ah, crap. I finish shoving some odds and ends into the bag and set it by the door. It's going to be a long drive tomorrow.

CHAPTER 24

Motorcycles are perhaps not the best vehicle for a road trip in winter. They are quite cold. I'm grateful for the several layers I am wearing, sweater stuffed under my leather jacket. My helmet visor is blocking a lot of the wind from my face, which does help.

I pull into the town of West Haven around eleven and decide to stop for gas before going to Astrid's. The benefit being, I could warm myself and freshen up before meeting her parents. My hair is fine since I braided it this morning to avoid helmet hair, but I do reapply a quick swipe of lipstick. I leave the bathroom and see pots of poinsettias near the exit. Never arrive empty-handed to a party, right? Does Christmas count? It's a gift-giving holiday, of course it counts. I purchase a plant and head back out.

A few turns later, I park in front of a cute, brick one-story house. It's a modest home that fits well within the neighborhood, with a few Christmas decorations out front.

I sling my duffel over my shoulder and grab my plant before walking up to the front door and knocking. A graying, middle-aged man opens the door, standard PTA dad appearance.

"Hello, can I help you?" He asks.

"Is this the Larson residence?" Oh shit, this is her dad. Alarm bells are ringing in my head.

"Will? Who's there?" A woman calls from inside.

"Just a moment, sweetheart," The man, Will, responds. "Yes, this is the Larson residence. What can I do ya for?"

"My name is Anise." I stick out my hand nervously, which Will shakes. "I'm here to see Astrid."

"Will? Who's there?" The woman attached to the voice appears in the doorway.

"Rebecca, can you go grab Astrid?" Will places a hand on her shoulder. "This visitor is here to see her."

She goes off into the house and Will invites me into the entryway. I wipe my boots on the welcome mat, hoping to not track puddles on the hardwood. While the outside of the house had few decorations, the inside is completely decked. Red, green, and sparkles cover almost every surface from tablecloths, to pillows, to hanging art. I stand in the entryway, plant in hand, waiting while Will hovers near me.

"So, how do you know Astrid?" Her father fills the silence.

"Oh, um, I first met her at her coffee shop in Boston." I answer, now unsure if her parents know about our relationship. "We became good friends."

"Interesting."

The awkward silence only lasts a few seconds more before Astrid comes around the corner, trailed by her mother and another guy slightly younger.

"Anise?" Her eyes light up when she sees me. I give a meek wave before she crushes me in a hug. I hold the poinsettia above my head, trying to save the poor plant from also getting crushed, while returning her hug. "What are you doing here?"

"What do you mean?" I ask awkwardly. "Last night you told me to come."

"Astrid, you goof!" The other guy laughs, clutching his stomach. "You got so drunk you forgot you invited someone to Christmas!" Astrid smacks his arm.

"Liam, manners!" Rebecca scolds, before giving me a smile. "Welcome to our home, we're happy to have you. Astrid, will you introduce us to her?"

"Yeah, everyone, this is Anise. Anise is my…" We lock eyes, a silent question. I take her hand and squeeze, a silent answer. "My girlfriend."

"I knew it!" Liam shouts, pumping his fist and jumping in a circle. "You can't hide anything from me, sis!" Astrid shields her eyes from her brother's outburst.

"Well, it is lovely to meet you, Anise." Rebecca smiles, clasping her hands together in excitement.

"Welcome to the family." Will claps me on the back and leads me further into the house. He takes my duffel and passes it to Liam, who disappears with it into the house. We turn into a living room with well-loved, but still nice, furniture.

"I brought a plant." I hold it out to the group, and Rebecca takes it from me.

"Oh, that's so nice of you." Rebecca smells the petals. "Not necessary, but very appreciated. Thank you." She sets it in the center of the dining table, amidst a plethora of gold tinsel and vines with faux red berries.

"I'd love to hear more about you," Will says, sitting on a recliner and gesturing toward a sofa. Astrid and I sit down, still holding hands. She curls up, but I focus on keeping my back straight with good posture. "Tell me about yourself. Where did you grow up, what do you do, and so on."

Talking about myself. My favorite subject. Gross.

"I moved around a lot growing up actually, never in one place for more than three years, give or take." Astrid's family listens intently, curious to learn more. "Coincidentally, much of my childhood was spent in rural Pennsylvania too, but I don't remember much about then. I live in Boston now."

"Interesting," Rebecca chimes in. "Were your parents in the military?"

"No." The room is quiet for a beat, waiting for me to elaborate. I decide not to. Instead, I smile and change the subject. "To answer your other question, I work as a freelance electrician."

"Freelance electrician?" Will repeats. "What kind of people do you normally work with? Small residential fixes or large commercial projects?"

"A little bit of both, but primarily smaller jobs," I explain. "I enjoy being able to work with clients directly, but it's also nice to take a larger commercial contract when I want a stable, long-term gig."

"Huh," Will looks intrigued. "I've been meaning to call someone about the lights in the laundry room. I swear the light fixture is-"

"Will!" Rebecca interrupts. "Anise is here on holiday, not to fix your light fixture."

"Don't worry about it," I chuckle. "It's no problem. I'll take a look in a bit."

"I like her," Will stage-whispers to Astrid, and Rebecca rolls her eyes playfully.

"Whoa, is that your bike on the street?" Liam reenters the room.

"It is." I turn to face him. "Do you ride?"

"Man, I wish." He dramatically falls onto the footstool. "Ma would simply die if I had a bike. Always wanted to ride one though."

"Never a moment like the present," I say. "I wouldn't mind taking you out for a spin if you're serious."

"Really!" Liam jumps up. "Could you imagine? The engine revving as the wind blows through my hair..."

"Rebecca, would it be okay if I drove Liam around?" I ask. "I'll be careful."

"Don't even ask." Liam pulls me from the couch. "I'm in college now, so she can't say no!"

"I was going to say yes!" Rebecca calls after us as Liam practically drags me outside.

Liam can barely stand still as I fasten my spare helmet tightly around his chin. Astrid stands on the front stoop and leans against the wall, watching me teach Liam how to hold on.

"Be careful, I only have one brother." She thinks a moment and then corrects herself. "Actually, drive recklessly."

She sticks her tongue out as I rev the engine. I pull away from the curb as Liam cheers. I navigate to the highway. The roads are clear since everyone is celebrating at home. I don't go very fast, cruising below the speed limit, but to Liam, we are breaking the sound barrier.

"This is totally wicked!" He cheers, shaking one fist in the air.

I chuckle, knowing that if there were other cars on the road, we would be overtaken quickly. Road signs pass, signaling the mileage to nearby towns. Danver Hills, twenty miles south.

We turn north, circling back toward West Haven. I lean down against the bike, allowing Liam to feel the wind against his whole body. He hoots and hollers, feeling the adrenaline that only a motorcycle can give you. When we park back in front of the house, Liam is still whooping. Man, this kid is great.

"That was amazing!" He cheers as his family comes out front. "She was just like 'vroom' and the bike was like 'vroom' and I am so getting a bike soon!" I grab my toolbelt from my saddlebag as I tuck away our helmets.

"Let's go inside, wild guy," I tease. "Astrid, can you show me to the laundry room?"

"You know you don't have to fix the light, right?" Astrid says. "Like really."

"I know," I reassure. "And if it's a big fix, I won't, but I highly doubt this is an actual issue."

"As long as you don't mind."

Astrid leads me into the basement. The front half of the basement is finished, albeit very simply furnished. Once you cross the threshold to the back half, the rooms are only framed, bare to the studs. A washer and dryer are along the wall with some lightbulbs hanging from the ceiling. I reach out with my powers and immediately find the issue - a loose connection between two wires causing the lights to flicker and a high-pitched buzzing noise.

"Oh, this will take me five minutes at most," I say confidently. "Especially since I don't have to work around drywall."

"Do you need me to shut off the fuse box or something?" Astrid offers.

"Nah, I'm fine."

Normal people would need to turn off the power, but I'm not a normal person. Plus, I could tighten this connection in the time it takes Astrid to find the fuse box. I flick the light switch to the room and use my powers to redirect all power out of the room. Astrid holds the flashlight as I use my screwdriver to adjust the screws inside the terminal. Once I am satisfied, we turn on the lights and all is smooth sailing.

"There, saved you a hundred bucks," I joke. "Anything else I should take a look at while I have my tools out?" Astrid rolls her eyes. I notice a large pile of Christmas lights curled on top of the dryer. "Why aren't your lights up? You're such a Christmas-y family."

"Ugh, don't mention the lights," Astrid groans. "Dad spent hours yesterday trying to get them to work. No dice."

I give her a look and pick up the strands. I find an outlet and plug in the cords, the lights don't turn on.

"What are you doing?" She asks.

"I'm an electrician, duh," I respond. "I don't do roofs, so someone else is going to hang these, but I can find the dud bulb."

"Anise, my dad was at this forever. No offense but you can't find the-"

"That one." I point to the bulb with the burnt filament, obvious once I felt the current stop with my powers. "Do you have a spare?"

"No way." She passes me a bulb. I replace the dud with a new one and the lights twinkle. "You're kidding me. Dad!"

Will comes downstairs and takes in my two finished projects. He looks between me, the ceiling lights, me, the Christmas lights, and back at me.

"Huh." He looks at his watch. "Hours. Hours screwing and unscrewing bulbs for you to just fix it and the ceiling light in three minutes. Astrid, you found a good one."

"Glad to help." I smile and pass the lights to him. "Now, unless any further electrical emergencies pop up, I am clocking out."

"Absolutely!" Will says. "Well deserved. Astrid, Mimi just got back from the grocery store. Mind helping her in the kitchen? I'm sure she would love to meet Anise."

"Mimi!" Anise grabs my hand and pulls me up the stairs, giggling with childlike glee.

We bound into the kitchen. Rebecca is chopping potatoes at the counter as an elderly lady simmers cranberries on the stove. She has thick gray hair in two thick plaits down her back.

"Granddaughter, I've only been gone for an hour." She opens her arms wide and Astrid hugs her tightly.

"I know, Mimi." Astrid takes a step back and gestures toward me. "This is my girlfriend, Anise."

Mimi scans my whole body, starting at my loose braid, down to my arms and feet. Then her gaze meets mine, but she doesn't show any emotion.

"Not often you meet a lightning strike survivor, especially this young," she declares finally.

I drop my toolbelt in shock as her eyes lock onto the scar curving around my palm and wrist. Uncomfortable with the scrutiny, I pull my sweater sleeve down.

"Accidents happen," I lie. "Sometimes work is dangerous as an electrician."

"No." Mimi shakes her head. "That injury wasn't caused by a live wire. That there is a lightning scar." Astrid looks between her grandma and me, confused.

"Anise, did you really get struck by lightning?" She asks, concerned. The memory crosses my mind, my hubris in the middle of a thunderstorm.

"It's a little more complicated than that," I deflect. "But more or less, yeah."

"Anise!" Astrid throws a dish towel at me. "You said it was a work injury."

"I was at work!" I duck from the vicious towel attack. Lie. "I didn't want you to worry. Look, now you're worried."

Astrid pinches the bridge of her nose, exasperated. Mimi observes our interaction, still not revealing her judgment. Rebecca passes Astrid a knife and directs her toward the cutting board.

"Chop those for me dear." Rebecca instructs, changing the subject. "Anise, dear, can you get the tenderloin out of the fridge?"

I walk to the fridge to retrieve the meat and feel Mimi's eyes trailing me. It feels as though she can read every part of my body. My hand goes to my bicep, where the last reminder of Jack is fading. Can she tell? Does she know?

Rebecca prepares a seasoning mix for the pork, and I rub the spices into the meat. Mimi stirs her sauce. Will drags Liam outside. The two of them find a ladder and hang the newly-fixed lights from the gutter. Astrid's vegetables go into the oven and Rebecca sears the meat on the stove. Mimi is hunched over her sauce, which she eventually covers and places in the fridge for tomorrow. By the time the boys have finished hanging the lights, dinner is plated and served.

The dinner passes normally, with light conversation from all and many questions about my life. Astrid manages to deflect about half of the probes, and I am able to find satisfactory answers to the rest. After dinner, excitement rises in the family as they get dressed to go caroling. They enthusiastically invite me along.

"Oh, I'm not much of a singer," I laugh. "But I'm happy to watch."

"Nonsense," Will says. "Everybody carols, family rule." I lock eyes with Astrid in panic.

"I got you." She mouths, and silently ducks into another room. She returns shortly with a small book of Christmas sheet music, complete with the lyrics.

"You'll have to ignore the piano lines," she whispers. "But this will get you close enough. You can read music, right?"

I nod and gratefully take the book. A few members of the family pass me odd looks, but don't question my cheat sheet. The Larson family joins with a few others and the group goes door to door. While I was the only one with sheet music, I pick up most of the songs pretty well, despite some people singing way off-key. Astrid was beaming the whole time, even as the cold winds turned her cheeks a rosy shade of pink. We held hands as the group finished the last house with an encore of "Silent Night." When it was time for the choir to disband, Astrid and I walk back to her house ahead of the group. We were close enough to make sure everyone made it home safely, but far enough that we had a smidge of privacy.

"Some of these carols are so strange," I remark as I pull off my jacket and drape it over Astrid's back. "Babies in barns, deer with red noses, I have missed out on a lot of Christmas lore."

"I'm glad you came," Astrid says, leaning her head on my shoulder. Our fingers interlock. "Next time though, let's figure out our relationship status before I introduce you to my parents."

"You're the one who blacked out after inviting me," I tease. "This whole kerfuffle is your fault. By the way, I fully expect there to be eggnog tonight. I did not drive all this way to not get cookies and milk."

"You are insatiable." She fake pushes me before pulling me back to her. "But yes, we do have more eggnog, and enough cookies to last us through the zombie apocalypse."

"I can only hope you mean that figuratively, and that zombies are not a part of your Christmas celebrations."

"You have so much to learn," Astrid sighs. "Without the resurrection of Santa Claus, how would we restore the sacred light to the fireplace?"

"Wait, what?" I turn to look at her, and she cackles.

"Gotcha!"

"You did not just-"

Astrid yelps and takes off running toward her house. I follow, gaining on her. I hear Rebecca in the background call out some kind of warning, probably something about the ice on the road, but Astrid and I sprint through the neighborhood like children who ate too much sugar. Slowly, I gain on her until I grab her waist and tackle her into a pillowy snow drift. The snow crystals reflect the streetlights, cascading specks of light onto her face. Her breath catches as her eyes meet mine and time stops.

"I love you," I blurt, caught up in the magic of the holidays. I mean it though.

"I love you, too." Happy tears well up in her eyes, and she laughs with glee. "I love you so much."

I kiss her deeply, passionately, craving her touch. As we pull away, I can feel the fire building inside me.

"How fast can we get to your bedroom?" I say mischievously.

"No way," Astrid laughs. "You're crazy, my parents will be home any minute."

"Then you better be quiet," I threaten. She thinks for a moment. "Tell me you don't want to, and I'll back off."

Her mind is made up. Astrid grabs my hand and we run together back into her home. As soon as the door to her bedroom is closed and locked, we are a tangle of limbs. She pulls off my sweater as I fumble with the button of her jeans. This isn't making love, there's time for that later. This is fucking. Quick and dirty. She's already wet as I slide my fingers inside her. Astrid tilts her head and moans involuntarily.

"Shh," I chide as I move my fingers deeper. She fists the bed sheets as her eyes roll back. "Be quiet."

Astrid hooks a leg around my torso for leverage and grinds against my hand. I decide to get my other hand involved, rubbing her clit. She bites her lip, trying to keep quiet despite the ever-growing sensation in her core. Her breathing quickens and I feel her clench around me. She gasps as she comes, but otherwise keeps the noise to a minimum.

After the last wave of pleasure courses through her, Astrid flips me over, pulling down my underwear. She pushes my hips open and goes down on me as if I were her last meal. I grab the headboard for support as Astrid bypasses every one of my defenses. She gives me a naughty look as her tongue flicks over my clit again and again. I swear this woman will be the death of me.

A few minutes later, we are both dressed and waiting in the living room as her family walks through the front door. Astrid smooths down her hair nonchalantly as I pour a glass of eggnog. Will clears his throat and blushes as he takes a glass from me. I sneak a glance at Astrid and realize she's wearing my sweater. I look down and find that I am wearing her shirt. Whelp, there goes the slim chance of having any discretion. Subtly, her brother sneaks Astrid a fist bump. Oh god.

We spend the rest of the night drinking eggnog and playing charades. Liam howls with laughter as Astrid struggles to enact a hurdler tripping during a race, but he doesn't fare much better as a florist allergic to bees. Will loses track of points by the end of the night, so we compromise on a rematch the following day. We bid each other goodnight, and Astrid and I retreat to her bedroom where I perform a repeat of our earlier encounter, except much, much slower.

N N N N

The next day passes in a blur of festivity and cheer. Ugly Christmas sweaters adorn the Larson family, and unfortunately, one is pulled out of storage for me to wear. Family pictures are done without too much of a hassle, and they pull me in for one or two. Will also insists on a few with just Astrid and me.

We sit down for dinner, complete with roast duck, sweet potatoes, green bean casserole, and of course, Mimi's cranberry sauce - which definitely lived up to its reputation. The family opens presents after dinner. I don't expect to open anything since I was an unexpected guest, but William snuck out late last night to buy a bunch of candy bars to wrap. It's a small gesture, but I appreciate the kindness.

After all presents are unwrapped and the paper collected, I excuse myself to get a drink of water. I find a glass easily enough and turn to the sink to find Mimi in my path. She watches me silently and steps aside to allow access to the tap. I try not to be weirded out by the interaction and fill my glass.

"I spoke to the spirits about you." Mimi breaks the silence. "They had a lot to say."

"I've never spoken to a spirit." I take a sip of my water. "Are they normally... talkative?"

"Divination is a dying art." She continues without answering my question. "Astrid knows the basics, but I wish she practiced more. The spirits can help guide our paths in this life." Mimi faces me with her expressionless gaze.

"Um, would you like a glass of water?" I offer, unsure of what to do. Mimi shakes her head.

"Your path is twisted and dangerous, you need guidance." Her ominous warning shifts the mood of the kitchen. "The spirits have asked me to give you this to replace what was lost."

From her cardigan pocket, Mimi pulls out a chain with a single jade bead. She walks behind me to clasp the pendant around my neck. The jade stone has small lines scratched into the surface in a design I can't place.

"Thank you, Mimi," I say, a bit confused. "It's beautiful. Wait, how did you know I lost my necklace?"

"I just told you, the spirits." Mimi waves her hand, dismissing my question. "You young people never listen. Regardless, it is important you always wear this talisman. It is said that when jade shatters, it has saved you from a greater danger. The pendant will protect you."

"Is Astrid safe?" I look at Mimi, concerned. "What do I do to protect her?"

"That question is the first good one you've asked all day." She softly cups my cheek. Her reserved demeanor cracks and maternal warmth seeps out. "And it's also why I know you'll take care of my granddaughter. Astrid gets into plenty of trouble, but she always finds her way home."

"I promise Mimi, I'll look after her." I feel tears pricking my eyes. "I promise."

"Oh dearie," she hushes. Mimi guides me to the floor, and we sit against the cabinets. "All will be well with Astrid. Let me help you now."

"Don't worry about me." I fake a smile. "Everything's fine."

"Again with the lies," she tuts and pulls me into a hug. "It's okay to be scared. Everything seems bigger when you're alone."

"You got all of this from a few spirits?" I ask. "I don't understand…"

"They also passed along a message," Mimi says gently. "Your mom says she loves you."

Somewhere inside me a floodgate snaps. Tears streak down my cheeks, soaking into the fabric of my sweater. A tissue appears in Mimi's compassionate hand, and I gratefully accept. I wipe the tears from my face, glad I chose waterproof mascara today. She sits with me for a few minutes, tenderly rubbing my back. I hear a series of quick footsteps and Astrid is kneeling at my side, pulling me into a tight embrace.

"What's wrong?" Astrid brushes my hair from my face, scanning for injuries.

"Nothing is wrong, granddaughter," Mimi answers. "I delivered a message from her mother."

"Oh," Astrid coos, concern etched on her face. "Oh goodness." She pulls me back into a hug, humming soothing noises.

"I'm sorry," I stutter as I try to pull myself together. "I don't know why I'm blubbering like a child."

"Take your time," Astrid whispers. I take a deep breath, blow my nose, and shake out my shoulders. After one more breath, I recompose myself and stand. Astrid keeps one comforting arm around me, and Mimi gives my hand a firm squeeze.

"You know, Astrid, her mom's been trying to talk to her for a while," Mimi chides. "If you were practicing your divination, you would have heard her…"

"Mimi," Astrid groans. "You know my divination isn't as good as yours."

"Well then," Mimi taps Astrid on the nose. "Practice seems to be in order." With that, she walks away as silently as she came.

"Are you okay?" Astrid wipes away a rogue tear and tucks my hair behind my ear.

"Oh yeah." I shake my head. "I'm good now, thanks though."

"You can always talk to me, if you want," she offers and plants a kiss on my cheek. "I won't judge you."

"I know." I smile as we walk into the living room hand-in-hand.

All of our bags are packed and sitting by the door. Astrid and I probably won't get home until late, but the day after Christmas is a big day in the cafe world so we need to get back. Hugs are exchanged between the group, and everyone shares how glad they were to meet me. I can see myself fitting in here. I'm struck by the feeling that the future might not be so bad after all. Once all the gifts are loaded in the car, Astrid gives me a final hug. Unfortunately, I need to drive my bike back instead of riding in the nice, heated vehicle.

"Don't do any stupid driving, okay?" Astrid warns. "You can just follow me back."

"Actually, I need to make a quick pit stop before I head back," I say nonchalantly. "Go on ahead, I'll catch up."

"You better not," Astrid scolds. "I'm serious, drive safely."

"Yeah, yeah," I wave her off. "Honestly though, I'll be careful."

"Thank you," she hollers as she gets into her car.

I follow her to the edge of the city limits but turn south on the highway as she heads northbound. The open road is desolate, empty except for my bike. After about twenty minutes, I pull into a small town. The dilapidated sign reads "Danver Hills." On the outskirts is a fenced lawn with gray headstones in a line. The snow is undisturbed, but the sidewalks are shoveled clean. There are no sounds here, no birds, no engines, no laughter. I dismount my bike and walk through the cemetery for the first time in eight years until I find the stone I'm looking for. I kneel down and brush my fingers over the engraved lettering.

My voice cuts through the silence.

"I love you too, Mom."

CHAPTER 25

The cafe is the busiest that I have ever seen. A constant flow of patrons keeps Astrid moving behind the bar. I've been promoted from busgirl to cashier so Astrid can focus on brewing drinks, but she still makes time to chat with her regulars and wish them a happy holiday season. It's crazy how many of the patrons come up to chat with me. Of course, there's always Dolores (five down is peony), but several other groups ask if I have a New Year's resolution planned and other pleasantries. I find myself enjoying the conversations, and I can see how this place makes Astrid so happy.

When the cafe is closed, I notice Astrid spending more time in the corner of the living room. She straightens up the makeshift altar I found a few months ago - replacing herbs, rearranging crystals, and polishing small trinkets. She'll whisper a few words or shuffle the tarot deck, sometimes dangle a rock from a string. I never ask her what she's doing, and she doesn't ask what Mimi told me. It doesn't bother me that Astrid is into the arcana, but I do think it's strange when I find herbs and salt in my toolkit the next day.

Meanwhile, I focus on blocking out the creepy warnings from Mimi. I still wear the jade pendant, mostly because I'm too lazy to remove it. The ominous messages repeat in my mind, making me jumpy and setting me on edge. Even so, I don't want to ruminate on the so-called message from my mom. I'm embarrassed that I was so emotional from that one sentence. Ghosts aren't real, spirits aren't real. Mimi was probably just making it all up to prank me or something. Though I don't know how she knew my mom was dead...

My pager buzzes. I don't have time to spiral. Astrid is on the couch, wrapped in a blanket with a romance book in her lap. I wish I could stay and curl up with her, but duty calls.

"Bye baby." I kiss her forehead. "I'll be back soon, okay?"

"I'll be here." She flips the page, engrossed in whatever scene is on the pages.

"Hey," I call from the door. Astrid looks up, wheels still spinning. "I'm glad I walked into your coffee shop."

"You're my favorite customer." She blushes, and after a moment, goes back to her book.

I place my hand on the doorknob, and something makes me hesitate. An itch in the back of my head tells me to stay home, to stay with Astrid, especially after what happened last time. I take a deep breath and look at Astrid one last time, etching this moment into a memory. Then I turn the doorknob and walk into the winter air.

When I pull into the marina this time, there is a prime parking spot in the front row. I shake away the bad feeling still nagging me from the back of my mind. This must be a good omen. Jeremiah comes bounding down the dock once he spots me in the lot. He gives me a side hug as I walk onto the shore, and I pat his back.

"We've got a surprise for you..." He sings, leading me onto the wooden planks.

"Oh no," I say, apprehensively. "I'm not going to like this, am I?"

"You're going to love it," he cheers. "Actually no, you might hate it, but Derek and I will love it."

Jeremiah escorts me past security and onto the ship. He giddily walks me down hallways without stopping to say hi to his coworkers. This must be big. We arrive at the door, and he knocks an odd pattern on the metal frame. I hear hushed whispers as the lock disengages. The door opens and I see the table spread with boxes and take-out bags.

"Surprise!" Derek jumps out with his hands up.

"Um, surprise." Oliver stumbles out. "You didn't tell me the cue."

"Obviously the cue is opening the door." Derek facepalms.

"C'mon, Oliver." Jeremiah shakes his head as we step inside.

"Guys, I'm doing my best here." Oliver throws his hands up as he takes a seat at the table.

"It's okay, Oliver." I pat his shoulder and take a seat next to him. "I was very surprised."

"Thank you," he says smugly.

"Yeah, Oliver," Derek says. "How about you tell Sparkie what we have in the boxes."

"After our debate the other day," Oliver monologues, "We wanted to know which of us was the true connoisseur, the true foodie, the true-"

"We brought scones and muffins for you to try and decide which is better," Derek interjects.

"And bagels," Oliver adds.

"No one wants your bum-ass bagels," Jeremiah jeers, nudging Oliver with his elbow.

"But I brought my toaster," Oliver mumbles.

"How about you start toasting the bagels as we try the other pastries?" I recommend. He seems appeased and starts slicing into the bread.

"Drumroll please." Derek stands as Jeremiah and I tap on the table. He opens a box and displays four round blueberry muffins. "In front of you are freshly purchased blueberry muffins from the French bakery outside of my apartment. They feature a delightful crumble topping and the cashier was also hot. Enjoy."

Derek does a short bow and passes the box around. I pick one with glistening berries and take a large bite. The crumb structure is moist without being too dense. The crumble adds a nice texture to the otherwise soft treat. My favorite part has to be the plump blueberries that release a slight amount of juice as I chew. I give Derek a thumbs up as I take another bite.

"For my acceptance speech," Derek stands and addresses an imaginary crowd, "I would like to thank Sparks for choosing the correct pastry, and to my haters, wherever they may be, I hope you enjoy your lesser snacks."

Jeremiah and Oliver boo at Derek, tossing balled up napkins and muffin wrappers. Derek curses as he dodges the projectiles, but chuckles as he sits back down. Jeremiah stands next and straightens his non-existent tie.

"Please give a round of applause to my competitor," he begins, extending a hand toward Derek. I give a polite golf clap. "His entry was pleasant, but my friends, I challenge you to demand more, to demand excellence. While I disagree with the notion of divinity on earth, I enter into evidence the closest that we can achieve as mere mortals. Behold... the lemon poppyseed scone."

Jeremiah gestures to the brown paper sack in the center of the table. Derek grabs the bag and pulls out a pastry before passing it around.

"These scones," Jeremiah continues, "are homemade using my mother's secret recipe. She is doing well, thank you for asking. Last night, she and I grated and juiced fresh lemons to ensure the freshest flavors for our consumption. Please take a moment to savor."

"No fair." Derek points at Jeremiah. "You can't play the sick mom card!"

"Watch me." Jeremiah winks and flips off Derek.

"I'll allow it," I judge. "But only because he went the extra mile to bake his own entry instead of flirting with some random cashier."

"These better fucking suck," Derek grumbles as he bites into the scone. "Damn it."

I raise the pastry to my mouth, and before I even take a bite, I can smell the sharp zest of the lemon. As I taste the pastry, I can feel the mild herbal flavor of the poppyseed behind the bright lemon acidity. Somehow, the scone still feels warm, as if he just pulled them from the oven a moment ago. The crumb structure is light and fluffy, without being cakey.

"These are both great contenders." My voice is muffled through the scone.

"So, who won?" Jeremiah leans in, eager for my answer.

"Wait!" Oliver brings a plate to the table. "I haven't gone yet!"

"Dude, get your bagels out of here," Derek groans.

"Now, folks," I scold. "Everyone gets the opportunity to compete. Otherwise, how would we have a loser?"

"Yeah," Oliver gloats, then thinks for a second. "Wait, hey!"

"I'm just teasing." I smile. "You have the floor."

"Well, Miss Sparks, I don't need the same showmanship as these two chucklefucks." He hands me a hot bagel slice from the toaster. "Plain bagel. Strawberry schmear. That's all you need to know."

"Cocky motherfucker," Derek taunts.

"Just eat your damn bagel." Oliver tosses another slice to Derek who catches it cream cheese side down, getting the spread on his fingers.

I dive into my bagel as Derek spews more profanities. The bagel is a perfect golden-brown, leading to a very satisfying crunch. While the bagel itself is a little bland, the strawberry cream cheese is pleasant in its mildness. The heat from the toast has melted the cream cheese ever so slightly, allowing it to soak into the dense bread. The dish is very simple, much like the speech that prefaced it, but I enjoy it immensely.

The four of us finish eating our snacks over light-hearted conversations and jokes. Oliver gets a lot of crap for bringing plain bagels over one of the flavored kinds, but he vehemently defends his choice. Apparently, the other ones are too "elitist." Derek calls bullshit, saying that no bagel can be more elitist than a, I quote, "pinky-up scone." This prompts Jeremiah to throw another napkin and it's not long before trash is flying again. I grab a napkin from the air and wipe off my hands.

"Time to put you in the dirt once and for all." Derek rolls up his sleeves. "Sparks, what's the verdict?"

The whole table turns to look at me. I don't think these three have ever been this quiet.

"None of you," I answer. "Derek, the muffin's crumble was sublime and contrasted the cake nicely, so you win the honorary texture award. Jeremiah, the lemon zest sets the flavor of your scone apart, so you win the honorary taste award. And finally, Oliver, your passion led you to allow your food to shine instead of all of the frills, so you win the enthusiasm award. However, none of you nailed all three. But when you think back to the croissants I brought, I think the winner is clear." I point at myself with both hands.

The men look at each other, and then simultaneously throw napkins at me. I yelp as I am pelted by paper products, not all of them clean.

"I call for a rematch with a neutral judge," Jeremiah yells.

"Any excuse for me to put the mack on my new girl." Derek does a little shimmy and Oliver smacks the back of his head.

After a final round of napkin dodgeball, Jeremiah and Oliver have to get back to work. I give them both a hug and wish them a fun shift, to which Jeremiah chuckles and Oliver gives a meek thumbs up. I help Derek pick up the scattered napkins and muffin liners, glancing nervously at the door as I do. I'm fine when the three guys are with me, but with only Derek, I feel vulnerable. Jack could decide to appear at any moment. Yes, my powers are back now, but what if that's not enough?

"He's not here today," Derek says softly. With a start, I realize I zoned out staring at the entryway. It doesn't take a genius to figure out why.

"Oh, yeah." I shrug and turn away, pretending I wasn't bothered. "I was just thinking about things. I'm all good."

"Hey." Derek lays his hand on my shoulder. "He won't hurt you again. The boys and I aren't going to let that happen."

Our eyes meet and I place my hand on top of his, giving a slight nod. "Thank you."

He nods in acknowledgement before turning away. I face the looming machine in the center of the room with my hands on my hips. Now, to fix the beast. The final parts I requested are sitting in a tub. Hopefully, this is the last day I need to work on this, although I will miss Derek, Jeremiah, and Oliver when it's done. But when it's done, I'm done. For real this time.

I roll up my sleeves and kneel next to where the resistor is screwed in. Derek secured a much higher-quality part that hopefully should be able to withstand the increased electrical charge. We'll have to see.

"Fuck." I drop my flashlight and it rolls away from me. Instead of crawling over, I instead lay down and stretch for it. The beam glints on a piece of metal riveted to the back casing. Huh, I hadn't noticed it before. Makes sense since it's not connected to any machinery or wiring. It doesn't really serve a valuable function, so why is it there?

I scooch in closer and shine the light directly on it. There's some kind of... etching. The glint from the flashlight is making it hard to read. I adjust the beam to get better visibility. "Property of Synergy Labs."

It feels like a truck hits me in the stomach. I struggle to breathe as the air leaves my lungs. I'm reeling as memories tear through my mind of the day everything changed.

"Now kiddo, I know this doesn't seem like much, but one day, this technology is going to change the world." An elderly man in a white coat lectures me as he adjusts his spectacles. He continues speaking to me, but I stop listening. I'm not interested in whatever speech he has planned.

"Come look at this!" A familiar voice. My mom. I turn and face her, still bored. I don't know why she made me come to work with her today. "Zach is putting the final touch on the it before we turn it on! Get over here, honey."

A young intern is holding a new, shiny plaque. All of the scientists in their starch white coats have signed the back, while the front reads "Property of Synergy Labs," with an engraving of their logo. The intern, Zach, lies on the ground and rivets the plaque into the back of the hulking device.

"There," my mom says. "Now scientists in the future will know who came before them." She gives me a one-armed hug as I roll my eyes...

I gasp as reality washes over me like a bucket of ice water. This machine. The casing is all different, but the layout of the parts is mostly the same. I now remember that I wasn't the first mechanic to attempt repairing it, and their changes are likely why I didn't recognize it sooner.

Oh god, what have I done?

I put my head in my hands. What was that old guy saying about the machine? What does it do? Damn it, I wish I paid closer attention.

This... this abomination was responsible for the explosion. It killed my mother and turned me into this electrical freak. I've been working on this for weeks, trying to repair a weapon. I can't believe I trusted Jack. All he's ever done is lie to me, and I played right into his cards. I told the Water Weaver this wasn't a bomb, but I'm not so sure I was right anymore.

"Are you doing okay?" Derek asks from across the room. He sets his phone down on the table.

"Um, yeah," I say, still frazzled. "I, uh, have to go to the bathroom. Woman thing."

"I'll walk you over." He stands and heads toward the door. While his back is turned, I grab his phone and shove it in my pocket. I don't have a plan, I don't know what to do, but I need to warn someone, anyone.

Derek leads me to a small room down the hallway. After locking the door, I splash some water on my face. Think. Think, goddamn it, think!

I grasp the edge of the sink and look at myself in the mirror. I'm not sure I recognize myself anymore. The person in front of me used to stand against Synergy Labs, and yet, here I am, restoring their prized discovery.

This line of thinking is getting me nowhere. The point is, the machine cannot be usable. There are too many reasons it can't exist. What if the Tributaries sell it to some terrorist or murderer? Or possibly worse, what if Jack uses it to create more of me? No, one thing is clear. I have to destroy it.

I take a deep breath and look at myself in the mirror again. Am I willing to put my money where my mouth is? I've told myself over and over that I'd put duty over happiness, even if that meant dying. Even if that meant losing Astrid. I allow a single tear to fall before steeling my resolve. This is my burden to bear. I am going to destroy that machine. If I don't die today, Jack won't stop chasing me until I do. Hopefully, Astrid will understand one day.

I scroll through the contacts of Derek's phone, stopping on Jeremiah. The line rings twice before the familiar voice answers.

What's up, Derek? Is she ready for an escort?

"Jeremiah, it's Sparks," I pause before continuing. "The other day, when we were talking in the parking lot... did you mean what you said?"

Every word. His voice is grave, understanding the gravity behind my question.

"This is your out, your plausible deniability." I wipe away the lone tear on my cheek. "I'm about to do something stupid that will get me, if not both of us, killed. I know you didn't sign up for that, so if you hang up, I won't hold it against you." I hear him take a breath on the other side of the phone.

I told you the story a while ago of how I joined the Tributaries. I originally thought that God was calling me here to save my mother. I thought that was the truth until after we robbed that first bank where we met the Water Weaver. I recognized her after we left, and I knew then that I misunderstood God. He will take care of my mother after I serve my purpose here with the two of you. If I lose my life in the process, then I will accept that gladly, for that is God's will.

He stays on the line. I sniffle as I try to hold myself together.

"I have received new information about the machine I've been working on." Deep breath in, deep breath out. "I don't have time to get into it, but the gist is, it must be demolished. If it becomes functional, people die. I need a way to get Derek out of the room long enough for me to sabotage it."

I can be down there in two minutes.

"Give me three." I dry my sweaty palms on a towel. "And Jeremiah? Say a prayer for us."

I disconnect the call and give myself one more second to get my shit together before opening the door.

"Thanks, Derek," I say. "Much better now."

"Glad to hear it." He smiles and escorts me back to the room.

The machine feels taller now, more imposing. Its shadow looms over the room, seemingly swallowing everything inside. It takes all I have to not run up to it with a sledgehammer, but I have to wait for Jeremiah. Derek doesn't need to be a casualty in my war. Instead, I act as though it's business as usual and start to unscrew every screw I can find. A few minutes later, a knock rings through the room.

"Hey Jeremiah," Derek greets. "We're not ready for an escort yet."

"There's been a change of plans." Jeremiah shrugs nonchalantly. "Oliver needs you in the galley, so I was sent to watch Sparks."

"What does Oliver need?" Derek scrunches his eyebrows, confused.

"The fuck I look like, Oliver's secretary?" Jeremiah jests. "I wish I were paid that much."

"Fair point." Derek shrugs.

"Hey Derek," I call from across the room. "I've thought it over and I changed my mind. The muffin was the best."

"Booyah!" Derek pumps his fist in the air and then points at me. "I knew you wouldn't let me down. See ya soon, Sparkie."

I hope this isn't the last time I see him.

"See ya." I wave to Derek, as Jeremiah closes the door. As soon as the latch engages, the air shifts to one of solemn determination.

"How long until he finds out that Oliver doesn't need him?" I ask, continuing to disassemble parts.

"Depends on how long it takes him to find Oliver." Jeremiah strides over to me. "Especially since Oliver's shift is over. He already went home. Tell me what you need."

"Take this." I hand him a pair of wire cutters. "Cut all the wires and throw them in a pile. The more disorganized the better. If you can cut a few into pieces, even better, but speed is more important than perfection."

We work in a heavy silence, moving on to slashing tubing, denting fan blades, and sabotaging whatever parts we can. Jeremiah grabs the gas can with the remaining nitromethane and dumps it out the porthole. He pours water down the fuel tank as I crush parts with a hammer as quietly as I can. Five minutes pass and a knock rings through the room. I freeze and look at Jeremiah.

"Five minutes?" I whisper. "I was hoping for closer to ten!"

"Derek," an unfamiliar voice calls from the hall. "Open up, man."

"Do you think we've done enough?" Jeremiah asks. "It might be time to run."

"Derek!" The voice calls again. "We got reports of strange activity. This is just a standard check."

"There's no way they won't notice something is wrong," I hiss. We're surrounded by the bowels of the machine. Thousands of dollars turned to scrap metal, complete with a nest of wires.

"Your call," Jeremiah speaks softly. "Do we try to run, or do I buy you more time?" My brain spins in a frenzy, looking at the pile of destruction around us. I close my eyes, thinking through all of our vandalism. It's enough. It has to be. I open my eyes.

"Run."

"Let's do this." Jeremiah cocks his gun and holds it at his side. He gestures for me to stand behind the door. He cracks it open. "Ah, Nathan. Sorry for the delay. Derek isn't here, vacation day."

"I saw him earlier," Nathan counters. "Open the door, Jeremiah."

"As you wish."

Jeremiah opens the door further, and Nathan steps in.

"Holy shit! What happened-"

Jeremiah pistol-whips him from behind. As Nathan falls to the ground, Jeremiah grabs my hand and pulls me into the hallway. I stand behind him as we quickly walk toward the deck, trying to look natural amongst his coworkers. We made it to the final set of stairs before we hear voices yelling.

"Nathan!" "The girl!" "Stop the girl!"

"Shit!" Jeremiah swears. He takes off, dragging me behind him.

The voices from behind grow louder, and rapidly shift to include those from above. We step into the sunlight and I'm momentarily blinded. Jeremiah doesn't wait for my eyes to adjust, racing toward the exit.

"There!" A man calls out.

I shriek as a gunshot rings out from my right. Jeremiah yanks me down behind a banister as more bullets fly our direction.

"I've only got nine rounds," Jeremiah states. "I can draw their fire for a few seconds, but if you sprint, it might be enough for you to get ashore."

"I can't leave you!" I start to panic. "Jack will kill you, if they don't first."

"Don't worry about me," Jeremiah rebuffs my concern. "I've been in worse scraps."

"They have guns, and bullets, and those shoot you!" I can't seem to get any air in my lungs. Where'd all the air go?

"Look at me." Jeremiah grabs my chin and forces me to meet his gaze. "You need to pull yourself together. Jack might kill me, but He. Will. Kill. You. Your bike is right there. You'll be faster alone. We don't have any other options, so when I start shooting, you will run faster than you have in your entire life, get on that fucking bike, and drive until you hit the Pacific Ocean. Am I clear?"

"Yes." I try to be confident, but my voice cracks. Jeremiah pulls me in and gives me one last hug.

"Go with God," Jeremiah says, solemnly. He grips his gun with both hands. "Okay. Three... Two... One."

Jeremiah jumps up and fires. I don't see what he does next. I have tunnel vision on the dock. Run. Run. Run. I stumble when the wood beneath me turns to sand but keep putting one foot in front of the other. I straddle my bike and rev the engine as my helmet falls to the concrete. I mumble a quick apology to Astrid. Out of the corner of my eye, I see men running down the dock. I peel out before they can make it to the lot.

§ § § §

The wind is piercing and brutal. I left my gloves and jacket on the boat, so I am flying down the road in only my bodysuit. My fingers are losing their color, but I keep my deathgrip on the handlebars. My hair whips around my face, adding to my frenzied appearance. I look over my shoulder every few seconds, expecting someone to come flying around the corner.

Was it all worth it? Jeremiah and I definitely fucked some shit up back there, but how long would it take to reassemble. A week? A month? A few years? How long is Jack willing to wait?

I reach into my pocket and pull out Derek's phone, dialing a number I know by heart. No answer.

"Please, please pick up." I plead as I redial. After a few rings, I hear a sleepy voice on the line.

Hello? Who is this?

"Astrid? Thank god." I can't help the tears that flow down my face hearing her voice, even if this is the last time. "I need you to listen to me and don't ask any questions."

Anise? Is everything okay?

"Jeremiah's compromised."

What? She sounds much more awake now.

"Shut up and listen! I don't know how long I have." I desperately cut her off. "The Tributaries are trying to repair a weapon created by Synergy Labs. Jeremiah and I slowed them down as much as we could, but with enough time, they might be able to repair it. Astrid, this cannot happen."

Come home, Anise. We can figure this out together. Her voice is shaking, whether it's from nerves or confusion I can't tell.

"I think you know I can't, babe," I choke out. My vision blurs from tears and I try to blink it clear. "Jack will kill me and anyone else he thinks was involved. I won't risk them coming after you. I'm leaving. I'm so sorry, Astrid."

Anise, don't say that! The seriousness of this call has sunk in for us both, and I can hear her start to sob. Every mile is another stab to my heart. *Please, just think this over.*

"Please know I never meant to hurt you." Three motorcycles swerve onto the road driving erratically. "Shit, they found me. Astrid, the machine. Don't let them fix it. Please, repeat it back to me so I know you understand."

The machine. The men gain on me, growing closer despite me maxing out my accelerator. *Don't let them fix it.*

"I'm so sorry."

I weave through cars, but they're tight on my tail.

Anise, no.

One of the men pulls up next to me, a baton in his hand.

"I love you."

The man jabs the baton into my wheel, toppling my bike. I scream as I am thrown into the air. Pain jolts through my body as I skid on the concrete. Dark spots cloud my vision, and every sound slowly becomes muffled. The phone slid a few feet away. The call history. No. With my fleeting strength, I surge electricity through the phone, frying the circuitry. Hands grab my arms and shoulders, roughly dragging me backwards. My last sight before I lose consciousness is the crushed jade bead that used to hang around my neck.

CHAPTER 26

"Who are you working for?" An angry voice.

"I told you, no one." An icy voice.

"Don't fuck with me, Jeremiah. I am so not in the mood." The first voice again.

I hear them first. The fog in my brain makes it hard to comprehend what's going on. What happened?

My eyes flutter open. The room is dimly lit with no furniture. Two men are standing in front of me. Dirty floors lead to a solid metal door. The paint on the walls is chipped and peeling.

"Why can't you accept that I don't need a reason to fuck you over?" I guess this is Jeremiah.

A dull thump. Someone spits. A splotch of red appears on the floor in front of me. How odd. I wonder where that came from.

"I am going to personally make you regret that." The first voice hisses.

Wait, I know that voice. Jack. No, no, no. All of my memories come flooding back. Jeremiah, he's alive! I remember running, then the motorcycle, then...

"Ughh," I groan involuntarily as I register the pain rushing through my body. It feels as though I've bruised every muscle I have.

"Ah, looks like she's awake," Jack croons. "Did you have a nice sleep?"

My body clenches as I see him turn and walk toward me. Instinctively, I reach out toward the light bulb above to fling a bolt in his direction, but as soon as I make contact with the current, every nerve in my body is electrified. I cry out as I convulse. I collapse, but don't fall to the floor. As the mental fog clears, I see that I am suspended by metal cuffs from the ceiling. Blood drips slowly down my forearms from barbs within the cuffs piercing my skin.

My bodysuit is unzipped down to my hips with the sleeves dangling loosely. My bra and the upper hem of my underwear are exposed to Jack's lustful gaze. I glance across from me and see Jeremiah in a similar situation, with a black eye and bloody lip.

"Do you like your new bracelets?" Jack mocks. "I had them made special for you." He taps my nose.

"Don't touch her," Jeremiah growls, pulling at his restraints.

I don't say anything. How am I back to this? Flashbacks of the last eight years flicker through my consciousness. I left him. He was gone. I thought I was safe, but I never really was, was I? No, every road leads back to Jack. I was stupid for thinking I could escape.

"Oh, silly Jeremiah," Jack whispers into my ear. He cups the black lace of my bra. "We're going to have so much fun."

I turn my head away, nauseated by his breath on my neck. He responds by yanking my hair to force my lips to meet his. I squeeze my eyes shut, trying to block out the sensation and failing.

"Motherfucker!" Jeremiah snarls. "You limp-dick motherfucker! What's the problem? Can't get laid unless you rape someone?"

"Excuse me," Jack mutters, his eyes dark and deadly. "I need to get back to work."

Jack slowly walks over to a table set up against the wall. He methodically runs his hands over the implements until he chooses a weighted baton. He taps the baton against the wall as he walks back to Jeremiah.

"Perhaps now you'll be more talkative with an audience," he purrs with venom dripping on each word. "I've noticed a lot of... suspicious activity coinciding with your work schedule, especially a certain masked individual making appearances. Did you have anything to do with that?"

"No," Jeremiah clips.

"Is that so?" Jack lifts Jeremiah's chin with his baton until he's looking straight ahead at me. "Can you lie to her as easily as you lie to me? Tell her you had nothing to do with it."

"I had nothing to do with it," Jeremiah repeats to me.

"Jeremiah, I don't blame you for not knowing this, but I don't like it when people lie to my girl." He draws invisible lines over Jeremiah's stomach. "I'll give you one more chance. Tell her you had nothing to do with it."

"I had nothing to-"

The baton cracks along Jermiah's ribs. He bites his lip to hold back a scream. Our eyes lock and I can see how hard he's trying to protect me, sacrificing his body.

"It's okay," I soothe, my voice quivering. "I'm okay."

Another crack of the baton. He grunts, absorbing the blow.

"More concerned about my lady than you are with yourself?" Jack observes. "Maybe she'll help loosen your tongue."

Jack strides over towards me as Jeremiah protests, throwing desperate insults at Jack to try and redraw his attention. But if one thing I know is true, Jack never backs away once he's made a decision. He yanks on the chain holding me up until my tiptoes barely reach the ground.

"What do you think, Jeremiah?" My body shakes as the cold plastic rubs against my hips. "Does Sparks deserve pleasure or pain?"

"Please stop," Jeremiah begs. "She didn't do anything."

"You're still lying, Jeremiah," Jack seethes and spits at my feet. "I'm getting really tired of it."

I can't shield myself as the baton swings toward me. With my arms restrained, all I can do is watch as the hard plastic knocks the wind from my lungs. I curse under my breath as I clench my fists from the pain. Jack doesn't wait for me to recover before he runs his finger along the lace of my bra. He pulls down my cup and my breast slips free. I squirm as he pinches my nipple and tugs. Jack looks over his shoulder and notices Jeremiah averting his eyes.

"Oh no, you don't." Jack backs up until he is next to Jeremiah. "You are going to watch every single thing I do to her. If you don't, I will line up every single on-duty thug and cheer them on as they rape her. And when they are all done, I'll have them go again. And again. Or..." He grips Jeremiah's chin and turns his head back to me. "You watch. It's up to you."

Jeremiah's eyes are filled with torment, but he keeps them on me as Jack returns to my side. I wish I could say that I stayed stoic and proud as Jack pulled down my panties. I wish I could say that I put on a brave face and raised my chin high. But the truth is, I closed my eyes like a scared child. His fingernails caressed my hips leaving trails of sickening goosebumps. I felt his tongue draw circles between my thighs, and I cried out when he bit down hard.

When I open my eyes, Jeremiah is still there. He mouths something to me, over and over. "Look at me. It's just you and me." I took a breath and stare into him as he repeats the mantra. "Look at me. It's just you and me." It's a small comfort, but it's enough to keep me anchored as Jack slides inside of me. Every time I grimace at a tug of my hair or claws raking down my back, Jeremiah is there. I disassociate from my body as Jack's thrusts jerk me against my chains, digging the barbs deeper. Warm liquid drips down my forearms and down my body. "Look at me. It's just you and me." Somehow, that's enough to help me hold myself together.

Jack moans contentedly as he finds his release. He fastens his zipper and struts around the room, rejuvenated. I'm exhausted, mentally and physically. I can tell that Jeremiah feels the same way.

"This could all be over," Jack says to no one in particular as he picks up a cattle prod. He adjusts the settings as he meanders back toward us. "Tell me what I want to know, and this won't have to go any further."

"Stop," Jeremiah whimpers. "Please."

"Tell me about the Water Weaver." Jack demands coldly. Silence. "Very well."

Jack lashes out, jabbing the prod between my thighs. Oh god! Fuckity fuck fuck! I can't think. I forget about Jeremiah and his mantra. There is nothing. Nothing except pain. I'm aware I'm screaming, but I can't stop. It won't stop. God, please, make it stop.

"I give up!" Jeremiah begs. The cattle prod is pulled away, and I can breathe again. I can think again. What was he saying? Wait, Jeremiah, no! He continues, dejectedly, "I'll tell you everything, just stop."

"No!" I struggle against my restraints. "I can take it. Jeremiah, don't say anything. I can take it!"

"Sparks." Defeat creeps into Jeremiah's face. "I can't let this happen to you."

"Shut the fuck up!" I shout, kicking my feet. "You say a single word and I will fucking end you."

"Can't you see I'm trying to help you?" Jeremiah pleads. "All of this has been for you!"

"Save the pious bullshit for someone else." Scorn fills my voice. "I never asked for your commiseration. If you want to do something, you protect her." My voice cracks in desperation. Warm beads of blood trickle down my arms as the metallic barbs cut into my wrists. "Please save her."

"Maybe some further motivation is required," Jack muses, his shrewd eyes analyzing our interaction.

Jack walks around me, dragging his fingertips along my back and then up my chest. His fist encircles my neck slowly squeezing tighter and tighter. Jeremiah breaks into a frenzy, eyes wide, begging for Jack to let go. I can't speak, can't think of anything beyond-

Blonde hair in the sunlight.

Her laugh after I make some stupid joke.

Holding her in the dark as she sleeps in my arms.

Everything worth dying for.

"Sparks, please." Jeremiah begs. "Please."

I slowly shake my head no. I smile softly, at peace knowing Astrid is safe. I close my eyes and wait for the darkness to seep in, but it doesn't. Jack releases me from his hold. I gasp as my lungs expand and fill with air.

"I've got this all wrong," Jack chuckles in realization. "This whole time I thought you were the pawn, led astray from my path by Jeremiah... but that's not true, is it?" He lifts my chin and stares into my defiant eyes. I spit in his face and am rewarded with a sharp slap to my cheek. The sting makes my eyes water, but it was worth it.

"No, no, no." Jack wipes the spit off and glares at me. "You were an active participant in this betrayal. But what I don't understand is your allegiance to this woman. It makes sense that Jeremiah is trying to protect you as he's obviously fucking you. I speak from experience that you can drive a man to do many things." His eyes flick down to my body before meeting my gaze again.

Jack saunters next to me and steps between my legs, forcing me to straddle him. He rubs his hands on my upper thighs, massaging the muscles, reminiscing about all of the times my legs were wrapped around him.

"But that's not right, is it?" He continues, caressing my lower back. Jack tsks as he palms my ass. "So the question is - what would make you so loyal to the Water Weaver? It's not like you're fucking her."

My stomach involuntarily clenches as he stumbles onto the truth. Jack whips his eyes to mine. After eight years of living together, he's learned how to read me and right now, all of the answers he craves are written on my face. He pushes me away in disgust as he backpedals away from me, and for a moment, I see genuine hurt flash across his face.

"Eight years," he whispers. "You were mine for eight years. We lived together, slept together, fucked together." Vitriol fills his words. "And you threw all of that away for some whore."

"I don't owe you an explanation," I seethe, red filling my vision.

"No, I think you do!" Jack roars. "Eight fucking years of my life. What does she have that I don't have, huh? Is she loaded? Fill your head with lies of how you're so special? Or is she just an easy lay?"

"You don't get to talk about her!" I struggle against my restraints, the metal cuts into my skin. "Not after what you put me through."

"What I put you through? Oh sweetheart, you don't even know the half of it." He cackles before lowering his voice. "Synergy Labs is gone."

"What do you mean?" I ask suspiciously. Don't listen to him. He's trying to get into your head.

"The big, bad Synergy Labs?" No showboating, no dramatics. Jack talks plainly and honestly. "They're all dead. No one survived the explosion. They're just a ghost story I told you at night."

What? No. It can't be.

"I did it for you, Sparks." He steps in close. "For us."

I lash out, kicking my legs in the air. My foot connects with his face, and he swears as blood drips from his nose.

"You fucking bitch!" He roars. "You ungrateful whore!"

Fury rolls off of him in thick waves. He pulls out a pistol that was concealed in the back of his waistband. Jack takes slow methodical steps to me, tucking the pistol under my chin.

"Give me one reason I shouldn't kill you," he commands in an icy tone. "Because right now, it's looking like a mighty fine option."

"Wait!" Jeremiah calls from across the room. I can see the gears in his head shift as he puts together this new information. "She's a bargaining chip. You have the Water Weaver's girlfriend hostage. If you kill her, you lose your most valuable tool."

"Jeremiah, shut up or so help me god," I hiss through gritted teeth.

"That's a fair point," Jack murmurs, pausing a moment to think. He returns to his overly sweet facade. "But that also means, I don't need you."

A gunshot rings out.

I scream as hot blood splatters across my face.

Jeremiah hangs limply from his chains, a pool of red spreads below his feet.

Jack grips my scalp and pulls my head back, with his other hand he smears blood onto my lips. I grimace as the copper tang pricks my tongue. He grips my cheeks and leans close to my face.

"You did this," he spits. "His blood is on your hands."

With that, he strides away and slams on the door.

"Open the door!" Jack commands. "Clean this shit up."

A few men come in and release Jeremiah's body from his chains. He falls limply to the ground as they drag him out of the room. I stare agape at the crimson trail that follows them. How did this happen?

Jeremiah... he's gone.

I crack. Sobs rack my body as I scream. Anguish. Grief. Despair. My broken heart fills the room as I scream as loud as I can, not caring who hears. Let them. I have nothing left. Jeremiah's dead. I'll never see Astrid again. My feeble attempts to protect her have all been in vain. Jeremiah died for nothing.

Everything that happened today runs through my mind. The phone call. The machine. The motorcycle chase. The gunshot. Again. Crying in the bathroom. Cutting wires. Crouched behind the banister. What was it he said?

Look at me. Jeremiah says. *You need to pull yourself together.*

No, I can't. I'm too far gone.

We don't have any other options. He forces me to take a breath.

But you're dead. We lost.

You need to pull yourself together. Jeremiah repeats, firmly. *Am I clear?*

There's no point.

Am I clear? Jeremiah pulls me in for one last hug before slowly fading from my mind.

Don't leave me again! I want to roar and gnash my teeth like a feral animal, but I know deep down that it won't help. Jeremiah wouldn't want this. He would want me to get my shit together and act like a fucking adult. Even if he's gone. Even if I am now truly alone.

Soft footsteps startle me out of my self-pity. I see a figure falter at the sight of the blood trail, before taking a breath and turning to me.

"You're really in a tough spot now, Sparkie," Derek says mournfully. He cautiously makes his way over to me. He holds up his hands, in one of which is a damp towel. "May I?"

I nod, and Derek gently rubs the towel to remove the blood splatter from my chest and rezips the lower half of my suit. He adjusts my bra to cover my breasts, providing an illusion of modesty with the lace. The towel is soft against my face as he wipes Jeremiah's blood from my lips. Neither one of us speaks as he cleans my arms and the rest of my torso.

"What do you want me to do?" Derek whispers, pain clearly written in his expression. "Say the word, and I'll get it done. Want a weapon? Send a message to someone? I want to help, I just don't know what to do."

"The Water Weaver," I speak softly, confiding in him. "I don't care what Jack does to me, it doesn't matter. I need you to protect her. Please."

"Are you sure?" Derek asks. "Is that all you want?"

"Please," I beg.

"I'll do what I can." He nods, taking a few steps back. He folds the bloody towel and places it on the table in the corner.

The metal door opens again. *Clap. Clap. Clap.*

"Can I just say how much I adore the sound of your screams?" Jack applauds as he walks through the entryway. "I hadn't heard them in so long. Thank you for the performance."

"My pleasure," I snip. "Unfortunately, I don't think we have time for an encore today."

"Oh, that can be arranged." I flinch from the venom in his words as he surveys the tools laying on the table. "Derek, I have an assignment for you."

Derek straightens up and stands at attention as Jack continues.

"As this whole... debacle occurred on your watch, I need to ensure that you were not complicit in its unfolding." Jack gestures toward me. "Such a simple test, I need you to hit her."

"Excuse me, sir?" Derek's eyebrows scrunch in confusion.

"Where was I unclear?" Jack lowers his voice. "Hit the girl. Unless of course, you care for her in some capacity."

"Really?" I force a laugh. "You want this sissy to hit me? Oooh, so scary."

Derek takes a breath as he saunters over to me, cracking his knuckles. This is going to hurt. He squares up, before socking me in the stomach. I keel over as the air leaves my lungs heaving in deep breaths.

"See?" I goad. Derek needs to be convincing. "That was nothing. I'm almost embarrassed for you."

Derek clenches his jaw. For a moment, I'm not sure that he picked up on my undertone. Then he absolutely decks me in the face. My head whips back with the force of the impact, and I seriously second-guess the logic of that plan.

"Satisfied?" Derek scoffs at me, putting on a show for Jack. My confidence visibly wavers, and it's enough for Jack.

"I'm sure she could take a few more rounds," Jack jeers. "But I am content. Thank you, Derek. You may leave now."

Derek rubs his knuckles as he walks out the door, sparing one last look at me.

"It doesn't matter how many times you punch me," I mutter. "I'm not telling you anything."

"I don't need anything else," Jack says flippantly.

"Oh really," I laugh, probably going crazy from several concussions. "You don't know shit."

"Hmm, I wouldn't say that's true." He leans against the wall. "You see, once I figured out you were connected with the Water Weaver, everything clicked into place. Remember the day I redecorated your apartment?"

"Yes," I say bluntly, narrowing my eyes. When he trashed everything I owned, shattered my viola, and cemented my decision to leave. Really hard to forget.

"I just realized, the blonde that helped you move out?" He rubs his chin in thought. "That was her, wasn't it? Nice ass."

"Watch your mouth," I growl, pulling at my chains.

"It always turns me on when you get feisty." His eyes are full of desire as he eye-fucks me. "But that's beside the point. While I was arranging your things, I found this and kept it for safe keeping."

I can't stop a gasp from leaving my lips as he pulls out a crumpled piece of scrap paper. No, no, no, no. Astrid's phone number.

"Thank you for confirming who this belongs to." Jack smiles and pulls out a cellphone. "Shall we give her a call?"

"Wait, please," I beg. "I have a deal for you."

"I wasn't expecting that." Jack pauses mid-dial. "Fine, what do you have to offer?"

"Let me call her," I plead. "I'll get her to back off and leave the Tributaries alone. In exchange, I'm yours, forever. I won't fight you. You can have my body, my powers, whatever you want. Please, just don't hurt her."

"Tempting," he stalks over to me and caresses my cheek.

"I don't want to fight with you, Jack." I nuzzle into his hand.

"You don't have to," he sighs. "All you have to do is let me be in control."

I lean closer and kiss him deeply, passionately. Though every part of me wants to hurl, I force my body to crave his touch, his embrace, until he pulls away.

"There's just one thing you're forgetting," he whispers as he runs his thumb over my brow.

"What?"

"You've always been mine," he snaps. I yelp as he yanks my hair back. "And I love punishing you."

Jack pushes me away and my wrists scream as the barbed cuffs bite into my flesh. He finishes dialing and presses call. I pray for her to not pick up, but the line connects on the first ring.

Hello, who is this? Astrid's voice projects from the speakerphone.

"Hello dear," Jack purrs. "I've been waiting to chat with you for ages. I'm so glad I have the opportunity to make an introduction. You may call me Jack."

Well, I'm glad we were able to make this happen, but unfortunately, I am waiting on a call from someone else. Sorry!

"Wait!" That threw Jack off his rhythm. His overly sweet facade cracks. "I'm the call you're waiting on."

Hmm. I don't think so. I stifle a laugh. She's totally fucking with him right now. Jack glares at me.

"I assume you're waiting to hear from a few of my associates." Jack adds the velvet smoothness back into his voice. "One of them is in the room with me."

It would save some time if you could put them on the line. She suggests. *That way I could make sure we are referring to the same people. You know how it is, everyone knows a Brittany, but it's hard to tell if you want the Britany with one t or Briteny with an e, or god forbid Britanie with an ie at the end.*

"I could arrange that." Jack grits his teeth, annoyed with the Water Weaver's nonchalant attitude. He mutes the phone as he walks over to me. "Don't do anything you'll regret." He unmutes the phone.

"Sorry to make you worry," I say, tears pricking behind my eyes. "My shift at work isn't quite finished yet."

*Ani-*She cuts herself off. *Sparks, glad to hear your voice. How are you holding up?*

"Been better, been worse," I chuckle. "Jack throws a weak punch." As one would expect, Jack picks that moment to disprove me. I curse as his fist lands against my ribs. Yeah, I should've seen that one coming. That one's on me, my bad.

Jack, tsk tsk, let's keep our hands to ourselves. Though the words are lighthearted, the Water Weaver's tone lowered for a moment. There's a chill in the air, but only for a second as she returns to her relaxed attitude. *And my second friend?*

"He is unable to come to the phone right now." Jack takes the phone back. "You see, he outlived his use. It simply had to be rectified. You understand, don't you?"

You must be really popular on the playground. The Water Weaver says sarcastically.

"Why, you interested in a game?" Jack taunts.

I'm always down for a round of dodgeball.

"No!" I interject. "Don't do it!"

"Quiet!" Jack snaps at me. "Shut your whore mouth or I'll shut it for you."

"He's going to kill you!" I cry. "No!"

The only warning I get is a crackling sound before the prongs of the cattle prod are buried in my side. I shriek as my legs give out and my body writhes from the current. Astrid says something through the phone, but my screams drown out her voice. Pain takes over every single nerve ending. The burning sensation penetrates my entire being, until the agony is all I know. A second later, Jack pulls away and I hang limply from my chains.

Stop! The Water Weaver persona is gone, replaced entirely by a frantic Astrid. *I'm coming! Stop! Tell me where and I'll be there.*

"We're aboard the *Tenacity*," Jack smirks. "I'll text you the name of the nearest port. Join us in an hour or I shoot your girlfriend."

He disconnects the call and winks at me. "I told you there'd be an encore."

CHAPTER 27

A few men enter my cell and unclip my handcuffs from the ceiling. I fall to the ground in a defeated heap. So this is it? The love story doomed to be a tragedy. I stumble along as the men drag me alone to the top deck. This boat is so much bigger than the one the machine was on. I don't even want to think about what other horrors are hidden inside.

The wind roars ferociously as we step out onto the deck. The cold stings my exposed skin, while the legion of men on deck are equipped with winter jackets and machine guns. The sun set long ago, but the moonlight casts a soft glow on the ship alongside the ambient lighting. In the distance, I catch sight of Derek. We lock eyes and he gives me a nearly imperceptible nod.

One of my escorts prods me forward with the nuzzle of his gun. I am led to a platform near the center of the ship and forced to kneel. I rest my hands in my lap and lower my head, trying to remain composed as I shiver in the frigid conditions. A warm jacket is draped around my shoulders providing a slight reprieve from the chill.

"Although I love how perky your nipples are right now, it's probably best we warm you up." Jack sits on the floor next to me. I scoff and shrug the jacket off.

"I'd rather die," I say stoically.

"Don't be such a petty bitch." Jack rolls his eyes and pulls the coat back up. "Shrug it off again and I zip it like a straight jacket."

I acquiesce and allow the jacket to stay. Jack sighs as I stare straight ahead.

"How did we get here?" He asks. "There was a time when I would braid your hair as you sat in my lap. We would stargaze all night and make up constellations. What happened to us?"

"Don't pretend like you ever loved me," I retort bitterly. "It's insulting. I've only ever been a prized possession to you."

"That's not true," Jack defends. "I loved you the only way I knew how."

"That wasn't love." I shake my head. "But it doesn't matter now. Whatever affection I had for you is long gone."

"I'll win you back," Jack promises quietly. "Once the competition is out of the way, you and I can be happy again."

Jack takes my hand and places a rope of black licorice on my palm. He closes my fist around the candy and moves to stand behind me. My stomach growls quietly. I take a bite of the licorice and feel a gentle squeeze on my shoulder.

A wave crashes against the starboard side of the boat. Dozens of machine guns point toward the water, searching for any signs of the Water Weaver. Jack pulls out his pistol and flicks off the safety.

"Please," I beg one last time. "Don't do this."

"At the ready!" He calls to the men in response.

While everyone is watching the starboard, I notice tendrils of water oozing from the portside. Drops of water slide into the firing mechanism of several guns and freeze. The tendrils retreat and all is silent. Another big crash on the portside, and tendrils creep out from the starboard. Another round of guns frozen. They don't notice. The men are getting antsy.

"Show yourself!" Jack calls, as he whips the jacket off my shoulders. He cocks his gun and aims at the back of my head. "I swear I'll blow her head off."

Waves crash against all sides of the boat. The salt spray rains down, tiny projectiles sprinkling us all with freezing water. The droplets splatter against my exposed skin and I gasp at the glacial sting.

Jack fires once into the floor inches from my leg. I flinch from the sudden noise. He yanks my hair to pull my body flush with his.

"Last call." He pushes the pistol against my temple.

One final tidal wave rises up and dramatically falls to the deck, flooding the area. Standing in the water is a figure completely dressed in blue. Gossamer fabric whips around her silhouette. A mask covers her face, but she doesn't try to hide her blond ponytail. It doesn't matter, I would recognize those eyes anywhere.

"Is my clock off?" She holds up her wrist. "I thought I had ten minutes left."

"That's my girl," I whisper.

"Fire!" Jack commands.

The Water Weaver dives to the floor and raises pillars of ice across the deck. Simultaneously, guns on both sides of the ship jam, exploding with cacophonous booms in the quiet of the night. Half of the men are now disoriented and left without working firearms. I see Derek leap over the ice and tackle a nearby goon creeping behind Astrid. Mild surprise flashes across her face when she notices, but she darts behind the next cover as more shots ring out.

"Get her!" Jack cries in frustration.

He raises his gun, but I tug his arm as he fires. The bullet flies wide. Jack curses in frustration. I duck as Jack whips the butt of his pistol in my direction and I slide between his legs. I scramble to my feet as Jack turns to face me, a cold rage radiating from his body.

"What's your plan, Sparks?" Jack taunts as he holsters his weapon. "No powers, you're still restrained, and any moment now, your girlfriend will be dead."

"I guess I'm figuring it out as I go." I quip, backing away from the platform.

My back hits a railing and I risk a look to the side. Jack pounces, throwing me to the ground. I roll with the momentum and kick his feet out from under him. He falls and I scramble for the gun in his waistband. His backhand stings as it slaps my face and the gun skids across the floor.

I desperately crawl away from him before a hand clamps on my ankle and pulls me back. He lays on top of me trying to restrain me with his weight. Jack reaches for my cuffs but when his arm gets close to my face, I bite down as hard as I can.

"Motherfucker!" Jack curses, blood dripping into the water coating the deck. While he's distracted, I stand and back a few paces away. We are both soaked from grappling on the ground. Water dribbles from his hair. I turn and sprint in no particular direction, just away from the monster behind me.

Flashes of blue are to my right, Water lashes out as the Water Weaver lithely runs between combatants. A roundhouse kick knocks one man out. A second approaches from behind. She dives into the water, caught by a wave. The Water Weaver somersaults back onto the deck a few yards down.

Derek is also holding his own. He traded in his gun for a knife. He slashes his way alongside the Water Weaver, covering her blind side and causing his own mayhem.

"Sparks!" Jack bellows.

I risk a glance behind me and come face to face with a wooden folding chair. I crumple to the ground, disoriented from the impact.

"Anise!" The Water Weaver yells in alarm. "Gun!"

"We could've had it all," Jack seethes as he grabs me by the neck. He lifts me to my feet. "Between me and you, we really could've been something, but you just threw it all away." The silver coating of his pistol glints in the moonlight as he gestures wildly.

"Get over yourself," I counter as I try to peel his hands off my throat. I hear a clamor from the side of the deck. "We were nothing! There was no us! Not one that mattered."

"You broke us!" Jack cries out in anguish. He shakes the gun in front of my face. "So I'm going to break you, and you're going to watch."

I'm unsure of what he means until he points the gun towards the side of the deck. I see Astrid sprinting toward us, trying to rescue me. She gasps as the gun is aimed at her, but she has nowhere to hide. Time stops. I don't think. I feel the energy stored in my lightning charm and I let it go.

Electricity courses through my body as the metal barbs of my cuff pierce my skin. The pain is excruciating but I push through, focusing on Jack. The gun is thrown from his grasp as he screams in pain. I remember every bit of torment he inflicted on me. Every time he used fear as a weapon. Every time he hit me. I press harder until I start to convulse. Unable to keep my grasp on the electricity, it dissipates into the air.

Jack and I fall to the ground. Every muscle aches. Jack staggers to his feet, breathing heavily. He grasps the chain restraining my hands and pulls me up. His hands weave into my hair and he brushes his lips against mine.

"Goodbye Sparks."

I don't see the knife until it is inches away.

Bang!

A gunshot echoes through the still air.

I glance to the side and see Astrid clutching a trembling gun. Jack stumbles as a patch of red grows from his shoulder. His eyes meet mine. Confusion, disbelief, and then realization. He falls over the railing. I watch as Astrid's face changes from remorse to terror as Jack keeps his grip on me. He drags me over the edge and I am

Falling...

Falling...

Falling...

Into the water below.

CHAPTER 28

There's no splash as I break through the surface. My hair billows in front of my face as I sink deeper into the blue ocean. I know it should be cold, but if it is, I don't notice. Maybe I'm too cold to feel it. It doesn't seem to matter though.

Should I be sad to die? Should I be gnashing my teeth and kicking my feet? That doesn't seem right. It seems so peaceful here, the water like a gentle embrace, a hug over my entire body.

Besides, I'm tired of fighting. Eight years of anger and resentment can be laid to bed. I can finally rest. Maybe I'll even get to see Jeremiah. I hope he made scones.

Astrid is safe, that's all that I care about now. She'll move on without me. Make a warm cup of hot cocoa in the mornings, experiment with different seasonal drinks, referee board game disputes. One day, she'll find another woman to warm her bed. And she'll be happy.

I smile as I picture Astrid ice skating next winter, laughing as snowflakes decorate her hair. Content, I close my eyes and drift away.

CHAPTER 29

I wake with a start on a beach. My bodysuit is zipped up to my chin, and I'm completely dry. My cuffs are nowhere to be seen. I slowly sit up, sore from the repeated beatings. I'm sure I will have an alarming number of bruises tomorrow.

I look to my left and see Astrid sitting on a log, her back toward me. Her hair has fallen out of her ponytail, and water is dripping off her ends into the sand. Her damp clothes cling to her body.

"Astrid, thank god." I crawl to her log, in too much pain to get up. I wrap my arms around her. "I'm so glad you're okay."

She doesn't acknowledge me, just sits there as I hug her.

"Astrid," I shake her shoulder gently. "What's wrong? Baby?"

"I killed him," she whispers. Devastation is etched across her face.

"What?" I replay the memory in my head. "You shot his shoulder. He can survive that."

"Sure," she says bitterly. "Until he fell several stories into freezing water."

"I'm so sorry." I comb her hair out of her face.

"I tried to find him." Astrid slumps her shoulders dejectedly. "After I pulled you out of the water, I searched everywhere. His body is just... gone."

"I can't imagine how you feel." I pull her in tightly.

"Angry." She brushes me away. "I feel pretty damn angry right now."

"Why?" I place a hand on her knee. "He was going to kill you."

"And who's fault was that?" Astrid stands abruptly, raising her voice. "Every part of tonight was a shitshow because one person was so self-centered, so deceitful that her headaches infected everyone around her."

"Hold on," I say, taken aback. "Are you blaming me for this?"

"Look around!" Astrid gestures wildly. "What part of this was not directly caused by you?"

"Everything I did, every single fucking thing was for you." I fume, pointing at her. "All I wanted was to keep you safe."

"You know what would've been helpful?" She shrugs. "Maybe knowing what was going on? Yeah, that would have been nice! Instead of blindly pacing by the phone wondering if you were dead, I could have been doing something."

"Is it so wrong of me to not want you involved?" I protest. "How many times did I tell you to back off?"

"You didn't say shit to me!" Astrid blows up. I go to speak, but Astrid cuts me off. "You didn't say shit. 'Sparks' couldn't even tell me why she kept going back to her abuser."

"Don't even fucking go there." I stand angrily. "You have no clue what was going on."

"That's the problem!" She exasperatedly throws her hands in the air. "If you would have told me something, anything, I could have helped you. We could've made a plan, gone at this together. But you were so insistent on being mysterious and aloof, that everything blew up in our faces. Now, Jeremiah is dead, and you can't take that back."

"Jeremiah died to keep your identity a secret!" Her face contorts in pain, but I keep going. "We were both tortured and beaten. Jack only had one question, and he wanted to know who you were. So don't pin his death on me because you weren't there when it happened!"

"But I should've been!" Astrid holds her stomach as she sobs. "I could've saved him."

"He wouldn't have wanted you there." I rest my hand on her back, rubbing small circles.

"Stay away from me!" She backs away. "You barely knew him. You know nothing."

I stand there rattled, my hand still in the air. I don't have a response.

"You knew who I was the whole time, didn't you?" Astrid snaps. "Did you enjoy holding that secret in your head, painting me as the fool?"

"I recognized you in Golden Capital Bank," I admit softly. "But Jack promised it was just that once. Then it wasn't. I don't know if you remember, but I left Jack after the second robbery, the same day. Then I was hoping it was over, that it was all done. It just wasn't..."

"That was months ago," she states coldly. "Months of you lying to me. How could I ever trust you again?"

"I'll tell you everything." I fall to my knees. "I promise. Every single detail, nothing left out. I'll tell you about my mother, about Synergy, answer every question you have. I'm begging you."

"I think it's too late for that." Astrid backs away from me. "I promised myself that no matter what, I would never murder anybody, that it was never on the table. I loved you so much today that I broke that promise. I killed a man."

"You didn't mean to!" Tears flow down my face. "You shot his shoulder."

"No, I meant to." She turns away from me, ashamed. "I was aiming for his heart."

"Astrid, please." I hug my hands to my chest. "I love you."

"I can't love you anymore." She walks away from me.

"No!" I can't breathe. I can't think. This hurts worse than anything I've felt before. "Charlotte!"

Astrid freezes in her tracks but doesn't turn around.

"My name is Charlotte," I sob.

Astrid lowers her head, letting her forced dignity crack under the weight of my confession. I think I might hear her crying too. She takes a shallow breath and then walks away, leaving me alone with my tears on the beach.

CHAPTER 30

I stay on the beach until her silhouette has long since faded out of view. I watch as the greatest thing I ever had disappears and I am once again left with nothing. I sit there until I run out of tears and my cheeks are dry.

She's gone. She left me. How could she just leave me here? Alone. Hurt. Shivering. She used to keep me so warm, but now, all I feel is cold. And alone. So alone. So cold.

Slowly, I shamble off of the sand and onto a paved road. I wander aimlessly, nothing tying me to a home. The ocean stays on my right, constantly reminding me of my loss.

A pair of headlights blind me as it pulls off the road. I hear the car door slam and hurried steps run in my direction. Someone calls my name before arms wrap me in a hug.

"Jesus, I'm so glad you're okay." Derek releases me and looks me over. "You're okay, right?"

"I'm fine," I say sullenly.

"Where's your friend?" He looks down the road for another figure. He won't find her.

"She's handling something else," I lie. "She's not going to be around for a while."

He notices my puffy eyes and the hoarseness of my voice. Instead of calling me out, he nods, choosing to accept my answer.

"Well things are crazy at work," Derek rambles as he leads me to his car. "Jack's missing, probably dead. Nobody knows who's in charge or what to do. Oliver's been calling my phone like crazy. I obviously decided to let them all fuck themselves and came looking for you."

"Thanks for the ride," I sigh in relief as he cranks the heater and points the vents at me. "What's next on your agenda?"

"I was hoping you had a plan," he said. "I don't have anything outside of work. Not many friends, my whole family was murdered, not really in the mood for a relationship, so I just worked a ton."

"You grew up in a crime family, right?" A shadow of an idea crosses my mind.

"A pretty successful one," he gloats. "That is, until it wasn't."

"Interesting," I muse.

My whole life, I've had one goal. Take down the bastards that murdered my mom and prevent them from killing again. What has that gotten me? Beaten, raped, nearly killed. An empty life spent running and hiding. Abandoned by my girlfriend. No friends. No family. And I have nothing to show for it.

I'm done. I don't care anymore. The world can go to hell. If nothing I do makes a difference, then why should I try?

Why can't I be bitter and resentful and spend my life kicking and screaming?

My hands light up in sparks as I ruminate on my malevolent thoughts. For the first time, I allow myself to enjoy the beauty of the lights enveloping my skin, the raw power.

I look up at Derek and see similar thoughts running through his eyes. With our combined forces, no one could tell us what to do. We could run through the streets crying out our anger, letting our pain fuel our potential.

"Say, I think I heard about a power vacuum in the Boston underground?" I smirk.

"A real shame," Derek contemplates.

"Maybe we should do something about it," I suggest, fake concern in my voice.

"I think we should." He grins cockily and leans back in his seat.

I turn the radio up and relax as we drive on the ambling coastal highway. The announcer's voice comes on loud and clear.

"Here we go everybody!

Three...

Two...

One...

Happy New Year!"

Happy New Year indeed.

Excited for the next
chapter?

Stay tuned for
FIGHTING THE CURRENT
Coming 2025

CHAPTER 1

ASTRID

Water. It has a spirituality. Water heals and revitalizes. Picture your mother's chicken noodle soup, or perhaps more relevant to my situation, your morning coffee. My family has always had a special connection to this element, so when the spirits gave me the power to control and influence water, it felt right.

My eyes scan the patrons of the cafe as I pull another shot of espresso. It's a busy day, a few more customers than I would normally expect this late in the afternoon, but it's nothing I can't handle. I reach out with my mind and take stock of the mugs scattered around the room. A few of them have gotten a bit cool, so I raise the temperature to a soothing warm.

That's what makes a coffee shop successful, being able to keep water at the perfect temperature. Not many people know this, but coffee beans need to be steeped at a certain temperature for a specific amount of time. Too many shops just boil water and dump it in! No passion, no precision, no care for the perfect beverage.

Not here, not at Brew for Two. I'm not messing around. Every blend is steeped at the optimum temperature to bring out the sultry flavors of the beverage, while tampering the bitter notes. Then, I make sure the drinks stay at the perfect drinking temperature so the guests can enjoy the coffee in their own time.

Of course... I do cheat a bit. Having powers does make this a lot easier. I can feel the ambient temperature of all of the liquids around me and correct them when necessary. Technically, I don't even really need most of the machines around me - I could just heat the drinks myself - but people would find that very strange.

The bell on the door rings, drawing my attention away from the cappuccino in progress. Dolores, one of my regulars, walks in. A prickly lady with her hair in a tight gray bun, but deep inside there is a warm and caring person. Deep, deep inside. It was hard for her when Edmund, her former husband, passed a few years ago, but she still stops by the cafe a few times a week with the crossword tucked under her arm. That crossword is the most important thing in the world to her, so much so that she won't let anyone help. Anyone except... nevermind.

"Good afternoon, Dolores!" I greet, hoping my happiness is infectious. "Standard black coffee today?"

"That will be sufficient." Dolores nods neatly and pulls out her pocketbook. Exact change, as always. She leans to the side and peeks into the back room.

"Sasha is helping out today." A fake smile is plastered on my face. I know who she is looking for. It's been months, yet Dolores always checks. I've told Dolores that she's gone, no longer a member of the team, but she always responds the same way.

"Let me know when Anise comes in," Dolores curtly instructs.

"Perhaps I could help with your crossword?" I offer. Stop asking about her. Stop asking about her. Stop asking. "I'm happy to give it a shot."

"I'll wait." She straightens out her crisp jacket, a bit warm for today but you never know the weather in the spring. "I know she'll be back."

"Let me know if you change your mind." I force myself to look happy, but on the inside, I feel a crack in my mask. I quickly pour her black coffee and slide it across the counter. "Enjoy!"

Dolores takes the mug and strolls to her usual seat. I deliver the cappuccino to a college student working on some essay and make my way to the back, picking up empty cups as I go. Sasha is there, scrubbing dishes in soapy water. She moves to take the tray from me, but I wave her off.

"Do you mind manning the front for a minute?" I ask. "I'll take care of these dishes."

"You sure?" She tilts her head and looks at me. It's unusual, I know. Normally, you can't peel me away from the counter. But after an affirming nod, Sasha bops toward the front of the house.

I slump against the counter, my shoulders sagging as I try to keep my composure from slipping away. It's been months, but I still feel the stab when she crosses my mind.

Her red hair flying as she speeds down the street on her motorcycle.

Her smirk as she teases me for something stupid.

Her sinful grin as she lowers her head between my...

Fuck.

It's been a few years since I took up the crusade of the Water Weaver, using my powers to try and make the world around me a better place. When I first donned the mask, I promised myself that no matter what, I would never kill anyone. After all, would I be any better than the criminals I catch if I did? No, it wasn't something I would ever consider doing.

Until I did.

For her.

I still remember the biting cold of that December night. The knife glinting in the moonlight, inches from her stomach. The horror I felt knowing she was about to die. I didn't know what I was doing until I pulled the trigger. The growing patch of red on his torso. The panic when he dragged her overboard with him, into the inky black water.

I dove into the water after them, desperately searching for any sign of life. Finding her limp body was the scariest moment of my life. I pleaded with every god I could name that she would be okay as I used my powers to draw the water from her lungs.

I went back into the ocean, searching for the man I shot... but he was gone. And I couldn't forgive myself.

So I broke up with her. After all the lies, cover ups, deceit, I was done. I turned my back and walked across the sandy beach, leaving her alone by the shore.

I tell myself every day that I made the right choice.

But every day, I'm not convinced.

"The crowd's dying out," Sasha says. I jump, not realizing I wasn't alone anymore. "I can finish the rest of the shift by myself if you want to bounce."

"You sure?" I snap my shoulders back. "Wouldn't want to leave you hanging."

"I've got it." She smiles, and for a moment, I think she can see through my mask. No, there's nothing to see. Everything is fine. I'm fine.

"Okay then, I'm going to do boring owner's paperwork upstairs," I chuckle. "Give me a call if a wave comes in and you need another pair of hands."

Sasha waves me off as I hang up my apron. I leave the shop and walk up the stairs to my apartment. It's still strange to me to have employees manning the shop on their own. I used to run the cafe entirely by myself. Anise would pop in and wash dishes when she didn't have a freelance contract that day, the customers all loved her. But then we broke up, and I decided I needed an extra set of hands. I hired a few part-timers, then a manager, and now I have a full roster of team members. I don't remember how long it took me to realize that I didn't need another pair of hands, I just missed hers.

But it is nice to be able to step away from the cafe. Go on vacations, take a day off, or just sit on my sofa and ruminate on the past. Business has been booming recently. Things must be going well, so then why do I feel like everything is wrong?

Mimi says that when it feels like the world is against you, it is time for a spiritual cleansing. Grandmas always know what is best, so I figure I should take a quick shower. I fill a sachet with rosemary, lavender, and sage, and tie it to the showerhead. Soon, the steam is carrying their scent through my apartment.

As the hot water flows down my body, I fight against the flashbacks streaking through my mind. Her body wash. Her hands. Water dripping down her curves. I dunk my head into the downpour, but I can't shake the sensation of her fingertips trailing down my back. Frustrated, I turn off the shower. With a single thought, I use my powers to dry off, directing the water down the drain.

I pull my hair into a high ponytail, pulling the ends to make it tight. It doesn't do any good for me to be moping in my self-pity. I broke up with her. It's over. I need to pull myself together.

I walk over to my closet and open the doors, ignoring the boxes of Anise's things. She never came back. She didn't bang on my door in the rain, begging for a second chance. She didn't ask for any of her clothes. I thought at least she'd come back for her viola, but I haven't seen her since that night on the beach.

Deep breath. Focus. I push my clothes aside and slide open the hidden panel in the back, revealing my Water Weaver costume and mask. The cobalt blue fabric glides over my skin, while the tulle overlay adds a subtle shimmer. I love the material that drapes across my torso, and how a second piece falls behind me as a skirt. It's so fluid as I move, it makes me feel lithe and graceful. My reflection catches my eye, and a wave of conviction courses through my body. My shoulders roll back, and I relax into a state of composure. I am no longer Astrid, I am now the Water Weaver.

The streets are quiet as the sun begins to set. There has been talk about new players in town, filling the void left after I killed the last crime boss. My informants say that it's a duo, focusing on illegal gambling and betting events. One of the pair is a man who comes from a long line of mafiosos. He went quiet after his entire family was wiped out by a rival gang, but for some reason, he's decided to reenter the game. Apparently, he also has a partner, but no one has any information on them. Nada. Zilch. Zero.

If you ask me, there's probably not a partner. Instead, the guy is running solo and using the elusive mystery of a second to gain more power. Typical scumbag behavior. However, I do make a point to do thorough recon before I make any moves and get the authorities involved, so here I am, loitering on a rooftop near the supposed casino location.

There's a rumble of thunder as raindrops start to fall. It doesn't bother me any, I simply use my powers to create an umbrella over where I'm sitting. The rain can actually be helpful - providing cover and distraction, preventing people from looking up, and also, supplying me with water. My powers can't create or destroy water, I can only move it and change its temperature. Unfortunately, I am quite useless in a dry area.

The sound of an engine echoes through the alley, and three motorcycles pull up in front of the establishment. I slink down the fire escape and crouch behind a dumpster. Leading the pack is a strongly-built man. It's clear that this is the leader. He pulls a razor blade out of his pocket and starts flipping it around his fingers as he strides to the door. On his left is another man, slightly smaller in stature, but could still handle his own. This second man appears to not be as well-rested as the first, with subtle bags under his eyes. On the right is...

Oh. Oh god.

It's her.

She pulls off her helmet and her fiery curls fall free, brushing the tops of her shoulders. She's cut her hair. It looks nice. She's wearing the same black bodysuit that she used to wear as "Sparks." It hugs her curves tighter than before, and I can tell she's been working out. She laughs as she pulls her cloth mask over the bottom half of her face. Though she raises her hood to cover her head, I can still see the glint in her eyes as she banters with the other two men.

She looks... happy.

I don't understand.

The one with the razor blade bangs on the door and a third man pops out. Typical greasy slimeball. He rubs his hands together before gesturing wildly at the man. I creep closer to hear their conversation.

"I know the payment is late, but it's not my fault," Slimeball says. "You don't understand what it's like working with Sammy."

"Don't blame Sammy for your own ineptitudes." Razor Blade steps closer to Slimeball. "He's never had a problem with any other contractors. Now, when can we expect payment? I'll give you a hint. The answer is tonight."

"Yes, sir," Slimeball stammers. "How do you prefer payment?"

"Bring the cash to the Lightning Bolt," the second man interjects as Razor Blade rubs the bridge of his nose. "Tell the bartender-"

I accidentally kick a rock that goes skidding across the road. Oh crap. Instinctively, I dive behind the cover of a building. I peek around to gauge whether the rock blew my cover. The three men are still deep in their conversation, unperturbed. But Anise, she's always been more observant than most. She steps away from the group, head on a swivel. I move behind the corner as she looks my way and I hear footsteps coming toward me.

Crap. Crap. Crap.

Out of the corner of my eye, I see a ladder with roof access. Good enough. I scurry up the rungs, my chest heaves as I flatten myself against the roof. This is not the game of hide and seek I want to be playing right now.

"Astrid?" I hear her voice call uncertainly from below. "Is that you?"

I close my eyes as if that would make me disappear.

"Astrid?" Her voice is quieter and hesitant, but she doesn't climb the ladder.

"Sparks!" I hear Razor Blade shout. "Time to go!"

"I'm going crazy." She mutters and I hear her footsteps recede. I lay there until the sound of motorcycles fade in the distance.

Anise is the mystery partner. It makes sense, with her obsessive need to keep everything about herself a secret. Heck, that's practically why we broke up. I mean, she was a part of the gang called the Tributaries for who knows how long. Combine that with her own superpowers, she's a natural fit. I guess, I just never thought she would fully commit to a life of crime. What is she up to?

Oh, Anise. What have you done?

ABOUT THE AUTHOR

Lydia Jo Wede has a guiding philosophy – write the book that you want to read. An avid lover of spicy dark romances, Wede has taken that to heart with her debut novel, *Igniting the Spark*.

Born in rural Iowa, Wede has always had a passion for books and for reading. While she originally worked in marketing, she would choose to unwind most nights with a book. It was out of this passion for literature that she began to write her first novel and fell in love with the craft.

Follow her on social media or subscribe to her newsletter at https://ljwede.com/newsletter/ to catch her latest release.